TRANSIT PASSENGER

ANASTASIA SHMARYAN

Order this book online at www.trafford.com
or email orders@trafford.com

Most Trafford titles are also available at major online book retailers.

Based on, real facts of the events of people lives in the XX-XXI Century.
Some names are fictional.

Printed in the United States of America.

ISBN: 978-1-4669-3286-9 (sc)
ISBN: 978-1-4669-3285-2 (e)

Trafford rev. 08/25/2012

 www.trafford.com

North America & international
toll-free: 1 888 232 4444 (USA & Canada)
phone: 250 383 6864 ♦ fax: 812 355 4082

This book is dedicated
to my late father Leonid.

Barcelona Aerial View 1

PART–I

One Upon Time
There Was a Family

CHAPTER 1

A taxi has stopped near Sydney airport; seen here a young man is getting off the vehicle. Next he takes out a red suitcase from the back of a cab, while is carrying a hand luggage. This chap pays the taxi driver for the trip, and stops with a slow by slanting, as looking around the area, he then—progressing. Given Australia's illustrious launched of the spring time, it come into view a beautiful weather, where at Southern hemisphere for infinity, but extraodinary in September being in nature. The sun sparks over and straight onto the surface ground; seeing rays are flashing, falls beyond a huge window and resting on the sliding doora. A reflection is sparkling into this chap face, while its image blindfolds him up for a second. Next he picks up stuff in his left hand, whilst tries to cover up his eyes. This chap slowly, but surely is striding into Sydney airport; at one fell swoop passing through the sliding door. View he remains on foot, when is headed for departure lounge. To describe him that is of a typical characteristic as it comes into view: he is in his late twentieth: 1m and 80cm or six-foot tall, and broad-shouldered. A great proportion of this chap's feature, of which he has a short haircut like army-style, his hair color emerges dark brunnet. It is drawn attention of the chap's facial that is light-milky, a fine distinction of his skin. As for the color of his eyes: are seeing—sea-blue by a lovely grayish within midst of his ogle pupils. In view width of his eyeshot that appear being great big by its size, and superbly wide-open. Other parts of he's facial appearance are vague of a bind measured by he has lengthy eyelashes that greatly curly at the end of it's tip, and mane seemingly alike tresses of his hair. He is wearing on set of clothes from top to bottom: matching by a pair of jeans, and atop a navy jumper be made of wool.

View in Sydney outer surface sensation of the weather be spotted pleasantly warm; while he is carrying a brown tinge on undercoat this chap has folded, and hanged down over his left armrest, apart from other of his hand luggage that being carried by him.

Eventually this chap looks around the airports that be an enormous area, there he is spotting one of monitors, which situated in close proximity. Then he has progressed towards it. Once he is begun reading on monitor up-and-coming of these scheduled flights; whilst the chap again looks across the area, and sights for that ticket-counter. It follows that he starts— is headed with his intention of finding that aimed ticket-counter. Next the chap began hearing swift noises coming from the landing, or take off aircrafts with made fuss among those travelers movements. Select he hears announcement via a speaker-radio transmits that he is able to pick up on his next flights and for all others, who in their turn encircled by groups of those travelers environs around the complex. Eventually this chap is begun striding without stopping directly towards ticket-counter that be positioned nearby. ticket-counter; follows he starts a verbal communiqué with one of those airport officials and himself that happen being a woman atop she wore basic uniform by a symbol of their airline, who is fully claded appearing in uniform. Apart from to be given some idea for her full constitution—spotting her intact body being hidden by that her figure came into view to some extent up and about to the waist, which have shown up. Aside from other half of her body which is hidden down, visible that the woman of the airport staff, stood behind the ticket-counter initiates, as turns her attention to him in a clear voice with is assured, hearing she makes analysis to him:—Good day. How're you today? Can I help you, sir?—Mutually came respond of this chap's, as he looks being hesitant, and him lacking of composure:—Good day, I need info of the nearest air travel to Europe? And could you, tell me, if I am flying through Mombai where is going to stop it in?And if not? Whereabouts these stops the airplane schedule to be?—This airport official's role seems being certain, and in compare—her head leaning down, while she is checking for his query. Concurrently he contemplates into her eye brows, when she pulls up, it's given impression of her being amazed by his reservation; but composing herself, while he reacts with a reply:—Excuse me, sir, is this your first time, that you're flying to? It is a E-ticket you're holding there? Is it not?—This lad's facial appearance has changed with more confident; still him being uneasy, as he acts:—Actually, not! Just the same, I wasn't flying for nearly two decades, only when I was a child. Yet, you haven't answered my question, whereabouts this plane is going to be landing for its first stop? It's a great of importance to me. And, yes, it's a E-ticket. I've booked on internet for my flight!— Facing the airport official, who has wore airline uniform, which be a symbol of her clad. Next this member of staff is raising her voice, just as dauntingly, has interrupted. Suddenly he's like others heard audibly message be made via a speaker. A lady from that staff has wore standard; ultimately once is re-collecting her, she's becoming less tense, and looks into the chap's eyes, she smiles and says into loudspeaker in an Australian accent:—No, sir, the plane certainly doen't stop in India, as, according to your itinerary your flight is scheduled to stop in Singapore primarily. And the next scheduled stop is to be planning—in Tokyo, Japan. You'll stay there overnight in a hotel-room that is included in the cost of your ticket. On the next day you ought to be flying from Japan airport towards the country of your destination!—As she is talking to him through a speaker-microphone, like this young man is listening carefully, that public in contrast is promptly encircled by, which are hearing noises. All over be heard earsplitting of the Customs X-ray machine, else a conveyer belt be launched in service, and trembled wind up in space by echo. A disorder of the conveyer belt that gave this chap also a break to be calm and collected himself, still he leans a fragment lower over this counter, while talks up with confident, and looks on the female from those airport officials and straight in the eyes with curiosity, as he means:—Thanks for update, but I have another question: could you tell me, please, where I'm supposed to I go boarding the plane from here?—Just now, the woman from staff bows her head down, while checks the info, and she's responding him by way of coolness:—Certainly, Mr. Borodin. But first, can you pass me E-ticket together with your passport? And now, place your suit-case up on this X-ray Customs machine. Fantastic! Now, tell me, are you going on business trip, or on holiday, sir?—This chap grins is replying with confidence and looking straight into her eyes, he comes back with a reply:—Definitely, on a personal business trip!—Even if, her head being inclined down, as she began to check up his ID, as hears from him positive reaction; just as her eyes brows pulled up, and so has her eyes in it's turn into open wide with intrigue. The woman, in that case again sustained and beyond self-control, she next replies over that counter:—That is must be exciting for you're? All has been done for you, Mr. Borodin. Now, you can go to gate-5, flight number 947 for you're boarding, sir! Enjoy your flight, sir!—He still with a grin, and is leaning to the right side and with poise he's replied:—I sure will! Please, give me a few seconds, as I need to double-check my travel documents if these all is very important my boarding pass! Thanks, for everything!—At that moment more messages have been made within complex, prompt the guy named—Borodin is listening with laziness. Seeing he picks up a hand baggage with extra stuff, and on foot began shifting away to that aim 'boarding gate-5.' Contrast this airport official's eye with brows get pulled up, seeing as her eyes is wide-open, still her she is watching this chap's steps, as he walks away, she is peculiar, and expressing her opinion to one of the co-workers:—This young man is fab, and good-looking, with great manners, and I find him intriguing, don't you agree?—Interim this chap with the intention of catching scheduled flight, on foot is wondering in the airport's sector; by stopping constantly to get a peek into large shop-windows, where he's passing near by, as the light is sparking via its glass with reflection that leans to him. He then walks into one amongst lots of smart superstores, matching extra brightness is flashing via shop-windows glass with its reflection that falls onto his face. This chap is—Egor Borodin, stopped afresh by 'Liquored shop', and looks with interest indoor; he then enters the store, whilst is paying money for a bottle of 'Russian Vodka'. Egor temporarily occupies a sit in the lounge, resting on chesterfield. Being bored he then is started reading a newspaper, which being placed on the table in café for everyone to take a quick look into abridge, at some stage of long waiting period for upcoming flights. Egor enduring and is sitting for some time, and patiently waiting in the interior of the a hall, and by now becoming bored, as a result of his inflexible joints that linking within he's muscles. Thus he next gets up of his seat . . . All of a sudden a little boy runs towards he's side, still, seeing right behind the kid, but on a full hand length from him, a young woman that has too stride out quickly. She tries to catching up with this boy, but its being visible it isn't so as to easy, he is smart and quick, but cunning. Where this chap get himself off chesterfield; next steps across to block off the boy's way, just where this youngster stops. The youngster looks up to Egor, as it gives the impression of without being shy, at same time is boldly seems to watch intently straight into Egor's eyes—has asked questions:—Who are you? And what's your name?—This chap bends down to view this youngster, and looks into kid eyes with a lovely smile, he then reacts:—My name is Egor, please to meet you! I am waiting for my flight. And what's your name, boy? Whereabouts you're flying to? And where's your parents now?—The youngster still being deals with boldly, but with curiosity looks at him:—My parent and I flying to Europe, and what about you? And this is my mom!-, he points his finger at the woman is standing near. Egor hears, that someone's from a distance strides in, he than turns towards the right side to view this new personality. He glances to this woman, whose at the age of her early thirties. When this young woman has come within reach of them, Egor twists to face her upfront. Despite being composed, all at once

Egor turns around towards this boy. Whilst he concurrently is facing the eccentric woman—Egor then starts dealing with both parties all at once:—Me too. It seems over there're all traveling to Europe, maybe we'll be boarding the same plane?—Together there all began hearing a voice using speaker, and announcement be heard in an Australian accent, about scheduled flights for those passengers. An interruption made shift their attention to the Customs X-ray machine, seeing next as a perceive sound noise, where everyone is begun hearing from conveyer belt with launch functioning again on with ear piercing in reverberation all the way through of the entire place. After a short break in proceedings, when everything seems be potentially settled down with them so as reverberation heard, to suit pro continuation of their discussion. Egor still facing both: this youngster along with the young woman, who happen to be the boy's mother, who smiles; shakes hand with Egor, as talks to him:—Thank you, young man for stopping my son, if not its absolutely impossible to keep up with him. He is such a disobedient and fast to catch kid.—Egor smiles again plus still holds his head is leaning to the right, as with he is gestured towards the boy's side:-That's okay. But he is smart, the youngster, I mean is he not? Excuse me, how old is your son?—The boy's mother reacts, as her head is inclined down, still watching her son's intention to act upon next:—He turns six next week, for that reason, my husband and we're flying to arrange a birthday party in Europe for him, that's where our all relatives live. What about you're? Are you flying on business, or for pleasure, excuse my prying?—Egor still holds his head that is leaning to the right, just as he's rejoind:—Neither I'm flying to Germany to meet my father and my other relatives, whom I have not seen for over two decades. I hope my family over there eager to recognize me, when the plane is going to land in Germany airport, to me being in a foreign land!—The boy's mother, who's name turn out being Rosie pulls her head up, and she looks with interest into Egor's eyes, simultaneously, as she speaks her head disposed down; concurrently, where she still is watching this youngster:—Then we all wish you good luck, Egor. Where's your flight to? Our flight N0 947. Oh, yours' too? Fantastic! We'll be flying in each-other company, than? On behalf on all of us good luck or maybe see you later, Egor!—Whilst those two strangers are walking away; Egor turns towards their side and watching, is following with a glimpse their foot-steps. Remarkably Egor then began laughing, the same, has reflected to himself:—This is really enormous?—Just now, Egor again is long-lasting seated in departures hall—roughly one hour or so—and in anticipation of it there for his upcoming flight. At this point he's body bown down, he then pops in the photo from his bags. At that moment Egor is begun examining the images with greatcare.

'I am flying to Europe to meet my family. I guess I delayed this trip for years, but now me going to see people, whom I have not seen, since I was four-and-half, and so it's twenty three years passed, since. Suddenly reminiscences of Egor's childhood is begun appearing in his subconscious mind, alike these footage from an old film, or it's set aside back, and rewinding to surge back by his recollections again: like he unbroken amid purpose that bear in mind of the past that he set aside, and are flooding in involuntary more and more in his memory. With the intention of reversing the time, this story begins, when I was not even born.

Going through old photographs in my collection that are least, I didn't come across a single, where my dad is with me and mom. It's always me and mom; or mom and my dad on their wedding day. Actually, technically I was, in that photo, given mom was pregnant, that I could be there, see me via her stomach. By the way my mother's name is Alena, and my father is Alik. 'Reminiscences of me being home with my dad and mom as one 'happy family', in the vein of 'a pretty picture in a golden frame hanged up on the wall'. Resembling to typical families, which gave the impression of being fond of that in most cases positive as undeniably it would ensue day-by-day life. But it didn't ensue in case of my kinfolk compare to other happy family story. Apparently looking back, and given of reflection I haven't got anything in common with others kids. A the true story about his family live was a farce, which affected Egor's whole life, above all about he's father back then.

Facing memories, which have effect made him forlorn, even being miserable for him, who learned by heart then. What is more touching in this story that all should value, why the hell am I telling every bit of it, that you should be bother to read, given that story is of unique events? 'Still I have gloomy recollections, but I recall my family and I had lived in a provincial town, somewhere in Eastern part of the Ukraine. There I was born, and my memories of old home-town, where I had spent the first five years of my childhood development. Yet, to maintain with the story of Egor's childhood, who behaviour always resembling neither to let vanishing all of his favourite bric-a-brac, wisely to be taken away by any, nor he might consider to be accepting stuff from the strangers. 'Rumour has it, that my close relative weren't teaching me about that kind of behaviour, yet my spirit for all time had suggested it would be the right thing:—I will do it my way!—As he meticulously be watchful in many ways, which develop into motivation, for him having fresh memories about hospital. 'Perhaps my dad wasn't an angel, who always scared me with his odd deeds. I'm not keen to argue, of my own principles it's my own forte. Still I gloomy recall of this day, when dad was tossing me across the room, and my memories started: me being in a lot of pain. I was only toddler, when this story begins, but I would be facing demons that are imminent.

Alena takes trip, and is travelling on a local train. View Alik is here travelling to his hometown. Whilst Alena is passing through in the same direction at train's carriage. So there conveniently those two have met.

Followed by Alena and Alik began dating for a bit; even if her guts feeling have told not to seek him. Then without telling him she went on holidays; but Alik kept calling in her home and looking for Alena. He almost tracked her down; and insisted for them dating. Within three months on their dating, she had found out that she is pregnant. And so she didn't have a choice, when she agreed to marrying him.

Their wedding was not a big one, roughly thirty to forty people there, those close friends and relatives. Unfortunately on this wedding Alena's grandma had vomited on her dress, which was being a bad sign . . . !

'What my mom has said that from the start their marriage didn't work.' Given that Alena has lived in a provincial town, where everyone knew her, and so she was embarrassed to split. On top she's being before now with a child; this was another reason for her not to break up with him.

When Egor was born Alena being overjoyed to see her son coming to this world. Given that Alik was married before, so that event being unhappy one for him. In view of the fact that Egor was born, his parents being supposed to record, which his birth was certificated in the Notary Office. While Alik is absent working; so Alena looks through ID, around in one of his documents, she found out that he was married before her twice, of which he didn't warn her. As expected she became and has tackled him, by which Alik tell:—I didn't back then thought it's relevant to tell you?—Despite of odds, she thought as the newborn grown-up, and so their marriage can develop. While the baby has been nurtured—but more troubles have grown in their relationship.

Once Alik came home from work; she asked him kindly to help her bath the baby, who was three months old then. When Alik removed the infant from tub, suddenly he has thrown Egor towards Alena, if she wouldn't pay heed and catch him; he could be hurt or worse killed. Then he put a heater down close to Alena's dress, whilst her fabric be caught on fire. Despite of Alik's cruelty, Alena has tried being collected for her son's sake, and he needed to have a father.

Later, when Egor was almost six months, Alik left for training course to another state; while he was absents there for a few days. Upon his return home Alena and her family had visitors. So they have got-together in her parents home, joking in the company of festivity. Later that night, when all have gone to sleep, Alik of a sudden has disappeared. Alena's late grandma has begun screaming on top of her lungs, given that before Alik left he had turned on the gas, but if any light a match their unit and the whole building would rap on fire or blow up.

CHAPTER 2

After unpleasant incident those two split up for a while. Alik had travelled to his parents' home in another state. While Alena has being left in her parents apartment together with her son. She has applied for separation, but Alik assumed that she need to change Egor's surname—to her maiden name. But she couldn't do it, given they were legally married that in the USSR it have not been expected.

During their first split Egor had fallen sick, and was admitted to a hospital. There he stayed with Alena for over one-and-half month. During the baby's illness—Alik has not come to visit Egor in the hospital.

Some months later Alena and Alik and their son Egor have reunited. 'My mom sometimes came late from work, and my dad would pick me up from pre-school after finished his job.

One day my dad had picked me up as usual from Pre-school and we went straight home. Upon our arrival to my mom's parents apartment, where I glance grandpa Leonid's was eating early dinner that Grandma Esther served him. Alik suddenly has become angry, and tossed me across the living room. I was flying all over, and end up falling down on a wooden floor, on the brink of the heaters made of steel. My memories started with my leg aching. I began crying on be unable to get up or caused by sore ankle. By which grandpa has got of the sit, and him being in motion; he then began arguing with Alik. They were shouting, I was crying. Next Leonid picks me up from; and he starts running via a front door. I recall this day: it was raining; while Leonid's being carrying me, and holding in his arms.

When we had arrived in a hospital that been located not far from home. After doctor did the X-ray, and examined me, he detected a fracture in my ankle. When Alena has returned home, I was already there, but no-one told her the truth, what really happened with me. So Alena went in pre-school and blamed there the teachers, who in their turn put in plain words to her that:-Egor left pre-school and being perfectly healthy!-

Alena tried being serene in the relationship, thinking it may well become stable. Given that Egor needed a mother and a father, thus she made an effort.

CHAPTER 3

Superficially to put in the picture, that every year on the first of month of May, or the Labour Day, which always be held for celebration in the ex USSR. It's become traditional for every Citizen in the country to celebrated May 1st, who exist. Besides I dare to say, as me wouldn't be possible wrong too telltale their folklore traditions still exist—even at present. Since existence by the nation of USSR, while these citizens celebrating '1st May Day' with that massive Parade on all the streets of every city, towns and villages, back then, once upon a time, as my parent married and lived together as a link—they were husband and wife. On that challenging day, Egor's parent used to spend first of May—Labor Day festivity with Borodin's family to snow up. As I could recollect, on that May Day with my own flesh and blood and I would commit to memory for a very long time.

In the morning, Alik has taken the three of them to the train station, as usual; where he gets them all set on the train. They have travelled towards the town, where Egor's other family from his father's side lived be not far removed from their district in a provincial town for the period of that time.'After our arrival to kinfolks place: they are greeting in traditional rituals of kissing and hugging, with meetings of that kind of joy, as they always have expressed so that saw me.

When the usual ritual ceremonial being completed, and they have left soon, except for my grandmother Dora, whose wish being staying home. Next they have vanished outside to watch, and were taken part on the demonstration on 1-st of

May in conjunction with the grand parade taking place the city streets outskirts in villages. It was a beautiful day on the outside. Seeing the sun is shone, where it's being unpredictably sizzling outside, and as for the sky: it be blue devoid of these giant clouds, covering on top and slowly moving ahead, which ought to be the forerunners of upcoming rain, but have been on the move. In unison as, they are seen people there who seems to have appeared in a festive mood. Those folks have been laughing, singing and dancing. In all over the places those public are spot, who being flanking and formed huge crowds, and saw those holding in their hand lots of colorful flags, transforates are fresh flowers or artificial; portraits, which exposed unlike features and unfamiliar faces had painted therein. He entire city' streets has transformed 'in a big stage performances'. Music come from varied places and resonance being heard, the street bands have played diverse tunes, by paying attention it have existed and well-known images of the Russian and Ukrainian folklore music, intended for that kind of celebration around many place, where persons would be headed for meetings with festivity prearranged purposely in centre squares, with an advantage always are in motion on these streets and lanes. By use harmonious melody be heard, as reconnect with accompaniment of piano-accordion, harmonica or the cords of guitar, plus in the course of other piece of music and instruments. every one around that area have heard other piece of music, jointly the meeting of some speeches that recited under shrill audibly via a microphone, with its echo vibrated as of altered angles encircled by contrasting ribbons and paper chain; besides the public all around the City. Mood among those folks are feeling great, beside it come into view having been on high, at one fell swoop, heard one and all sang, and being dancing in combination with tunes, as it gave the impression they're like flowing with the ear-splitting harmony. Advance is crucial that public in the streets have not suspected, what on earth odd to be of outcome, which have taken place, and occurred around. Bar it's being in some way atypical in the course of a hot weather conditions that felt for the country existed rare of those previous years then all were ignorant. While the folks resided, then the entire point of their live haven't got used to heat, an indication, which were period of a cool weather on spring by the USSR. Still from time to time during summer, in favour of the family and me it's be supposed to available this Labor day festivity taking place on the first on May day exhibition parade every year, be nearby a part of the country tradition, at the time in traditional way, in the vein of the folklore, in view of the fact that every citizen likely dedicated to it, and it have not, as they been forced to carry out with it, or as they were give the lowdown, since they just be fond of being entertained by by enjoying themselves there. Ahead of all on occasion too get a few days off, given that its turn into holiday in the Soviet Union, for those citizens who desired having a rest from work. In actual fact what's critical in this story that they've reappeared indoors of Egor's kinfolks dwelling first of all they done: have switched on television, siting and relaxing with a stare on screen. Conveniently on TV have viewed, rather odd appeared in the news, saw a newsreader made broadcasting:- "It was a fire in one of 'Chernobyl's reactors . . ."—In the room respectively the Borodins become on state of high alert. Being a kid, not even three-years of age at that time, I couldn't figure out on disturbance, which being exposed upon their faces. As has made somebody believe for those be kind of distressed, view expression of vertigo, as they're frown meant with a sign on their faces are:—Why my relatives so scared?-, I bear in mind ad nauseam: white-stone of their skin tone. Dimly if shocking now grandma Dora began crying, when my parents are tried calming her down. After the Borodins are begun talking, as their expression given the impression of being seriously pre-occupied with some reflection of panic that become visible up on their eyes. Once news was shown on telly completed with a recent broadcasting which my family again underway of are listening to radio, where again they have heard of in the vein of statement, with speeches, by more details as to focus on: radiation levels be external. Here also talking about the 'air-pollution' readily available over, as be pointed out more serially, which previous was reported. The newsreader, on prime time has spoken with agitation the comes a warning:-"Little kids, shouldn't be attending, pre-school, or nursery school and even primary classes at the local Schools. Not by any circumstances, until further notice with instruction from the Government will be recommend. equally, here are further instructions, in aid of the Ukrainian Government also of the USSR Government, concerning that urgent matter!—After stops Alik switched back on TV, despite they've seen news in advance on telly, but now the family anxiously being watching that screen. On TV screen has shown a frame, whilst there plainly to be written:—News—extremely important!—It has passed a short while, as this newsreader appeared on the TV screen again, who's emerged being a man; and attend to viewers is coming to a hold for a few seconds; he then takes intense breathing, even as he regularly tolerant:-"Women and children, added to those elderly and sick citizens—must stay home, with windows and balconies should be locked hermetically. As for the dust inside their homes, one and all should wash the floors and leave them they aret, twice and even three times a day. All one must be very careful and not to go outside only without important needs for them . . ."—This reader non-stop has explained with more in details the situation:—Too much dust in the house, can raise the radiation to a very high level, and could be dangerous, not only for yourself, but also can put your kids' life on a huge risk . . .—A newscaster brougt up to date for viewers, and has assumed with the aim of spared there—radiative leakages from the nuclear station's reactor had by now got onto atmosphere, which occurred earlier than the twenty-six of April 1986, of Chernobyl's power plant, from the time, when radiative leakage vanished up onto environment was on a very high level in the air and underway to re-locate above and afar. This reader continual is saying:-"Those, with breathing difficulties, among people from asthma sufferers; as for those folks with hearts problems—you must stay indoors of their homes. Cloud full of radiation had moved beyond Belarus, where on the go to re-located ahead and beyond, headed for Western and in South-East parts off Europe, potentially on the way to the Balkans. The reader calmly of his speech, by extra an news and has well-versed to audience:-" . . . it wasn't an explosion on power plant' in Chernobyl!"—But my family knew damn well that—definitely it was a blast in one of reactors . . .

In spite of hearing about Chernobyl catastrophe, those three are supposed to return back home at the same night, but seeing that place to be located further into a remote town, where they both should go to work the next day. So, Alena took a 'gauze cloth', while has put over Egor's face, seen as it's be able to cover his nose and mouth wholly. Given to a hint that I was only a kid back then, by which I couldn't become conscious on thus genuine circumstances of the incident that occurred around, except for every individual is depressed? Whilst I befall be restless and miserable they wore masks in advance, than our trip begun, as those three headed for train station to catch a local carriage. There she tried to comfort Egor. 'Mom explained to the point that I must keep still, on top of the whole thing that made me puzzled need bear mask on, it's just for fun too they arear masquerade obscure, as said by her—sequence of events. Back then potentially in that case its being true, while they are walked at first to the train station; and those three of us taking sits in the train carriage on the passage back to our home town. Once me being forlorn and I become attentive to the other kids, and saw even adults have put on gauze cloths, which covered their oral cavity, like me. By seen so I thought to myself folks might headed for a party.

The next day, and for about a the week ahead I stayed at home, seeing as I haven't been attending pre-school. My mother couldn't stay with me, for the reason that she may well go to work, but my dad took a leave from his job, and so that dad alongside my grandmother Esther, has taken care of me.

Many times I have made an effort step in balcony, but the door and its knob has been hermetically locked up.

Alps Photo

PART–II

When Chernobyl Struck

CHAPTER 4

Catastrophe in Chernobyl had left traces, as it have effect on one and all there, who were afraid come out on the outside, only when it was necessary for them—going to work or shopping. 'While our hometown be located not far away from Chernobyl—less than two-hundred-kilometers off a radiation zone. Over there the Local Government requested the public, who lived within a close proximity to Chernobyl power plant for help with evacuation process in order meant to evacuate and moving out those residence of the away, who have stayed there predominantly of their life and shift them out towards new location. In accord with the local ruling demands intended for that public, whom being residents nearby the Chernobyl plant, and had arrived in order of becoming volunteers to help throughout that mass evacuation with moving those citizens out to other locations. Alik and Leonid were on industrial unit, where the plant's association together with admin have raised that crisis amid workforce apt to become volunteers, in order to leave for Chernobyl. At the same time the factory's admin have objections for Leonid's expedition, be that as it may he sensed of duty upon himself and being readily available travelling to an aimed place. Instead industrial units admin felt have expressed objection, due to in excess of his aging. Given to a reflection of him not getting any younger he by now gone beyond sixty years old . . .

My entire family being watching, once Leonid left for Chernobyl. In spite of the fact that grandpa Leonid's trip was cut short pro homecoming at the same day, where those folks in charge there, gave the orders if anticipated in aid of thus Chernobyl evacuation process have decided for Leonid to leave, seeing as 'him being an elderly man, which might become dangerous' with an effect on his heath. So with concern look: one amongst staff a man stated, who's giving the orders, spoke Russian:—Leonid вы пожелой человек это—небезопасно для вас!—And thus precisely what it's become; also there're in charge having evidently disputed of. About my other grand-dad, Josef, who in contrast has emerged being younger than Leonid. So that Josef has been forced to depart for Chernobyl in order to help with evacuation mass process over there. Chernobyl area have long-drawn-out between the region of 50-250 km, throughout some parts of the Belarus too was effected; where on higher level expanded beyond far-off the USSR, simultaneously thus clouds headed for Europe, or where else. The whole country with regions in close proximity, counting Zhitomir—have declared: the state of an emergency with an extreme ecological disaster. Effect in excess of an ecological catastrophe, many citizens from other far states of the USSR arrived in a bid to assist there, and to provide the main needs by critical medical aid for those citizens, who existed in that zone, as those refuse to give in defy radiation pollution, also through some of sporadic fires, which have arisen on the main territory around these places with it's environment . . .'

Looking up into the skies can glance blue white clouds, which have become visible with the shape of crafted cob webs; and lying on the atmosphere amid slow to be able seen jerky in motion; the sun is spot radiating. By reflection as it falls onto running water, other than on substance glass, where beyond—with sparkle; as people right to be heard all over with echoes around beong made. In contrast these settings contained by built-in from parts: of the skin texture and externally within mane, which have explained carefully by those coordinators, might contained most of the capacity via accumulation areas contained by irradiation towards it. All together it have served, like of some notion by filtering device for the process to facilitate, so as to force for people, which are having near, and must be served the persons as a protection shield. The volunteers weren't given adequate set of clothes from anti-radiation protection. Its by all accounts be a requisite to create effort during: hair and their skin, as those had produced it with the purpose of to prevent radiative element aligned with chemical via infiltrate getting through under inside skin, which been unable to penetrate, and being advancing internally into parts of persons body-organs right through those folks well-being with hot-blooded effect at this time down to them. The emergency squad has given mission to organize massive stations, which has intended for: washing the public, whose resided there or worked near—predominantly by warm water showers and disinfective liquids. The fokls, who are working for emergency evacuation crew gave to wear special costume with equipment, which have been capable to shelter those initiation off radiation, with they're wearing set of outfits as a part, which used for their safeguard the skim gas-mask one at a time so as to protect against exposure to radiation and chemicals, otherwise penetrating below and in persons internal body-organs. That crew of volunteers, who walk off that plant from be covered themselves touching by radiation and chemicals, of which it has emerged from the air, because those would mortal of dust. In accord to their opinion that might be restricted within a hazardous factor: cause it now had developed into more deadly for those citizens health . . .' As they have heard water poring by sound is exaggerated, listen to a steady rhythms of running water are running from showers, where a flash of light would spark all the way through these white feathery clouds to be spotted. Temporarily, the Ukrainian Government gave a mission to organize massive 'washing stations' designed for cleansing those citizens. Thus it has emerged cleansing method by simple using warm water with showers those general public in anti-radiation disinfection liquids. Readily available folks be wash off with extreme care predominantly via these showers, where in some areas have built with extra Russian YMCA: bathhouse. It's spotting the substance that enclosed a unique remedy of the liquid, which helped to wash out thus radiation elements the length with dust of surface away off peoples full body and coats of their skin. With the purpose of built-in of skin texture and hair, which the coordinators have given details meant for the people, who been full of most accumulation capacity areas off radiation resource through and excessively filtering. Enhance by using thus protection shield used for those folks in order to cover and it have worked pro them. The folks from the squad determined to reach that public, where bathes and evacuation process to be arranged. Seen there're hosepipes with water pouring in excess, as drops bursting of light is radiating through, at the same time shell, while it's sparkled. The team sense of hearing din, since having the power on high capacity: been seen staff responsible for an operation on high intonation talks at the top of their voices, via loudspeaker said in Russian, since deal with a those huge groups of folks:-That public, who lived in unsafe zone within region or near the site of Chernobyl. Those remained follows those from in a close proximity to residential areas!—A stop, as he next began counting regularly the citizens, declaring, which's held in hos hands in a unique fluid:— Товарищи, проходите вот туда для обмыния! Каждый из вас берёт эту жидкость—специально предназначенную для мытья своего тела. Это—своего-рода, защитное средство, которое убережёт вас от проникновения в ваше тело— радиации, а также химикатов. После ополаскивания тела: просьба—необтираться насухо! По-скольку ваши вещи могли бы подвергнуться радио-активному заражению, в этом случае—после мытья вы получите свежее бельё, а вашу одежду—придётся сжечь!—The residents then were invited to get undress—on taking their clothes off; as those persons who have bathed with warm water by unique cleansing fluid, which could help to get rid of exposure towards X-rays radiation— against the chemicals too. Through first step on cleansing and purification process were completed and rinse must be done by warm or cold watering; by next step their physical check up for the general public that have been prearranged, intend for them on set of fresh clothes. Also citizens have been requested to stay put wet, not by any natural factors been a reason drying up. As these old garments worn by folks, which are supposed to getting burnt—decided by those in charge, who having believed that general public were dressed in fresh clothes, which must be destroyed by fire. 'Despite the effort of that rescue crew, who have ineffective to burn it. The effect groups became scared on level of radiation, which to be getting higher along with dust that, might surface from these ashes of an occurred fire. Meantime that crew given orders not to make extra fires there. As a result capacity of that radiation level can be adjacent have increased to maximum. Apart, it's already subsist on extreme high level set of radiation exposure elements by. Sparks of light was being reflecting through the trees and glass or via a glass. Those locals from zone within the region of Chernobyl with all of their possessions have got requisited, to depart from area in order to move out the public to new places. Except major of the inhabitants, who have reluctant to move out far-off, mainly those elderly citizens, who build their life in Chernobyl region for most cases. The general public involving those, who have not got close relatives, or they're just unenthusiastic moving out to new places, with the intention of re-locating those refugees, apart from their own homes, else out off their lively-hoods . . .

'Except grand-dad Josef, who's medical test didn't pass for him so fortunate. After few months passes, Josef began feeling funny, while being forced to do a medical check-ups and blood test also. Once the medical test be thought-out by doctors, who found out, as their diagnosis been a progressive form of cancer, which there have become aware of in core of his internal body-organs. Once doctors painstakingly examined him and separate done an extra medical tests, which searching on Josef abnormal state; him being diagnosed of a progressive form of cancer, which have established internally in his body, which already with a cause of swelling. To be more detailed its found in Josef bowl—as a result of with blow to his life it have spread of malignant cells, while these cancer cells as had already destroyed his health, without him being aware of a crisis. When Dora and aunt Tanja learned about that awful news they become upset, except for Josef, who couldn't believe it that is all true, why thus has turn out to be so as to a way in the course of misfortunate for him? Although, gran-dad Josef had travelled as far as Moscow, for the second med opinion and to the last minute being in hope for life. Except analysis he received on firmation, by which they've made a diagnosis—its still be alike. Dispite Josef was alarmed, but made an effort staying positive, he suddenly has tried, in every respect he's not hidden his true feelings from every, it would glance a sadness in his eyes.

Shortly, those locals have given the lowdown of unlike version of 'horror story', what has really occurred over there, while they were convenient in Chernobyl, while being able witnessing first hand every bit of catastrophe that taken place there, which being made the Borodin family shivering with fright, as with an advantage of partaking, cause they were, by means of blood running through their body.

Back then time passed by, as they start hearing of unpleasant incident at odds stories, which have taken place about high level of radiation.

When either mom or grandma would go down to the market, where those locals ought to predominantly buy food with extra crucial stuff on or after. Seeing in markets those residents would search out or check—ups thoroughly for every small piece of groceries, as they might carefully chosen vegetables that have grown in the fields. In town using milk and similarly products, which contain of dairy supplies between that public, it's also being a great concern, among whole population, counting the local Government has grown to be in a state of high alert. As the product intended for poultries plus other type of meat, one and all become on alert to purchase all bric-a-brac. As the residents would come down to market, neither indisposed to buy provisions, nor devoid prior thoroughly its being a check up. Foremost by the special health authorities, either doctors, or registered nurses. Even if, there be signs of warnings, which have been glued up on the walls, or in various of public places and gatherings, often mostly in Market places. chief via broadcasting on the radio they listening a lot to other sources that often would be heard, as a reminder of news broadcasted or visibly, in public house by a dictating tone flat:- "Продукты питания, включают: мясные, птицы различной породы, молочные продукты, сыры и иные продукты— поступившие из близ-лежащих районов, в направлении зоны Черноболя—недолжны быть: либо приняты—либо получить разрешение на продажу своих товаров питания, никому из жителей—не выдавать . . . !"-

Within a year after Chernobyl catastrophy, almost every single residents in Chernobyl, Pripjat and it's nearby areas were evacuated—due to radiactive fallout there. For the period of a year Chernobyl, Pripjat and nearby surrounding areas—have turned into Ghost Towns . . .

CHAPTER 5

L ikewise, as I have brought up before my aunt Tanja was 's coeval, whilst my relatives from both side evenly have celebrated their birthdays in April. To prolong with the story: my aunt Tanja was married. Much later on the same year of 1986, at some stage in the events she met a young man. Rumour has it that time necessity be ticking out for her, seeing her still being a spinster, so as she grow to be concerned, that she would turn into an 'old maid', as a result—aunt Tanja decided to tie the knot with this young man. What brings to my mind that I learned by heart: parents with their ancestors from mother's side and me on our have exited left for aunt Tanja's imminent wedding ceremony. They all have caught the morning train, soon arrived to his grandparents, whose being another relatives from father's side. Dora, he's grandmother invited all of them to have refreshments; but after a while my dad came from the kitchen, while being holding a glass already filed within unusual to pallor liquid, which he offered my other grandma Esther 'something for a toast drink for Esther "Lehiem!"—He has said by way of sarcasm. After fifteen minutes passes, Esther's cheeks become apt shade of pink on her cheeks, it's be visible, but not from her thrill, rather in the vein of blood flash, caused by a touch of disturbance by means of making her being unwell. As a result skin colour on her face has dramatically altered—into pallor, seeing her eyes befall being colorless. By inconsistency observable spots in front of all. As for Esther's breathing it has become frequent, while she slowly changed to shallow. If anyone could stare directly and inventively into her face they might observer that she being out off breathing, as shallow. She is feeling very sick, but that was unusual for her, seeing her being always a strong woman, and not only physically. As a result, she has emerged unfit apart been unstable. Even if, she's being talking to my other granny Dora at first, but then abruptly Esthers' left the last, whilst begun under her own steam headed for bathroom. Upon returning back her physical condition hasn't improved at all. Esther suddenly has set off again to the ladies rooms. Walking back, I is over heard her talking:—I tried to vomit, but could not . . . ,—and she sustained more:—My breathing, oh-oh . . .—Her breathing grown to be shallow and frequently being intense, while it become visible that genuinely her health being poor, but she tried compose hers, sustained articulate is meaning:—I don't have enough air in my chest! I feel like I'm gonna die. I'm in pain. My back and stomach is hurting. Please, Alena, ask your Mother-in-law to let me have a rest on their sofa. After, I might and shall be feeling healthier, before the pair's marriage ceremony goes ahead. Alena, ask your relatives to get me a glass of water, pronto!—So, he's aunt Tanja, has not got many of her best friends, who might single her out, on top make promising to stand up for her as the best men during the wedding ceremony and Matrons of Honour, so she ask for my parents go ahead of their honour,as to be carrying out responsibilities at my Aunt' Tanja's wedding day. The wed's couple Marriage Civil ceremony takes place at the Registry Office, where they've accepted this pair, as well guest in celebrating mood, during, which Alena and Alik are suited, as they having become witnesses on Tanja's matrimony with her future husband vowles. Acting, this wed couple has signed a marriage certificate by complementary in their passports that needed for this kind of formality, my parents follow next a comparable procession, as the maitres of honours' tasks have to be. For the civil ceremony that always should be the most momentous part of the wedding that has passed in traditional Russian gala, and brought into play then, which always was traditional for all those invited guests, who come into view are retaining in high emotional state and festive spirit. When civil part of the wedding ceremony has near ended, those guests, who are drinking champagne for the Newly Wed's happiness, who just have tied the knot. Seeing as granny Dora stood beside grandpa Josef, are crying. I couldn't value why, but all the same it's become thrilling for me in attendance to be able observing that chapter in my Aunt's live—at first hand. In a bit this married pair along in the company of guests are arriving from a Registry Office, where act of their marriage ceremonial—significant; and taken place with all those invited guests, who have been present at the get married. Veiw they all and I are arrived back to granny Dora's place for that reception.

'The Reception', for this pair be embraced, and allegedly held at the location of the backyard of grandma Dora's place. Whilst it passed with the toasts of drinking, assortment of like chalk and cheese courses of dishes, which have been brought to the tables, and served to those guests to enjoy that banquet. In a while those guests demanded for the Newly wed that tied the knot pair to dance their first dance as a husband and wife,. They also demanded for the Maitres of Honour to dance next, after that they ared pair. And here comes out of ordinary piece of act: my dad with the sarcastic smirk, in that case he made declaration by motto in front of all guests:—I'm not going to dance with Alena. If she needs somebody to dance with her, she can find anyone, who's willing to do that? If not, Alena may find herself a creature to dance, or she just can hop alone!— Alena being humiliated and wordless, even as standing close, at the same time holding him and embracing the child in her arms, but unaware how to act, unconscious she on the go with dancing accompanied by me, as a partner. To the revelation of all those guests a lad has approached my mom and invited her to a dance with him. Except his dad, whose that idea seems to be shown a selfishness, or rather of an amusing astonishing. On the contrary, neither dad has found every bit of that lad's deed impropriety, nor by being fond of. In its place, Alik's bias start by a clash promptly: at first with the chap, who's defend mom, but dad verbally abused the man and then tried to provoke this lad, whose being publicly paying too much attention by dancing with Alena, while Alik by means of challenging this man to a fight with him. Next Josef, has walked in them and reminded my dad for:—Alik that is not a public gather, it is your sisters' wedding after all! Stop now a spectacle behaviour! And better watch for your son!—Ultimately Leonid has approached Alena by her invited too dance. While both are dancing to a waltz, and engaged talking. I was busy helping out my aunt Tanja, with making her happy and enjoying her wedding. I started to recite one of the longest rhymes, that I have learned in pre-school, because my purpose be just to pleasing her, and I have succeeded in that.

Egor didn't see Esther, after the events and excitements, during which they were part of a wedding celebration.'When the next I have got to see her, she still looked pale and into the bargain her cheeks turn into being pink. She's talking to mom:—My condition wasn't improving and I still feel terrible. I'm scared, cause my state of health become even worst. Your father and I are leaving. So, look after your son, be careful, don't do him, or say no matter, which to provoke your husband, by getting Alik angry . . . !-

Except for Alena, who's already being upset: first of all, cause her mother being feeling unwell. For another reason, that my dad, who earlier was rude to her and humiliated in front of our relatives and other guests in attendance; where Alena is standing within a spit distance from them. As wedding was coming to an closing stages; except for Egor's parents and he absolutely not are nor in humour to departing home. And those three have decided to stay in Grandma Dora's place overnight, at once for the second day in favour of that marriage celebration.

In point of fact in Russian traditional, some of those guests, mostly, who were very close or among parents, or other relatives, who continued in that festivity on the second day of the wedding.

There 'all you can eat' with preparation of cooking and drinks, which be left over from the previous day.

The next day all the food and desserts, that still to be fresh and endlessly need to serve the guests, who would arrive second day of the wedding for that feast, since everyone acquaint with the legends of harmony to do. The invited guests, who would come back on the next day for the carry-over for festivity of entertaining begins once again. plus alcohol, in any case, if there are much left overs or not, the people still buying, with thus drink to make extra toasts. In relation to my parents and myself: we being happy to hang about for the second day in the row promptly. Given that both of them were the matrices of honour, with me, who also being the bride's nephew after all. So my parent and I are wished maintain with festivity all for the newly tied the knot, who in the past become—a supreme married couple. Meanwhile, Alena has made a call over the phone to find out, how is her mom, Esther doing, and whether her condition has improved. But Leonid, has lied, and enlightened her with a contrasting version of Esther's state of health . . .

On that grounds later, Egor had learned, that Leonid did not wish to upset his daughter, pro Alena's implied:—Don't worry, everything is good. Your is resting, the whole thing will go away. And how is my favourite boy, can you pass him a handset to me to talk?—She pass the receiver to her son. Leonid's kept asking questions, and at the end of their phone conversations, he said:—When you'll be back, today? Darling, I'm longing to see you, and so is grandma Esther!—Though they could not suspect a thing, but this wedding to be converted into foundation for Esther's far-reaching long suffering in forms of a chronic illness. It would take her many years too come to terms, before she has gone through dissimilar type of healing. Apparently it's all aimed at given details her being alive, which hooked on—a prospect for Esther . . .-

Meantime Alena still is ignorant, what lies ahead, at the same time so be fixed as to exchanging words with Leonid on the phone:—Papa, please, look after mom, do not be bothered about us here, we're okay! And we will arrive back home today . . .-

I won't comment, but rather carry on what occurred after our coming home. At first they have spotted Leonid looked worried, followed behind by Esther, who next is emerged in front of their eyes approaching out from extra bedroom in that flat of ours. They couldn't imagine, for only twenty—four hours Esther's appearance has changed dramatically. It's essential to point out what she might felt by getting through of pain, thus disturbed her. also it was visible how much stomack-ache of its suffering by hot and bothered her. View she has tried to overcome a painful indigestion and day-by-day lose lots of weighty.

In the long run Esther's look not only altered be pale, instead in a prudential light has gradually grown being a changed self: seen in her eyes overturned, and she would react aggressive to her family, is pickying on mom, whom she couldn't recognise if all of those in her is agonizing ignorance. What I obliged to explain to your view that during the first year of Esther's hard battle against poor health and suffering, with it's consequences; it's become quite the opposite for Alik's, whose never looked more an pro this situation; so Esther's emergence off pain being kind in favour for him, would scream coming out from hers and Leonid's bedroom: with such an agony on or after as a result, which she must being suffering. To get finger-food to consume by and large for Esther would develop to an awful stomach-ache through real torture be a great deal. It has resulted for her direct follows use of a primitive method was using enemas. As a result of her condition has become unbearable, when Esther's consumed catering once she would start digesting—process of delightful cooking be a real torment for her, as the only method she saw—enemas, which could be a remedy—instead of healing. Then she thinking then in nasty incident off abnormal state with an agonize hurt; at the same time she's being feeling kind of a relief, by which hopelessly she tried pull off by her hopes, except it was not the cure that she needed. as a replacement for heal she used a few dozens of enemas, if not—hot water bottles despite the fact it's contained by that primitive methods, which she used to in a bid to smooth thus aching of 'cleaning' and 'washing' process via her stomach with water. Even at present time they would appreciate that, if it wasn't for these enemas, Esther most probable being dead years ago. Taking in pain-killer pills its seems being irrelevance for Esther's, still extremely painful would fall out incredible caused her have a poor medical condition—stomach-ache. Whilst in contrast for Alik it seems gave him satisfaction. For Esther in contrast, pro tem was on loose-fitting as she's being sluggish off thirty-kilos, in total weight loss being, like formerly her body mass more or less, whilst of her usual body load that in the past she weight over eighty-five kg. To view her close anyone could shed tears that she doesn't need 'a weight loss program.' Thus must wicked way for any human being, consequently part of her losing being risky, as to her health most of all by well-being that focused to be disturbed. With bated breath that at current days, she couldn't regularly consume cookings properly. Still after level of tests followed by a surgery procedures, which have to be acted upon on her. Esther hasn't gained weight back, despite of all the treatments, which she was going through, but remained being slim. During all those years, and would-be still now erratically the illness have entirely changed not only her attitude, but her as a woman's state of mind. Compare to earlier times Esther was tending of become destructive, and she would scream often during night and days, which meant it has caused her dire stomach-ache, by which she remained looming cause off abdomen, lacking of properly been functioning. Being in poor health that effected Esther's felt moaning, which made her behaving abnormal.

CHAPTER 6

The time bypass quick, when at last came the last days of June, which happen be my birthday. It's appeared that a big birthday-cake had now arrived, with chocolates, and varied of lollies, soft drink, which were stored and set aside. While the toffee must be waiting for me in the fridge, which mom along with dad have bought prior to that exceptional day for me in store, I thought. Egor awaken early this morning as usual, even supposing its to be a beautiful mid-summer time outside in the company of the beautiful month of June and it has also advanced his Birthday that he anxiously being waiting for. Each one in his family unit, since they supposed to leave for work, thus in the house have no-one being left that could stay home with me. Apart from that exceptional day my main concern become for Esther, who's already remained being in poor health, and for that reason alone, she is being hopeless to look after me. That's why I supposed to go to pre-school, even though it was my birthday; so both my parents obliged to go to work, and in my state of affairs, virtually the same was for grandpa Leonid, who still being attending his occupation. Where relationship of his other grandparents: Dora and Josef, whose too have worked, cite to, given that their home to be located at distant in another district. On that foundation I was intend going to pre-school five-six days, by which me being very happy there. Anyway I was glad to grace with my presence pre-school on a daily basis, except for weekends, when I would spend time with the family. I is imagined having fun there, how I in company with my friends take pleasure of my desired cake, and consume chocolates, while sharing supplies alongside with those teachers, and nurses; by the way those last two dearly being fond on him all the times there. Routinely Egor's parents have been getting ready going to work, seen then Leonid's clock be shown 7.30 a.m. in the morning. Given that mom well under way be supposed to start work-in on this day earlier—in that case seems my dad supposedly ought to be taking me to day nursery, well . . .

Alena politely has asked Alik to take Egor in pre-school, seeing as she then is fully claded her son in a brand new set of outfit that set pretty on for a three-years old boy. On this day be wore in nice attire, which were manufactured from abroad, being shipped from the USA from close relations, before send via parcels to Borodin in the USSR as presents for Egor with a bonus in common with other bric-a-brac to boot. So this kid in compare looks be suit for a special occasion. Undesirably, back in the former USSR, just then pay money for garment; plus erstwhile alike stuff, which was its own trade in from abroad, there was all but impossible get hold of these items. To find and purchase nice clothes from abroad, or to come across some delicious supplies was particular difficult too, whereas to reveal it would cost dearer and to be more costly. Since on that time it was impossible—as those would call it over there 'to get it'. Given that paying a great deal of exchange notes, called 'Rubbles', still hassled for it, which is equal to or even extra, so both of my parents' earnings were with at least a sum for six months of their salaries are supposed to, counting Leonid's earnings into extra, coming to equivalent of a sum in total for a year existence of my kins income. To keep up with this story, by which period expands, once everything was set amid rations and mom being supposed to take with me in pre-school. So goods has been packed prior by my parent, except when we all being getting ready to leave, when dad abruptly in full swing begun screaming on top of his lungs at me, for talking by a tone of hatred. He has insulted all of them with vulgar and abusive words Alik being cursing all of us, mostly dealing with grandma Esther and mom. After the whole lot off slur with Alik's decree he hope that Esther, whose in his Russian words, must die:—Какого чёрта тебе здесь надо, старая карга? Почему ты не здохнешь, Эстер! Убирайся отсюда прочь, иначе, я за себя—не ручаюсь!—In dealings with Alik's awful conduct towards me he is shaking me, abruptly I began sobbing, as those two were crawling, since revealing that me being extremely scared of him.

After having left home, Alena grown being troubled and afraid for son's well—being, and so, she asked our neighbor, whose owned a car:—Can you, please, drive my son and my husband to pre-school. Today is my son's birthday. And I really wish for my son to be happy on this special day!—This male neighbor seems being happy doing her a favour, especially, like hearing that Egor is the birthday boy. Even if, he is getting ready taking his own son too pre-school, when he has let known:—I'll take him there, cause I'm driving my son Ludwig to the nursing school, whilst it's on my way to be. Seeing they've lived not far away from the place where pre-school is located. So Alena come across, and get your son in my car! Let's keep moving on from this backyard, pronto!—It seems the whole thing have been settled; after that this male turns to face Alik implying:—Put your son inside my car! What you're waiting for?—Instead of putting me in neighbor's car, Alik—on that stand-in is gnashing his teeth. There is taking place incident: he then began to hit me over my upper back or below buttocks. It's being aching, cause I endlessly sobbing even louder and heavier. In that case mom has grabbed me away from dad's hand, while is trying comforting me. I could not stop crying, while even our neighbor, Jura, who has become irritated; seen as next he began whisper onto Alena's ear:—I can't stand and watch, how he hits and disdains he's own son. I can't do such like thing, as I will teach your husband a lesson. He'll remember for the rest of his fucking life! I'm a father myself, may not be a perfect example, but I could never lay a finger on my son. Put Egor inside my car, Alena!—Next Jura is twisted back to facing my dad with his fists which become visible, while he has ascend straight to him, seeing as followed by him saying in out loud voice:—Get the fuck away from my car, before I regret to do something with you, and I should forget that you're, Alik—my neighbor. I'll take your son to pre-school' without you! Fuck off from my car! You're, Son of a Bitch!—

So, my birthday be ruined obviously by my dad, I felt on that special day, its turn instead to be the worst day of my life. I could not stop crying for a full day in the row, neither enjoyed a yummy birthday-cake, nor being in the company of my friends there, who have cheered me up with pet chocolates to munch.

Later this afternoon, on which instant Alena arrives to pick up Egor from pre-school a teacher started one-to-one with her, of a warning:—Mrs Borodin, I am giving you a last warning! Don't allow your husband bringing your son to 'Pre-school', without supervision either by you, or someone else. Because your son was very upset the whole day in the row, today:—He was crying whole day in a row, shuddering, as many times visit the toilet. Egor even wet his pants once, which is very unusual for Egor. It didn't occur, since Egor was younger than one-and-half years old, where the first time he had been attending our Nursing School. A men, by name Juriy, who's brought today Egor here, was really worried about your son's welfare, and told us the whole thing that has occurred. So, I warn you, before we're taken any action to bring your son in the place, either yourself, or anyone in your family, or someone else, that you trust with Egor!—

CHAPTER 7

A few months passes, and they are started to hear stories, which worlds apart more or less exaggerated with the reality about other incidents, on the topic of irradiation the, on top of they have got used to live in accident.

In the interim, while Alena or Esther would go down to the market, since the Borodin lived in a provincial town, the people there predominantly have to buy groceries and other necessary items to eat. In view of that walking down to a market the folks would always cautiously checking every bit of products, vegetables specially, which have grown on the fields. As for the poultries, or other types of meat, the person cautious were buying provisions, which they have paid money for it. While the milk with a range of products, which contained dairy food just before the residents were using, amid the folks become a great fear for everyone in district and the local Government, were on the state of a high alert. The residents within the area, would come down to the markets in order to buy or sell instead they weren't buying groceries, not without carefully acquire scanning: first by those specially authorized persons from the health dep: either by doctors, or nurses. It's emerged warning, which were glued on walls, where viewed a lot by those locals of placates in public places or gatherings. Specially these listing with warnings in turn would hanged in markets as a reminder, as importance of the news, which the inhabitants regularly were listening often track broadcast on the radio, or by other way of statement sources, to be heard as a warning:—Foodstuff counted: meat, poultry, milk, cheese, and vegetables, or groceries, which had arrived from nearby the locations of Chernobyl zone, neither to be accepted in, nor to be sold to the public, or its going to be legitimate to make sale by anybody!—

After a catastrophe struck in Chernobyl, the nearby area citizens tried to ignore, have not purchased provisions, which been sold by unknown sales persons, not without proper certification enclosed authorizations. An included variety: like lollypops or other items, and must be sold on markets openly. general public, counting my family, were really scared; and worriedly waiting daily for the news, either to be reported at some stage in broadcast on TV or radio of any news, which would appeared or have explained to them. as a result started to fall first casualty—in neighborhood, amid our acquaintances. To my family misfortune this was not an exception—as evil had not missed us.

Not a very long time after, my grand-dad Josef's sister or my Great Aunt Bella had passed away, while Alik alongside Alena have been present there at her funeral. Those two initiate of this deceased woman's daughter, whose happen there, as also being my grand-dad's niece, Vera during their exchange of grief the last one tells on hers panic, that a while ago she had got as being examined by a Doctor for a scheduled medical check-up. During her medical examination doctors had found a lump within her breast. Given that she is only thirty-three-years old, and already has a beautiful family with two kids, her being pregnant with a third child too. In spite of odds Alena tried make sense, as lady looked so desperate, which has discussion in a soft voice:—Believe me Vera, you must not think negatively of your condition and be categorical. The doctor gave you hope, and I believe that it looks hopeful, there is always hope that the whole lot you're getting through is going to be fine in the future, I advice you to rely on God's mercy that He—Almighty will be gracious to you and family!—Alena then ads infinitum by talking with her, and started telling her a story, by a similar mistake that had come to pass years ago with Esther:—It's like your situation, Vera when doctor's detected a lump in her breast, be fond of an advice to carry out by a surgical procedure. Years ago the only trouble, which she a vicious arisen was surgery removable, but all seems to be fine back than, many years had passed. Now she is still fine. My mother keeps on too well, being in good physical shape even now.—Besides Alena tried to look at her situation in a positive light, but it seem terrified her:—Vera you must believe that jointly with you're family and kids will be fine for many years to come . . . —Then again she's my dad's cousin, as I felt obligation apt for conscious what's being happening around, just then, I daringly asked her on the matter:—I wish to find out and to learn, what death means for? My focus, what happen, after your mother had died? If Great Aunt Rose is coming back alive to be with us or she is not?-

A few months passes, while my parents have existed for nine out of ten on their ups and downs at home in their relationship. Above all after dad came back from the hospital, where he has got thoroughly med examination, after he was taken a trip to Chernobyl's neighbourhood.

CHAPTER 8

One night, while playing with me mom clued-up me that she is having a baby. Then Alena pretence to freeze with a grin, and in aloud voice invites me to have a chat:—Do you want to have a little sister or a brother?—I've become more than ever astonished and speechless, all the same, I grasp now that may perhaps having my own little sister or even a brother to play with her, or him, and teach the baby the whole lot I new. given that I'll be the eldest and ideal brother, who could take care of her or him so as to protecting the baby. Is thoroughly making absorption, I start suddenly laughing:—Oh, mommy, is it true? That I can have a brother or a sister? When? Mom, where are you going to buy it?—She still has glowing of a conceivable delight, when assumed:-Yes, but do not break this surprise, yet! This time it's definitely a girl and you shall having a little sister. From a source I have had a dream and saw a little girl. I believe in dreams, and want this little baby!—That turn out to be the most wonderful news that Egor didn't hear for a long time. Suddenly, they are turning towards the front door, as him being in the hall sited. Over there yonder opposite from us I've spotted dad, whose stood in the doorway, and was listening carefully towards our chat. Then suddenly, he's green eyes turned brown; abruptly gave the impression of being like a predator, where Alik on the move on foot towards mom's footing, and is looking at her, he then alleged:—So, it's really true, that you're pregnant? Really? Don't, we have got other problems in our lives to worry about? You're definitely not going to give birth to 'this' baby! And if you think, what you just said, it's not going to happen? You're mistaken, my dear wife. As for you, Egor, get the hell away from her, or you, bloody! . . . —I began crying by Alik's reaction, while both: my mom and dad began raising their voices. Though, I have tried to keep closer to mom, instead she is demanded me to go away to Leonid rent room. Being there I couldn't hear a word, what dad is yelling:—You're, bloody . . . If you're not going to make the abortion, you don't know, what I'm prepared to do with you? Do you understand me? I don't want this baby, and I don't give a damn, whether it's a girl or what ever. Tomorrow you must go to make the needed arrangement for schedule time to visit obstetrician, on your abortion! But if you should refuse my claim, Alena? Demit you, I could just . . .—Next he in full swing, starts hitting Alena: smack! While he is also screaming, with cursing her:—I hope that you die, as you're undertaking this abortion procedure. But if its not going to happen I shall force you to do that, without your consent, off on my free will. Besides I believe, your precious mother and you for the company will be dead soon. You're bloody demit people! I will deal with all of you're: one by one . . . !—After that Egor has heard loud that ensue—Alena sees to in hot-tempered voice by shielding hers in opposition to Alik:—You bastard! I'm longing to give birth to this baby, from the time, once I believe it's going to be a girl. I've already a dream about this new baby, even before Egor born!—She stops exclaiming for a minute, while breathing deeply, Alena hysterically is meaning:—Also I saw a dream about him to be born, giving birth to a beautiful baby boy, the absolutely copy of a son, alike color of his eyes and hair, that looked like a picture of our Egor, who has got sea-blue eyed and white skin and I even saw his hair, the absolute copy, the same as painted portrait of him, on the time when he was born. Like our son I have seen this time again a little girl from another of my dreams. And this time again, I saw a lovely little girl! I wish to bear for another child. Even supposing, the obstetrician advised me, despite the outcome, if I should get pregnant or not that it has to pass at least four years, until I will be giving birth to a new baby, as it makes nor difference to me, if it passed four years or not? I'm also aware, on the danger, to my they well-being and I have to face. I am willing, also to take that risk, cause this is my life,not yours, Alik! Thus far they're talking about life of this baby, that I am caring inside me!— Before long Egor began hearing resonances of screams, its earshot of he's mom voice. Thus, I felt like to run directly towards living room her and helping her. Save for Leonid who at that point stops me assured me by telling him:—Don't you worry, Egor, she is my daughter! I'll never give that bastard or anyone else the satisfaction to offend, hurt or touch you or your mother. Stay here with grandma, until I'll be coming. My boy, do not leave the room by any arisen situation!—Egor be worried for his mom become reckless, and start to cry again. Still Esther, be unaware, but she's being able to hear, not all phrases, but enough to figure out. As she is always kept asking me what they're saying, and who said what to whom. Being a little kid, I could not become conscious, why and whom is right, and who is wrong. Him lacking by unfamiliar through such vocabulary of words, consequently, Egor have neither sufficiently being an expert to judge by these enlighten word-by-word of a colorful vulgar Russian language, nor could understand what they are saying to each-other? It seems like some of these tongue being odd for me listening to that. After that he began hearing scream among the resonance a quiet tone of a voice, taken place in the living room, but have proclaimed also angry words spoke negatively, to boot by means of Leonid. Those echoes of yelling are coming from the living room. Followed by rather of an object that knocked down, or someone has fallen on the floor. Just like that Egor hearing, which is on the high-pitched line:— Papa, don't do it! Stop it, he isn't worth it to fall for his tricks!— Soon those ear-splitting yells have stopped. Next Egor saw Leonid enters back into the bedroom. Except he appears pale and angry. He still being hot and bothered by each one over there yonder, and finally ran into the living room. Then I sneak a peek on my dad's face—its be converted into green with anger attempts, and it has gave the impression of Alik's eyes—

changed. Shortly after Alik went to the kitchen, and Egor quietly follows him as well. Its be visible Alik's being making tea in a jar, but its emerged unlike, of which I used to drink, for the most part it's contained more than usual as of some tea-leafs, in contrast it's emerged to be short of full-size quantity wateriness, which have developed into a murky, as its contained not a full cup of that unknown liquid. Thus far, Alik has drank it all the same; next he grins to me, and kept doing it, as earlier. Then he looked at he's son with a smirk, as he let know:-You see, everything is going to be fine, son. Go back in the big room and start to play with your toys, Egor!—The moment Egor returns back into living room let Alena know what he saw:— Daddy being made some odd drinks and very dark tea . . . —What have effect later Egor doesn't recall, other than that he heard a bit later, Alena and Alik start arguing again; but this time, Aliks said:—When I come, back from work, tomorrow you need to tell me, whether you've decided to go ahead with the abortion. What's more, if you're decided give birth to a baby, in the situation, either I would personally take care of an abhorrent situation that has occurred, or look after the problem from other potential. I'm making here a point, if you refuse do abortion, but willing to give birth to it, I'll pack up my set of clothes and leave for my parents place!-, Alik stops; then takes a deep breathe, while becoming angrier with fury in his voice, he declared to her:—And yet Alena, you're likely forget that you have inserted a 'spiral', other way, or other this baby could be born with defects it's one point. My second indication is that you're, dear likely have forgot on my trip to Chernobyl, where I have worked with others with the emergency assistant crew, and took part there. Thus, its a real chance that radiation might have got into my internal body. I want point out that I'm not even aware of my own fate for the future? But you want to take risk—giving birth to a child, in any case of consequence from X-rays, follows effects from all, which occurred over there? Besides the effects, which might appear later from that event? Are you, crazy? What is more, I am not even sure, if this baby is my? I'm given you a word of warning for the last time! Look me in the eyes, when I'm talking to you? Do you grasp, what I've just said? Decision is up to you Alena? Think carefully? You've the time either to break that circle, or decide the fate— until tomorrow what to do? My, dear Alena!-, these last words he's said with biting wit. But Egor tried not to listen what's going on their argument, as ultimate has covered his ears over with bear hand. Alik likely has bashed Alena, that's why she tried not blaring, cause for his sake, as a result has left the room without delay. He was set out to bed earlier that night, but falling asleep; hearding that he's mom was crying, following her being shuddering with gulp his of air befall into deep sleep.

The next morning I saw mom, who has been worn a bandage upon her left index finger. On top she has got a bump black eye clearly visible roughly over her left eye. Until recent days her left finger is half-lying on a fragment bend downwards— Egor believes that Alik broke it then, on the same night, while thrashing her.

A few days pass, while Alena being on foot, all at once strolling—conveying Egor's baby-trolley to pre-school; while she's placed him in a baby-trolley, she talk to him:—Sweetheart, today is a hard day for us, so you must stay overnight in pre-school. Cause, I won't be able to pick you up today from there. But tomorrow, you will be back home, as always, you have to behave well in pe-school, while staying there. Listen to the teachers and be a good boy!-

'At first I didn't pay attention, if it's being a real discussion or just a joke. I couldn't imagine, that she or somebody from my family, wouldn't be attending there and unable to pick me up from. Egor maintains being in 'pre-school without suspicion, as usual happy enjoyed him amid all these play and games, music and lessons habitat cookings. With an accustomed day nap has included of many other things, like its typically I would be able to find it, which I could systematically attend it. But then the evening draw closer, and its be time for Egor to go home, given that all those kids in the group, including he's friends, had left for home, been picked up by their parents, who still arriving, and the kids are called to get dressed, since they hading for home. But nobody being in a hurry to pick me up from there. This new teacher, who came to pass here be as a substitute from Egor's familiar nurse-teacher, where he has got usued for few years; new arrival has educated as us following her to another room, this's where the teacher has brought me in—there being surrounded by other kids, whom I saw and met before, seen that few amid them were not from my nursery group. The remained broods there're either older than Egor, or babyish. Searching the room I've spotted a baby-boy, who is standing up above the bed's bench and shaken it; and has appeared around one-a-half years old. At first the boy is howling, then a baby in bed gradually stopped, and looks towards Egor's stood. 'Soon I start to get worried, when taking a view from the window, where I have spotted outside already grown to be a twilight. Thus I realized that I still being stuck in pe-school; even if, I loved to attend it on a regular basis or I dare say—full-time. After these groups have finished watching telly all have a snack: warm milk and small sandwiches, as those kids consumed biscuits.

Minutes later, this new teacher gave them go-ahead watching television again. Before Egor could even figure out what's arranged, it was the time for those kids, counting him too, getting ready to sleep in their bunk beds, and to lie down in there. At that time it's struck Egor, while starts to remember, what Alena telling him all along on that morning. So, it was true. I latent 'staying overnight there. out of the blue he began crying and each moment more heavier and louder. Within a short time the teacher being unhappy with Egor's deeds, even if she let me know:—Egor, everyone have told me that you're intelligent boy, with good behaviour. But today with such behaviour, I can't believe, its all true? You're disturbing all the other kids here, Egor, cause, they need go to sleep! Your loud cry, and wildness! Also you were not only disturbing other kids, but also breaching regularity of disciplinary behaviour here! Didn't your mother tell you earlier about it? Cause you must stay tonight, and you will be sleeping in here, did she not?—As I've heard the whole thing her been telling me well, neither I could believe it, nor want to, that's really happening to me, or its like become a bad dream for me?'—He kept crying, and would not stop. Until, the teacher took my hand and has insisted him to go out and following her, seeing they both on foot exit are all through the corridor. They were came together in this office, which has usually been occupied by the principal, who's often would take me around, where she often had awarded me with similar certificates, with an upper hand of sweets, while she becomes impressive with astonishment in the vein of:—Egor, today your performance is perfectly ideal. Here is your award, come up and get it! You deserved it. Herewith is your new rhymes, with lyrics for the songs for you to learn, because I believe in you, Egor! Also here is the chocolates for your special performance today!—But on this picky night I've not been invited to the principal's office to meet her, who I believe was fond of me. A reason for me coming here with this teacher be that I haven't behaved in a proper way. In effect, I wasn't conducting myself, cause I have disturbed other kids, who slept. Rumors has it that sobbing have troubled them, as she point out they could not sleep, as Egor woke them up from you're howling. The teacher takes a deep breathe; she then alleged:—Egor, what am I going to do with you? You, seems to me a smart boy, but I won't be caring you around, as I usually I do bear those babies. I see, how upset you're, but a solution to that is: you need to stop crying, and get to sleep. Cause tomorrow, when you are going to wake up, except you must be aware, here those kids will be waking up very early in morning, there're rules here. How you will to do it? And I see you're distressed? You might feel very tied in the morning—it is one point. Secondly, its already past the time, since you have to be in bed to asleep a long time ago. So, Egor stop, crying, and tell me what should I do for you're to stop being upsetting?—I couldn't work out, if she was talking to me or to herself. So, I acted in response frankly, my shoulders are shuddering, and looking directly into her eyes:—I want to see my mommy, and

I wish for her to come here, and take me home? If not, I won't stop crying!—A lady teacher began shaking her head, and didn't look pleased of my disobedience. Still she is thinking about something, she then said:—It's impossible, Egor, your mom is not coming today to pick you up. You have to stay and sleep here. You don't have a choice. Then again, I might call in your home, and ask, if she will be able to change her mind after all and do that. Do you want me at your home? So, Egor I could make that call? Do you remember your home phone number?—I have stopped sobbing, even if, I look in her face acting in response:—Yea Mrs. Petrenko I want you to call my house, to beg mommy coming fast and taking me home. Positively my dad or grandpa Leonid instead can come too take me home?—Given it's restricted only five digital numbers, despite that I was slightly over three-years-old, I did remember my home phone number, that seem has astonished this pre-schoolteacher, of my ability in knowledge. But, in contrast she is being unhappy by my behavior; despite of her displeasure how Egor has behaved, she has decided to make a call, cause she understood that it was without a result of her tactics to deceit me, or fool me around into a trick. At last, she have dialled my home phone number, and talked for a short time with Leonid. By a teacher's second attempt there was Esther, whose heard the phone ringing, and picked up receiver. Over the phone, she has explained the situation to the teacher, until today, I wouldn't know, if she had acquainted her with what happened; yet an educator looks nervy, her cheeks grown being pink. Following the teacher has dialled unkown phone number, and begun talking to someone, is asking:—May I speak to Alena Borodin? Thank you. It's not a problem, good, I will wait then!—In a minute she began talking again at one fell swoop I've heard afar on the line mom's voice, so me became restless and being annoying. I reached for the receiver all the time, until she passed it to me, but then finally I is listening what mom has to say:—Son, how are you doing in kindergarten? Are you all right, son? I can hear by tone of your voice that you are crying. Stop sobbing, and listen very carefully. Okay?—Retorting to her, Egor began talking fast before she changed her mind, by saying:—come here in pre-school, mommy, please and pick me up! I'll be a good boy, and always listen to you. I'm begging you, mommy! Don't punish me! I won't go to sleep, until you come! I'm going to wait for you. When you're coming to get me from here?—When I have spoken my shoulders trembled, with the breathing been intense, by which half of argument become shallow frequent breathing. But Alena's respond shocked me:—Egor, I can't come today to pick you up. And I am not punishing you, darling. I'm at Hospital right now. But tomorrow, I promise, either grandpa Leonid or anyone shall be definitely coming to get you home. Don't you worry, we all won't leave you in pre-school for a long, I can safely promise you that! Trust me! Just wait until tomorrow, and behave they arell, while you'll not even notice, how quick the time is going to pass. Sweetie, I'm bagging you, be a good boy, make me happy and stop crying. Listen to your Teacher, and go to sleep, now!It is too late, while you need to be strong. Yes?—When Egor heard he's mom's shallow voice, as talked, he has realized that she was being sick. thus Egor's raised a question, again:—Mommy, what is wrong with you? Are you sick? What is it, tell me? You're having temperature? And so you won't be coming to take me home, or you will? What's about a little sister or brother you promised to buy?—He talks with desperation and antiquity, which has felt in his voice, and is waiting, that Alena will change her mind at the end. Then it hit me, as I've recalled, that she gone in a hospital, and figured out her possible being unwell? Alena responds with being affectionate, also softness has heard in her voice:—No, darling, I'm not sick, just my tummy is hurting that's all. Don't worry, son when I'm going to see you, my pain shall disappear. As you'll take care of me, won't you? And I will feel well again, good, it's a deal? Now, Egor calm down, and if you'll for my tummy to get better, you have to reassure me that you will be listening to the teacher, and go straight to sleep, after we'll end our phone conversation. Will you do that for me? What I just told you, can you promise me that?—He replies, still being heard with extreme angst, which completely astonished her:-Yes, mommy! I promise you listen to the Teacher, if you promise instead tomorrow, I'll be coming home? And you'll be waiting for me there?—Alena on the line, is laughing as responded with assurance to him that tomorrow will be exactly, as he asked it turn out, she hasn't breached her promise to him after all!

Over time Egor became sick: saw red rashes over he's whole body, with resting spots on his skin, which effect have caused high temperature for him. Alena called a doctor. When doctor arrived for a quick visit for check him up, follows has done him medical examination—Egor being diagnosed with German measles. 'Too my sufferings being added that mom could not stay to take care of me. As a result my dad has claimed an absent from work to look after this sick me, on grounds of thus family circumstance Alik being granted with a sick leave intend for their family doctor's in order for him staying home with the kid. When Alena would remain at home before going to work, Alik acts as if he is an excellent father in front of her pretending and fool each around that, may well he was in his own way. After she would set foot off and leave home he is either yelling on top of his lung at me, or start teaching me enunciate rude words with an obscene language, on top too cursing, and swearing at every in mom's family.

One night, after Alena arrived from work, Alik has prior stirred Egor against Esther, and send him off to her room to say:—Grandma, when are you going to die? You're already a walking corpse. Ha—Ha—Ha!—Then, Egor covers with illustrious, given Alik talks in his ear softly is half whispering, so that no-one would be able to hear. Then he sends him to Alena to insult her:—Good boy! And now go to Alena, and tell her ... —Being only a three years old kid, actually I have no idea, what's good to say—and what is evil. I was hostile, and said to mom in a clear, loud voice:—Alena, you know something, you a bitch! And a bloody whore! Daddy hates you, and we all hate you!—Her face be transformed into pale—I saw expression, by which her mood has also changed. Besides tone of her voice became irritated on a way she start talking to me. Alena has not done hard for my discipline often, but this time she was irritated at me with an angry of bitterness. Despite of what Egor genuine has said that, honestly regrets and comprehend her very, as these means, but at that time I was only a child, thus event could not happen being conscious to twig of thus meaning for those words, which has brought a nasty reaction from mom, since my dad taught me these proverbs been to blame. at that time she has responded instantaneously to me:—Egor, you a very bad boy!—Next she grabs my hand and taken me to the corner that has always being the place for my punishments, when I would be naughty: so she left me in that part of the room and by strictness of impatience in her voice, commands Egor to stay still, until she would give me go-ahead to leave the corner and being liberated from punishment. Egor has reacted—become upset, and is crying, then he's begun plead his mom for forgiveness; despite lacking of grasp, as him being blameworthy for? Except Alena, who retorts fairly the opposite be firm, but haven't looked in Egor's eyes, as her been enraged. She is warned:—Egor, if you ever repeat those words again, I'll resolve to grant you by a punishment!—Also Alena has alleged that she may decide to leave Egor over night in pre-school, and only pick him up on Fridays. Sadly, he believed that she has strikingly able to a certain extent to do so by way of telling him the truth, cause once, a short time ago he stayed in pre-school overnight, where he over-heard unlike stories as had a chat with other kids, who told him why they left to stay there. Being only a kid, it terribly has struck Egor, so as Alena to give her word—and is capable stick by that. Then unexpectedly Alik turns up, and walks him out towards toys. Egor still is feeling upset, and hysterically being crying. Abruptly be heard as Alik began to scream:-Alena, you a bloody bitch! Don't ever do that to my son! More, I've decided to make an appeal to a Family Court, and I'll be taken custody for Egor! You not feet enough to raise him, and it's precisely, what I'm prepared to tell there. I'll tell the same in a Court-room that you're whore, and undeserved to raise a child. I hope you will die soon.

Too bad, you didn't die, through you're abortion procedure. And if that won't happen—being a vampire, I'm willing to evaporate blood, and all the energy out off your fucken body! You'll weight no more than fifty-five kilogram. I can promise you that!—As upshot by the pair started argueing. Next to be heard Alik's rude words not in favour of hers, there being also heard and argument: predominantly both are verbally abusing each-other. Also both are screaming, but Alena is over yelling on Alik by watchword:-You will never get take my son away from me, because the Family Court is always on mother's side. Even if . . .—She's fiery and ruthlessly being arguing, by calling him:—Alik, you a crazy man, who's unable even to satisfy a woman!—She has sustained in colorful vulgar words—making clear to him that she never was a whore and never will be. As for he's 'atypical sexuality' Alena enhanced, by which she has doubts about him being a real male, in view of the fact they have to check him out by a doctor-specialist in that area. Above all the verbal assault Alena is too held him so that if she could neither trust him with Egor, nor will she be able to leave her son with him alone in a single room without a proper supervision,she's declaring never ever in his care, even if they must live separately from her parents. Seen both are barring temper involving their infuriation—emerged on Alik's expression has gradually altered—to green, as color in his eyes—changed to brown. He quite the opposite has stopped arguing with her, seen that Alik underway to their bedroom. Barring Alena, is followed Alik to the bedroom, as she hooked on as is given him lowdown above her character:—While we're on that issue and I thought a lot by long-standing idea of divorcing you? I keep staying with you Alik, only, cause Egor needs a father, thus he would have a full happy family? But my reflection now is—for my own happiness, and Egor's too. But I don't have to take that shit from you anymore, until he is growing up?—So she won't stop in the mean of the cruel words, of which Alik payed attention by hearing it; as she's filling him by meaning that she hates him and his guts even more than he does her. She then turn that talk in bearing of a real hatred in dealing with him:—I've never loved you, nor intend to do so sometime! So, fuck you mother-fucker! You're dirty and awfully smelling bastard!—Whilst Egor, neither was heard Alena talking with anger and disdain, which being directed towards Alik, nor himself ever saw his parentd arguing candidly, with ferocity—mostly in front of their son.

The next day dad let us know that he's absent from work, then I left home in mom's care. Although mom loved me dearly, she still was mad at me from the earlier incident, which's happened yesterday. For now I over-heard a new conversation she had with grandma Esther, when the latest one said to her:—It's very sad, that bastard is teaching him those rude and horrible words to say towards you, and particular to me. I was crying by hearing what Egor told me these awful phrases that bastard taught him, I would not like or even wish to repeat that. On the other hand, you must recognize that Egor is just only a little kid, who is barely over three-years-old, and for that reason—he doesn't even realize what he was saying. Even so, you must now stop Egor to repeat these non-sense ever again, particular what he said yesterday. Try to be firm with him, don't punish him harshly. Make him to be occupied with books, toys or other he's stuff, to what he used to do in pre-school. even if, Alena you need to go seen a paediatrician and ask them, if he is feet enough to get back to surroundings, which he is felling relaxed, by nor means, you know if Egor is sufficiently well? But once he is feeling well enough, don't hold him any longer home, just send him back to pre-school with lots of reason to reveal to a doctor, of what situation you're existing in.—Later that night, when Alik arrived back from work, I is playing. As he comes within reach of my site—since he want to teach me telling to others with of verbal abusive language, and is insisting:-You must repeat these words, which I have just taught you—this time say it to Leonid?—Absolutely not as I pushed dad away, as it seems that I felt like not to repeat it anymore, this's not funny, so I come back with a firmly respond:—Leave me alone, to play! I don't wish to repeat suchlike words! If you want to do, go and say it yourself!—

'For the next few days I wasn't feeling well. But after that, those three went for scheduled appointment to the doctors. Alik has too accompanying mom and me, instead of him going away working. Once medical test be carried by our local doctor; the three have gone down to the Cafe, while Alena ordered lunch for those three, seeing Egor is sitting on the other side of the table—just opposite from his father's position. After mom brought the soup with divers cooking and placed it on the table, dad began to feed me, though I didn't need that favour from him, cause in pre-school we all have taught to eat by themself and being, as independent, as possible there. Once he open my mouth allowed dad to feed him, Alik instead abruptly be converted into aggressive upshot, as he pushed a spoon inside Egor's cavity of the mouth so far inside, by which he felt pain on skin tone as well in all spots around his lips, also inside jaws and gums, on top of his cheekbones and else. As for my lunch this food has spilled over my jacket, of thus incident I begun coughing and crying at the same time. Alena has lost patience. She then gets up from the chair around and grabbed the spoon out from his hand, as has assumed to Alik has pointed a finger at her son:— . . . to get the hell away from Egor! You're basted!—All that ordeal and mockery be done by Alik's deeds towards his son didn't in the least off disposition to have their feast, in fact Egor being distressed, though, but felt hungry, since it was usual time for him to consume lunch. What Alik tried to prove by thus conduct we both unaware of, even now, possibly he just felt like it to pay them back, or maybe he was for all time greedy, crazy with jealousy. That's the best way in he's opinion making Egor shed tears and suffer, with Alik's intent to spoil appetite for both of them: for hers and he's son. After thus unpleasant event Egor began less be in touch with he's dad. Even if Alena being absent working, in view of a previous episode he keeps asking Alik, how long before his mom is coming home?

CHAPTER 9

What basically I wish to keep posted of that state of affairs with the aim of the relationship between Egor's parents, which have lacked of achieve, neither they being unable to bond in a bid to stabilize, nor seem improvement in their liaison. During that time, Egor's reflection and hopes were, quite the opposite: instead of bonding with a view to bring Alena and Alik together by connection, as a substitute state of affairs become unbearable for both of them, which have lead to separation. A view: winter has arrived—but the festive season been coming to an end. Here it's already past the New Year and the Orthodox Christmas with the Old New Year celebrations being on its pick. Sees winter, be surrounded by lots of snow, which fall out om the event—and happen just a week after the old New Year, which usually to be Celebrated. That event ensued in a cold month of mid-January of 1987, surrounded by masses of snow, which saw remote, in fact been in the midst of that thickness' layer of white cover up on the ground all over the place in the streets, and even up on the roofs of the buildings. As it has given the impression of been like a magnetic power, been demanding me to go downstairs, and play with snowflakes or just to be carried away on the sledge along with fluffy snow surface there. While I watched from my room's window downwards to a backyard—it's just clicked me with an idea to ask dad to take me for a ride on a sledge, which have always given me joy in that kind of action pro excursion on top of it. I have also being enthusiastic asking his dad to take for a ride on the sledge, in the region of city hub that, spree Egor loved it very much, seen outdoors was plenty of snow as it is nor being a very chilly winter on this calendar day, nor more than minus -10 Degrees C, compare to those previous days, and it was Saturday. Adjacent to our town emerged be a tiny via estimation, for that reason I only getting ready to put in the picture for dad . . . At the same time, Egor has been distracted he's mother, whose in her turn in advance made warning that he can't go for a walk off now, because she and he's dad decided to split, while be supposed to reside separately in differ cities and house. Alik be supposed to move out form our place and live remote of our state, while they are going to remain where they are they arere. Unexpectedly I'm having befalls silent, which I became conscious of their intentions with her meaning, as well that's for thus entire family there being a propos, but logical, even for me more than ever just then a real experience to deal with. Soon after Alik has made clear that simple himself, he is sorting out of he's son and wife, as they are separating, cause he to be moving out. In a difficult situation Egor has been helping Alik packing up his stuff into the suit-cases. After a while Alik grabbed some of he's belongings and moved out in corridor. Despite all the odds, earlier occasion dad left I even run in the entrance open the front door for him that he would not be leaving without him hugging and kissing my cheeks. Alik cried; following waving up his hand, where attending to face me with tears run down he's face:—Goodbye, my dear, son Egor!—

They were married almost five years, but through that have split three or four times. This pair lived separately, Alik would move to his parents hometown, where's Alena be staying with Egor in her parents flat. Then Alik and Alena have decided that was enough, cause she just could not take it anymore.

Even with the aim of Family Court procedure be started by going through final stage of using the fill divorce papers with the intention of ending Egor's parent relationship. When divorce process being terminated it has made sense to me; even then it didn't occur to me authentically that my life will not be the same. But I couldn't believe it, or maybe I didn't want to accept the true in all me paying attention to, as a matter of fact—the entire state of affairs with a view to those maters, papers have been signed. As far as this divorce record that was received, except meaning if it's being a game for me or possibly a bad dream?—Meantime, every day Egor would search out and learn a lot of new things, but strange and too gist: why all these serious consultations intended for? Along with these unknown things would not click for me or signify no matter, which? About my parents divorce—at home: rumour has it all, and yet I could not figure it out, what's next to come?—

CHAPTER 10

The time slowly, but surely is passing by, when I have turned four-years, already, is apparently begun asking questions about: 'what divorce means' between my pals in pre-school? Area under discussion I covered with my teachers apt, who explained to me. And it struck me, since they've finally told me—then I began comprehend that my dad is not coming back to live with us, nor will he be present too watch me growing up, neither.

After six months had passed, since my parent finally got divorced; they have become liberated from each other. For time being, in the face of the whole thing I is kept waiting for dad to show up, still imagining that he might appear one of those days to pick me up from pre-school that he always had done it on prior occasions. But he never appeared, as I have not got a choice, while trying to get used to my new life without dad being together with me, by seen for my part of grown-up. It's even perchance appeared that I might not recollect for being missing dad so much, because for me the most important thing in life—to stay together with my mom. Despite of a challenge with myself, as I tried to hold on to my reminiscences of my dad, by keeping his picture as a visual images, which kept my brainpower: remembering him deep within my mind this is all I could do, and intuitive it at all times has been my wish. In view of the fact that I do have a father, and his name is Alik, so matter being significant to me, given that majority of those kids in pre-school, who were my friends there have got fathers, who lived alongside with of those and raised the kids as well. It was quite the opposite—without a result to solution at my home, which me being surrounded by a family, which I have enclosed to live with. Time and again I would look at family photos, and sudden start calling him, when there image of my dad comes into view: he's positioned on it covered in company with others. I would straight start call his name, as his face with a moustache became visible there. Be well acquainted with Alik's feature, I would not need neither recalling his portrayal, nor to stop thinking about him. Provided of meditation that I felt like to preserve his picture in my mind, trying hard to keep hold on to it, be kept, too save dad's image very deep in my subconscious and never to stop thinking about him. what ever the case was I tried make my family aware convincing them, that was my wish to be able very often remind them all of dad's present, this is what I want. Being that as it may, what ever the case was, together I have committed myself emotionally to memories of my dad, seen I is resisting, mother prolonged conversation with grandpa Leonid than would usually divert that debate about my dad—going on into a different course.

One day mom has bought me a projector with a collection of fairytales. And every evening mom has demonstrated these to me, still it was various of only either show on the wall, or midway intended for access of the door, which be painted contained by white color, where upon its surface has been covered with linseed oil, which made nuance extra glossy and smooth. I was excited, with the aim of a new hobby, and nearly occupied the all of my free time, but it turns out being worthwhile watching these tales. The minute I would be home, either after coming back from pre-school, or on the weekends, particular, while winter still being in its euphoria weather was chilly, or with raining outside, as this new hobby made me excited and hectic. That activity in due course helped me put aside other unwanted ideas, which have disturbed me for sometimes; added too from insulting queries unlike with mockery between other popular matters. Soon I started to forget all on raise questions, which now and then be a grown up person, valued more than ever, that it was the most offensive part under topics for discussion by everyone in my family to talk about my dad. 'Over all I have accepted that its being a good idea to distract me from the pain and depression, despite a separation with my dad, which's caused me a lots of hurting moments with a hobby that helped me prevail over especially from disturbing thoughts with intolerable, but to boot of sharp memories about him. For the families, who parents are getting divorced it affects first of all the kids. When this happens, is this leaves a scar which leaves a deep wound and unforgettable hurt in their hearts and souls, which might stay with them eternally, even it would never to be healed.' Meantime Egor is busy with excitement, when every time Alena would invite for demonstration of his favourite fairytales. Then, she made rules—when and how to watch these tales as it was always: the fist part emerged watching these—not before lunch or dinner; as for the second part to view it, after ceremonial dinner or tea. For him its like to be able travelling into a 'fairyland', possibly him being like a typical kid and engaging in their dream. Likewise mom was never mad, which being a help, seeing as she always have hanged about along with me in high spirits, and she knew well that children my age would visualize stuff, as too living within a 'Dream World', thus be a part for those to prolong period to grown up slow. Also I believe that she herself cherished with me, while watching fairytales, she's being dreaming as well of her own venture. Except to destroy a 'new imagining world', will by the same token loosing their strength, all together, most likely the kids grow being adults, who are able to kill off 'their moral ethics.' Some parents would shamefully haven't got a slightest sympathetic or inspiration, how the whole lot stays inside broods mind, every word of thus wicked verbal communication—less confusion, with its key point, how or why? With no in the least idea some parents are ill-advised not hypothetically assuming even, which might destroy the child's mental acceptance of wisdom, or could cause breakage off their spirits, as well devastate of their mental strengths of moral values. See them maturing and so it can break kids beliefs in good. Once those adults call the kids liars, facing thus effect upon kids are feeling designate along by their magic world, of what effect of that must be in time, as the kids creating around themselves. Adding together too their values in beauty in truth and morality. Like they would build castles of dreams and magic of they're own creations, its just like breaking a crystal ball, when them getting destroyed. Also visualizing how their dreams are supposed to smashed, or like sand castle,which getting ruined crumbled or spread out for good that might exist deepin kids's subconscious. But too bring up the anger and fury, towards their parents, or someone, which would call youth 'nick-names', it's like too be spectator: intend for'The shatter of imagine world, where at times, in the vein they would let go of they're believes in good, leaving them out empty—only with evil inside!'Still it must have become a painful transformation, more than ever for those teens and for youngsters else. It come into view—through their wounds won't be visible, since it should be placed not from faint the body, but from inside, very deep, where sole of those and sub-conscience are located. So majority of those heartbroken teenagers would maliciously may start with their own fury so as to attack not in favour of pitiful individuals, but for a majority adjacent towards their parents.

To retain with story as an interim measure returning back to fairy tales, I tried warily to memorize these lyrics, so far as I could, and me likely be able to bring about exercises by my excellent memories, which have power over a base for my future upbringing, and retains inward, how I must deal with. Egor really has a believe its turn into a great idea, that she helped me to overcome later by distorted issues, and built a base, what I have learned by heart gen that I'm still pursuing, by a loat from his nostalgia. He would learn new things in pre-school, that he used to attend for a few years: he started there, since he was an infant—from nursery, and alike other kids from his group, who mostly were of early on age or among the group in common with him. Teachers there would reading books to the kids, and tales, which seems to him being getting excited listening to these more attentively. Then the rest of Egor's group would listen to the teachers, which have read to them. 'While watching these tales that I have come across, and got learned to like that stuff very much, so he became a great listener, and to be an admirer.

Upon Egor's return home from kindergarten—he would run promptly into his room, whilst there on the screen have appeared fairytales, which pictures are deliberately with fully set between diverse colors being unimaginable feelings for him undescribed. Despite inconvenient, where our two bedrooms building emerged undersized being with its illustrious gauge, hasn't been converted into a design to facilitate for these kind of things, still effect being enormous. Yet, demonstration of the films essentially from a projector, pictured on tapes fully in color down the film between lines—subtitles. Just as well this has meant the world to Egor, and to his upbringing. I couldn't be happier to get hold control of tales. Apparent it wasn't just a toy, as in my dreams tales have been a reflection that being cherished—of a real mode by my mind's eye. Just then a lifetime ago—being a child, slightly over three-years of age; despite of that I've already become acquainted with Russian alphabet. Whilst I have also begun reading on my own. That time seems to be running fast, when later on I have grown up progressively, as turn four-and-half years, been watching the fairytales; and become engaged to be taught rote with lyrics of rhymes from poems. The entire volumes were written by those famous Russian poets with harmonious of the flowing lyrics. From now its being down-to-earth a job for me that I've learned by heart the whole of these written lines. Still every day I couldn't wait for the show to start with my favourite 'tales' amid main agenda that myself being counting, where I enthusiasticly whole day in a row—my view on these again. Just to raise the key points, given I could read on my own,equally, as those pupils from the fifth grades, even if these tales written in Russian. Thus I put aside in a relaxed mood of my mind, surrounded by so various of mixed images as to maintain the tales. Be in company with flashes of tales, in next to no time I forgot what I was searching:—Where's my father? When he is coming home to play with me?-

CHAPTER 11

After more than a year of the former illness with a result of he's sufferings, my grandpa Josef passed away, just two days after his birthday; as a consequence, grand-dad Josef was the second casualty among my family, as an effect of that tragic explosion occurred in Chernobyl's reactor. By means of the tragedy that struck—grandpa Josef died, this had occurred in mid October of 1987. After Alena and Leonid had received such dreadful news both of them resoluted travelling to Josef's funeral, in order to give their last respect to thus dreadful disease. despite my parents already were divorced, inexcusable for me to declare, with an eye to my parents haven't been living together any longer, except tragedy come to pass, nor the future have looked dodgy for both of them to flourish equally in their relationship, as a pair; the length of devoid neither affection between them, nor regards to one-another, still mom and dad not any longer grasp and in favour of both getting re-united even for my sake. Except for grand-dad Josef, whose funeral Alena and Leonid graced with their presence; saw his departure still had always made me committed to memory, as a great person, lacking only him, but also for our entire family, which was left off them. Personally I will always admire him in my heart for who he was: a great and courageous men, considering that he was my blood relation—grand-dad Josef!

Very soon I stopped asking question about: where's my dad, or when he need to come visiting me? And why my grand-dad Josef had to die, in tandem with about other unpleasant subjects. But after the projector had appeared in my home— nothing seems to interested for me except my fairytales.

Basically you may call it inspired by my dad's image, reproof that still remained in my mind. Just then, be grown up without a father-figure, the only men in the house the role suited, that I should look up to that—grandpa Leonid. By the same token I was always scared that one day mom may leave me too. Thus, I have pushed myself to please her, being proving to her, shown—I am the best son in the world, that she can be proud of.

CHAPTER 12

Pro tem, Alena's private life during that time, since her divorce from Alik—she has several proposals of marriage. Those guys, who came across they are not the first one to make such a proposal of marriage, and precisely ought not to be the last one either. To commence with at least back then, for a example, Alena has attracted lots of attention by many among those Russian chaps, who would tried hard to get her attention in order to notice them, as she even having raised issue on a marriage proposals from some of them to boot. At this time one among few of the Russian guys has actually attracted mom's attention in our ex—town, located in Ukraine. Despite the fact that, this chap being tall and good-looking man: as for the color of his eyes its nuance would appeared sea-blue, but contained by a dark nuance upon he's hair or shotten, likewise fold on me. She's fallen for this guy, whose name turn out being Alexander—, as she described:—A great proportion!—Alena gave a first impression being liking him very much. The man Alexander would come at her job range of time. Often than once finishing working day him either was accompany Alexander for a pleasure tour as would invite Alena in a restaurant to join him in company, involving many other places for their enjoinment. Before long she has really fallen in love with him, as their relationship gets more into a romantic involvement between those two, and it's being flourishing. At last Alena and Alexander leaned into each with sparkle of attraction, as magnetism have drawn the pair close to each other, as they forget about the whole thing round them. Grasp they are not alone in location, and feeling only magic of their presence. Alexander next started slowly to brush her lips with a kiss, while they have advanced further into a deep long-lasting that kiss. Followed by this pair pour into a full of meaning kissing, as too forgetting. they would appear as a pair in public, around them outer walls, that public saw inner, which have to stare at this pair with jealousy . . .

Eventually Alena and Alexander have realized them alone in his space feeling at ease and uninterrupted within their intimacy. Alexander then starts slowly brushing her pour into a kiss, as further into deeper longer passionate kissing until . . . The pair continuing dancing slowly, seeing as each slowly are getting undressed. At that point a magnetism bond those two, at the same time as they pour into a kiss, as their hands move fast. They're looking desperate and hungry for love, while are mutually slowly sliding in the bed. Full moonlight is passing through window—excels beyond with its reflection be sparkle into that bedroom.

Divisive, one day during lunch that has prearranged for Alena along side her client, who ensue to be one of mom's dealing cohort and woman. Given to consideration that she worked as an economist, in addition with her duties that she performed in order to execute an Annual report, which was counting quarterly reports in combination with bookkeeping, and too monthly financial details with other tasks. While working in that company, where she has been obliged to make balance reports, or else, where Alena was employed, which her main duties designed for, as her need proficiently accomplish topics with expertise, by which she would spend years of studies.

Going back to her meeting: a chat with this lady client, who happen to be Alena's client, to both of their amaze at the entry has appeared that Alexander-character. Once he has appeared there this woman, whose being sitting nearby mom, seen her expression, in contrast became pale at once. Even if, he asked mom to leave at once, except Alena is that kind of individual, who doesn't leave without hearing groundless explanation by her finger pointing. Thus Alena, decides to stay, and find out what all that odd frown expression is meant: eyes blinking with face mimic, which have effect here. Boost Alena be aimed on it Alexander and her barter mimics between the two. The instant Alexander has left that restaurant this young woman then began telling her a story about his personal life, as picking on he's habit. The woman used to date him a while ago, when she wasn't married: then they've got involved, as bond between them grew into a romantic one, the same as they became a couple. Then one day she found out that he is a professional gambler: he used to win large amonts of cash, but mostly losing to gamblers, who would travel from distance roving and change cities or could go secluded in a bid to make kind of playing cards or unofficially for luck picking him; or debts, who was a major gambler. Though, Alexander wad beaten many times during playing card games, but at the last time when he gambled away all in one's a large sum of money. In good time his mother died, by a cause of distress, and heart attack that be related to her son Alexander's dealings and bad habit, he's about losing her apartment, where his mom lived for years, and gambling away negligible. The client more or less is said:—If you're looking for that kind of life? Alena good luck to you! Don't forget, that you have a child to bring up and rise. As for Alexander character—him being a professional gambler, I personally could put myself and my son's life on the line, cause these sort of persons that he is dealing with, likely putting the lives for both of you and you're kids on that table to play, or undergo in a deadly risk!—Hearing thus revelation Alena befalls in a state of a shock, and is decided by having searched for the truth, and chinwag more with her about his character. By and by Alena arrived to his apartment is buzzing; shortly he opened the front door. When he saw her in doorway, his face suddenly turn into stone-white, and he is begun rushing her out. Alena is at a complete loss, and without delay demanded to let her in his apartment, which in no way he has refused.

By a short disagreement Alena daring revoltingly—pushed Alexander aside, and proudly on is stepped inside. Walking into living room Alena is spotting a trio among young chaps, and a middle age man seated around the table, whilst others have seated aside on the chaise lounge, and intently watched toward a wide table. Alena also glimpsed poker cards to be positioned, which lying on the middle of that table. Observing that scene Alena has changed her mind in a flash, as a result insisted heart-to-heart with Alexander; instead she given the lowdown for Alexander, and is asking him to meet her to chew the fat. When this pair have eventually met, Alexander wouldn't deny, is openly acknowledged that he's daringly quitting gambling. She, in spite of his hope being that kind of a self, who was nuable easily to trust a sole taken account of an eye to Alexander that deceived her, just he has betrayed her. In its place, Alena decided to get separated with him. Above and beyond, she is thus kind of an individual, who would be apt firmly said to, what she really thinks—straight in the face, without being a hypocrite:—I'm asking you're not seeking for me any longer, Alex!—It follows that she added, doubly:—I have lots of problems on my own to deal, burden on shoulders: my mother is ill, I've an old father, who's having a drink more than usual, do not forget a have child, whom I duty to raise him on my own with. So, I don't need new stress anymore. All I want is a peaceful life without new traumas. So, from now . . .-, She then takes a deep breathe, turns her head from to side, in a mournful voice:—it will be better for both of us to part for good! Alexy it's my final decision!-

CHAPTER 13

One day Alena decided to make a call, but before dialling a number she has enlightened Egor that, is determined to talk to Alik. 'So I've become nosy, but agitated at the same time, and very excited about that too. Though, is I kept asking her, whether I will be able to speak to my dad, of what she's come back with retort:—Of course you will, silly boy!—After a short awaiting she has dialled number, as began speaking with one over the phone, and to Egor's surprise this important self happen to be his dad. At last Egor has got a chance to speak with my dad; when I earnestly asked him, if not he is coming to visit me, he replied, that would be better for him will be taken a trip towards his town of dwelling for a visit to see him and grandma Dora, and have their home with aunt Tanja there as well. Egor's spirit improved into high, and so he could not wait until they are having intended for exodus as to travel visiting the entire Borodins family.

With a long period had passed that I got au fait on this day, but I have got to miss attending pre-school. In view of the fact that Alena and I were heading for a visit to my dad hometown, where Alik and these rests of he's family dwelled. I've wore the best suit that have been kept in the wardrobe meant for a special occasion. On one occasion I looked in the mirror: the attire is sitting nicely, and so have I in it, display of outfit shown to be suitable, and designed for me. He distinguished be happy with himself after all—standing in front of a mirror.

Soon those three have arrived in rural place and next they are just before in dad's apartment, by seen me grandmother Dora start kissing me, while she also cried, and so has my aunt Tanja. Although, she is holding a toddler, which's being resting on her hands, and sleeping. Other than when I enquire:— Ainty is this a real baby or a doll?—She made a laughter then acquainted me with that new realist infant, whose appeared being a girl. So she is my cousin, but the girl is a very miniature to be carrying her around and for me embrace it seen the infant being up, where I approached to take the baby at my hands, instead ant Tanja declined of implying that:—Egor, you a child, thus I afraid that you may well drop this infant, my daughter on the occasion?-

After a while Alena enlightens Egor that she and Alik with Great Aunt Eugene are going out for a while:—While you must behave well, and listen to grandma Dora, but not to disturb this infant.—And so, I be left at home under the care of my grandmother Dora and Aunt Tanja.

Period in-between mom and dad together with Great Aunt Eugene are taking a breath of air and strolling towards the train station, where the restaurant-buffet has emerged been located. By taking a seat—follows those three have become captivated in a serious argument amid them. In favour of both party's talk, Great Aunt Eugene is decided intervene by turning into mediator, since talk between my mom and dad hasn't gone smoothly as not achieved its aim, as they were using firm language, which become an objected alone from its. Alik, in spite of his protest has finally agreed to give his authorization for Egor to leave the Soviet Union in a bid to travel abroad; but not without extortions: in persistence, Alik has demanded, firstly:— . . . me to be given a big amount of cash, so that I will buy for myself a car and will be able to drive in the region of anywhere, as I need travelling. My second demand is: you must register the property in my name only, core existing of that apartment of yours, where you have lived for many years in the town, and still do right now. And since its be located in the Ukraine, so, I will be able to own this place—after you're four leaving the USSR . . . ?—Ultimately, two bedroom flat that he desperately fancy be registered under Leonid's name back then just when they are used lived here, the flat belongs to the 'municipality Government community housing'. As a result, it is not being possible by any circumstances register the apartment under my father's name.

Still, in the USSR rules and in accord of with the Law: all the public sector just then had been under regulations and strict control by the Government, besides it's being supposed to inexistence way of life by these private sectors, counting the 'Real Estate', which being a negative aspect in here. consequently it was impossible in any circumstances for us to reassign the unit, which he's raring to get into his ownership—in no way abiding to his demands. Next Alik added more wishes, which has suited him:—Importantly, you as is to be extortion, and liberating me from alimonies with emancipating, which is a burden for me and my family, that I pay to Egor through you, and into your Alena account, since we were divorce. In accord with the Family Court's decision, is I obliged make payments every months, which I being supposed to transfer in Egor's account until he turns eighteen years Majority!—She, interim listens carefully to all of he's extortions and statement; but she acknowledged, in spite of their has wedlock failed, Alena promised to get all done. Except she is requested for a period of time, to be able accomplish some of his demands. Alternatively, Alena solicited Alik to give her some time despite of marriage failer, in order to be able achieving these demands, and to make the result effectively—first of all those two went to the 'Notary's Office'.

Followed by the Family Court, where my mom and dad sign up an agreement, among them, by which my dad was emancipated of alimonies and payed to me, with advantage, she's released him from further payments have meant for my upbringing, as in accordance with of the USSR Law. In their agreement my dad supposed to pay for my upbringing alimonies in advance, that a total by a large amount of cash, which contained by the fund. In view of the fact was that they're departing from the country, so Alena has 'liberated him from a burden', in compliance to his words—essential. In due course by an agreement was sign up, accordingly I have left in my mom's care, and to be within her Custody only.

CHAPTER 14

Here is Egor's recollection how they left the country of their birth.'Meanwhile, it had passed a few months, since it's all happened, as I wouldn't become conscious that my dad has nor longer being part of my life. Alik, then again from previous day started to make phone calls to me every week, initiation on or after that time, since our last visit to his home-town.

In the long run: the last time I saw my dad, was on my fifth birthday. He has arrived on one occasion, without warning to visit me at the end of June 1988. On this particular day, that befall was my birthday, I myself being in pre-school as usual, when those kids from my group with me in company, just prepared getting to have a day-time nap at mid-day, for that be done, by rules in brood bedroom, where our beds conveniently situated here. Still I was partly asleep; when the governess wakes me up, during I too learned that an important person arrived to pick me up. Also she is allowed me to go at the rear of corridor to the corner. Still being stunned, though, but other than that I turn hurriedly headed for rear the room to see, who disturbed my nap and could that be?—Entering the room, where to be located principally for parents and guest, there I glansed mom and my dad, who are standing in a cheerful mood. I jumped up directly onto my dad's hands, seeing as I began hugging him. I also have learned that my teacher gave consent to leave for home. Dad has helped me to get dress up and the three of us have left for a walk in the park that been located close to pre-school, but on the opposite side. I enjoyed myself on the merry-go-around and have joined on other attraction. My dad had brought me a present and by coming to my home we have a lunch for the five special of us, as a real family does, and to celebrate their son's birthday. Apart from this party in pre-school was, where prior to dad's arrival the teachers in company with kids jointly wished many happy returns for me, and they've taken delight to share my birthday-cake plus other sweets. Upon our arrival home together with my dad, I then asked:—As it conveniently is my birthday, I wish for dad to be placed at the best sit in the house, as he is the most important guest . . . —I've brougt to standstill myself partially, with sentences then despite abruption, be based on my knowledge, it couldn't upset me after all. As the whole truth must be that Alik, whom I was waiting to see keenly for a long time, and missed him terribly, as he at long last has appeared. Until this present day, also my dream came true, at least then, on Birthday. My dad at last has come to visit me, in spite of whole mess, I could not get in touch with him prior, except I've felt like to tell, what my birthday-wish was all along. Alik has held him, temporarily on his lap all the time, and ever since they return back home: they are sang together, and have a chat for a while in each-other's company.'Alik asked me, whether I have missed him, while I also thought about him and still remembered him, since they are part? I have been glad to react with a reply to him, as truthfully, as I may could, have said daringly:—Конечно, папа, я тебя никогда не забывал и всегда буду помнить тебя Но почему ты ко мне так долго не ехал? я тебя ждал, а ты не ехал? где ты был всё это время? Спасибо тебе за подарок, мне нравиться эта машинка, что ты мне подарил. А знаешь, папа, мама купила мне прожектор, и мы часто смотрим сказки, я почти их все выучил наизусть. Хочешь, я прочту тебе то, что я выучил напамять, папа? Хочешь?—When I has asked over dad with an eye getting back-up from him; once he looked at me with an admiration as is overwhelmed to learn thus in his turn, whether I am familiar with famous Russian poets. with Pushkin's fairy story, where these rhymes specially I knew that well. So Alik invited:—Правда, сынок? Ты знаешь наизусть много сказок? И сказки Пушкина знаешь? Ну прочти, если знаешь: У лукоморья, дуб зелёный, знаешь такую?—Contrast he is focused on, he still gave the impression of being astonished and unbelievably shocked by my account. Dad sustained to be in a state of a shock, when looked like with a strike of bewilderment that, has shown all in his turn what he heard, which was unbelievable, also it came as a surprise for him. Else he learn how much of progress, I have made for those time, since his walking out from us. Despite the fact what he discovered, as next he recollects himself from the shock; then has took a relaxing pose on the chair put a smile, he then has ducked towards me, that sign meant for me to go ahead, I need to start execution of the poem:—Ха-Ха-Ха. Конечно знаю. Прочесть тебе, папа, да?-, while I made a posture, by holding my head straight up, in tandem and began to recite that rote of rhymes having read it clearly and loud:—У лукоморья—дуб зелёный, златая цепь на дубе том! И днём, и ночью кот учёный, всё ходит по-цепи кругом. Пойдёт направо—песнь заводит, налево—сказки говорит. Там—чудеса—там леший бродит, Русалка на ветвях сидит . . .-

Thus, has been the day when for the last time I really saw dad for the last time. Despite the fact that I had enjoyed his company and shared my happiness with him, I also saw that he cried, as I recited it from memory of my favourite fairytales. Then this moment of our final meeting I keep deep in my heart, that time when for the last time I saw my dad, much earlier than my family, and we've prearranged for the departure from the USSR. I guess destiny has quite a sense of humor sometime.

By this means few months passes, and its become unpleasantly cool outside—seeing Autumn has arrived. Its loom that season being visible outside in all the places surrounded by amalgamation of ginger-and-chest-nut colors, besides it's just usually chosen to describe amid that confined public in Europe: the velvet season. In the long run the one subject matter that's clearly comes back of my reminiscences, when I was learned from mom that me 'ought to be available for due the last day in pre-school for me to be able attending, since—they should be leaving our town soon, as to leaving far away. I was very excited and could not wait until that trip ought to start, and kept hassling her with heaps of questions. I was felt like to know all about upcoming trip abroad. She smiled, and has responded:—Our family, to start with: is going to travel scheduled on a train. After that we shall be flying on the airplane . . . *!*—

Sheremetyevo 2 Airport

Nighttime in Vienna

PART—III

TRANSIT PASSENGER

CHAPTER 15

An ultimate had forced Borodins to flee after all in the
USSR was slowly fallen apart.

They left a year before the fall of Berlin Wall, and two years
before the break up of the Soviet Union. 'We were officially
then stripped of our USSR citizenship, following of Passports.
The only papers we have left with was—'Loopol called an
Israel Visa. Only then we could arrange for our departure. In
our visas stated that we are—'Passengers in Transit'. In view
of that, it's only have past few days, since I learned of my
family's trip out of the country. Before leaving Soviet Union
they were have left all of their savings in the Bank, furniture,
and apartment, which went to the Government.

We practically left with Birth Certificates—to prove that
we were alive. Finally this day arrived for my family and me
to leave, that marked launch of a 'journey', that I have not
even imaged it could be thus hard-hitting. 'A whole morning
mom and granpa Leonid be supposed to packing belongings,
also to point out the heavy suitcases. Those lasts two gave
the impression to have been so busy, that I felt as left out by
means of being in a state of loneliness, contained by seclusion
and bored too. Given that they have not even got time looking
at my side, though, I was anxious to help, by getting involved,
but I would not dare disturb them. and so I have watched TV
before they sold it to the Russian next-door neighbor. Until that
time to that event on me had an effect a male singer appeared
on TV screen, who's sang back then about Fatherland, to which

I didn't pay attention as he sung, or to he's lyrics, herewith that piece of music hasn't attracted me what so ever. Soon after I switched the television to another channel, and be able watching the kids cartoons with several extra programs that I had not learn by heart. After a while our TV vanished over there to next-door neighbor, and I became once again bord with nothing particular to do, on top of that haven't got a clue how to be active?—Thus me kept is assessing myself: how to fulfil that emptiness, which delimited and spontaneously structured by vacuum of time. Abruptly my mom convert it to me by implying:—Egor, you, have to learn how to pack up your personal things, plus unpacking these too!—In fact, at that point I understood significance, that was my duty meant for to be taking care of my own stuff.

At the end of the day—when outside become darker—the truck has arrived. At long last Leonid and Alena began moving all the stuff out—from their once controlled dwelling, where they have lovely hood during the family get hold of it until now.

Alena has kept busy helping Leonid outside, where they have positioned their personal belongings into that truck.

Once I've taken the last look towards our previously owned apartment, facing the place I was born, and grew up there; that over my live around the first five-years of my life there, but in its place of distinguishing my home, as an being our livelihood, which I used to remember, all that appeared in front of my eyes what have left in around been an empty place: without furnishings, or other objects that at all times I saw inside, now its just an empty space. Soon being outside having not realized, though what I heard just than why those neighbors screaming to us with tears that become visible in their eyes:—Goodbye! Dear friends, take care of yourself, good luck! They are hope to see you again one day!—All the neighbors, who came to say goodbyes to us were also crying, as a replacement for could not wait to leave. After our family went inside the truck, when the vehicle started slowly to leave the fellow citizens, who're kept waiving, while this truck being accelerating and we were heading for the main road.

Every bit of the time all I've been doing in the car, being looking in the car-window, and patent following by those road signs, which came into view from nowhere maybe from side to side of there a truck, is travelling at the side of road where I catch sight of cryptograms and odd symbols.

Later that evening all the remaining members of our family left are already to be found inside the train, where's being travelling in these same carriage, at the same time as they are all have been present in a close proximity to each other, in the same train carriage. Although, rather unusual spoiled our family's ideality—followed there by abruptly the lights spotted disappeared, but when they have all looked in the window, there they are saw, that the train has been passing through a tunnel. Except for me, seen that I was unaware what route we're having travelled, but somewhere, or what . . . ?-

Much later on the same night I have been placed to sleep above on the upper tier/store up and it's to be situated inside the coupe in train's compartment, while this coupe have reserved for us a while ago before this event, for the entire family to be able travelling together, with the exception of me who's being ignorant of the whole thing.

CHAPTER 16

In the morning when they arrived at last, at Moscow's railway station, nearly for occupied day in the row I've not seen my mom. Since she's disappeared I become as be unaware at that moment, where on earth she went? But next I saw her appearance on foot back to join our group, I is begun to feel confident, and too believed:—That now everything is going to be okay!—I have not even become conscious that my family actually situated in the heart of Moscow. Perhaps, since it was my first visit to the capital of USSR, where that place gave the impression being weird and wonderful for me, some noise be supposed to perceive sound with diverse types of public convey or private transport, with ear-splitting clamour and rattle coming from those high-risers, or other giant high-rise buildings with look alike construction. also I become aware of enormous city centres, with it's giant diverse statues and memorials, which resting, while being lying on by representing unfamiliar individuals on upper bronze. Thus kind of transient impetuous life there I have not been used to in view of the fact that they arrived from a provincial town aggregate seems is feeling that it poles apart extraordinary for me. While Moscow gave the impression of being one of the majestic city, as equally unadapted, on top in unfamiliar conditions, which scared me off by observing in the region of a metropolitan—in this capital city. My grandmas' sister whose name happen to be Eugene as well my Great Aunt, who were chatting to a stranger bloke. Except for mom, whom I gaze at face, then it has struck me with realization so as to she has looked discontented. Out of the blue, mom left the circle, where they're all having mutually stationed, as she madcap in full swing being in motion, and changing direction. followed by the sight, consequently I became apprehensive, when asked Leonid:—Why mom is walking away from me?—I held aside dire thoughts, and accepting wisdom: now the only family circle, which enclose from what used to be facing a Big familia—have only left, folks, who are standing there: mother—Alena; her dad and my grandpa—Leonid; with grandma Esther; her sister, whose name being—Eugene, and is my grandma sister's husband. This man I don't remember, except I bear in mind that he's name being Mikhail. But next a touch of realization struck me: I became aware that this last pair won't be travelling with us abroad, whom I was being acquainted with undoubtedly.

In the meantime Borodins have spend the first night in Sheremetievo2 airport. All of my family members have taken seats in the Departure lounge, except for me and grandma, cause we both could not sleep in this stupid and rough place, on top of uncomfortable means of chairs sitting on there. Still being at the Moscow airport in Sheremetievo2, temporarily, the next evening, which be by now the second night in a row for us. During waiting period for our scheduled flight on the night before our leaving abroad it was being depressed, except for some rough position in the airport complex that I keep in mind so we all were: just then I had gradually lost my two milk teethes there. These two teethes fall out and all of a sudden from my low gums abrasion gets open blood being spiling all over me: first lying on the jacket, where stuck all through down and straight on top of my jumper, even onto my hands. Egor wasn't crying at first, has befalled only in state of a shock, but at that same time the cause from it came for me, as a surprise. Notwithstanding, Esther is expressed her thoughts and said:—It hasn't been an awful sign!—She was always and disappointingly still being a superstition person. Soon Egor has become apprehensive—minus very tied, as it felt freezing, and upon my skin surface have occurred goose-bumps, as my whole body is trembling. In that case out of the blue I started to cry:—Mommy, I beg you to take me back home in my own bed, cause it feels cold, as well I'm shivering and very tired. And into the bargain I have lost my two-milk teethes, and so my gums have became swollen, particular the low one, that's situated below and the second underside. The blood's still flowing out from the space, wholes, and also it feels inside the mouth there up ache it at the empty where's my teethes are situated prior to:—Mommy, please, I want to go home to get warm under the blanket to be able sleeping in my own bed!—He kept sobbing and with desperation looked in Alena's eyes. But it not has occurred to him at that point of time that what I have requested—my kinfolk have emerged helpless to fulfil it: giving of the view of the fact that to return back, there once their former home wad—near by, but it's being impossible to reach it. As a result of getting so much distress, on top experience of losing my two milk-teethes from the low gums, at the end of a long day, seeing as I have fallen a sleep after a long and tired waiting, me being resting in mom's arms.

'The next morning mom woke me up early and be clued-up that it's time for us to fly. Rumour has it: I learned that my family and I have to catch the flight to Vienna, in Austria, from Moscow airport. At that point in time I was unaware whereabouts Vienna have situated. Together with my feedback I have felt a mixture of excitements and nerviness from all latest and unheard words, as a result these all state of affairs scared me possibly will lay ahead for of the four us remained. Finally my family having said goodbyes to the Great Aunt Eugene in company with her husband—Mikhail. The last two kissed me and gave me exhortations, as relations often like to do:—Look after your grandma and Leonid and after your mother too. Listen to them, and be a good boy!—Each person surround us in full swing being expressing some thought of grief, while I could not value such a meaning of that precious moment, why not?—

By that time pro my entire family that left of four, which I though to myself:—They're the only four in the whole world, who left out, of what was my family whom I trust and can I rely on!—I set off deeper in my heart, even if those four of us have found, and by now are occupying sits in the plane.

When finally the plane took off: suddenly in full swing I is begun experiencing awful pain, while somewhat have cracked inside my ears. At that point I have realized that genual I could not hear with high-quality as before, whilst facing this condition made me also scared to a certain extent. Providentially for me rescue, the flight attendant came straight to our seats, who has brought me a lollypop and a glass of cold water, as saviour. Besides that last advised me to drink it very slowly: drop-by-drop. Apart from that a new and special excise, which called 'Steamship', once I agreed to learn if she hasn't skilled me, how it should be done wholeheartedly. And yet I know, since I got to learn it well that special exercise that helped him open up thus eardrums implementing it's a compression, which grasp by connecting the 'air-pressure' unite sledging the eardrums as pushing pressure to the air. By this means, she gave me advice, how it should be prepared—it goes like:—Close your nostrils with your hand, inhale the air to the full within your lungs, by taking a deep breathe. Now, hold your breathing for few seconds. At this instant, breath out!—Increasingly I began feeling a touch of blow in my ears: my eardrums of your own volition clicked, then it cracked again be save this time in full swing that I have got my hearing back. Gradually Egor began felling tired and overwhelmed from excitements by a strange experience and sensation, which have been so hard for me figure out and explain to mom; as outcome he's fallen into a deep sleep.

CHAPTER 17

For Egor woke up only just before plane landed in Vienna, with cotton buds still are inserted inside his ear-holes, into the bargain Egor was a bit disoriented.

Before they are left the huge field, where landing region and they are actually got off that plane in the location of Airport of Vienna, where they are began walking towards the entrance of that Complex, the pilot from that charter plane called our names. At the start my family had been surprised, as they are all turned our heads towards a person, who called on us staring with wonder. Egor's grandpa Leonid alongside Alena have stridden back on the way to this pilot, whose called upon them, while this man returned back our precious family photos. 'I would not have the slightest clue even today, how possible they are could lose these precious photographs. other than that Pilot also has put in the picture to an interesting Russian proverb:-You're having returned back to the plane, by walking forward and backwards, since being a pilot for years, they are very superstitious. As I know for sure, what it's means, you'll be going back to your homeland, in the country of your birth, some day! That's inevitable!—The instant Borodin step into the interior of complex of Vienna's airport where Leonid's being incapable catching our suit-cases, as they are discover news to come without delay towards a special meeting place in that airport complex. Every single of us left our suit-cases behind, and there're on the other side of the airport complex, where that meeting point being situated and taking place. By arriving at the key point site, where they are have been informed to come straight ahead. There they saw there lots of people, who are standing by adjoining these diverse groups that they have encircled and formed among each other. To our revelation they are discovered that all among those present spoken Russian there. Though is I felt confused and apprehensive, seen near such outsized number of individuals, who come into view being stranger to us, still they couldn't figure out what is going on around me, as a result I've clung closer to my mom. Apparently they have noticed a few strangers amid a big crowd, and footing beside there, who have been standing apart from others, as on the opposite side amid those remaining in a crowd of people, whereas jointly with us also stood in line. All those migrants, just have been facing us, as they are also being facing each-other. Besides they're have invited to stand-in and form these groups to get in huge line, that's exactly remind it me of the times, when I used to go in pre-school, in contrast seen so many adults struck me, there being rather peculiar about all those within formed queue have me made realise, as thus has nothing to do with those children line up there back then. A single one, among those few standing apart from all of us, despite hearing the man spoke a foreign language, and also being participating in other persons conversation, then suddenly interrupted them. This outsider begun asking questions, and is particular being addressed all of the maintained groups within formed circles around there, including my family and me too. Those few gentlemen have been dressed decent: one of them worn a dark coat with a scarf, which's knotted all around his neck with a knot, but those two remained are wearing a jackets or coats, in keeping up with weather conditions in Austria. There a silent eyes-examination were between all of those remained public, which have done, one of them is begun attend towards those groups there:-Who of you, people, are willing migrate to Israel? Please, come just before those people standing on the right side. And for those, who are willing migrate to other foreign lands, please, step forward, start walking to the left side. So that they will be able to see how many of you're have decided migrate elsewhere in the world, except for Israel?— In fact most of those people from the form circles, who are standing near them, underway walking directly towards left. Anyway, pro their documents, which all of those had in their possession, what they arrived with. Equally, there's being stated that all of them with my family integrated, those members' have got visas-invitations from the Israel. It has appeared predominantly those persons, including my family, who have joined the group alongside others, consisted by a majority of people, who aren't really enthusiastic or unwilling migrating to Israel that's being greatly visible. This stranger, whose began to count all of those remained folks amid these groups, who are in attendance. For those rest of folks, who are willing migrating somewhere else in the world, except for Israel, the retained groups of folks counting our family too, while put together all assembled majority. The strangers look being unpleased, still with peoples' decision, one among them has address anyway:—You will—He then, sustained:—So, you have made your decision, but, please, once more, think carefully, before you make up your mind, only then you need to decide. The final solution be whereabouts you really want migrate to?—Then one between those remained families' who have been represented by the family of three being talking to each other in a very soft voice, suddenly have left that group from folks, and already started to move away by distance from the main group on the left, and they are shifting, and headed for right side.

When Egor turns and looks up towards the right, he only saw a few families, who are in attendance, but enclosed merely that, there're standing over there yonder with their intention of made decision migrating to Israel. At that point in time, I have not got even the slightest clue, neither where Israel ought to be located, nor what is going on and happening around me the time. In view of the fact that my family has not got the time to clarify, caused the whole situation being too serious for these matter discuss it openly, or talking to those strangers about it, as a result the contact between Borodin's have subdued, as they made contact by gestures only, then all with them being doing with each other. In view of the fact that Leonid was the leader of our family, as people usually say—the 'bread-winner' as the central figure, who is to take the matters in his own hands, on behalf of the whole members of the family to be very sure. This has become up to him to make an important decision about the future for all of us. Even from the start of our journey he has already made up his mind. Beside, Leonid has decided for whole family migrae to Australia. Given that, there down under, so far away, lived his mother, who just turned ninety-two years, amid other members of his family, whom Leonid hasn't seen for years, so he missed her too those relatives so deeply. And by the persons, who have stated those from formed groups, that they're having to walk towards one more end around the airport area, where luggage collection being situated, in order to pick up their suitcases from there, if they're craved to get hold on to our stuff. By more important issues, which after they're should be completing with vital procedures, and they've required to start walking onto the main point place. One of the leaders prolonged, and into the bargain instructed all, they also be supposed to getting transferred, whilst vehicles ought to be conveyed our family towards places, where they are supposed to be stay, as an process before called for. During intended period, it become essential, which have taking place there to the full in a bid obtaining thus first step with the aim of being able commence the procedure, linked with temporary filling these forms for that process, on top substantial documents, in favour of authorization in order to enrol for the entry visa towards one among chosen foreign lands, without consider for waiting period for all those newly arrived migrants plus those folks, who have stayed in Vienna, for a while. All those by now turn into public from the mention groups, including us set in motion under their own steam on away, as fast as they could: every family to change directions. Set by forethought of Borodins are following others that it took them less time to find their way toward a luggage-carrier. Given the Borodins haven't disembarked, after their arrival that they got a chance to pick up their baggage from carousel. By so following others, they have been able to find much quicker that pointed out place in airfield, without getting lost in a foreign country.

Above all for the Borodins, who have only just arrived from a provincial town. When Egor's family have stepped outside to breathing fresh air, while they saw prospect on time frequency definition between Austria and Moscow that has accurately two hour on the negative zone, and for that reason the time in Vienna be very early morning, the same precisely, ever since they were left Moscow airport in 'Sheremetievo2'. The whole thing around us seems to look for him weird and wonderful, that to be encircled, while happen fast for me, despite of all these new meaning and perceptions that I've not got a twig. As for my family they haven't got neither time, nor patience in the least for explanations to shed light on . . . Meanwhile, outside I spot a man, whose sold chest-nut, and him being frying these items in a pan. Smoke's evaporated and flew up in the air toward my nose, while the steam made me feel warmer and draw me in the direction of it. I wasn't quite sure even presently, if it's being mentally, or maybe I have imagined things, which drawn my attention. On the other hand, it make some people think the way they want to see it. As for the reason I inhaled that aroma and by my curiosity asked to pay money for new objects for me, handle fare and ate it. even if I wasn't hungry, seen that odd grub, I urgently fancy it to try. Alena and grandma have emerged unhappy with my caprice. Leonid on the other hand, moved with me to the foreigner, where bought these chest-nuts balls, which have operated via frying on thus flames of fire. Since, it was frosty outerside. They've ogled tiny chest-nut balls with a steam raised straight in the air, like a mist, as a result it made me feel warmer and satisfied. While I dare taken these chest-nut in my hands it's felt hot, even 'to hot too handle.' Still that little things would not scared me off a bit, in contrast light ginger-brown color balls being uncommonly for me to grasp that such small chest-nut balls apart from used not only to play, but can be to consume it, by being helpful with its warming up process of my internal body organs, precisely I have effect on such effect took its toll: I curtly began sense it. After finishing my morning snack, I asked for water, as this was my first experience in a foreign land, while thus cooking made me thirsty, or that all developed into my mind's eye?—Then it's struck me, those civilians, who encircled us and have spoke a foreign language, herewith I was unfamiliar. Still, it didn't occur to me, that people around me speak foreign languages, except for Russian that I was acquainted, but me absolutely not be able to interact with unfamiliar person, as it made me feel ignorant. Despite that state of dealings I found myself be upset, it happen had not been for long. Besides it didn't even occur to me that mother can speak German. As it came to me a bolt from the blue, when I saw Alena verbalizing in a foreign language that I couldn't understand: it was in German. Despite of my wonder, she implied:—Geben, zi mi bitte, wasser!—So, I could not imagine and could not get over it, when I be heard her exclaiming in German. In a while, the four of us have gone back inside the airport, but we learned by authorities of:—You must wait for transport, that gonna to convey all of you're to hostels, which situated in the heart of Vienna.-When your next in line is coming. evenly, the authorised self resolve to transfer you're, along the way all set to explain the whole thing, to all there. The folks must distribute your baggage along with you're. But you're all having to go, and waiting remote!-

The Borodin stuck at the airport, knowing its temporarily. Here's a security guard, who has warned them to shift outside and wait there; but its been cold outside. Then the Austrian man became gracious towards me. so this security guy has allowed me to stay interminably inside airport: at least for the time being before a transfer van ought to arrive, and accordingly those strangers, who made clear to everyone amid the Russian migrants that drivers from the transport have expressly reserved, as are going to convey all of the newly comers from offshore, alongside our family to the places of settlement. That be organized individually for those, alike us, who have arrived today. There have in a foreign country, with unfamiliar language spoken; since Borodins being called— Transits Passengers, this is precisely, who they have turned out to be at that time. Within spitting distance amid migrants emerge those, who subdued are waiting any longer, I held they have got large amount of cash to pay in front, in view of that they being taking ahead of us, while they are kept worriedly watching and waiting for our next in turn in the queue to come. In Vienna like those migrants, counting Borodins, have arrived a famous Russian singer with he's wife from the USSR. But Egor believe the pair flew all over on the same charter flight, as the Borodin have, as they have spotted this couple even before, when they had a rest in the Moscow Sheremetievo2 lounge. 'Then again earlier in Vienna airport's arrival lounge, I wasn't paying attention at first to this pair. When he turns bend forwards to the pair's side to view he's being placed again, on the second time looks closer, and he is recollecting himself at once, and having said about him just then, whilst watching him TV, precisely on this same day prior, to our exit from the state. Evidently it had past only couple of days, since I saw him on the screen, when the vocalist was visible on TV, where sang contemporary genre songs, thus realization being strange for me. In one go I become nosy with thrill: the singer was in attendance, who being placed in arrivals lounge right in front of my eyes, and I begun to speculate if he will be in concert, or some part he is predisposed to sing right now at the Vienna airport? Then it's being clued-up to us that the famous singer is leave-taking for an international concert tours. Also the Borodins heard that the Russian singer together with his wife is supposed to transfer as priority ahead of other famylies amid whom in the line counting them. Barring Egor's family could not care less for this singer and his wife, cause they being feeling tied and cold. With all those encircled, who have been anxious, just by the look at their faces anyone could read:—What the future holds for us? What will happen with our fate?—It appear that all being pre-occupied deep in their thoughts, counting Borodins. At long last, each family, who at the same time have been waiting in a queue to be transferred, instead have driven away by this van, and ahead of our family. A vehicle emerged mercedes-benz brand, so van has dynamically left with those folks aboard—headed for anonymous places, by which those migrants who just have intend to be settled. While the Borodins, who have arrived in Vienna on this same day, as others, found themselves in a similar situation, or by us it's called—'in your shoes', ensued. Folks from establishment are supposed assembled by decision, vis-à-vis for that having enforced steps, which have to be taken for those newly arrived, together with my family too, who already have settled in Vienna a tad, or correlated for the procedure: to fill in papers to handle and resolve made. The family learned that their stay in Vienna have intend—for at least a fortnight.

CHAPTER 18

In the meantime, Leonid enjoyed himself by visiting a brothel, be situated on the other side of the street, just opposite from our guest-house, where my family having placed to be staying there in hearts of the city of Vienna.

One day shortly after our arrival Leonid took Egor for a walk, while those four are passing by a brothel. There I've spotted the women, who worn heavy cosmetics up on their faces. As for their red lips the skin surface contained too much make-ups with lipstick, as a auxiliary upon it on top of, that each one being outside could notice them from a far away distance. Those women have wore in accord of fashion also worn very long boots, that have covered their knees up to thighs; seen that nuance, which these long boots bona fide, as painted with have been mostly contained black, and covered by lacquer that looked bright from it's blistering shine, so that everyone in the streets being able to spot them, while those ladies exposed themselves from a long distance in direction of us. some of those women' have been dressed in winter fur-coats. As they have begun unbuttoned their winter coats, accordingly, it's ought to appear with a view underneath they have been wearing very short skirts. Even anyone can look at them from top to bottom are naked bottoms, covered only by pantyhose. Thus, one and all take account of me as be able to detect those ladies, who even have got there adgies, so tight be seen that it would stick inside to their assholes. At one fell swoop, the odd looking women also wore boast by wide smile and having chat in German, except I could not understand a word as those were saying, when I alongside Leonid have passed in close proximity from them. In mind anyone could analysing those women being dressed alike in recent porno-films. Specific of season outer surface that be late autumn, where surrounded by Europe, as it seems in the most part be unpleasantly cool and windy, with plenty of rains falling down on that surface. As the nature gave the impression of being remarkable, the flowering shrub onto falling either when the wind is blowing shrubs away else where, or already they're laying down on the naked soil. Symbol these hedging plant color yellow and tint of brown, which flowing seldom in the water or by the side of above can be spotted, where's the streams were flowing over along the parks, or on the naked fields, or within surface in the forests beyond from trees. Tree leaf failing down on the ground, in view of the fact that forming outward show of a circle around trees with mix of red and dark-yellowish, or by a touch, as these have often altering into a brownish flush upon it's covering. It like artist has brushed with its tassel, as done a colorful illustration—superb side that can draw everyone's attention.

One night, a week after the family accessed in Austria, Leonid has brought me inside a weird but intriguing build. I couldn't figure out of they're behaviour, and thought to myself that those persons chatting cheerful tone with smile, for their motive happen to be just good friends. Entering there be heard boast played music that audible range of the sound being fine-tune, but ear-splitting, but from where about site in that building it's draw closer on or after unidentified sets. Here I also could hear those public chatting in German, I absolutely did not understood a word of this foreign language. One among those ladies get closer towards me and has caress my hair. Meantime, Leonid has interacted in German to the lady before, when they're began laughing. I become confused, though, but period in between have caught in a moment as asking Leonid to take me back home, but he would not listen to my plea. Leonid being engaged in a deep tête-à-tête with a stranger lady. A short while after, he bought himself a drink and for this lady, at that time I told him:—Grandpa, I want to drink the same as you've?—Leonid produce a smile be wide, as his 'golden' teethes, which be made of brass, has appeared being visible, and he reacts:—Alright than!—He then has brought me a drink. When I sip a bit of liquid, which tasted of bitterness, then I turn my head away, cause I didn't fancy of carry on drinking that liquor, because in my mouth it's taste felt disgusting, and I've felt nausea. Accidentally twisting my head to the other side off my seat, I glance a lady be station in front of by facing bloke, whose have been standing in front of me but near the counter bar, whilst chap has passed cash to other man staying behind the counter: thus money hand. Before I forget A lady sited near most recent man who has grabbed two towels plus keys from the counter bar. Next those two at once are walking away headed for the stairs, as he is embracing and touching her. After they both are started ascending upstairs, even if a have passed by, I still couldn't distinguish the duo retuned back to that bar. Being a naïve boy it could not occur to me her reputation that coupled with . . . Except nothing seems to interest me any longer; then I turn at the back rear and once again shufti Leonid there, who is kept talking to this lady. By getting real confused and bored stiff, I just want to leave, thus I said it to Leonid, he looks at me, as his features didn't show any kind of satisfaction, even so he advised:—Just wait a bit more, we aren't to staying here long, as we'll be heading home!—Alleluia, sooner they have gone rather than later. Once they are arrived back to a guest-house across the street, Egor is felt like to tell all about his new practice over there. Except for Leonid, whose started shaking his head steadfastly, by looking to him everything ought being visible, he gave the impression of being dull. Impossible to tell apart, it's like a full fixation being plainly reflected on his face that he is not being pleased with me talking too much. Thus Leonid simply wished for me to shut up, and definitely not bestow about our previous adventure to mom, incidentally they were in that weird place, since the family lived in a guest-house, surrounded by the other folks, who have got ears . . .

After that episode, Leonid would not take me in this place, where in excess of it seems be in my opinion weird, but wonderful to any further extent. During our stay in guest-house I would spend time with mom and grandma. Except, family wouldn't stay all the time at guest-house, normally they go out, either for a walk nearby, or just in the region of Vienna, where lots of times they would go leisurely down to markets or shopping centres.

Practically every day Egor would exit either with Alena or Leonid for things, with every moment—it was obvious that Egor became unbearable: trying and insisting for the family to pay money for items, which come into view in the windows, or stalls. Then promptly he would alter into an egotistical wishing for stuff, which must be owned by Egor. 'In peeking varies of yummy food, I would never grasp or even image, when staying in Vienna and have to smooth the progress of me being able discovering lots of beautiful toys that would existed anywhere in the world. Thus, I have become impossible to deal with every time, when my family refused to go out with me, and pay money for items, on which I kept staring, and pressuring them to get, me what I want it to be mine. In that case Leonid explains:—Egor, we don't have an adequate amount to be able buy you things, each time we go to the streets, or what ever you wish. For there's a limit to everything, including sweets for you, desirable toys mainly! We aren't in the position spending money, cause of your caprice, and I mean it; you mustn't insist us to buy lots you want it? I wish you to remember, son that we won't be buying stuff for you! But if you agree to go out with no insisting and pressuring us to pay cash for everything that you fancy? In that case, your mother or I'll go with you, and even grandma will be happy too take you out!—So I have not been pleased at first with his response, but later appreciate, whilst they would go away from home regularly.

Once, those four a big familia' have travelled to the city centre of Vienna, given they haven't got enough money, of the low-priced public transport there for us to use has been always travelling from side-to-side on underground, of which to be unrestricted taken a trip on 'the metro'. When we draw closer on foot to an imaginary place out towards the exit, I realized that us having been touring around the city for many hours in the row, into the bargain I want to visit the loo. As people usually say:—When the nature calls . . . —On grounds being just a kid, I asked grnadpa to take me to the loo. I couldn't grasp at that time, that for my 'natural world needs' be perfectly normal, while there anyone could charge you money for a visit to the toilet, but living in Vienna it would cost you money or 'shillings', which was currency exchange back then in Austria. Temporarily be spectator here, I saw Leonid talks to a bloke, who's being dressed in uniform. Lacking of ability to understand German, I'm not at all caught a peek of the expression on the man's face in the uniform who's nodded his head, which meant one thing—he is given me okay to visit the loo—for free. When mom and grandma next too have appeared and jointed our group. As a result they both are most likely feeling need visit the loo too, Esther primarily with her poor health, so they applied to this man. Foreseen our intent the Austrian man, who has wore uniform turns facing those, who have stared directly towards that side, where my family stayed. Next I witnessed my mom well-advanced starts talking to the man in German, as she has tried to explain somewhat to him. This Austrian inspector, shook his head, and collectively is I spotting facial expression on the Austrian—altered; then I realized that my family must pay him for a visit to the loo in 'Shillings', which they have not enough money for it. Yet happen a twist by the Austrian man abruptly turned his head aside, where he saw Esther. It's become visible, that her look being pale like a sickly creature. Because her poor health being engraved upon her facial expression and in her eyes too. That's why he possible felt for her, and as a result he hasn't charge money for Esther. But the bad news be spendthrift of not left much cash inside our pockets, also it cost the family a great deal of shillings, seeing that they are unable to afford paying for their lunch; though at that moment being just over five years old I realize thus tough on us. I still keep in mind those words came from mentor grandpa, who's right, as warned me not a long time ago:—Not always we can get, what we want? There's a limit to everything!—

CHAPTER 19

Time running fast, and so our stay in Vienna was coming to an end, though for their stay there a fortnight. Still they have been clued-up, that soon our family should to be moved to another location for delays in dealings with advanced affairs intended for a process to fill in documents.

During the night in Vienna being raining cats and dogs, at one fell swoop, in the air was cool contained by frosty temperature outside, as a result asphalt has become slippery. That effect of weather conditiond outside still be sensed unpleasantly cold, with difficulty for the folks, who are experiencing extremely slippery pathway, and danger to be walking or drive in.

The next morning, grandma Esther has taken on me with her shopping to buy: bread and milk. She had lost a massive amount of body weight, cause her being experiencing dire pain, as she felt in her stomach, thus she hasn't got a choice but to take too many of these prescribed pills and getting kind of relief, as agonizing at least for a while, most of which be the pain-killers. thus, she was unstable as of prescribed medications, which her being taken these regularly. Likewise she appear being slim and unstable, as a consequence it become beyond Esther's power. Seeing as I only being a kid, thus weak, who's unable supporting and holding her, while she walked, as a result me befall being unsteady through supporting for her. On their way back to the gest-house an accident occurs, as he is tried crossing the road alongside Esther. Suddenly she is slipped, thus Esther be unsteady, as it gave the impression that her be unable to hold balance, consequently she has fallen in the middle of the road directly onto her leg. 'I become afraid and a bit scared, cause it have emerged around, as we two got stuck in the middle of the road, seeing as those cars kept functioning rearward in close proximity from us to frontwards and beyond. It seems that she tried to get up at first but obviously could not, I too managed to help her out along with all my strengths and power that I have. One way or another—Esther has managed to raise up on her feet after a few unsuccessful attempts. shortly those two are began walking as heading towards guest-house. On their return back I begun acting quick, from Egor recalls and repeat what had ensued with Esther during her ordeal on the streets, followed by the story, which she is shown to them her injured leg, and expressed concern from that previous fall. The family is getting dressed in; and having taken her to a nearest hospital for check-up. When the Borodin arrived in hospital, a doctor first examined Esther, he then has sent her urgently to carry out an X-ray. After the results came this doctor explains to us that she has fractured her leg. All in the family befalls in absolute disarray, and positively a nurse instructed in that case has lied down onto Esther's leg a plaster, ahead the med staff provided with two crutches, which customary second-hand be a support for her walking.

The next day due to no time after accident those two folks arrived in our place to enlighten:—About a trip to Italy, that you are supposed to take, like the other migrants . . . Compared with your documents,where clearly revealed that your stay in Vienna is a transit. So in accordance with rules—they have to be transferred to Italy pro further process to fill in these forms. Even if, you are supposed to travel soon. But sorry to say, it is not possible in her condition, its even out of the question, at least for now. And as for the time being . . . -, has over and done with his speech one person, who happened to be a gentleman. After that with thus discussion a new person, who happen to be a woman:—Well, it concerns you're near future, you can't stay any longer in these same place, where are you living at present?-, She has stopped for second looked around, then continued saying:—They have to move all of you to a new place, at the location of the Austrian Alps mounts. It is crucial for the time at least until your wife's condition improves Mr Leonid your wife and your mother Alena, special. Mainly until she isn't recovering completely, when Esther will be able to walk on her feet, without plaster and stretchers too. Thus, cause of her—the family won't be allowed you're travelling to Rome, in Italy of that condition. To your information, all the other migrants, who arrived before your family or together with you ought to be travelling on the train from Vienna to Italy. Cause of accident, which had happened with Ester, they cannot allow her, which means for your family travelling in such conditions this would be too risky . . .-

After those foreigners left harve still being sitting on a couch, and becoming even more confused from that argue and the news, that they are just heard. Essentially they're having discussed, mostly about what do Esther and Leonid, but Alena also is participating in that family affairs.

At the next evening after those visitors left, I learned that my family should be going out. Mom reached out in one of these suitcases and pulled out exquisite looking set of clothes and has told me to wear it. I have also been instructed to comb my hair for the occasion, after looking up in the mirror, me be pleased with myself, seeing as my appearance seem given the impression of looking very nice and they all well-dressed for the near to occasion. As soon as all four of us exit faint; then we caught a taxi at once for the first time, since our residence in Vienna started. Given a chauffeur has driven us around the city. In the interim I was restful seated in a cab, me saw attention-grabbing places that passed by just in front of my eyes: boutiques, shops, with lights in the region of metropolitan. Given that its glimmer came from upon the trees being full of wind-around were visible outside, and so specially for Christmas decoration. There Illuminations sparkling with brilliance, which these streets even more eye-catching and looking festive, as the shine commencing by it's should be enough virtually to reach all avenues alongside the lanes, as light up the entire area. Even if, outside sense cool, its was far long from Christmas and the New Year, but too the entire festive season already started celebrating earlier, elsewhere in Europe, and at the heart of Vienna to. So I only grasp—is looking through cab-window with admiration, and me in step of prying: by a wishful thinking to myself that, I have never been to these places before, whilst Vienna looked immense and a gorgeous city in my eyes, with us having layed a foot readily available. While we bypass the city centre in Vienna, I is noticed these trams, which are travelling throughout most part of the city all around—going by, to be challenged at one fell swoop, having faced up to and avoiding the banks of Danube—river, Leonid has explained to me this river is called. When for firstly I heard, that tram actually has its own sole signal. Along way unusual emerges, as the taxi driver non-stop is driving towards the embankment, and when I looked in through cab-window—I saw along with it's reservoir of this Danube river that being long drawn out, while stretched the length of it banks in Vienna and likely farther ahead. Danube river be surrounded by the waters, where have upcoming forth by amazing reflection below bounded all through the water from illuminations, while these shiny lights resembling from curtains of hub and the streets, so the entire city become a giant reflection well-located in the water with it's glowing lights. Meantime, the cab kept advancing, as it's approached a park, where out of the blue has appeared a 'merry-go-round', but bigger and to my render speechless very tall and grand with it's size, and as we used call it high 'the devils wheel'. I could not sit still without be excited; no less, I is longing for that kind of thrill to enjoy myself on. Since, when my family and I had left the country of our birth, the lot around me passed with such distress. Here in the park somewhat has appeared—in front of me, rather incredibly giant, I have felt like it's a far removed from world that I couldn't expect to see. Next I saw a chance to escape reality, which's surrounded me, and to be in high spirits, at least for a while. Since I became this lonely sole, with no my friends around from playschool, who I missed terribly, as well being left to myself, cause I didn't make new here in Vienna, the realisation made me miserable. As I have got an idea—thus new world should turn around along with my melancholy, when I would be circling up and down with rotation on that beautiful and beyond my beliefs far above the ground a 'devils-wheel' carousel.

On our arrival to Vienna's town hall, where the reception to be taken place, in which the whole evening passes well for my family. Period in-between and I to join company with all those other among invited guests, who have present at this reception, where they're enjoying themselves. During that event at the reception party Egor family are watching concert, especially organized for folks like them—for the emigrants. Readily available appeared to be present singers, who sang with the fine-tune cords from the guitar with such melody, and piece music under the accompaniments of the piano-accordion among the professional musicians, as their execution on a grand-piano being excellent. Prolong, readily also being performances of Russian folklore songs, as they all were dancing by that well executed by artists, who ultimately rehearsed before that concert started upon the stage, to boot readily available few of the artists recited lyrics, and poems. Among those migrants, being see sociable folks, who had wrote even poetry and lyrics themselves, which they recited in front of all those guests, with great performances some of the poets too. Except, a short while after that enjoyment being spoiled by religious words, which I start hearing on the topic of:—God is the only one for each person, for every religions, denominations, while they are must be tolerate towards our believes. And those, who are going or already Apostates in the God's beliefs, will be punished at entrance towards and on the gates of the Heaven . . . —Add to high reverends religious studies. In level-headedness, I chosen to be deficient and naïve, as well, what they have talked abou; by hearing for most of their speech, all those purposely provided with, plus the unheard of new words, aimed of all high reverends made me dazed, still they're kept talking on-on-on . . . Except, a thing that occupied my thoughts just then have to join the attractions. I peeked it recently, prior to this cab had passed by and brought us here, and I cared only about one thing when my family ought to take me round the corner in the park for a ride or two on it. Later on all those who present were given gives, mostly— clothes. Alena rising has got a good quality, practically anew trademark coat, that was in the fashion then, as it would been in demand, and so has Grandma, whose received garments. Those persons, who are present at the reception received something as the remembrances of that evening. Else those guests, who are present, together with us having given the 'Bible', which been written in a foreign language, but already translated to Russian. On this reception they are got to met a family that contained fourteen people, seen there eleven among them—emerged their children. Though, this big religious family had travelled from USSR, and spoken Russian, but they belonged to a religious 'Cult'. We have got acquainted by one of the family members with their believes in 'God', even so, it wasn't particular they adored and worshiped Jesus Christ, nor they believe in Thee either. It also being revealed, when have raised issue in favour of their young kids; and one asked:—Whether those kids belong to anyone?—But elders of family member retort, and claimed all of those kids are theirs, since their family fit in of a massive one. They are learned that family has belong to a religious sections or 'Cults' called 'Сектанты', with the intention of avoiding being prosecuted with have to be discriminated as of many ways pro in the USSR authority—according their explanations. Given there the Borodins have met a woman that prearranged reception, her name turn out being Katrina Hermann, who had converted into Judaism ensued in Jerusalem. She is known as a local Austrian who's also being one among the famous personas in Austria, whose became beyond her title has invented, as her being running a charity given to kindness. Herself to be the most known country's philanthropist. This Austrian lady be sighted in the age of her late-fortieth, or most likely in early fiftieth, and by analysing her become visible: she has light skin combination of blond hair that Ms Hermann perhaps was tinted it time and again.

Later on Egor and he's family have cultured that streets, or locals in German, as Austrian called—Schtrasse and it gave the impression of be remarkably freshly clean avenues plus roads, where they are passed on our way back from the reception, the some people even called it 'Streets of Millionaires', and a park nearby. Conveniently for the Borodins came to pass via diversity with lots of splendid shops, officers, boutiques and gorges amid high-elevated buildings, where lights seen even more brighter, followed by taking place surrounded amongst these on the local streets too. They are went to these streets, which it's got the name after those they arealthy and famous and they are enjoyed the view of, not for the reason that they are became jealous. As to observe weather on the streets looked impressive on top, which fall upon be unimaginably structural with it's festive point of view there, it's done I imagine could attract countless of people. Me personally have not got acquainted well with either of folks, which these streets were dedicated to—if they existed, I hope? But I could not care less, I stared being modest, but at the same time eager to ride on this high 'devil's wheel', since my Leonid earlier had promised to take me into the park. Then again, at first they are went to the post office, where Leonid and Alena waited get connected on the phone line with a foreign country. The woman, who's worked as phone-operator, or it's typically be said switchboard operator has informed them that are needed to wait for a while, before it's be able to get connected. After nearly one hour waiting in there she finally calls our names. So, I have over-heard what he talked to those folks on the other side of the line, because its turn up they have rang from Sydney, located in Australia. Soon grandpa Leonid got frustrated and asked and me to leave him alone as let him talk to his relatives without witnesses, except me being nosy for those persons said to him from the other side of the line they are never resolved to find out. I was unaware why he has refused to be heard, of what secrets he told during the phone talk that being out of reach. In the face of what have happened earlier they walked towards the park, whilst mom has put in the picture to me that this playing field called 'Luna Park'. After a while Leonid joined us also, as advised me to wait before he ought to pay money for our tickets on that pending ride in. Lucky he didn't pay money for my ticket only for himself, since me was obviously underage, thus I be able to ride for free. When Leonid and Egor both jumped in a 'devil's wheel' the booth gave the impression of being not bulky amid it's size, but it was enough to be able fit in at least four people to place inside. Then the wheel started lifting us up higher and higher, as their cubicle be far above the ground, cause breathings has stopped for a second, with Egor trying not to look downwards. As at that juncture without warning the carousel would stop by itself and they would stuck hanging up on the top on a height, above the ground while Leonid wouldn't dare shake cubicle, since him being afraid and possible I get scared of capacity, or start to panic, and cry. They stopped on top of near to sky, as I measured, but not for a short time, when abruptly that Devil wheel could start be in motion again, and at the same time their booth have dropped down, seen by every moment lower and lower towards the ground. Egor starts feeling butterflies flutter inside his stomach; every time, when carrousel bunged, where they've hung up atop for a short while, still booth would declining down slowly, but surely, yet it would gradually coming down to land. It's being an amazing experience, feeling like that it could just takes your breath away, with sense of butterflies be flutter in your stomach always,when the high'devil's wheel'-device' machine switched on, or climbing beyond the ground higher and higher into the skies!

CHAPTER 20

Period in-between, less than a month after Egor's family departure in a foreign country, which have effect in a changed episode for Alik.

Vis-à-vis going back to the past events, on seventh of November 1988, while in the former Ukraine usually was celebrating the Revolution Day. He's aspired to give the lowdown that Alik has arrived in their ex—town with a visit to them, not even aware of Borodins departure. He kept ringing in our former home's door bell, but couldn't comprehend why not a soul is opening the front door there. Then our former neighbor—steps out of her apartment and begun exchange a few words with him, entailc with news:—Алик, вы напрасно звоните в дверь. Вы что ничего не знаете?—This lady neighbor has looked with peculiar on his behavior. In spite of the fact that, Alik seem being ignorant, she constantly in opposite tells, because in contrast he still look ignorant when he said:—А, что я должен знать? Где все? Почему никто не открывает дверь? Я приехал к сыну и привёз ему подарки! Скажите, а что дома никого нет, сейчас? А тогда, в котором часу они будут дома? Когда прийдут?—Alik is pushy asking being in a cheering mood and he would kept looking all the time towards the door, when before tried to say impressive, but he is disrrupted by our ex—backdoor neighbor implied:—К сожалению, вы опоздали, Алик! Вся семья вместе с вашим сыном—уже почти месяц, как покинули эту квартиру и уехали Заграницу. Разве, вы не знали об этом? Не смотря ни на что, вы сами во-всём виноваты! То, что произошло между вами—это меня не касается. Конечно, Алёна поступила немного жестоко. Однако, вы сами разрушили своё счастье. Вы издевались над своим сыном, не говоря уже, что он— невинный ребёнок. А также над своей женой, и её семьёй. И вам некого винить, кроме самого себя!—She's speaking to him in a language of brutality in her voice by accusation towards Alik's previous behaviour, as its spottea by sign of reflection in her eyes:—Что же я наделал? Я потерял свою семью—а главное моего сына! Наверно я Егора больше никогда не увижу! Что же мне теперь делать? Как же мне дальше-то жить?—Alik then slowly fell begun to collapse down on his knees, while tears already being visible his eyes, in the vein of crying with his shoulder shuddering. As a result he became distressed by the news and resulted in a state of shock and has been broken-hearted for a while, until this neighbor given him a piece of advise to leave now, despite of the whole obsession that his done in the past, but exceedingly to think carefully for he's past mistakes, to live in this world, as beyond uphold himself also life for a future ahead.

For the time being Borodin being ignorant of the incident with Alik over there. Instead that quartet willingly moved to the Austrian Alps mountains, where they were placed in a 'Winter Hostel' which has situated on the Low Valley, within not so isolated from the usual Ski Resorts, so that they are would not be disturbing those, who ought to arriving here for Holidays, or ski trainings. The place where they have got an offer, as its being vacant to move at the Austrian Alps to be situated not afar on isolated area laying—used for German-Austrian linking through border surrounded by a district for tourists, in view of the fact that the region be supposed to readily available for skiing since all over the World always come here. From time to time some famous sport celebrities, or even rich and popular with men and women, who would travel there in Austrian Alps mount, especially for training otherwise relaxing and skiing just for fun, when those with aspiration running down the hill along the ski-track. The Borodins disembarked from a van that brought them to Austrian the Alps followed by, as they have been placed in a single-room in the hostel, but it's looked big with it's gauge size, where to assist those folks, but to restricted, who to be arriving three beds and a stretching-bed with other basic attributes.

The first few days they have lived in thus circumstances, but later the manager in a practical eye of Borodins situation, which have found themselves in: with Esther being in poor health, and a five-years-old boy, he decided to offer their family moving into double-hotel-room, or to be more correct a hotel-suite. To be frank 'hotel-suite' didn't look like a suite at all, that room emerged spacious be supposed to facilitate those guest resembling of home-stay, where they being placed, cause situate haven't brought an old Austrian owner any bonus income, so it's more precise to describe a plus with a minus. Then again the Borodins have got two rooms at their disposal: a dinning-room, with a table and four chairs, a lounge, as they be given as a chest-nut table, dresser-table, a mirror, alongside the usual stuff, that hostel being for their ownership to facilitate tenants, and it was not unusual to find in any other hotels, and additional bedroom too. That be a double-room be furnished at Borodins disposals to dwell in. Chosen by a capacity alike bathroom be joint, indoors has included a toilet. They have shared a bathroom with other residents of the Hostel, where a bucket too has been placed inside the hotel-room, just in case. In contrast, there be too match of the guest-house in Vienna, where they had settled in a comfy room, and importantly the object to facilitate the family enjoying here luxury. Apart from furniture plus other stuff which they're needed, there in front has emerged the fireplace—with a real fire inside, where its also been sight with brown dark-grey logs, which came as a part of making the real fire with its flame for more effectiveness. Despite of their joy, Leonid received a warning about to be cautious while making fire; other than worry in order to keep the fire on functioning, as so Borodins have followed order on given advice. Yet with apartment the family became apathy as to be functioning effectively, while they should regularly throwing extra logs contained by as to facilitate that intrigue fireplace. Thus Leonid and Egor would go outside to collect these wooden logs, which's already been chopped up; followed by next step all these set with stuff have to be placed in a hotel-room and by the fireplace—for that system function out properly. Practically every morning Leonid would go outside to chop up wooden logs, he then is collecting it; but I always following him and revealing for my part with motivation to work, as I have tried helping him out. A few times I even stand in for Leonid to see how he tears apart these logs. I have got drawn in to make myself an effort to be in a plain sight close at hand, while trying getting involved working shoulder-to-shoulders with Leonid. I was then collecting wooden logs, then would bring these collectively into one heap; at the same time me being capable carrying these bric-a-bracs upstairs to our hotel-room. That's why in our room they've felt warm and comfy particular, the instant the snowfall emerged outer surface, or even snowstorm could whiteout next to path or small, laying on the ground. Saw the winter have got ahead with it's euphoria, as the family would play along making fire flames ample by kindle of the wooden logs in the fireplace. That set out well with its greatest part, in tandem thus heating up process for the room itself functioned, on top of it made us feel hot and thrilled. Being an electrifying feeling, picky to hear how these logs inside a fire would crackle, at the same time as the colors red-with-bluish tongue of fire being sighted, by reflecting with dazzling all over the place, like the shadows should become visible the room exactly surprisingly that made it of more brighter shade inside. hotel-Extraordinary view being equally with our mutual feeling, as they would help ourselves to have a big smile of delight. Then it would come the time gainfully, when masses of snow being visible outside, with a peruse from the window to our family with those residents of the hostel would go in the backyard to play with convenient snow, and were creating the snowman or snow-women: place in the middle of these snow dolls—stick with carrots instead of placed a nose in combination with black charcoals as a substitute for the mammies eyes. Family would also make the snow balls, in one go the Borodin's at full blast throwing set of snowballs at each-other, plus at anyone who are dare passing near by . . .

'Leonid in time even found for me a sledge, and would take me for a ride on it. He would either pushed me down the hill, or just take for a ride towards town, where they are usually made our shopping, buying food supplies with extra indispensable stuff, which they needed the most. Occasionally Alena may well too taking me with her for a ride towards a town, even if distance between hostel and the town are measured fairly accurate of three kilometres, with me on sledge and smoothly glided upon the surface that covered with fluffy snow, since resting on the blade; whilst walking by manage to convey by a sledge, while me being placed private ans conveniently covered on top amid a mantle by feeling at ease seated inside that sleigh. That snow itself has been so white, as sparked with it's shine, mainly feels the weather when it's without a gusty wind. In spite of be frosty temperature where the sun shone downwards on that snow, its like pouring of discontinue overflow with such a ray of brightness that come across like a dazzling spark, which reflected by varied of colors. Virtually all the times those are have to put on sunglasses, bar devoid the sight protection of it's reflection can appear straight into the eyes, thus ensue to get blinding us up. Thus admiration not have rather being all positive, except in view of the fact that whiteness and vividness from the snow, which have an effect on as of it's reflection turns out to be abscessing for my eyes, but has warned me that it can become harmful, if I 'm not be careful and refuse to put on sunglasses. Perhaps Alena was right along with her remarks, cause before long I come to feel like is impulsive blindfolded for a moment, while I would dare stare directly towards thus snow, which by resting on the surface ground, like the white giant blanket wrapping by way of it's coating partly a secluded region, at the side of more or less in the region of the entire environs to boot. When mom would take me for a ride on this sledge, I always being in high spirits with excitement from that feelings, seeing as the snow has falling on top of my winter-coat plus on my head and face, like remote I would take a gulp of fresh air with so as sense like, despite the fact that cold winter felt in the air, which gave you a small fracture of a strength coming from the mountain long-life extension. hence the family openly declared in another place, that's be truly a common sense, but it was not a fantasy. At one fell swoop my head be spinning around from all thrill. Back in the hotel-room my ogle would still be rewind it's pictured with its reflection of such white-blue or lilac with vary of shadea. It has altered and formed in a shadow of these snow flakes would come into view. Upon our return home from the excursions on mom's and myself cheek would for ever and a day look natural cherry color, while she would carry breed odour in company of the snowfall else.

This way I always learned by heart illustration of Alena: reminiscent of her be supposed to carry that aroma of winter showing into warm place in the midst of it's given flavour to flying remarkably in the air, which's important by winter, as has provided a great deal of impression. It was always deep in my mindful, since my childhood's earlier days, I had at some stage in existence been at home with her and surrounded by family's dwelling then. From time to time Leonid would clean outside the annex all through entrée of winter hostel, where plenty of snow fallen on the surface ground, and he would use a spade, which has made from wood, it seems that specifically been used for shovelling the snow. Esther, in contrast become disabled constantly using two crutches for her walks, when us three could spend the most part of winter in the house.

CHAPTER 21

Time in the Austrian Alps have passed quickly, as Bordins haven't seen that Christmas is arrived. They in contrast, wouldn't celebrate Christmas openly back in the USSR, like they used to celebrate the Orthodox Christmas from the seventh of January each year. For myself it was an astonishment, as it's being put in the picture to us that here in Austria, in the regions between the Western to Southern parts in Europe, even beyond—those nation started to celebrate festive season on the eve of twenty-fourth of December, as it came as a surprise for us, in chorus festivity. Temporarily a massive Christmas-tree be brought from a forest in close proximity, once the woodland wardens and local Austrians went deep into the woods to find the one and only Christmas-tree to facilitate that have covered with snow upon its branches, when the Austrians found it. Then the tree be placed in the middle of arrival lounge, of hostel's foyer. A Christmas-tree being decorated with diverse color glass-balls, which each tint be of: white, green purple, red, blue. View atop of tree's branches of a highest branch an Angel's statuette, where a starlit was placed too. For a Christmas-tree it's be decorated with the balls and other decorations in the midst of these bulky branches with lightings, which hanged full wind-around the tree; it has glimmered with pride by overflowing by magical colorful illumination all around these bulk branches. Those per head, who stayed in our hostel gave me a lots of presents, and I've become nuts with excitement and kept myself occupied unpacking them by hiding all these gifts being given for me. Then I would go down on my knees to sneak a peek and check under my bed, it's where I can hide these. Before mid-night arrived, one and all, who then have stayed at the hostel came down to foyer for that celebration of Christmas Eve in Austrian style, with masses of alcohol drinking, as those locals called there 'Schnapps'. After that those locals have served fat roasted ducks to the table, filled inside with apples that were baked. As those Austrians traditionally ought to bake a goose in a stove, and folks have served fowl hot and straight from the oven, or old style kiln.

At mid-night all and sundry is still sitting and offer each-other with gifts, the same as wishing good fortune, also health and happiness for the future. By seeing as jubilant Christmas party, I kept running backward and forward to pick up my presence from under the Christmas-tree, and all the residents tried to brush my cheek by a kiss or in the lips, since their ritual for good wishes be allowed in old Austrian traditions. Upon the New Year celebration Leonid has got in a bad temper, as rums gave the impression that earlier he spoken over the phone with his relatives, who has called upon us previously in the Hostel from Australia uninspired him against us. After finishing his phone conversation Leonid began arguing with Esther, as earshot been heard then, he become in conflict with Alena. Given that locals together with those guest; a man among an individual family, for the most part said by focus on us:-That he wishes to hang about in Austria longer, and objects for the three of us to arrive along there—down under . . . -He's relatives have expressed wishes for the three of us travelling either to the USA, or any countries around the globe, where we are choosing to go, except for Australia. Rumour has it that Leonid's family over there, were not in favour of us to come. And he began crying, and alleged that his adopted mother, who has lived—down under, turns ninety-two, so she wishes to see him, before she would pass away. That incident couldn't spoil my festive mood, since that night be supposed to unique, given that New Year Eve party is advancing in spite of everything. Three of them spend New Year in company of these two families, who too have arrived in Austria earlier than from USSR are, living here for about a year. All who being in attendance came to rejoice the New Year Eve, and to have a good time here—laughing all the way. At some stage of the festivity in a gather the guests sang a lots of songs with folklore music being heard, and under accompaniment of guitar. Afterwards all guests moved out outer surface where have formed a group leading a circle around Christmas-tree them being a joyful mood, as the Borodins would by custom having done yearly in a row. All of them sung in chorus, then being leading circle around-and-round a dazzling Christmas-tree. later all of us began playing games by throwing snowballs at each-other, as too likewise against anyone who have the guts pass, and laughing on the way. That kind of happiness being very much in my favour, as they arell as for every person who participated in that New Year happy play. I being sent to sleep, seeing as time was very late, after midnight with good and happy thoughts. Even if like this previous disagreement, I have missed Grandpa Leonid, but wouldn't dare say anything to strangers to spoil their mood and humour too. They have become aware explicitly that, his family in Australia stirred Leonid against the three of us. Since phone booth be situated outside of our room, in corridor on every floor within hostel, thus Egor didn't hear what exchange of words between Leonid and his relatives were about? Forlornly my family has been unaware, where about he went. But in a while they've found out that Leonid gone without stopping towards the town at the Alps and in the Brothel.

The next day, when it's already dusk, Leonid has returned back home, and at night he is begun packing up his things. Meantime Esther has witnessed his objection, she then comes with word of warning to him:—Hereby, situation, we have found ourselves in, where you brought us along, is unbearable, thus, it's you alone have been responsible for all of us. Specially now when we're staying in a foreign country. Likewise, you too Leonid . . .-, She has spoken with sadness that being heard within her voice. But Esther took a deep breath; and next has wildly, entailed:— . . . that was your idea for all of us to leave USSR, we all were living with satisfaction, and have got a roof under our heads, but were forced by you to wander and doubt with unknown fate that we now are going to face in future. On top of our hardship we lack of travel document and cash—makes us all, you too included, in trouble! Now you want to leave us in thus circumstances!—She continual, and is accusing Leonid, despite the fact that he has put us in deprivation now, but when he leaves us, he will regret, what he's done towards his family, mainly to his daughter and grandson. Thus Esther has looked distressed, and become alarmed by the situation, and begged Alena to stop him. Being worried Alena has appeared pale and excessively dull, as watched severely for every shifting he Leonid doing. Retaining in rank of my memories: I was sobbing—while I trying to cling on to his suitcase, but Leonid became like a madmen and grabbed the luggage away from me, and quickly under he's own steam towards the door. Alena alternatively—thinking about just for a minute. In that case Alena stops him at once, she then firmly is articulating:-Papa, if you're willing to leave now, don't come back to us? Cause you put us in the situation, where we are don't own a house now, nor jobs, and most important we don't have the passports or ID to travel with. If you're going to leave for good, just tell us the truth, and tell right now. I will find the way to be able return back to the USSR, us applying through the Soviet Embassy, and we all are will beg those nation there returning us all back home, in our town, before it's not too late. On top I would beg the officials there, in the Consulate to give us back our flat!—Without warning after these words Leonid throw it his suit-case on the floor and with anger left the room, shut the door with a loud chatter behind him, while I run after him, still being distressed and kept howling. After the tag on of thus earlier incident of a quarrel between Leonid and all in the family—time has passed calmly but monotonously, without any excesses. But Egor's relations dynamically, and have felt fantastic somehow.

Thus previous ill-fated accident that stroke Esther, after she's got a nasty fall in Vienna; kaput on her left foot whereas she fractured her ankle. The family kept well, Esther contrast after a fall has become disabled for the period of one-and-half months. Still she used the support of two crutches; but she's remained lonely in the Alps. Cause it was hard for her to walk, thus she spends most of the time being seated indoors.

A while later, when the plaster has got removed off from Esther's knee, over and above being already walking on hers own feet, despite that Esther has given a walking stick; otherwise, thanks God she has got that cane for support, or else she would being unable to hold balance. Even if Esther constantly has relied on a walking stick for a while, except for her been standing on foot, she excessively lamed for quite a long time. Esther for her rarely with a view of traditional festive season haven't been completed yet, since the previous festivity followed by—the Russian Orthodox Christmas arrived, and the old New Year Eve festivity begun next they're looked forward to rejoice. My family and I have also been celebrating that every year, for that reason the Borodin's family were earlier than bought some poppy-seeds and extra sweets, by tradition desserts with other special sweets, and also baked yummy of be diverse cooking,as part of typical party in the Orthodox style New Year. At some stage of the festivity the Borodins alongside neighbors having half-dozen drinks of Russian vodka, without me, given I was allowed for my toast lemonade only, that adults having made toasts for the Old New Year and to our family health, as they're sipped to our family and everyone's jubilant, and to good fortune. For the guests, who then opportunely being celebrating. On the Eve of the Old New Year that usually takes place at mid-night from thirteenth to fourteenth of January. Alena, meantime, has invited other Russian families, who too lived in the same build as they're, but I being forced to go to sleep, earlier than those begun that fortune-telling ritual ceremony, which is a customary in folklore traditions held back in the USSR and other Slavic Christian Religious. At that special Festive season, amid Christian Orthodox cultura time to celebrate customarily folklore that being highly regarded, by their beliefs, which be supposed to signify religious festivity in the company of Christian Orthodox Churches, as those believers were celebrating from mid-night—spending the whole night; where between others up to early cock-crow, when the rooster would start off singing—and shown extraordinary with that ritual to look at. Candidly, I was intrigued by kind of tradition that attraction me with it's magnetic power, which demanded me to be there, to be able witness with my own eyes breed of magic that fortune-telling—in procession. except to my ill luck, I wasn't allowed watching ritual ceremonial regularities of a fortune-telling, instead I have got marching orders to exit indoor. As for ritual in keeping with the traditions by individuals, who they were in attendance, as imaginary must be a glance supposedly visualising into folks future, who being hopping for those as chosen partners in imminent marriage. Presence of children to be forbidden; then again the kids could have a glimpse, only through window, and obviously from outside, since being a little boy, I would not dare go outer watching what have effect inner by mid-night, and so I went straight to bed . . .

CHAPTER 22

It gave the impression of hearing announcement that made, anywhere volume is on high definition that heeded must be exaggerated, but at the same time it seems resonance have to be arriving from out of space. Except it becomes visible that Egor could not figure out, if he be supposed to at the absenty, or still is flying with his mental picture within the past, it's like he has got caught betwen the two dissimilar world: of thus actuality along within the past . . .

A sudden, someone began to pull up Egor's sleeve jumper. Only that unintentional act made effect on him, thus has brought him back to reality from his deep thoughts. Then he suddenly becomes aware and start hearing, the plane's engine makes noises and these following effects, jointly with traits at this plane, which's heard being speaking through speaker-radio. Egor then turns-off as is switching his attention with a stare towards the one who's disturbed his feelings. Flexibly pulling up he's head over seat Egor has spotted the flight attendant, who come to pass being a female, and she is leaning over too get hold of him. As seen him in her company when at last he is paid attention towards her. Next a stewardess began speaking in tandem is yelling with a concern look straight into his eyes, while right to be heard:—Excuse me, sir, you seems be occupied to a degree? Didn't you listen to an earlier announcement that was made. I'm wrong about that? Are you okay, sir?—Egor, instead gave the impression of being absentminded as apprehensive in her eyes, when he's reaction being:—I am fine, thanks. What's going on? What announcement?—The stewardess's head is a bit inclined to the right, yet her being progressing towards him:—You have to lock up your safety belt, cause the plane should be landing soon. And, don't get up of your sit! As the plane's Capitan will make statement?—Egor has looked earnestly her in the eyes, at the same time as listening with attention:—Why? There's anything wrong? Are we in some kind of danger?—Stewardess gives a big smile as her head is a bit inclined towards the right, she then in a more relaxed tone says:—Oh no, nothing is wrong, it's just is a tradition here, that the Capitan with the Pilots are greeting passengers.—Egor becomes more relaxed, sesn he's head straight up:—Thanks God! All righty then. Thanks, I may do it, as you advise.—Meantime, the aeroplane with non-stop of its course flight for at least an hour or two, while all these passengers there in got back to their seats. An extra thirty minutes passes, all those passengers are still having taken the weight off he's feet on their sits, fares with Egor built-in there. And so, the red button which was yellow color previously, suddenly is changed into going red; then it's turned on by itself and begun to flash with a siren, which brings to attention all of those travellers including Egor. It sounds as if Egor has heard a signal, then a speech near-term of wherever interior of the plane, still Egor won't identify himself being in the atmosphere. Those travellers on the flight began hearing speech, that is making this Capitan of the plane, but our main character's attention is focus on the button, as he looks straight forward him perceive sounds with a speech, as volume has become increased through that speaker-radio, which still is on, as a result of vibration from the echo moves around compartment of the plane, as the are passengers watching and listening with intent a button, as statement follows:—Good evening, ladies and gentlemen! This is your Capitan speaking! I would like to inform you all that very soon our airplain will be landing in Japan, Tokyo International airport. So, please, take your sits, and lock in you're safety belt. Plane is flying at the altitude approximately 10,000 feet, temperature outside is minus -58 Degrees C, and the wind is North-West. As time in Tokyo now—is 22 hours 40 minutes, when evening time there. The time difference between Sydney and Tokyo is eight hours on negative. In the best position, I would like to remind you: before you're going to leave the plane don't forget your stuff. And you must wait for a while before your turn comes to walk out to leave the plane. Thank you for your attention, and I hope—all of you being enjoying a trip with our air travel!— Indeed watching through an skylight what's occurred beneath and beyond there, where City of Tokyo amazingly became visible . . .

Soon the complex of the airport also appeared underneath there on the surface ground.

Despite of Egor has disembarked from that plane, still he is remaining by the side of the Tokyo central airport. As a requisite procedures Egor between amassing travellers get through the Customs Officials, where excessively out for the Quarantine. There to hint from the interpreter, whose be supposed to pick up his luggage from carousel, which being designed for travellers, in order to pick up stuff from a luggage-collector. Obviously those passengers ought to be flying through changed routes travel to, as a result the previous guy has asked to forming circles among persons along for the ride, who are going travel one way, or the another—in separate groups, in accord with their place of destinations. One of those formed groups, where Egor has sighted to be found in, that contained of a large circle of people, among whom standing and awaiting being two nuns. The interpreter has in words added and up to dated the passengers, to facilitate of their next flight that is scheduled for tomorrow, in line with Japanese time on mid-day: for they are leave twelve o'clock—noon. At last but not least, every single one those passengers from the flight N947 have been up to dated that those must be transfer at the hotel and placed within, where they be to able resting and stay overnight. After few hours have passed, since Egor arrived at the hotel. From there Egor has been re-located over night stay, prior to and in accordance with for the next scheduled flight of their destination. In the hotel lobby concierge has told Egor that he is ought to be placed in room number 22. He starts to reflect on it to himself:—What a grotesque?—To deal of what's be said, he feels that has enough of alarming news, and what he also saw, and above all—feeling dead beat after turbulence too since he could not recover due to jet leg from flight, and after he is decided to switch off TV, except for the touch lamp is still on, when finally he is closed his eyes: In its place his childhood memories once again start to surge back, he is kept remembering the past, like that tape being rewinding in he's mind back, and flooding—filling mind into the core of his past memories onto the presence conscience . . .

CHAPTER 23

The Borodin have been informed, that soon they're needed to get ready on time for an air travel to Italy. Basically they've completely forgot about arrangements, were living comfortably in the Austrian Alps hostel, and enjoying a carefree life up in the mounts—faraway from troubles and other nasty situations without dilemmas, that families had to face. For that reason, just back then it's all started over for us like it was on the verge of a new journey, as it has been previously done: again, they are supposed to pack their personal belongings with extra stuff. 'Grumpily for us, one of the suitcases that they are brought with us got broken on the way just then, since we were situated in Austrian Alps Mount, where they are have not got a chance or money to buy a new one. I let slip that this Austrian man or should I say being the owner of the hostel, where the family stayed for almost two months then, and who was good to us seen our fiscal difficulties, and offered us with formerly owned suitcase. Also Egor's family have been enlightened that they obliged to wait for transfer outside that, is supposed to arrive and picks them up. In keeping up with that facts the family be supposed to transfer with all of their belongings to the Vienna airport for the scheduled flight towards another foreign country—Italy. Ahead of their hard luck: the family has given notice as a warning, despite the outcome, if it's going to take place—either very 'early morning, or very delayed util night' but we must get ready first and await for the transport to arrive without delay there. In so doing, every night for about four days in the row they have been waiting for transfer to arrive, that be supposed to picking up the family up, and other people also, who stayed at hostel and conveying those including us towards the Vienna airport for the scheduled flight to Italy. The Borodin's were advised at some stage of the phone talk with this one be in charge in the course of action for their document procedure via an interpreter:—Folks, who are undertaking the transfer for your family and other people towards Vienna airport, will arrive to pick you're up between 12 o'clock from mid-night—to 3o'clock in the morning. As you all must be ready on time, and waiting for a van, cause the driver, who is in charge for transfers won't be waiting long for you're! That is your duty to get ready in advance with your stuff, and your entirety family need come outside and are remaining there, until transport arrives to pick you up.—For the weather itself is seen snow and windy conditions—since it is still winter outside, herewith befall on frosty month of January in Europe. The heart of the winter, as I say often: with plenty of snow cold winds, as they exist in the midst of frosty temperature outside. in its place to talk about Alps mounts, where the weather was nastier and colder, then it's surroundings of metropolis. I still commit to memory that place no other than from first to last with warmth and contentment of all these times that they are spend up there by the side of that Austrian Alps uphill within the Low Valley.

In doing that, every night the family would waiting for a convoy to bring them toward Vienna airport. Expect that for the past four days the Borodin's did not catch a sight of the transfer. 'Despite all of us didn't sleep—still we have being in good health, as well as we could in that condition.' Yet I felt tired in frozen in sub-zero, as the only positive, which have come out of this situation being that Leonid single-handedly waiting outside for transport to arrive. Otherwise I have nor idea what would be resulted of arrangements, neither of a scenario, which supposed to be frozen, devoid of sleep, else other harmful factors. Just to reverse at that time when it's all began I was sleepy, as they hush sleeping, and tried to be calm for Alena's sake. Since the entire family still was resided in the hostel, but they were forced to move in a single room, which by it's size being big enough to fit there for the Borodins to stay. Suitable, but inconveniently I shared the bed with mom on bottom of the row, while Leonid was resting on the higher tier, where Ester in its place, being sleeping just beyond with the low base down layer of bed. In the evening, while they would wait for transport to arrive, I was getting fully dressed up with having worn a cardigan and atop winter coat, thus me would be seated clothed either in a hotel-room, or in a lobby, while worriedly watching either towards the door or window. Due a long course in anticipation of waiting, I would get tired eventually after 1 a.m. o'clock in the morning, then would slowly fall asleep . . .

Once I scampered back and forth around the lobby—playing on my own, pretending to be a pilot, suddenly I'm spotting Leonid there, who is talking over the phone. I've brought myself to a halt, as has blocked way in foyer, still I was unable to hear. Follows that I have decided to move closer to him until I could hear, what Leonid being saying. While he is talking in Russian, I overheard everything that he being saying. He's voice be irritated if I didn't tell it to one on the side of the line, and listening carefully. 'Leonid is talking with galling, that for three nights in the row our family had waited for transport, but none cite of that transfer been seen. Also their exchange of words vehicles seem to be in a hurry coming here and to pick us up. He has been supposed, that if 'those in charge change their minds, and let the Borodins extend their residence in Austria, even supposing at Alps mounts for our family to be considered to stay here up to the end of process of the registration period, on that procedure to the body dealing out as filling in travel documents . . .

Then he finally delivered apiece of news to the family that he just received, and I became conscious, that we are forced to leave that cosy and comfy place after duo months since they are stayed there, but we be supposed to take a trip again, as crossing through new boarder. Eventually, it come on the seventh day when the van finally has arrived to pick us up, still, earlier than this time pro our waiting period ended in the afternoon. This driver called us as we learned from that have phone dialogue before arriving. See the Borodins's being depressed, but were ready and waiting for a van outside in the backyard, and conveniently their new endeavour started once again.

CHAPTER 24

Though I have gloomy recollections how our voyage went all together. At long last the Borodins have safely arrived at the Italian airport, which is located, of course in Rome. At the same flight together with our family have been travelling many other persons along for the ride, among whom were those Russian speaking refugees, as the Borodins being later learned about it.

Eventually the Borodins disembarked from the plane: when shortly after the family is begun under their own steam towards arrivals lounge, where have got instructed to do so. In that way they are noticed a few individuals have been footing aside, whose met us from that charter flight in a bid to they are welcome the entire group of those, predominantly among Russian migrants obviously, who also have arrived in Rome, like us. One person in particular amongst the previous 'meeting and greeting group' has spoken Russian with an accent. About those two are being polite towards us during, on the other hand they couldn't understand a word in Italian, they are interacting in. But in unison those few kept watching for everyone movements, in conjunction with seldom have discussions with each other in that extraordinary, but unfamiliar language. By that time when all the compulsory rules being done, as previously to form and line up group among folks, as they have been asked to walk together with our baggage, by following those as guides towards the coach-buses, that being standing on opposite side from entrance to the airport. It appears that all fuss and preparations they been made for those Russian migrants, who have primarily arrived from Vienna. In a short while predominantly all the passengers, which have arrived from this charter flight they're comfortable placed inside the coach-buses. In view of that they are all have been informed, as these buses facilitate with the intention to transfer all of us, as should be headed for the hotels. That coach-bus has driven for a while, then at length we arrived towards a very high and a massive building where's the gauge was concerned. But the minute the bus has stopped near our family being informed that's conveniently close, where should be our final destination to settle in at least for a time, as they're having conveyed along, and contained by other passengers too. briefly they have observed hotel's construction within surroundings that itself looked grand; but I can't recollect how many storey in actual fact it had. Folks from association that looked after the refugees and migrants, who have asked us forming again those outsized formed groups from those expatriates, where every family member being given keys from their hotel-room, that being intended for all of them, including our family too. From my re-collection that I have off pat, that they are have been placed actually up on the seventh floor, and any couldn't imagine how they are able to climb upstairs heading towards hotel-room. To our wonder a lift to be there for our movements, which functioning regular. That made the job much easier for us bring these suitcases upstairs, if not what would happened to Alena and Leonid, who being major dependable, since the hardest job has laid upon them to lift up heavy stuff. Too cite, how difficult would be for them particular climbing upstairs onto the seventh level together with the heavy hand baggage. So they have been placed in accord in a single hotel-room, not allowing for of how many members of those families ought to be consisted. Since issue turn out be unhappily for us, thus Leonid has misunderstood, as carelessly and unthoughtfully he explained our family's situation to those individuals, who being in charge to deal with those migrants' affairs mostly with the newly arrived wanderers? Thus, be there inconvenient the four of us them were forced sharing a single hotel-room. Given that our family has been appointed with to share a single room on level seven, they apprehensively wanted to observe where about they have been placed in. Once they're have walked on the first time in hotel-room they've spotted a list is hanging down from the inside of the entrance door, which being covered into a thick plastic with all info upon it's being written in Italian. In that way, they are also noticed one double-size bed and a stretching-bed. In the interim, at the start my grandma complained about this room, except for Alena, whose contradicted her by protesting:—How lucky for us they were given us an extra stretching-bed for me and Egor with a family package of mattress and pillows, is even better than we've expected?—Next observing around the hotel-room they are also spotted that two paintings being hanged: one of each have been situated within the middle upon the wall at the hallway, and which detained being visible from a short distance, the moment someone would entered that room. And as for the second painting it's being placed here. in view of what have been visible as distinguished upon the paintings they are able to catch a glimpse of visual pictures. By seen these images more closely It be visible that upon both of the paintings have got diverse sketches, which presumably symbolized all over the country-side of Italy, and places of its provinces so the whole thing traced being climax. For hotel-room itself looks wide, with central heating be convenient. It has felt warm in the room, cause that set of heating to be helping with a warm up process, which have reminded them of the flat they possessed in the USSR. The bed itself that situated parallel with the window being a double-bed size, while for the bed-spread which emerged there also has neatly covered on top of it. Despite of the color on here being purple with the same shade that has matched painted paint on the wall. Handily on apart from inner color painted a fine distinction of a light yellow, that made material a bit more cheerful. By fixing our eyes on more around they've found a long list dangled at the heart of the door, be covered with plastic, and hanging down from inside of the entrance door towards facing us, where a text contained written in Italian:-'Occupato', or analogous. The room itself was large of its gauge but dark thought, a glow they have found lights in, possibly the reason for that, seen the room has been painted in tint of bluish-purple, or should be of the curtains, which they fell off, as a result obscuring windows and the balcony, which made the room darker even during the daytime its obvious sighted, they are have noticed it when for the first time they've walked in. Yet here to be a plus they've found a phone in room that functioned to their surprise. As for the bathroom itself handily there're saw in readily available full of toiletries such as soap, bits and pieces by clean towels for their needs and usefulness. The moment having got settled, they heard a knock in their door. Leaning by way of unbolting a lock, on the threshold appears be a middle-age man. Given he spoke Italian that they couldn't understand a word, not at all whilst the man applied to us by saying, he has been holding out a guide that of listing is illustrious, which being written in Russian, he hand it over to Leonid. With an eye to contained instruction from the society, which gave the impression of being in charge for migrants, who's arrival in Italy to be unheard of, ahead specially for those not have acquainted with rules along with list of procedures inside of this hotel. In booklets plainly up to date:-Vis-à-vis all of you're as payed guest staying in the hotel . . .—There be found reminders:—schedules and introductions for their interviews.-

Down in foyer they have met a young family of four with two kids, they presumably are the same age as Alena. While amid them was a youngster, a boy lesser infantile than I have. Seen him being crying regularly, while his shoulders shuddering, and many times he asked his parents taking him back in his own bed. And so I started reminisce of myself: at first in Moscow airport, later in Austria, follows back then I had said these same things to my mom. I was by now five-and-half, as the little boy—was only hardly a bit over three-years of age, so I have felt for him. Shortly, the Bordins have met in lobby a family with their little girl, who's being the same age as this former boy. Alike this little girl, who's scarcely over three years old, this same as other boy was, and she's seat next to her grandmother, while the last peeled her an apple, but this girl has patiently been waiting to start eating it. She is kept weeping now and again, presumably her being tied and cold, or hungry, I guess she's sick with fever. I still remember her . . .

After the mutual introductions they are have been informed to go downstairs in a restaurant for all those migrants, counting my family be supposed too have ceremonial dinner. I then again be thinking to myself, if have situated in lobby, what this someone'a meant by 'going downstairs'. Nonstop I'm being walking with my family, but haven't had the guts to ask any questions, for the reason that I felt by now very hungry. When they have taken seats around the dinner-table have their own seats with accordance of that listing by those strangers, folks, which's the organisers and in charge for all the migrants being present. So the organisers got in front of those persons, including our family and some among them continued with counting all those guest at the table, who have arrived at restaurant for that feast, still, in control double-checked, in case if missed some between registered persons. That's why I have taken a seat near mom, but she was busy reading the menu for an upcoming feast that to be for the four of us, but it's being written in Italian. Besides the family is seated on the other side of the table from other those groups among other Russian migrants, who have happened found themselves in a similar situation, to Egor's family have to: 'for now, my family tried to be acquainted with those Russians, and have exchanged words with them. Before long of waiting for feast, readily available that supper at last have brought to the tables by the serves contained of food preparation. Trying rations I become disillusioned saw what kind of cooking the serves had provide with. Actually the full menu, which those have made available us with, neither contained any meat, nor whatever thing it wasn't nourishing. though if I was a kid, as a quantity of served rations hasn't been enough too satisfy my appetite. Besides everyone being given a glass of water, but before the end of that 'great dinner' they have been served with tea. As luck would have it at least it contained sugar in there. Like this 'great dinners' which ought being served to us this evening, they are supposed to consume cooking and 'enjoy' not a whole week ahead to come, for the period of our stay in hotel. As they are unaware off forthcoming on the first day upon their arrival in Italy while they have resided in the hotel for a few days. On the first week, since the Borodin's arrival in Rome, they were appearing in tenure, and have already obtained many scheduled interviews. As the Borodin's have got to learn about procedures to being able assimilate with set up process to fill in an imminent travel document for those nomads and the Russian-speaking, who have chosen migrate to a foreign country, which to be issued and bring about appearing in as a major factor for Egor's family that, need to stay in Italy, by means of their status being known—'Passengers in Transit'.

At some stage in few days in a row, all evening they would come down to hotel's lobby to converse with other Russian-speaking, who have stayed in Italy also. They're talking with the Russian interpreter for a while, and having well-versed her of many interesting facts. She unrelenting gave the lowdown by trying to explain to us, where next that last has twisted towards me:—Since four of you left the USSR, not considering, if you accept at existing your father's surname or not? Even if do, given your mother won't be inviting your dad, that he has no longer been living with you're. In that case you must change from your real surname Borodin—into your mother's maiden surname?—Alena, in contrast has become sceptical, if it is a good idea to change his name: The earlier agreements had been, that since she got marriage, followed by my birth, during which her official marital states and bond with my dad, regardless what and how he behaved. And up till at that time, she's being certain, that I must bear my father's surname, so with this name I was born, that Egor must stay as Borodin.

As for the furture, in Alena's belief: anyone could believe, that I would be identified as an off spring. hence it must be bad for my reputation on top for the future to come, particular when I grow up. Eventually, when the interpreter asked for my permission I responded as candidly as I could:—I'm totally agree with my mom's decision, and she needs to be undertaken my affairs, on my behalf.-

Crucial to draw attention to, that during the first few days of our residence in the hotel—neither of us could speak, nor understand a word in Italian, at the same time as they're tried to communicate with those locals or with any, who spoke foreign languages. Just then by means of they have a language barrier, given lack of communication, that brought us to a point of desperation, so either of us be unable to find the streets names, which we were seeking desperately. Borodins were obtained a mini-dictionary one for each family members to grab. Alas, I was unable to get a chance to grab one, since me being under age. Rumours has it that for these famous historical places, which the Borodins were heard so much as Italy's culture, as they ought to visualise, who fancy visiting Rome, but my family being unable to find much of televised facts about these places. Public transport, on the other hand wasn't a requirement for me to get worried about, given to concern that me being five-and-half, and according to the Italian Law those kids, who were under eight years weren't obliged to buy travel tickets. In view of that, Alena wouldn't bother to buy Egor tickets or paying for their tour, which they took, as could travel on a range of public transport.

'During Borodins stay in Rome's hotel, they would go often for a walk in city centre, or to market, where they're desired to buy yummy stuff, which have tasted fab, with ice cream amid. Since having winter outside been of its euphoria in Italy, by observing the picture via the glass, while they would go inside a warm shopping centre to hide from despair. Often they are would catch public transport: bus, or the metro while they would travel to the Market places, which to be located at the heart of Rome. The whole lot being presented to visibility they are considerate to be altered from what they have used it overall at the Alps, which emerged in some ways it being they weird, at the same time wonderful, with unfamiliar have brought up ignorance of the Italians among us, who made us undergo by disadvantage.

CHAPTER 25

The Borodin's wouldn't pay attention, as they stayed a full week that has past, since their arrival in Italy.

When Alena, Leonid and Egor have left the hotel, where they stayed. 'Egor is holding mom by the hand. Alena has engaged talking to Leonid, while they constantly are under your own steam for quite a long time. Even if, Alena has brought along book, which she is holding in her hand, it materialized a tiny and mom explained to me that its a dictionary, or called mini-dictionary, with no advantage. Yet this trio have felt to be insufficiently experts, who have also become disorientated, in what direction to go. 'When I tried to get involved, as thus asked them questions, but they both have ignored me. With my next query Leonid and mom stopped, he then, shockingly has asked me:—Don't you see we are looking for a place to stay, and to move out from the hotel, if not, the four of us including you too, should be sleeping in the streets. Don't disturb us or or else interfere in banter. Do you want to sleep in the cold weather, and you know it's winter outside, aren't you aware of that, or not?—I've become confused and could not comprehend, what he meant by that 'sleeping outside', but mom continued with serious tone of anxiety implies:—Stop it! Stop being silly!—These were the only words that I have heard from her. In this state resulted—they are kept walking for a while, than they are caught the bus got on it, and non-stop being travelling for some time. At least I've got a chance to sit down, not have to buy me a ticket, since I still being five-

and—half years old for that reason everyone around could see even that the bus-conductor. They're having continued travelling on the bus for a while, and when finally got off, where by looking around next those three began on a long walk. 'After under our own steam the three of us began strolling this time on foot on the way to unfamiliar distance, then I began to get restless and cranky, asked to give me a touch of food, cause I being already hungry, could not keep quiet. A negative point to their misfortune as those three neither speak Italian, nor English, then they could became more confused of the situation, they've found themselves in being unaware either how to act first, no where a direction to exit might be. Surprisingly something is struck Leonid seeing him with a grin, while he shown his golden teethes', which emerge in front, he is assumed:—I have an idea, what we need to do, and whereabouts' the place us to be visiting. First of all, check your dictionary, what's called in Italian 'the market'? When next, they are asking the strangers, whereabouts location of a nearest market from here. Doesn't it not sound good to you? Come on. There's nothing for us to lose anyway. Let's do it!—Once Alena has found the words, that they are having, learned from her seeking for the place to be called 'mer'kato'. Short-term, those three are begun crossing the road to the other side, and tried to get around the corner. When surprisingly they have noticed those two black men, as for me it become a bit outlandish to see folks with unlike color of their skin tone. She kept looking towards them and then said:-Listen dad, can you see those two black African men, they are walking on the opposite side of the road? I can bet on, that they speak Russian. At least one of those does. Why aren't speaking openly to them, and see if they going to respond? If I'm wrong, I lost the bet, but if I'm right, in that case, you shall listen to me. O.K. Good, it's a deal?—given Alena started asking in French that she new merely a few words:—Excuse moi, Monsieur, parler le François or de Russie?—To my surprise one of those two African men, react in repond:—О, да, конешно! Я понимает по-Русский!,— Indeed they really have. Then in a relaxed voice one among twosome, who to our amaze have a word enough in Russian. I feel like to explain that am neither racist, nor do I no matter which anti folks with diverse colors on their skin. yet, what I'm trying to emphasize so far that, before my family left the USSR, I was born and raised in a town, where only lived roughly, nor more than 100,000 people. At some stage all those time majority of population with me counted haven't seen, nor come across to meet individuals with different skin texture colors, except for these Korean, who were born in there. As a result, it came as a shock to me, when I come across for the first time to meet those men of African appearence, who are for real. Briefly a discussion between Alena and those Africans of a this delicate story tale; which they're having been happy to share with us. Whilst one of those new acquaintances was dating, and he felt in love with a Russian girl, whom he had later married. He stops; taken a deep breath, then has continued with his story: that's why he arrived here in Italy, and has waited for consent migrating to any country in the world that is willing to accept a young couple—in order to settle down and build a new live along with their child, except for his county of origin, that's Mozambique, in Africa. Logically, at some stage in a discussion those two Africans have asked that trio:-Что ви трое деляете ви Италии?—Given she won the bet, that has a discussion, responded:—There is a junction nearby, I'm willing to explain, for that reason it shall go on-and-on-on . . . —First of all, we came to Italy, and there aren't three of us, but four. And secondly, because my mother has also arrived with us and together to assemble—we're a family. Unluckily, my mother couldn't come with us, and since she is feeling unwell, and so we left her in hotel. There we have actually stopped, upon our arrival here. I want to introduce my father to you're, his name is Leonid.—This one Africans has approached Leonid and shook hands with him, and they're introduced themselves. Like foreword mom is sustained talking to those men of African appearance:—See this boy here is my son. His name Egor. But now, straight to the point . . .—Next one of those African men for the second time asking question:—Where about are you staying now? And why you're looking for this particular address?—Alena is maintained talking with those Africans:—At this moment our family live in a hotel, there are other migrants, and mostly those from the USSR. Instead, our family have been given notice that our time is running out. So we're all must to move out from hotel, as soon, as possible. Also, because, within a short time there are going to arrive other group of migrants, this hotel should accept new migrants, and offer our room, which's meant for them. Meanwhile, we are searching for other Russians, who at the moment staying in Italy, and so we arrived earlier then they're having. A while ago they've left a message for us, as well as for those others too who like us came to Rome a short while ago. The people came from the same town where they are've been from, which located in the Ukraine. We personally acquainted with them, and our family had met them many times before on lots of occasion, when we lived there. All we want to do is to find the acquaintances of ours' and asking them to lend a hand, not only do your bit to employ us, which's very important for us currently, as chin in of somewhere to live. To our bad luck, we aren't rich, and in a great need of cash to survive in Italy, above all as its winter now!—She then is taken deep breaths, still be anxious, with desperation means of:—As I said, we have arrived in Rome only a week ago, much later than other nomad, cause my mother fractured her leg in Vienna, thus, our remain had extended in Austria. That's why, we have settled herein and wait, until we're reaching our goals for the entry visas to Australia. And as you realize this is, where where we're hoping migrate and to build a new life . . . -, Aimultaneously when next I look into Leonid's face I grasp that, he has emerged being not overjoyed with her talking. Thus Leonid barges in and prevents them from talking, then rather what he has said in German, that I could not understand a word:—Stop that talk group, you must not tell family's secrets to strangers!—Has said Leonid. interim, Alena has prolonged discussion with those Africans, as incredibly puts that discussion into rightly unrelated direction—asking them, whether they both are familiar with a suburb that they're seeking for. Although those two African men haven't heard of this suburb, but they've promised to be helpful finding it. Indeed they have spoke a little Italian. Shortly they have found that place with the help of those two African gents. Sadly the Borodins acquainted individuals, have neither been home, while those five counting the African men were seeking them, nor they have been pretending to made an excuse not to open the door, after saw them getting ready to come in.

After the Borodin return back to hotel being, under supervision of those African men.

Much later, as those African men have left, those three retun to hotel, follows are finishing thier deliciously nutritious meal in the restaurant, Leonid again has reminded of the previous conversation that she has with those men of African appearance:-You have a long tongue. Why in the world did you tell complete strangers, gave away about our future plans. As I won't be pessimistic, but you told them whereabouts we may possibly migrating to—could be dangerous for the lives of all of us! In a foreign land you've to learn trust only yourself!-, Leonid then added auxiliary more by a Russian proverb:—Там, где знают двое знает и Свинья! Поняла Алёна? Разве я не прав?-

At the same evening, after supper that alike previous meal we have had, as mom took me downstairs with her, where the foyer has been located to the lounge, and by seen her talking over the phone with an important person, at first. A while after a lady has appeared in front of us from nowhere followed by—she has approached us and said to her, then they both began chatting at once. Alena's look be of concerned during their discussion, and she was asking for help, and uttered being keen as to find for our family somewhere to live?

To discover suburb of Ostia, specifically the station called 'Lido de Centro' being very difficult. Since the Borodin's were a week in Rome, seen as Leonid, Alena and Egor became disoriented there. As this trio had been advised beforehand by the two African gents that at first they need to walk towards train central station, where they are catching the next train to a location of an Ostia suburb. It's spot on what they have done, according to the first stage of their advice to get and finding the intend place. Besides, they were travelled roughly for thirty-minutes, except have made a mistake on their way. Given to selfishness of Leonid, who's being an energetic one, who has puzzled us by means of his behaviour. His action seems to be, it's hard to find the right words to describe, I wouldn't be wrong to suggest that Alena and Egor have observered Leonid, who's being distressed and reprehensible. What Leonid has done next, was unbelievable: after the train stopped at 'Lido de Centro' in the suburb of Ostia, he suddenly jumped off his seat, where start marching directly towards the exit, then he opens the train carriage's door. While the two of us haven't got a choice as to follow him out. Leonid then stepped off the train, and walked into the train station. It have ensued Leonid either misunderstood those Italians, or lost in translation, when have not payed attention toward the station that be supposed to the right place to leave the train, or just was impatient and could not wait any longer. It seems that Alena, too absolutely has not got a clue either what to do next, or where to go, or where about the location of that aim place. At this moment she in full swing has remembered advise, which been given by those two African men, so that's been a second stage of theilr plans. Next and around on the path towards hostel that they are supposed be heading for what seems to be situated in close proximity, or just two minutes by walk from that train station. While, Alena looked in a map, tracking—and observe surrounds, ensuing she realized inconveniently all the directions being written in Italian, that these writing inside made her confused, in any case it was save for to her say:—Apparently they could travel out of Rome, ahead, I'm not so sure, whereabouts a place be located, but they were not there yet. More to the point where's direction they are need to go, to find this 'Ostia' place? That's could still be more stops to follow ahead . . . ,—that ed except for: on that particular day the train did not go off to Lido de

Ostia, at least they are never will find out, whether it's true or not. Or perhaps, since they have neither familiar with the area, nor were acquainted with time-tables, basically with this foreign language, which of course is Italian. Leonid said:—Что ты смотришь на меня, Как 'Анна Каренина' на Паровоз? Разве я не прав?-, As he looks towards Egor—hearing Alena expressed by an odd look, but tried not to argue with him in any cases. At that point the place they are arrived in was a huge area seeing there of many construct building, mostly with five or even more storey. Seeing there are also situated a big shopping centre, also by other diverse shops, medical centre, add to hospital, with many business like offices, be located in the central district—of the residential suburb. Then again, fear to get lost along in the area has been holding us back, and so they still could not leave this train station and tried to communicate with the train station-Master. On the way this quartet were lacking of language and barrier of snags, which neither of parties understood each-other. It comes into sight a remote and crowded area of concrete substantial location in a unfamiliar area for a quartet. By which we've mutually become of confusion, as somebody put an obstacle, which being connecting us the way to, for us to be fond of as are supposed overcome, it's like too jumping over a high hurdle there. In spite of a mix-up, this train station-master called a man after all, I suppose he was his assistant, while he said to him rather in Italian, by that understanding with the aim of resolving the assistant nodded, seen he then left quickly. After a while the previous man came with a middle age person, while this last one to our surprise spoken little in Russian. In good time those four have found one that owned a car, and they're turning into high spirits, this Italian being able give an opinion to Borodins, who are listening, but they haven't recognized, this car owner intention. 'Him being polite, given that most of those Italians being real gentlemen in dealing with women, when he's invited us for a ride in his auto. This middle-age Italian with a view to has driven meantime to that aim place, as the quartet have been worried that lost a chance to find it, and kept looking through his car-window with interest. Next this Italian in his turn tried to keep up with talking, mainly referring to Alena and asking her odd questions, at the same time—staring at her via the car's mirror, and fussily examine her methodically: from head to her toe. A tour didn't take them longer than ten minutes, sooner than later that trio have arrived in expected place for the most part looked of an desolated area. Where this middle-aged Italian has drawn attention to details where they've arrived in. The minute that quartet got off a car in front of they're eyes aroused build in between, where have come into view balconies and mansards, over the roof to our surprise colored up on exterior with apricot, where equally were other buildings, which raised nearby. As the Borodins walked into backyard linking buildings they met a young Italian man, who's emerged in he's late twentieth or early thirtieth, a good-looking chap with black curly hair and dark brown eyes. He is standing in front of them, and talking with a few people. View he has got open atypical features, with extremely white teethes, while he would open his mouth to smile contrast to his olive skin tone. This middle-age Italian fellow, whose brought us over here, equally interrupted their conversation, when is attend discussing with him meaning of a foreign language. The Italian fellow, who's name turn out being Maurizio, has introduced him to those near, except for him all that same has been unable to understand a word likewise, as they are. By an audible range, but to our misfortune he has spoke Italian and perhaps in English, but to the Borodin's it made nor difference, it seem they could neither understand both of these languages. Seen this middle-aged Italian is Italian fellow, whose brought us here started conversing with the young man directly, while they're tried hard explained earlier than situation to him, where they have found ourselves in that he heard the story from us before I suppose. This Italian fellow then turns to them, it gave the impression of being examining the three of us—from the toes and up to the heads, other than that with hand gestures he has been unspoken, as he tried to explain, as next have pointed out to follow him. Adding together the last, who not has obviously appeared pleased, as he kept saying over:—Kabish? Kabish?—Leonid has commanded Alena and me not to follow them, they both have left outside to wait for them in the backyard upon their return. interim, as they have waited, Egor is spotting a short woman, who's appeared tiny and slim, passing nearby. You could think—she bear similitude to a kid as of a first glimpse, the effect of her height and look, instead she not being in the slightest. As they've drawn closer attention to her countenance its looked like a drunken one. It also looks like that it 's being ruffled, as she just has only woke up from sleep; into the bargain her breath reeked terribly from alcohol. telling about her: hair color appears being dark brunette with a medium haircut. As for her eyes color it's glimpsed being sea-blue, at least Egor thought so just on that point. 'Lady-luck'. The same token, about she is enlightened them on, as established herself to them, though, her name turn out being Francesca, who declared, when recollecting herself. in point of fact I was troubled to shake hands with her, while, she gave the impression of being weird . . .

After Leonid came back with this Italian chap, mom and I decided to goin and inspect the flat that emerged to be vacant, as has offered to our family sake to stay in. They are kept climbing the stairs and at length walked headed for rear an extended corridor, made attempts to find out, whether they would be having a chance to reside within one of these apartments, but when the mid-age Italian fellow translated to the other young Italian fellow, expect that the previous man whose reacted rather by conforming to facilitate, which the three couldn't recognize. He then in his turn began shaking his head, and they understood his responds to be negative. Egor too doesn't figure out what the heck's going on, when they being asked crawling even more upstairs, next they are finally walked onto attic room, where they come across to view this room looked remarkably enormous and open with its two windows, which have seem be a balcony, but these were not. Once observing a space that emerged as if this room was neither clean enough, nor been enclosed any beds in there, where they be supposed to sleeping on, on top of the whole thing else other furniture being also missing, as they are relied to find in that unit. where it has looked as an empty place, as well as untidy. Even so to all negative in there has been light; while ceiling become visible far above the ground, not low. While they have glimpsed up there on top of the surface a few of wooden planks be visible, it also likely staved prior to, where have plunged forward via all over the ceiling also towards apex of the roof. As for the room itself: it's like as if it was constructed from side to side of some thought of a geometrical matching in a form resembling of—rhombus alike. Momentary disruption, whilst now it's essential as Egor recalls, and stress that attics constantly remind him of a workshop: where up till now in analogous places for those famous painters, who had potentially used to exist and create their art paintings a star like: Van Gough, Salvatore Dali, and Francisco Goya. Where they would had painted some of their famous Master-pieces with stunning success; plus their work-creations with unique upheaval—they enriched the history of Arts, to promote: a culture of their contemporary paintings. The world Master-class artists had brought phenomenon results in places likely, which they were gone in. For the Borodin adversity absolutely not had been as to the famed artists, just ordinary people of provincial town, who are looked in way, which intend to exist, on top being in great need for a warm, and comfy place to sleep in, and a bit of nourish to get fed with. There's a Russian proverb:-"Не хлебом единым—жив человек."—Deprivation for all, in there it's being not fairly true. 'At least not in our case and condition that we have got caught at that point.' What's more they are learned, the lights would disappear more often than not, when its happen they're needed to go down stairs, which has been located a few steps underneath that attic's and to press the button for the system to switch on back the lights, as the central electric heater, be situated at the rear corner, amid combination of its corridor that being jointly specious. At some point in the time as they are resided there, on condition that into I would purposely run often towards switcher being situated, while determined for myself off; then on the rear back that electric button emerged rather peculiar and at the same time for me unlike, to some reflection of a mystery. A push of that button become visible big by its range, which shown great fun for me pressing it often. I spotted that switch be tinted in ivory color, while I have off pat; it seemed every time me rub push button, I would always imagine that its base deep-seated in my mind if item was really made of 'ivory'? For the draft of time, they would be informed ahead of their taking part on that subject of sharing the rules: a toilet, on top of the shortly the family, given that in have situated a community bathroom, where those be supposed to divide such a procession among other residents, who together with us too are have resided on the same storey-floor. Except those, who lived at the same time away from us, which by the way be fourth floor, in attic-room, positioned on a peak, where ironically be located of the fifth floor, it something like piece, and where they were supposed to exist atop of that roof. At the same day, as they have returned back from 'Lido de Centre', where Egor saw attic-room, so for those four beside are first in turn for their 'last supper', in this hotel. Except during dinner it's still be served cabbages, which caused Esther assumed so:—Lets get something to eat now, because they are never know, how long it would take for us, Egore they are get to'the place. They're even won't be unable to have, neither time, nor cash to buy some food.

Perhaps they will force us get hungry, too our bad luck...-

After 'a nutritious supper' they took off with all of their belongings downstairs, where a truck has been waiting for us downstairs...

Although, it's has been also arranged prior to send our family a ute-car to pick us up, given that we disregarded another driver, whose being send by this ex—aged Italian, whom they are met while travelling towards Lido de Centre that arrived to transfer my family together with our baggage, as to moving our family out off the hotel away.' Towards the end of the day, they have been able to move out from this hotel.

They have tried by the same token verbally with the driver of the truck. So far Egor and his family tried to do what any could in this situation: after they is exchanged a few words with an eye agreeing to the right price gladly for both parties. As the vehicle seem be more alike a Ute with its basket-body—to the rear of the car, and onto the open air.

Travelling towards suburb of Ostia, especially destination within the station of Ostia and the aim place ought to be located near, but they are found that trip hard indeed, as it's being far distant from the city centre of Rome, and from the hotel in general, where they had to stay for a week, after their arrival in Italy. Herewith the Borodin's language barrier, add to they're lacking of money and communiqué, which have made them helpless to fall in with: at least it's always hope—the family has found a low cost that they being able to afford. Despite the fact they have paid the driver in part off the cost, which they are supposed to give in cash, in keeping with agreement for their transfer, and the second half of cost they're though spending for their new place of abode. At the end of the day, the Borodin's being relocated to new place, that to be found outskirts of Rome—in the suburb of Ostia. During our transportation, on the way to a place that came of dealing, we have found out that a new dwelling been located nearby Ostia train station. Meanwhile, Ester and Egor were placed inside truck's cubicle next to driver's sit, with the vehicle's shape be a ute. Except for Alena and Leonid, who climbed up onto back of the car, which have situated of that painted red, where the two have taken seated onto basket-body. Follows that the driver has started the car slowly, but surely, and lorry is in motion out toward new destination, as its engine switches to be accelerating in due course, herewith their luggage sited in. That they're having stuck between stuff, soon have set into main freeway. Soon they've already moved towards the main road. As the ute-car is accelerating, as been able to view far removed from heart of these streets, and having passed through unfamiliar squares with old structures, to the fore from side to side of those ancient architectural monuments, which's famed by

Italian conventional past sculptures. In due course of driving, truck has set into the highway and kept speed up away to the route of . . . Upon our arrival in Ostia's hostel; at the same night we all saw again this same person, whom wewere met earlier in the morning, once for the first time travelled here and tried to exchange a few words through phone-interpreter, vis-à-vis on meeting within their agreement, somewhere to live and other indispensable expanses, which be in a fiscical support of our family. For now, they're temporary awaiting downstairs until Maurizio handed the family keys from that listed room, on top they have been given an extra bed sheets plus pillows in the middle of this room spare with stuff a single stretcher-bed to boot. Where Esther was quite the opposite unhappy, being earlier, on our arrival there in the morning for the first time in attic-room, just then quite the opposite of not have been placed a single beds, in fact the vacant room was empty from top to bottom without a single furnishings. As the time came to protest they couldn't verbally communicate with the Italian manager, lacking of the gen language and confusion made us helpless. Hearing of situation, which they have found themselves in would not allow to give them a proper explanation by an Italian man, who is complained, and the only choice, which's left for Egor and he's family to make hand gestures. So that they are tried to explain the situation to Maurizio—using hand gestures, but he didn't look pleased at all, and he kept repeating over and over:—Kabish? Kabish?—She comes back with him:—No, Kabish!—After all thus confusion after a long wait those grabbed luggage seen as they began climbing upstairs. The moment they are entered inside the attic-room my Grandma became discontented and agitated. Despite all odds they are at least have a place where to stay in, instead of being outside, she start to complain at ones, take in hand to deal with Leonid. Next in the row she began arguing with my, saying something like, why she wouldn't look clearly on conditions, before bringing the family here. So far I'm convinced more then ever that Esther misjudged the place as sustained disagreeing, as said:—This room appear to me being as to facilitate us all, thus laying on ground of unlikelihood to be able existing in such a place, but also relaxing in such poor conditions! Where're your eyes before that?—Besides she insisted, that they are have to return back to the hotel that they are just arrived from, and request applying towards the admin that allow us stay here, until them being able to find a suitable warm and comfortable place to live in. Except Leonid doesn't listen to he's wife, being in its place him together with Alena left downstairs to pay for that lodgings. Their purpose being, cause its needed of paying for this place that were simple told, so they've left given notice, about our first payment, which they were required to make upon our arrival in hostel's build. It seems that was not as much to pay as they asked for. Even if the room didn't look quite a perfect place, yet it has got some potentials. Also to reveal it's just being a small fracture from cost that hypothetical are supposed to make out. If they were agreed to go ahead with a Russian man, whose made an offer to help them, suggested in point of fact have predictable for. Then, Leonid couldn't tell the whole truth, how he came across—what kind by means of its turned up to the family in order to be moving in Ostia suburb . . .

One evenings, shortly after their arrival, during our stay on hotel Leonid met in lobby a few Russian men, whose probable came there for a visit, since those previously guests within there. initially as Leonid has inquiried, about accommodation, while one among new arrivals, which was a man had offered to help to find us rooms. He invited Leonid travelling with him to suburb of Ladispoly, where the Russian migrants have been placed to stay at that time of their settlement over there. Just the once Leonid travels to suburb of 'Ladispoly', as Egor is re-telling, with a site over one hour travelling on a train from Rome, where predominantly the Russians have resided in the region of. In any case prices for dwell there being offered to pay for a single room and to share indoors with more people in two bedroom apartment together with other families were utterly unbearable and impossible for our family to pay, budget was tight pointed out to be choosy in our situation with Esther being sick. Meantime, this man called himself a 'маклэр', which means in English person, who acts as mediator by recommending a business deal, ought to get out of that deal a fair share of about 15%, or even more commissioners for its profit as of it and us. But this 'маклэр'-man asked beyond than he could chew, then he be supposed to get from dealership. Hearing the owner spoken Italian and grand-dad Leonid was unable to understand a word what both the Russian dealer and the Italian owner were saying to each-other. This con man obviously just has taken advantage of the situation that they found them in, nor Egor believe he felt for neither, all he want to achieve that to make a quick wealth out of our misfortune. This erstwhile man saw that the family happen being from province and thus trusting people, who misunderstand such kind of skilful intricacy, which were used pro that cunning crafty to make profit for himself. Into the bargain this Russian man has smelt money-making out of that dealership him being able proceed initiation on their awful situation they've found themselves in. It appeared that he has been acquainted with the knowledge of the Italian and possible in English too, and it's exactly what he's made him a superiority over us, without doubts. Undoubtedly, he decided that they were the right people to be able making profit out of our hardships circumstances. Then again, as he's letting Leonid know that its going to cost us amount of $US 500 Dollars for a monthly payment. In that case, 'маклэр'-man has declared just then it still too much for anyone in a position being able to afford to pay it, and as for us it was utterly without a solution.

Going back to previous discussion—alas Esther being unable work out of the situation, cause by sickness, which made her thinking unclear either. Since in her reflection of thus place it have not been the right decision that Leonid made, but in fact it was her, who misjudged it. As a result, Grandpa and mom did not listen to her and began to settle inside attic-room. They were shocked, when saw three stretches—beds in this room, after they have entered inside.

Period in-between Leonid has brought our luggage upstairs, and then they are not down again, and by the time of his return he has brought upstairs a bonus fourth stretching-bed, that was given by this same manager Maurizio; indeed they are becoming amazed. Seeing as other forthcoming of the situation have not been, as bad as they were expected to find that at first: at the same time they are found blankets, only three of these, and akin cushions, if not too forget there are four of us. Temperature in contrast, within the room felt chilly, as didn't make a different as from outside, where it's appeared that steam seem to evaporate up onto the air, that's being visible every time, as some of us is breathing or start to talk. Also, apart from the heater that being just only a small single one of it's size, it haven't made inconsistency at all for warming process within the room. Room itself comes into view to be big enough, where gauge is concerned, which have appeared alike been formed as a quadratic rhombus in the midst of roomy. Herewith the ceiling be situated far above the ground, which has made it as an open space up toward the roof, where over are visible two wooden planks—as a result draught coming from windy, or snowfall that leave the Borodin's with no solution to them to be able heating up the room that came from a single radiator. Still it's should help with warm up, but it haven't changed, so that get warmer indoor either start of heating process around the room. That absolutely not, in such freezing condition to make ourselves to get the space heated up by every inch in the roomy. Given that it's being bitter cold in the interior of this room they all decided to include tea to warm ourselves up provisionally, as a result they are have send Leonid finding a kettle, or rather similar. In the meantime, Alena tried to unpack all of stuff, which they have brought all along—is trying to make themselves more comfortable in the attic's. And if given to consideration that it's being already dusk, but not has been late, as on the other hand they are still felt very tired, as a result they have intended get ready to sleep soon. Opened one of suit-cases and reached for sheets, with pillow cases, covers two of blankets, which they have brought all along. As Leonid return, and he has brought along a kettle right away be filled with water, that immediately connected it to the electric system's rosette. Lucky for the Borodins that have brought a mini-boiler that be supposed to plugged into electric rosette, in submission to be able boiling water for drinking tea. 'When the kettle began to boil, at that same moment the whole electric system got off. In the room became dark and I couldn't see, where I was stepping on and in what track have to move to.

Alena start running towards the door, after she left, Leonid too being following her, as closing the door behind. The room be seized through a complete dark, on top silence made situation even more scared than it was already being there. My reaction toward being: as all stopped, as for my breathing: it's develop into more frequent, as I could not see, and figure out what's going on in room, or anyone being there?—In spite me be scared of the dark, I have begun to move quickly, but without warning I collided with Esther, whose in her turn being holding a kettle with hot-boiled water in her hand. As a result the hot water has spilled on my left knee and slim onto my toe, as a result thus following burn, which being already formed some place: beyond my knee within leg between the calf and the low foot, at one fell swoop as starts too burn instantly. At that time rapidly the light turns back on, in due course my mom or Leonid pressed this big switch back on. But it would not interest me just then, cause my left leg is hurting from a burn, which I received, and me being yelling. At that time of Alena's returned back me being crying, and I kept howling, when she grasps that I've got a burning incident and something is off beam. It follows at that point she runs directly downstairs to other neighbors, who they live in the same build, where the Borodins were placed near to the attics, but on lower level and parallel from the stairs; then has rushed down stairs to those neighbors, whose apartments are situated on level lower than attic-room, and close to, but opposite from the stairs, at the same time this way lead to them as well. Shortly upon Alena's return back and holding a gauze in her hands, when asked me where accurate the spot of burn, which hurt. Seen a burn, Alena began rolling up straight Egor's pants. It has emerged the burn being a severe one, he felt being awfully tender though, within area of that wound view be the hot and it has bothered his foot, where located resting on left leg: between the calf on low foot of the surface skin. Examining locality of Egor's burn, see it's emerged to be gone red, which lying on his skin, along with smear that arouse, and began changing terribly to bluish trace, down the leg's area, and in front of their eyes. At that moment attic-room enters a woman, dressed in fine, which I have never met. Yet at least she is begun talking in Russian with an accent. By the same token the Borodin's have understood her well enough. Still, she has stopped from putting the lotion into the gauze moisten of vodka to this wound, instead she's being advised her to take me down stairs:—Пойдите, вниз у ванну комнату с ним, и подствьте его ногу под-струю холодной воды, до тех пор, пока ожог на ноге не утихнет. Позже, прикладывайте марлю с водкой к его ране!—So, at first mom constantly washed this burn with colt running water, until thus nasty burning with pain at least to be subsided. The woman sustained with advice:—And only after that you can put gauze with vodka to thus burn.—This eccentric woman makes plaine for Alena. Despite mom's effort I still being distressed, with my ache thus disturbed me. While me not having grasp that woman being holding a large bottle with a liquid in her hands. This Polish lady reached out to they that bottle, which she is holding, but since being able to read I glance there—its sticky label printed tag: 'Russian Vodka'. even if the lady is offered to us a bottle for my cure, mom has reacted, which our family also had brought along with stuff couple of bottles 'Russian Vodka' with they. A Polish lady smiled; then has touched my hair, is implying:—Не волнуйся, парень, всё будиет хорашо с тобою. А сэйчас ты должэн идти с мамой униз, и она будет мить твою рану холодной водой. Да? Хорошо? Ну, пошли?—

The minute they moved down stairs this woman kept talking to Alena, while the last one has held Egor's foot under cold running water, from the tap. This woman has also advised her to take me:—Tomorrow go to Lido de Centre, and arrange the appointment with a doctor for a check up, for your son's burn, in case if there is going to be any complications in the morning. But for the time being, at this moment you need soaking the gauze into vodka, and put moist towards he's location of that burn . . . !-

I'm still being apprehensive from burn up and pain, as it felt freezing, and so I asked to make my bed, because I want to get to sleep. Besides I asked mom to stay closer to me, and hugging me. I start sense much well again and warmer to be cared by her, as long as possible. Even if me had fallen asleep, but woke up during the night, insisting for mom taken me to the bathroom, seeing that's took it's toll of thus cold temperature inside that attic-room, it seems I felt the needs, when the nature called visit the loo.

As Alena opens the front door, surprisingly few bags appeared, which neither of them have expected to find there, nor understood, where it's came from? The plastic bags full of items contained provisions for us: cartons of milk, bread, cheese, butter, by yogurts, like chalk and cheese varieties of jams, bread-rolls with other yummy goodies also. Those foodstuffs are given away stuff, which having touched by those Polish migrants generosity, who also tried to survive in in a similar way, but willing to share supplies with the complete strangers, as we were. It was touching to help the Borodins family at that point of their endure hardship, and they did a humane gesture.

The next morning Egor with he's family tried to find out who be are so giving, in that case they feel like to express their gratitude face-to-face to those Poles, who were so kind and gracious to them. Alena couldn't hold her emotions, and even was crying, and so being Esther. Residents, which are stayed at hostel predominantly are as of the Polish origin, just equally understand those four lacking of other lingo except for Russian. Apart from those Poles amid others around that Hostel since there also lived one family from Bulgaria, and people from the f former Republic of Yugoslavia.

As they have arrived on day before it was already dark outside, and they were not observe a clear picture: what the place looks like. Even so, there to be found out conveniently near contain by two buildings, which shared by vast size backyard with its second block, there have also been situated apartments, but very first class as appeared furnished and it has being great inside of it, be a superior than a typical hotel where they have stopped upon their arrival in Italy. Over and above I can safely declare that inside these apartment to be even enhanced than in Austria Alps hostel could ever was.

The apartment blocks in the second building looked like the 'Real McCoy', these flats sited with three in corridor, where inner private saw living room is linking to bedroom, and have enclosed in it's own bathrooms. As to bring up practically in all apartments there's being also positioned balcony, which made it's more attractive for those, who want to lease in order to stay in there. Each bedroom in the second building's block also has furnished with: queen size beds, mattresses, cupboard, of requisite bits and pieces be there too. The whole lot what people needed to exist contentedly in that apartment, with even more, provincials, like they could not ever dreamed of to be able exist. Occupied by those Polish families, who lived in the second building as have approached them, and have started to converse with them. The Borodins introduced themselves to those Poles; seeing that make conversation between them commence on making in a pleasant and respectful a note of for the most part with those Poles, since of them spoken in a broken Russian. Besides those Poles tolerantly, other than open-mind intend for the new family by describing right away on this former middle age Italian fellow, whose brought them here on the morning before, to be as expected and supportive once one among them observed our situation, that they've considered him in high regard. In links of his dealing affairs they also warned the whole family that old man was involved within the Italian Mafia, which by caution of concerned, caused Alena more than ever must be very vigilant, since—he is not the man to be trusted, if he shall offer her a job, in fact that's precisely what he did on day Egore. One among those of Polish origin have prolonged on gossip and alleged of this Italian man's disposition, of which got a mistrustful reputation between general public; as rumours has it that residents have heard compared with him having an important effect of big bad businesses. In dealings to his dealings: he might bring to some terrible consequences. If she would ever ought to be in agreement with him. Thus, without prior notice the middle age Italian man arrived in his car and has appeared in front of the form group of people, who they arere standing at the backyard where has begun talking to them directly. Thus far this man shown up in cheerful mood smiled when has loomed to the whole group. Seeing as they are on the contrary, became silent, all together confused too after hearing a story about his character, but most of all of he's connections. Other than to come back with him, they are instead nervously have stared and could not work out how to behave next and how to come up with a respond? One among Polish neighbors, whose has few minutes ago spoken to Egor's family begun take directly in his hand to deal with an middle-age Italian man, who had only yesterday was most helpful towards our family by the side of Lido de Centro train station within oral translation. Except for today: ever since they are become known of his links and dirty business; as lack of unawareness how to conduct themself, instead they've become at a complete loss what say to him, as a result Alena began communicate with gestures using hands the, as the rest of this family be sign with their eyes and nodded of heads, which leaning towards one of those Poles, whom they being permitted to speak up on their behalf to this aged Italian man. Still a man of Polish origin has spoke to this Italian middle-age man, just as this last being listening warily, and ensued; then again, have scrutiny him more intensively, once come into the sight, as he's features altered for a moment. This Italian man goes round to face Egor's family, and looking into their eyes, next he's said goodbye to them; given that he left quickly. The Borodin's are unaware without having a hint, what purposely he said to an aged Italian man. Nor could they understand a word, what has made him leave in a hurry either, and never come back in hostel-flats in Ostia, since. This other Polish guy name Vladek, whose stood nearby, and is listening to their chat to our conversation, very carefully. He then come within reach of by motto rather in Ukrainian like; despite he understand Russian, but would prefer to chat in Ukrainian, if they don't mind? That exchange of greet between those Poles and Bardin's; still proceed it, when he has been willing to affirm what this pervious Polish neighbor were plainly put in the picture for our family. Besides he evidently explained to Alena: this Italian middle-age man was trying to get her into a dirty business, as he was going to set up Alena with whom she must dealing with, which can involve her for upcoming future having sex with men and befall into a trap by some plan of slavery trade meant for using women, thus supposed to give pleasure to men or him ought to be setting up her with, or maybe even worse unlawful deals too. By wrapping up he warned them:—Alena, you should be afraid of this man, who just left and never to get involved or even talking to him again, and also with other Italian men, whom you never met before.

It's obvious, seeing you aren't aware what kind of awful things that could happened, not only with you, but for your family also!—At one fell swoop, he introduced him by letting know that his name is Vladek, like his intention must be of unwilling to scare they, but gave them a word of warning; he then smoothly changed unpleasant subject, to let them know that:-Я понимаю по-русски, но предпочитаю общаться по-украински, вы не против? Моя бабушка, мама, да и я сам—родились на Западной Украине, в Карпатских горах. Я очень часто, каждый год, приезжал к бабушке в гости на Украину.—His mother and grandmother and even Vladek, himself—all were born in Ukraine, at the he's western part within the Karpaty Mounts of the Ukrainian border with Poland. Besides he has put in the picture for Egor and he's

family:—When I was a boy he used travelled every year to visit
my grandmother in Ukraine, particular Summer time, while
School holidays set off"-, Vladek continued and is telling them
that: I live here in the hotel-apartments with my family: with
my wife and two sons for almost two years.—He then brings
up to date:—Being here in Italy for so long time we all of the
Poles new mostly the whole lot around and protecting one
and all here, but you should trust when you're get a warning
not to get involved with foreigners. Most of all, seeing as your
family arrived from provincial town, but you aren't aware of
living in Italy, where: these principles and rules in here. You
must be very careful, whom you are talking, but importantly
with whom you're acquainted or going to get.—To prolong on
telling about Vladek and his family unit: one of his son's was
nearly that same age, but him being a few years older then
me, and his name is—Janush. Some among those Poles have
joint in chatting with those patrons, who actually have invited
the Borodin's to come for a visit in their apartments. Set the
Borodins have declined invitation, but promised to visit them
in near future, given that Poles are neighbors, and might come
up, only another time. Even so, the Borodin's be happy utterance
with those Poles have come to meet on the way. They are also
be grateful to those neighbors of Poles origin all for the whole
thing; then politely inquiry pointing they the way towards
the train station. In spite of unpleasant news, that being heard
previously they headed for the direction to catch a local train
within a positive mood. One of schedules plans, that they are
have made for this day was travelling to the Lido de Centro for
a visit to the doctor, pertaining of my burn. Afterwards they
caught the train, but to our amazements it took them a while,
as they are have passed only two stops to our conveniences to
facilitate—as Egor family now have arrived in Lido de Centro,
that's made them relieve and dumbfounded at the same time.
By every minute the situation becoming even more interesting,
because Esther was also travelling alongside, when they are
decided to book for an appointment not just only for my burn,
but also to exam Esther's physical condition, who's clear-cut

by means of contracting doctor for her check-up, with her ill health by unsettled stomach ache that still being bothering her on a regular basis. In the same train carriage Borodin's have been meeting one of those Polish neighbors, who's being sitting with them all the way and turn out speak Italian, she too has travelled in the same direction as they are. So, Egor alongside his family get the prospect to invite this Polish lady to be translate for them, as soon as they are going to arrive around. Meanwhile, they have spend at least the whole afternoon in the Lido de Centro on appointments, except that was not pleased, cause they are supposed to pay for a visit to the doctors a large sum of cash, which of course they are not attained in the least get hold of any, even a fracture of it in cash, but after that they are all intended for lunch. 'It seems that mom become troubled, observing that I paced for an extended distance, mainly woth my leg burned, as a result she suggested me being obligated having a rest, thus she insisted for Esther returning back accompanied by me in Ostia's hostel. Then again I was not so excited returning back with the last one, surprisingly grandpa Leonid is offered taking me with him on the way to backstop.' So, together this pair have discovered a travel routes from Lido de Centro by a type of public transport, which complete opposites in unison as they are travelled on bus, which has operated directly on route to Ostia station, whereas even seen been supposed to go by our building, with on farther more distance to hit the road. The news being received, added to our jollity: a bus has operated along the route, that allowed it to stop near the hotel in Ostia.

Meantime, being in attic-room it have exposed to me that we should be living there forever, for how long we all were unaware? Except it has emerged to my family and me that we not having got other alternative or choice, by means of merging with thus circumstances, as they are got use too. Although, the situation with switcher here, at first has become weird for me, but later on I would run just for fun downstairs, and even found that amusing, like some thought a game of guessing, thus very often I would press this big button, while measured of an entertainment that I know how to occupy myself with, even if it's grown into fond of new 'adaptation toy' have to switch light on. To our adversity these same happened repeatedly on the next day and intend for other days too; seems it to occur when all other residents, who have also dwelled in their flats would return back from work, while make the use of the electricity, on top of utilize the running water. Rumours has grown to that reached them, as heard from dome of those Poles, which whole water and heating systems has been connected within each other, the attic-room has the last place, where the lights would being kept on longer for our needs been available. Aas a result, the intact electric system worked as an economy for entire residence, when suddenly it would get switched off by itself, it's made some kind of warning for them, as they arell regulations for every resident, who reflecting upon it through ed staying at those apartment in common with our family not to extend lots of energy, when it's be used for electrical appliance. At least they've got some luck by twist of fate, where been given a chance to use the commune toilets, which situated on both sides of corridor—taking place every floors, instead, the Ladies room to be situated near to steps, which lead towards attic-room—to be a plus, but for Gent's toilet within a length on the other side of corridor, which was a minus for me. Anyhow, someone of the residents would decide to carry out by means of ebb and flow in community toilets, such as: grooming, combing hair or washing up, or tend themselves, or else to have taken shower. Myself in contrast was not forced to wait in the queue, until any of those folks finished their grooming, or other needs.

CHAPTER 26

So far, they manage somehow, at least for Egor's sake not to have problem what so ever, given to reflection that for the most part during the day time or on occasion in the evening, when 'nature called' me be supposed to 'do wee' inside our room, but I haven't forced to wait in a queue, resembling one and all in that affair. Ultimately Alena has suggested during the night, or unexpected conditions to place a bucket into 'attic's' just in case for 'their comfort and needs', that purportedly assumed, and without problem, for all in their family with her decision been suitable, and in high spirits that scheme I made efforts. It appeared that the light during night time would get off, given for their need by glow to be on not crucial, in the evening, many times, either me or Leonid would go downstairs to switch on to be able highlight with lights in attic-room. But a lot, as soon as the lights would suddenly got off, though it didn't bother them much, since they are got used to it. 'Cause of thus frosty cold's become our greatest fear and enemy besides.' I even have stopped counting, once I begun to do that, how many times the light would got off. For that reason, many times, either me or Leonid would run downstairs to switch back on the lights, because all those residents in hostel being depended from the main electric system, as I used to call it a 'big switcher'. about expenses, which the family being supposed to spend every month for lodgings or at least for every fortnight, to facilitate a bill that have included electricity and water—merged, at least that been kind of a positive news for our family. Although it was in some way attic room, seems not have the luxurious place to reside in, but when it came to the price being also reasonably cheap, compare to other places. thus they felt that have superb place to live and a real bargain compare to other nomad. Nearly many time all those residents have experienced economy to electrical appliances, while every tenant has tried not using too much of energy or at least lessen their usage either for water, or electrical often, given that's become indispensable sparingly using the electricity and by saving on. But for the television set only, as they are would expect. Thus hardship they exist a few nights, being not used to that Egor's and he's family, as a result of the situation for a while, due to the fact that they haven't got alternatives. Be at the heart of winter with euphoria, they have stayed in an odd country with a foreign language, with the aim of neither of they could understand a word, nor speak for these matter. Except after couple of nights have passed, since accident happen with me, I over heard that I stressed to Leonid and Esther about that environment they are existed in, but seen thus they couldn't stay any longer in attic-room for the sake of our family well-being.

The next morning Alena with Leonid asked me to look after Esther, whilst they have left them both under supervision of one of the neighbors.

This duo among Alena with Egor are aimed traveling to Rome to have a word with a leader, whose being in charge for immigration procedure for the process of fill in travel document at the Org that looked after refugees and migrants for assistance. Alena and Leonid have found the one, who was in charge in order to ask for help. As she began re-telling their story, revealing of the condition in which the family have established themself in. Even if the Italian woman listens charily, but shortly this leader from Org began making phone calls, followed by she has given an advised to Borodins:— . . . your family need moved out off Ostia. Now you need to pack up luggage, cause you're to be relocated—from where your current residence is, to another more guarantied of convenients for your needs place.—Leader also added, that:—Later this evening the transfer will be arriving on, to transfer you're family into warm and comfortable place, where's you would be staying safely for a while, until the next available living ought to be vacant. So far it's be decided either way or the other, what going to be for your family later?—

'When mom and Leonid came back from Rome I tried to tell her all about my plans, plus I have done, while she and Leonid being away. She visibly being busy, for a reason that she has not got time even paying attention towards me. Though she would not let me finish with my story, when has enlighten me to pack my stuff up, together with all of belongings to be ready by getting fully clad, as soon as possible, because our family is moving out of here towards another consign. All that fuss around made me confused, while I could not comprehend what's going on? When the next I looked closely what Esther did, she was also busy packing up our stuff. shortly, roughly in an hour or less they are started to take downstairs our suitcases one-by-one. Those entire residents of hostel began to leave their apartments have approached our family taking place at the backyard, when next they enquired:—you're all going away from here? Whereabouts you're travelling? Have you found yourself another rent?—Alena come back with a reply seeing sadness in her face, but sincerely, she alleged though:—Actually, they have nor a idea where about they are've gone travel to? Yet, our org promised to find for them a place, where they'll be able to stay for a while. Cause in attics is freezing in sync it's winter outside. But God forbid, they are can catch a cold, possibly even worst. In other words, they would all become sick, and even could catch pneumonia. My son, Egor has got nasty burn, my mother is sick. And to our hard luck, they don't speak a word in Italian, in thus circumstances, we all might get very ill, God knows what else can happen with us. Given to their hardship, lack money for food too pay for the visit to the doctor, that makes them vulnerable, while they're can't rely for help on anyone for these matter!—She stops for a second, and took a deep breathe, though, looking sad, but she still continued speaking:—Although, attic-room isn't worth it to pay a penny for it. For that reason, they have intend to stay whereabouts your org is sending us to. I hope, that soon they are'll be able to get out of thus nasty situation, in which we are found ourself in. Even so in spite of hardship, we're all happy to have met all of you; and they are wish you all the best in the future. So, thanks again for your the kindness. So long, friends!-

Shortly after a ute-car has arrived to pick them up, and those four are taken off again towards a mysterious place.

CHAPTER 27

Trip didn't take very long, roughly twenty-five minutes or so to travel, at one fell swoop they saw the van suddenly turns left. Next car drives towards a Monastery. That realisation came when they saw within spitting distance, there a large size bell is emerged just beyond the roof, where has placed above on a transparent huge vacuum space, along with a big Holly-cross that being hanging over. This Bell has been situated above entrance just in the midst of between the roof and the main entrance towards the Church, and the Cross happen to be visible even from far expanse, cause it's radiate with light. While, edifice be painted in dark color, most likely in brown, as it already has been evening, and so I couldn't see clearly the exact color contained by the external. A roof top was painted with light grey, me being not quite certain, or just mistaken. When they are walked together with the driver in direction of backyard of the Monastery they are glimpsed two nuns even from a distance, who have been standing and waiting for someone to arrive. Those two are dressed in a lengthy black color dresses, which its measurement being lengthwise longer than their cuffs, the nuns also have wore robes. Around their neck's and upon their heads are covered, which bear a resemblance to long shoals, there in between it's being visible white color, which covered almost a fracture of their faces: this same fair being circled upon their long shirt-front, which those nuns worn at the top of their robes. Also to be made of wood a brown Holly-Cross that sighted is hanging around their necks. After those nuns saw the family, began greeting them, as are waiving hands to the best of their abilities and awareness how they arelcoming everyone, including them. In spite of their polite they're welcome, they could not understand a word what they saying, still, they are begun to smile and shake hands with them, as a mutual introduction allows to act on by etiquette with someone whom they are have knew, or would like to get acquainted with for the first time. up Apart from shaking our hands they also bothey ared and began to speak either in Italian, or Latin. I can't be so sure, since I've being unable to understand a word, and so hasn't my family. Even so, one thing my family did comprehend it good that in front of them; given that being definitely a view of Monastery without doubts, whether its Monastery for women—it was a mystery for them then, as yet—important?

Period in-between, one among those nun's patted my head, while other nuns seeing are embraced Esther, and having patted over her upper back and on the shoulders with care. I think they were aware that she was sick or an important person had informed them in advance about our family situation. Having been nice and polite those nuns helped they with the baggage too. One of those nuns has placed them in two separate rooms: for mom and Esther ought to be staying in separate rooms. It seems that for gentlemen, she has meant being addressing Leonid and me—in separate rooms, but not without the help from, or I should bring to light through a Russian translator. Once grasp, that I am not aimed at seeing my mom I began to cry. As is I kept crying more and more heavier, until one of those nun's at first knocked on the door, at that moment she opened the door surprisingly, where she has entered as emerged in room, which I be supposed to share with grandpa. This nun appears being in the age of her late fiftieth, when held her head straight except leaning to the right, and has composed her hands together tight. While, she began speaking directly to me, except I could not understand her, by lack of a foreign language she spoke, and the realisation made her doing next: she lifted her left arm then straight with her gestures pointed them to the door. Leonid, possibly grasps the nun's intend and without delay started following her, though, I tag along only a length behind them. When both of them walked along the corridor and being following nun at the back, until they've reached rear the door, which led towards an office. A nun take good manners, when has waved her arms, and made them known, inviting two to enter inside an office. Facing that at first she's walks ahead of them, near the entrance to a room like an office she has changed the places with ours, and stepped aside to make the way for both of them; she then softly closed the door behind him. And with her bob and curtsy the length of her right hand that waived towards the armchair, that they are translated, that it's being permitted for they to take a seat. Once all of them sit down on the table the Nun dialled a number, as they 're heard she began to speak, either in Italian or other lingo. They're begun staring at each other, instead she's composed herself, while meticulously examining me. After nun has completed which has given the impression of being analytical me, in my opinion it has been Leonid's turn for her to be able examining by her too. Once they both have got more relaxed: grandpa and I begun observing round: the room itself be big, and the ceiling was very high, where above a chandelier is hanging above the floor the room and brighten it up, for that reason curtains are off it's obscured windows. As a result the moon light couldn't be flashing in inside the room: only gloomy reflection stayed upon curtains like shades that I have thought. Observing insight they have come to conclusion that room signify a library, the surface of the large bookshelf being tinted in brown, but with chestnuts tint upon it, like it's be made from mahogany tree woods, and are fully filled with it's books. And as for the table it's being analogous to color of the bookshelf, in conjunction with the objects seem be made from the same wooden material—armchairs equal have felt soft and relaxing to sit on, its being covered in the midst of dark brown leather, or I don't know—rawhides?—Meanwhile this nun has begun speaking over the phone, while they earnestly are listening, except those two haven't understood a word, for patiently waited until they've got a chance to speak up. Anyhow she passes the receiver to Leonid, and I over-heard what a man voice, who spoke in Russian, on the phone is telling him. Leonid's responded that they are glad be invited to stay in Monastery. Though, my grandson is distressed, cause he wants to see him re-unite together with his mother, in the same room. You see she is my daughter, of course. Otherwise he won't be able to sleep, and he shall cry for a long time. About my wife, I ask for your consent to stay at that same room where she is!—This person, on the other side on other side of telephone line happen being an man, who has translated those facts at some stage of discuss in Russian to Italian—with rearwards, he also let Leonid and Egor that this nun, who's sitting in front of them is no less then 'Mother Superior' herself, which made the duo uneasy. Yet 'Mother Superior'in her turn has delivered to them that they're have got inform by a Russian interpreter—her rank in the religious world being high regarded, and at the monastery be picky. And so, by the gestures, which Mother Superior has made, when begun shaken her head that's being visible, except for Leonid's request so identify if that she's approved by means of to some degree. A translator's voice of on the phone line be supposed to in turn deliver back to us what's being her respond. Mother Superior stops for a second, whose in anticipation become for this translator of delivering in succession to adult and a child. She then pull up again her head, and tells:—As for your grandson, its promising, I don't object to it, they are allowing him to stay in his mother's room, given that he's just a kid, as we've wholly realized—a child needs being by his mother. Concerning your wife, senior, it's impossible that you will sleep in the same room. Since, you're all in a sacred place, in fact we won't permit it in here, neither for you, nor for anyone else, to commit sinful wicked matter to be in present and in the Lord's hands! Remember you're before facing Mighty Thee, where here at the house of God!—She has stopped for a second looked though towards me and—serenity. Next by recollecting herself once again contined with a talkin:—About our rules in here you should be having breakfast nor later than 8 a.m., Lunch about 1 p.m. And most to consider is that supper you must be nor later than 7 p.m . . . . !—The nun stops for a sec., and starts changed into a softer, has in more relaxed voice:—The nuns and I personally hope, that you, senior, and your familia will get settled for a while here. As if there's anything else that your family and you'll be needed, don't hesitate asking the nuns. Also, in relation to you're family affairs, tomorrow your wife will be examined by a doctor, and so will be your grandson. For this moment, I wish you're good night, Senior!—She then turns to face Egor and gave him a smile, and with her gestures showing towards the door. 'Thus has also meant that I have been endorsed to stay with mom in her room, otherwise in the monastery cell. When I entered that chamber, where mom was waiting for me, I glanced there a clean and bright room. Where in front of me only two beds are standing parallel and apart from each, while on the wall—just in the middle between the beds up have spotted a vast brown Holly-Cross hanged midway—between the ceiling but higher than surface floor. Still these beds are singled in sizes, which made from timber beside with two bed-heads, as a part for convenience. There have appeared covered on top with bed spreads, which looked sanitary and tidy and gained by an improvement as being comfy and relaxed beds. One of those nun's later has brought me glass of warm milk and biscuits that nutritious felt warm inside and satisfy my appetite, as made me feel sleepy. When I finally lay down to rest up on one of these beds, it felt very comfy, and relaxing, though I didn't feel tired and sore on my leg. In a short moment after I began yawning, and then finally falling into a deep sleep.

In the morning, when I woke up, mom insisted that I should make bed by myself, she has also said to me to remember, how I have done in pre-school, soon after finalizing with grooming and brushings the teethes, he's whole family move down to ger breakfast. Not before I was examined at first by a doctor, who couldn't verbalize in Russian, even so with him close by has been present at our convenience a shipshape looking gentleman. Whilst the last has been wearing decent outfits in a light grey suit, by way to show up color of his hair being light blond, likewise has. He has at the same time been interpreting for both parties. Once this Italian doctor has done examining me, he then made clear to them, on the topic of my burn, that it's neither nasty, nor severe wound to be concerned pro further complications. Even so the doctor still hads prescribed me a cream, which he advised applying again and again towards injury, accord in where burn being located for a quick healing. As a final point the doctor is also believed, that my wound shall be healed at no time at all.

There're having advised to take a walk around the city and enjoy ourself. After doctor's check-up with good quality nourishing breakfast: mom, Leonid and I decided to go for walk, except for Esther. Even so, they have been warned by this nun nor to be late, and return on time for the supper herewith.

On this same day the nuns believed that our family being in luck, thus they are glad to join a group that organized excursion in the region of Rome, picky to our handiness in Russian. On the other hand, the time has past slowly but surely in that Monastery. I am not aware up till recent days, whether, it was the monastery for women or else? By this means they have stayed at the Monastery in a row for at least ten days, where they're felt comfortable and protected from the world . . .

So, the next time when they are have called pro scheduled appointment to the Org, once again they met there this same Italian lady, who conducted an interview and has been also in charge for the process of filling in documents for our future travels. Rumour has it she clued-up that, vis-à-vis the place they couldn't find any available for the family, as a result— once again they needed packing their personal belongings up and move towards former housing, at the location of Ostia, in these same hostel-units. When the family heard of that news it plunged they in a state of a shock. Once again, Borodins endeavour started from launch: they are said "Au revoir" to those nuns at the Monastery, and we thank them for takein care of us, and generosity. Whilst the same ute-car with the familiar face of a driver began accelerating to hostel in Ostia, that being placed in the same bloody attics, but at least not get for long, as Borodin are guaranteed . . .

CHAPTER 28

Its seven days have past, since the Borodin's first moved into the inn, located nearby Ostia train station.

After that at least few nights had past, and they are have been forced to leave this place not a long time ago. And that time once again already they are have arrived back to the same hostel—apartment and moved back in attic-room. As soon as they are finished unpacking luggage some of those residents, whom they met at home then came up to our room and invited they for a drink to their apartments in the second building. There have lived a Polish family of four, who invited them upon the first morning of their arrival in the hostel nearly a couple a weeks ago. Once again the Borodins being invited to one of those Polish neighbors, at this time they could not resist be invited, and have decided to visit them. During their discussion with those Poles they put in the picture for they a story, about how they have happened to immigrate from Poland, most of all come to cross and pass to be in Italy. Conversely, it has been nothing compare to what our family have gone through, but they wouldn't dare to interrupt, or somewhat enunciate to them. They have also talked about, how their Family has ended up to be in Italy. On top they have told they, shortly after their arrival in Italy that place has been recommended to them, and so for over two years they have resided here. Consequently, they're wrapping up that they accordingly since staying in this Hostel-apartments for quite a long time. One among these Poles also sustained chatting, when just then out of the blue they began to cry, one amongst those started, while she commits to memory of members of their families whom they left behind in Poland and have been unable seen with them ever since. It passed quite a long time, and ever since, they have been missing their relations terribly. Towards the closing stages of that conversation, they have informed they—very soon are going to leave for Canada, what their aim and the plans being concentrated on, but they shall be glad if they are would occupy the flat after their departure. For that reason, they are assumed that this family for real to leave the apartment in order travelling towards Canada. Instead they are have been deceived, again considering wrongly as they are folks being really from provincial mainly.

After receiving the unexpected decision from their organization, which by the way—has called 'Caritas', they called upon the owner of the building as well this manager of the hostel-apartments, where they stressed about, that they have already payed for the accommodation.

Rumour has it those Poles given a three weeks notice that hypothetically be supposed to leave in three they areeks time, so as they would enjoy one whole week to stay, basically for free without being charged for the apartment, only after their departure, in view of that.

It seems that few days had past fast, but the Borodins become impatiently enthusiastic; and couldn't wait, until a Polish family is going to leave. Seeing their apartment, has been remarkable, just 'a heaven', compare to attic's where they were moved within and still are existing. It gave the impression that, other residents alongside those Poles, didn't mind, and were taking into account for us—the Russian family should move in second building and live beside them. Or possibly, since one of those Polish man, Vladek, who's family been scheduled for the flight to Canada. He's appeared being kind of a person, whose most of the times has got in troubles, especially after being drinking heavy, and he would make live of those residents impossible. For quite a long time he was employed at the 'Fiat factory', that be situated just about by twenty minutes away from our hostel. Despite he's weird behaviour the fact he has been a good car mechanic, which has been his main profession he would earn money for his family and himself, not as much as those local Italians, who have had permanent jobs, but enough to be able survive financially secured, as too living a normal life. From time to time he would get drunk and looked for troubles, and that kind of behaviour sometimes could lead to arguments, and even resulted him too start a brawl.

Convenient roughly there resided a family of three people, who have stayed in Italy for over two-and-half years assumed the person that called from their Org represented migrants, which were linking of Polish descended, or else among other European countries. But they cared less for that matters, who is going to leave, and who is to stay? In view of the fact the Borodin have got themselves in a desperation that being keen for a warmth and comfortable apartment.

Suitably for them, at long last came the day, when that Polish family is leaving for Canada—after a long wait, it has turn out for they to be possible!

In the afternoon everyone, who is staying home just then, they have gone outside to say goodbyes to the family that leaving. They wished the Poles: success, and along the way safe landing, for the reason that they need it, after all they being on a familiar terms with them, given that aimed for Borodin's upcoming journey. As they are have clued-up Borodins, that after the family moves out of apartment, they will be able to move in. They're remained in high spirits by receiving good news. Even supposing Egor and his family were thrilled, still they've waited for approval from the manager of these hostel-apartments and owner of these buildings. Despite that those Poles would leave earlier than they are expected, and they have got the 'green light' at the end of the day, and in our turn said goodbye to an attic-room, which was our place of residence for few days. Where I was so adverse to burn my leg with boiling water. My family and I being temporary placed in the office of manager Maurizio, while awaiting too they are briefly met again the short Italian woman by the name of Francesca, whose being a drugs addict, still, she gave they the keys as spectator taken a quick look towards our family, whereas they are with a happy mood have at long last moved into that apartment. Alleluia! Its materialized that after all these long and freezing condition that they are got through, as they arell as nightmares, in common with exhaustion from those movements and wanders, they are have been rewarded. After a long wait they are have found a comfy and relaxing place be resident for, that assist's exactly being alike. Indoors of the apartment appears to be encompassed by two enormous rooms, one of which— bedroom, where these four fab comfortable beds are placed to sleep on. To depict a next room has looked even greater, where of ceiling far above the ground to be hanged a chandelier. They have spotted that the floor layers of these large Dutch tiles mosaic, and being collectively combined with varied colors: such as rich apricot with nuance pro brightness of brown and cream that matched alongside with the paint color outer the surface on thus walls, as they arell come into view being rich apricot. What's more inside the lunchroom have already been incorporated a TV with a remote control that they are never in reality dreamed of to lay hands on. Equally in there being situated a full-size kitchen where handily be roofed the whole lot that they are only could imagine, plus a working fridge with other indispensable appliances, and yetmore. Among that be combined from the lounge room surfaced an entrance to extended balcony that link that they are shared with one more family, which appears being nomad of Polish ancestry, they lived with their two kids. From balcony conveniently they are able to enjoy a superb view surrounded by a wide area of the Adriatic Sea, which outer surface wouldn't disappear beyond of horizon. In the bedroom's interior with a view to a joint door with the aim has lead straight exit towards the bathroom, that to be found around, then again saw externally towards inside within of a joint, but on the same time it divide the apartment in favour of commencing for our natural needs. Through in one piece objects in the interior bathroom, which being painted in the mother-of-pearl blue nuance that being made of ceramic craft, while flash of lights would move towards through a tiny window with the intention of reflecting around this bathroom by the sunshine. They're differentiated that in this bathroom apart from the shower surrounded by a cubicle, a bath-tope additionally was placed there too, for residents' want. In that toilet, or as Italians called it 'stanza il bagnio', to boot even an additional washer being placed within too. So they've measured sort of improvement to be able enclose their own bathroom, rather than sharing with the entire centre of residents, where's those folks waiting until their next in turn among the queue. Plus in the interior of that apartment both the rooms to facilitate, where have found outsized in its gauge—by a heating set consign there, which has given them satisfaction being in warmth and comfy. From lunchroom have got a direct entrance toward it's large size balcony, with higher than entrance, where be hanged pale curtains, which made of material from tulle with a spare would blind, conveniently color of, which's matched the color up on these surface walls, in the best position of a dwelling in there.

CHAPTER 29

They would travel regularly towards the town for scheduled interviews in the Org for Refugees and Migrants. Yet, as they've arrived in Italy with no legal documents, which proved our identity, only with 'the invitation from Israel', as our travel document, as a result haven't tot permanent residency in Italy, as with well as permission to work there on legal terms. Not considering of the 'Invitation from Israel' and the 'Visa' for procedure of the documents, which ought to be processed by fill in thus paper work, neither of the following association in Italy being in favour intended for the admission of our family, nor our needs, but itself couldn't being a guarantee helping they for that matters and needs that they are have got some thought of Status, being able to find a job. For that reason alone lots of times they are tried to get help within the organize, which seem to look after the migrants, those folks in charge from there, include the Rabbi, who eventual comprehend that they are not really. From now they're tried selling whatever it's possible with of our luggage,in an attempt to purchase bread and milk. I still imagine clear the color of our bags, seen all of it's being dark navy blue, and the only two remaining of these be evidence for dark cherry color, as these suitcases most likely being made from leather, which had travelled with this family, and brought those migrants here. Only one luggage, that poled apart from others, since they are also possess it for a short while, while had travelled with from the Austrian Alps to Italy. The luggage itself has been a large size, which being decorated with mixture of colors. First of all they are sold that suit-case, that they are brought along with they from Austrian Alps. I had set aside thinking about that light brown mixed with grey color luggage, that was given to they by the owner of that Austrian hostel on Alps mounts, except they have not got options to choose, as they were forced selling it to pay money for bread instead, at the shop nearby. Rumour has that it would not help they much financially, they are have been unable to earn money; so that decided selling the bed sheets afterwards, which they had bought from USSR, before their departure, which has been made of flaxen fabric. even if, they are have evidently been aware as beddings especially some of the textile need to be worn in the near future. Since they have got in their possession according to previous count: ten sets of these things for the four of them, given that they couldn't get hold of that any longer, barring to see options, to our disillusionment failure had emerged. Thus they are have been forced to given that away for sale, due to be scarce of money, and too unconventional options in our circumstances, because our family were helpless coping with. In the face of all the effort, the sale process not have done go they arell, cause they are being unable to make enough profit out by selling couple of bed-sheets that could earn some cash in a bid to survive, or to pay our expenses for the matter. As people would generally say, 'what goes around—comes around': the same goes for the opposite, plus those too. The family began to panic, seeing they have not got the slightest idea what to do next, or to expect sooner or later:'How to survive in such extreme situation, without knowledge of foreign language? Without money, above all with no a job for our fiscally support? And to talk about apartment, where the family only just have moved in. How they are be able to afford paying for the dwelling, which was occupied by them?-

At the end of the day the Borodins have looked, and thought charily to find a way to be able paying off fees. Above all how survive, for their sake?'An option on impact, Leonid and Egor woud walk almost every evening in a row, where they were headed for near bread-shops. Except on the opposite side from our building have located one of these shops, there besides they are would wait for until the shop-keeper going to lock up. Closure of the shops was a perfect time for our family, whilst one of the shop-assistants meticulous would put out in rubbish bins a quantity of clean or untouched bread or bread-rolls, which there were left overs. Those two would bring in a few of plastic bags with they, which are clean, but having saved it especially for bread or a lot of similar, filled in bread all by taking these stuff home with they to consume for our feast or tea. Once of these nights, when a solo neighbor was returning from work, by means of become a spectator for that image, as a result he has grown being distressed by that image, which he witnessing, what being taken place just in front of him with an idea to himself of thus outcome for they. Later that night he knocked in our door and had long discussion with Leonid and particular with. My family felt humiliated and distress, in spite outcome of the hard situation, they have been ashamed 'to reach out hands' for help anyone for matters by extortion or soliciting. Even if he witnessed they there, he asked Leonid to follow with him to another neighbor. Once they are stepped inside he's apartment, he let those others know who have being present there—straight ahead, without wasting time, about our, family situation, while he has witnessed over there. The Counsel of those Poles has decided to help they by giving a few addresses and we've resolved get charitable help not only with provisions, garments, plus other stuff, which are also being in great need.

The next morning Leonid and I left for train station, as prior were instructed and we headed for the town. The ostia train station that experimental by me not for the first time, because on that occasion it was poling apart. In due course they have found the aimed address, that those Poles gave it to they. Just before enter into that building, I looked up on top have spotted it of the entrance I'm spotting a sign a pretext that could be read it: 'Humanitarian Organization'. Building itself came into sight being huge, but they have got inside, where's in point of fact looked like more of a warehouse, with plenty of be at variance shelves there, full of fridges, and more of technical equipments—packed in by these cartons boxes. Readily available they are also spotted shelfs filled up to the full with provisions, and clothing had been represented by dissimilar sizes start from fashions to old styles to extra moderns, with its colors are filled up with many other goods, which I saw for the first time in my live. Here is emerged individual, who's begun addressing them in Polish. Then she has quickly realized—. In that case a woman composing herself, by way of has spoke to them in a brogue Russian:—What can they do to help you're?—In spite of those Poles good intentions and them being franke, Leonid has felt humiliated, and being explaining proviso that our family found in. In that case she was begging them for a humanitarian help. Besides this lady from the charitable org offered they packed food—prepared in advance (like it ought to be served on the planes), then has asked over, whether they are need extra clothing, particular once observing me she wondered if I need an spare pair of jacket, or trousers in larger size. In view in Leonid's point of view I'll grow up quickly, that wash pants comparable would be fine fitting me. By the time of our homecoming, we are eventually have many bags too along with like chalk to bits and pieces: from food such, as cheese to cloths, even blanket, pillows, to coverlets for the bed. The utterly delicious yogurt, which they are also brought with they, in actual fact, I tested it for the first time, since the Borodins never have got a chance to eat it, or to buy these delicious stuffs, which I enjoyed ingestion it with great enthusiasm.

CHAPTER 30

Ever since that day they are moved and resided in the flat; just then they are could not asking for better way to live. Shortly after moving out of attic's—the family has settled in the 'Real McCoy'. The Borodin's at last have left for a visit to Vladek and meet his family; given of his self-interest that he has insisted upon it. Entering their apartment they are saw again this Polish lady, who brought a bottle of 'Russian vodka', the night when I had burned my leg. She has been sitting around the table and drinking from a glass, I not aware what kind of liquid she contained inside her glass, but I can only guess, that it was vodka. They are took a sit and the conversation began, though, as I was asked to leave the room and aren't playing with Vladek's eldest son—Janush. Alena expected to be coming on later, for the reason that she has hectically busy with food preparation of their dinner. Despite the fact that promised to come down to his place, soon she will be free from the house work, Vladek decided start on conversation with Leonid without hers presence. Egor is unaware off what has been the motive amid the conversation between those adults, but later I learned that the main point of their have a discussion was about me. And to be more precise, a propos for my education. Vladek made clear to Leonid with:—My son Janush is attending the School. Leonid, why your grandson is not attending the School? Cause you're now in a foreign country, which requires understand Italian. Unmoving, how Egor is going to learn to speak Italian by staying here? Why don't you, Leonid, take your grandson to the nearest School to make query there, if he will be accepted. I'm willing driving you there, even help to translate for you, since you don't speak Italian."—Leonid is grinned, saying: Thank you, Vladek! First of all, I need to consult with my daughter about that, and see, whether she is ready to agree? But thank you, in advance for the advice!—To the happiness of all of they came soon and the conversation started once again. Vladek also explained to:—Even if, your son is only five-and-half, thus he needs to be around children, not to mention, if you're going to stay in Italy for a while, and who knows for how long? Most of all, your boy needs to learn speak that language. Besides you have to find a job to be able surviving here!—Once they are came back to our apartment, the conversation commence, mom has questioned me, whether I would like to attend a school. I was a bit shy, then again, playing with Janush downstairs made me realize that I miss my friends back from pre-school and I desire to attend a real School. There was not any doubts about my decision. Obviously, they were desperately needed it to earn money to be able purchase not only provisions for consumption, but along with paying for the fare, plus usual costs intended for the housing, by covering for Esther's medical expenses by means of occasional visits to doctors.

One morning, a few days later the Polish bloke Vladek was waiting for their outer surface. I couldn't comprehend, that he has possessed a car, seen that's being painted on it silver color sedan, I believe the brand of it's to be—'Toyota', but to my misfortune I was unable to read at that time a foreign language. Except that his car was not a bran new, none the less, it's being in a good condition, and while Vladek has accelerated, whereas its being going smoothly indeed. Though, it has not taking him too long on driving, from the time when they are left, but after fifteen minutes have passed Vladek, and came across towards the Monastery, the last stopped than in close proximity of that assemble. Even from a distance they are spotted a Monastery whilst Vladek's car driven closer towards the build that has become evidently elevated and immense within it's gauge, being laid of the dark brick with a heavy roof apex, which also painted in dark green color. For the main building complex— surrounded by it's annex outhouse to be laid and originating of dark brown shade bricks. When they are approached the office block towards the entrance the first thing, which being spotted by the side of the façade of it's a bulky size Holly-Cross that hanged higher than have the focal point and beyond of this assemble. Such having passed the front door they're walking into the edifice, where I spotted straight down the floor, which have been covered with mosaic, which being laid from the combination of diverse colors linking these tiles that matched a quadratic outline. Walking boot into assemble, halfway of the surface, be prearranged a circle in the midst of different colors arranged within be skilled at ornament amid these mosaics: by amalgamation pro dark-red, green, by which looked like grouping a bouquet that being formed as of diverse colors of existed flowers, though it must reproduction. All the same its still glow. It seem that the important persons perhaps washed and cleaned this surface ground—regularly. As to glance Vladek is uncaring, to non-stop strides ahead, while they are following him to. But all they are kept walking along the corridor: they'ae glimpsing numerous of doors and shown the way towards different offices. Alena dressed Egor in trousers, bright-color shirt with long slaves where's tied up a knot, and on top I worn a dark navy jumper, along with dark blue scarf knotted upper part mid of my neck, plus being a alike color to be worn by me winter hat that matched my brown warm jacket. Given to reflection that its still has surfaced winter in Italy the outside, but on this particular day weather surfaced be frosty cold outside, and remind it me of a weather, to which I used to experiencing. As a result I have been fully clad atop with a winter coat, in accordance with the weather in the region of Italy. Once they are stepped inside an office, there they are met a man, fully clad in a dark color costume. But next to him have sat two men, who worn ecclesiastical long brown color robes with long sleeves, like usually the Priest or a Clergyman is carrying out on. The previous two have also worn a large

Holy-cross hanging around their neck, that made me feel shy and a bit confused, and so I tried to keep closer to. Indeed, the place became known as sacred, at the same time; conveniently in there has been functioning a school, separately as they were teaching there. Those Sanctimonious men have come across directly toward Alena and Egor, one of them begun talking to our neighbour in Italian. Vladek after being carefully listening, he then turns facing them, and with translation has attended to Alena:—We recognize an extreme situation of yours. Even so, you have to take your son for a visit to a Doctor, where he have to be examined by one of them. You also required to bring back here a Medical Certificate from there, a propos your son's health. What's more you should to buy accessories for your son's use, you need to get: a writing book, pencils and pens, eraser, scrapbook for drawing classes, plus more necessary items, which he will be using in his studies at school!—Next Vladek, turns to face those sanctimonious men who are clad on robes, while him looking toward them, and sustained with a talk. An Italian man is reacting that resulted on me. So, those have learned with Vladek's translation:—What is more, your son have to wear a school uniform, which contains: brown color costume, or at least similarly shade trousers, and a light shirt, maybe blue, as well as a tie, which have to match with the compulsory school uniform. These gentlemen also want to know, how old is your son?—Alena turns her head towards me has looked me in the eyes, she then solicited Vladek to translate:—I'm aware what you're saying, in regards to wear a compulsory uniform pro schooling's attributes. And yet, since my son is only fieve-and-half, as a result he's being underage, but I only hope that you can make an exception for him. Or at least you may resolve to be more sensible, relating to our family please?—Her look turns into concern, she then deeply with a shallow breath continued:—I would like to stress, that my son is growing up without a father above all our family also in a great need of money. And so, I'm genuinely would like to ask you to be gracious towards my son and our family, and let him wear, whatever we can afford now, and also postponed,

at least for these moment, until they are will be able to buy
the necessary uniform. In relations to my son's age, as I have
mentioned he is five-and-half. So, he has only experience in
attending pre-school in the USSR. To our misfortune my son
doesn't speak Italian.—One amid the sanctimonious men in the
brown robe spoken by asking through the Polish neighbor:—
My first question is: where about are you residing at present?
And secondly, how long you're intend to stay in Italy?—Alena
wists then glanced at Leonid, as the last swiftly has reacted
implying:—They're have been in Italy for over a month. And
waiting for compulsory formalities, compared with affairs
of processing our travel document. Though, they are are not
aware how long they are likely to stay in Italy, nevertheless,
they are really would like for Egor to attend your school. I,
myself am personally can bring Egor to school on time, given
that we're all reside close from here, in the same building
where Vladek and his family do, which's at the Ostia station,
in apartment 22. Ensuring to my grandson's situation: Egor is
only a child, but if it is compulsory in there, we can promise
to deliver a medical certificate from doctor to you. And on the
subject of required attire he shall be wearing it, when he'll be
accepted at your School. For my part I promise you. Thank you,
for your time, Signore!-

The next morning mom and I have left for the bus. Given
the two could not wait longer for train to arrive, whilst they're
needed traveling so far as Lido de Centro for a visit to a doctor,
with dealing to be given a medical certificate for Egor's sake.
'One point we have got hold of a required certificate from a
local doctor, seen the family and I already are returning back,
when unexpectedly I glance through bus window and outer
surface sighted Leonid, whose being waiting there at the bus
stop. Though, he got upon the bus, by carrying in his hand
a plastic bag with a startle inside there, but Leonid looked
cheering, but I dare to ask him:—Leonid, what are you holding
there in your bag?—Leonid gave the impression of being an
affectionate to me and also in high spirits, and in his turn come
back with:—Egor, you don't need to worry about buying the

school uniform. Here, in this bag I've got for you brown color trousers, a couple of blue shirts and a brown color jacket. Aren't you happy, Egor? And what about you, Alena?—Indeed I was pleasing, while responded that I am glad, but then quick turn this banter into another direction of my experience in Doctor's office. Besides he acquaint they with the address, which they are have found out accepting from those Poles, who gave them address for that charitable org—'Caritas', where he has got these garments.

By this means, soon I began to attend a school in the Monastery, which gab situated in Lido de Centro in the middle of the suburb of Ostia. From this day on, Leonid would take me to school in the morning, where the lessons start approximately at 8 a.m., until classes to be completing, predominantly for the time he waits opposite monastery school, which has shared that same backyard conveniently near, as he would pick me up from, and getting me home.' Even if I couldn't tell about my experience on the first day of my studies at this Monastery school, since in fact I remember that our neighbor Vladek has drove his son together with me and grandpa Leonid therein.

Meantime be in school I would feel energized, but clearly I kept in mind that for my part neither I have understood hub words, what the teachers explained to other pupils, nor I'm being able reading books in Italian, whiche tried educating me to accomplish it. In any case, during our session-breaks those pupils would have lunch at Monastery's cafeteria, even conveniently that feast in common with for my part I have enjoyed there being. Its indispensable to put in the picture, while in the classroom during the lessons by carrying out I've tried to look at carefully, with these subjects by selecting sensibly, while he would try there interpret what did those say? Or could be the meaning foreign words in order of forth? While the teachers made disparate kind of gestures, or would mimicking by addressing that to me. What is more complicated I wish bring to light that many times the teachers exemplify to me from the books enclosed by a range of images in, where I along with other pupils have being engaged in written texts inside, plus colored pages, which captivated my attention. Whereas I would always tried hard to guess it by decipher through their gestures in my mind of their quiet voices, to be able to comprehend, by trying to repeat some of proverb or motto amid these words to remember it. Many times, when one of the teacher's would show me some pictures, whilst I have always tried to guess, what it could be: one way or the other.

In contrast, very often they would travel to Rome by the local train. It was my favourite time, and I just loved to travel on the train, as they are would take walk on the market or towards shops, boutiques, they're absorbing lots of varieties: via the shining shop-windows within decorations, which having attracted so many: from different walks of life with some of it's diverse and inhale tempting aroma substance, which emerge in front of our eyes and would come out from round the corner—flew up all the way through that hooked up into the atmosphere.

CHAPTER 31

One of these days, whilst Alena, Leonid and I are travelling on the train, as usual to Rome, as the three of they would spend all but half a day especially on market, there they're found to be located very close to the central train station in the hearts of Rome. Thus key place that they are more often than not would visit to be planned to Market places. While walking around they are would absorb these vegetables, and also inhale it's different aromas, which demanded they to walk directly towards it counter and to be close near at our convenient. Even if I never came across or caring for these being existed, finicky that rock melons, with it's dark grey thick skin, which's amazed me, or any other exquisite types of such different varies of food products, which Egor never have even saw when the family lived in Austria. Seeing as Alena hasn't got a stable job in due course, and lack of money they are created an aspiration not got to get hungry, and to be able to find the way delivering a quantity of nutritious provisions on our table. They are found out a propos that location of the market, where at termination of the sale or closing time those sellers would put some of their fruits and vegies and the rest of other unwanted items or left-overs within, either by throw it out in the rubbishes, or at special formed places, where's it being organised heaps for discarded stuff there. Contained by these specially organized places, where they are able to find like chalk and cheese varieties of provisions, whereas all the sellers would put their unwanted stuff by making heaps from such things as: tomatoes, cherries, lemons and cabbages, with many other varieties of nourishing stuff that they are be supposed to collect in order to bring later home to eat it or for cooking. Apparently some of the foodstuffs materialized to be either soft, or not in the best shape, so the sale-persons being unable selling in consequence to the consumers, exacting for those individuals, who are supposed to be very choosy, or else a category of perfectionists, or who have been disagreeable or indisposed to pay in Italian currency for these stuffs. Except of lacking being choosy, as cause of it appeared with the aim for they have of a great in need something to eat, at least at that time. In effect these groceries have emerged, as good as anybody can get for their feast. Apart from fruits and vegies few times they are even found a carcass of pork, but for most of the times chickens, in addition to animals protein, as well as other type of birds, or their parts too that in advance being packed in plastic. To boot there they are have been able to find full carcasses in one piece of chickens, otherwise just their legs and extra other parts of the poultry's, such as duck's with other types of birds add to, where they are spotting flesh of meat from these carcasses. By the next step, they would wait until the rummage salesmen might throw their stuff onto rubbishes, or within especially organized heaps of things down there, where they are supposed to choose the best from thus stuff to be able taking home for our feast. Given to consideration that they are not have in our control a car just then and it's being easier said than done for mom and Leonid too lift an unbearably heavy stuff. Besides afterwards travelling with that stuff all the way to our place, and by carrying its upstairs. In view of the fact only negative in that situation was our flat that be situated on the third floor, but lacking of functioning escalator there, so Leonid and mom would lift up these items, as a result it's usually they are would get full bags, which felt quite heavy. To bring up that mom has emerged a young woman, who was inept carrying the heavy stuff, which have a weight roughly thirty kilogram, or even more. As for Leonid, whose being an elderly men, sixty years old—going on sixty-two, but despite everything he together with Alena being supposed to lift the stuff on or after markets or elsewhere up one by one bits pieces and carry upstairs. It has been times, when they are under our own steam with the aim of the length to come within reach of the local train. Being at the station I would look rather with envy tons of Italian ice-cream contained canister of mixed taste with such a wonderful taste like chalk and cheese flavours amid it, which one of my preferred desserts being delightful 'pistachio ice-cream' more than ever, I also would not mind at the time countless in favour of other types of yummy sweet deserts. Then I have tried not to annoy my family, sooner or later I have come to accept reality that they are been in a hard fiscal situation: if any among my relations could do it, they would buy it for me thus ice-cream, the moment they are should be able to afford it. So, I have patiently waited for that moments to arrive. Momentarily I could visualise—or be hallucinating of that mouth-watering coldness ice-cream—then out-of-the-way. Meanwhile they would expected, the time passing quiet in Ostia place, first and foremost after thus incident with my burn. That change of scene around they not taken place, and yet the whole thing slowly has been getting back to usual life, but instead they are have coming to terms with our existence. Also they've lived in harmony with those Polish neighbors. My burn has nearly got healed—in next to no time. Other than I still being attending the Monastery school with my neighbor and friend—Janush. Now I being in the company with Janush its obvious they are became good friends. Besides from the time, when Janush has owned a bicycle, I in my turn wouldn't dare ask him leasing me it for a ride. Cause Leonid, promised that I will have one too. For my bolt from the blue—I believed my Grandpa!

In passing the days, Janush and Egor attend school, as have become aware that many kids, who also were students there as becoming known to me from the Polish speaking community, where they well-read in that. Save for me to say that, soon I start to understand Polish language very well, be keen on talking with some of those residents from hostel, mainly to their broods, who emerged being my age. It sounds that if in earlier days, when they have lived in the USSR, while attending there the day nursery, where predominantly my ex—teachers were speaking in Ukrainian. Or other team of workers have verbalized apart from the Ukrainian—in Russian with second principally spoken language between inhabitants, who being there, which for my five-years of age have not only lived there, at that point I learned to understand Italian very well. So, it didn't take me long to verbally communicating with those kids amid residents in the buildings, who spoke: Polish, Serbian, plus many international languages, else identify similarity between those Slavic languages for that matter. But given to my selflessness that I spoken Russian, which of course has been my mother-tongue, enhance, in the course of the Ukrainian language. To understand Polish was also fundamental for me in order to be at that time do outside there being able communicate: in Bulgarian and Serbian languages, and it's sound popular among the Italians, that's why I tried very hard to learn Italian, for that reason alone I have felt obliged being able staying in touch in Italian, particular during school sessions at the Monastery. Which evidently knowledge of the two mix languages on the other hand—helped me speedy to get adapted to Polish language to understand, the whole story it have got similar words, know how to find in Ukrainian. Yet overall those words they could recognize, while listening to those Polish residents, who would interact with each-other. With my effort to learn and to be able interacting in Italian, except I still couldn't pick up the words, since we've only stayed there approximately one-and-half-months, where it was not easy for me to learn a foreign language. I don't know, it's mix of global languages, which's made me at complete loss, suddenly I felt being uncertain, but not without hope. Moderately in school it's differentiation between me and these rest of pupils, most of whom have lived in their country of birth, and gained from being Italian kids and were Italian Citizens. On the other hand for individuals like me with that worldwide group of migrants—being transitory passengers ahead of our hardships. Even with language barrier from the start, in spite of odds by our disposition has not make me feel an outsider, in Italy. Constant bizarre arguments and misunderstandings that would often occur between myself against those pupils at Monastery School, or with the Teachers, conversely, it would not make me feel low, or less of a human being there. Even if I was neither citizen there, nor have I felt like, being to put-down, or anyone tried neither to humiliate me with insignificant remark, nor make mockery over me in front of others at any times, which I wasn't aware. Likewise I felt as equally being accepted among the rest of other students, even as the public elsewhere, as they were saying in the society, whether it's being situated at School, at that apartment for that matter.

Despite that the Borodins have lived in Italy not very, a bit over one-and-half months, not only Egor has got friends, but also Leonid found himself friends: and not only between those Polish patrons, or the Russians, else—amid the foreigners but from the local Italians.

CHAPTER 32

Once upon a time, when Leonid and I would take a walk to the beach, we have stopped and admired magnificence and saltiness of the breeze that come within reach and in the course of the wind as of the Adriatic Sea. This two of a kind an old man and a boy just couldn't move away from there, as something kept them still for a long time, and they would serenely looking straight forward in the direction at length of the distance from the sea. An particular, when they are able to view the sunset, a view sun is still in zenith, and slowly moving down, with it's huge ray of light has reflecting, as being reflecting from sunlight whilst nuance of blue-greenish color sparkling of the Adriatic sea. Next just in front of our eyes the sky from blue color ought to fade, changed slowly into pink with combination of chest-nut and orange shade that still being flashing with its brightness, but then surprisingly apt turn into amethyst. Thus fascinating picture took Leonid and my breath away on top kept back our mind through thus spacious horizon and sunset by glued both of they to that beach too. That kind of a picture from an 'natural painting' has become visible alike been undiscovered beauty. But they are would miss a chance, just taken to indoors with environment enjoying every moment of it, where they're having felt delighted to be part of such a great moment in history. An old man and a boy look at that are compared to visibility of the horizon, between it's merge of 'that deep flow together with the Sky, the Clouds, the Sun. Plus on full central of the sea'—the picture comes into view just be superb.

Meantime, still living there Egor and Leonid met an old local Italian, just prior they have underway to leave. This old Italian man, who happens be in close proximity, has possibly listened to their talks, then himself started conversing with them, but they couldn't understand him at first. Given to his reflection he spoken Italian. Eventually realizing that they couldn't comprehend him, he suddenly too has began to speak up, but in poor broken Russian, he most likely over heard our exchange of words and picked up, when I have started a quick discussion with each other in Russian. This old Italian man, whose in fact understood little in Russian language, that for both of they have an unexpectedly surprised too learn. It seems that they are come across to meet him one of those days, when my Leonid be extremely happy to find out, after they are hearing him speaking in our language, on the other hand, for Leonid it was unusual initiated in his character, who's want to get closer acquainted with that old local Italian man. After that day Leonid would spend most of his time either near the beach of the Adriatic sea, or in other places, where this old Italian man tried to help. This old Italian gent, then again happen being a pensioner, still worked these days by knitting the nets or fishing, and than after catching them either set cooking fish that being suitable for eating, or foremost would bring from the Sea, which he would fry his catch of the day with fish on the open bon-fire. Very often Leonid has been taking me down with to see him where they would spend lots of times all together. He has also enlighten they, that long earlier than they are met, he saw few times how they would pick up bread from the rubbish, as too feels for our family. And yet, many times that they would spend with this old Italian person, while they are have got carried away by playing either soccer, or any other games, which boast popular there. Besides this old Italian fellow introduced me and Leonid personally to one of those man those famous soccer player, whose lived in the suburb of Ostia, but later had shifted to Florence to play for a soccer club there, is still he's favourite player, and their beloved fellow citizen from the local community. In spite of our friendship that got busted, when one day Leonid and I came, as usual to visit this Italian man, who emerged—drinking wine. Those two were invited by the old Italian for a drink. Being a kid I only tried a little bit of his lilac, but I couldn't drink it. Leonid, on the other hand has accepted invitation to be in the company drinking wine with him, as some thought of gesture for a friendship. They both have had few toasts on the way, and after a while the old Italian man brought up a story of his life: The story begins basically, when he was a young lad, during the World War II, and lived under the regime of General Mussolini. At that time many of those young lads, who's families had been rich and famous in their cities and some of the people of provinces in Italy, and into the bargain to have connections commencing the High Ranks among their local Government. For the time being, his family were pour, its come out too the light dead of his father just earlier than the World War II began, he was the only one, who left being the bread-winner for his family to take care of. Even so, the Mussolini's regime forced our Italian fellow to become a soldier not only that—he got involved with the World War II. in any case of he's family situation. As a result he had been sent to war under command of the German fascist command to fight against the USSR, picking on Russian territory. Those citizens hadn't been forced or obliged to the battle, when the War II in Europe had only being underway, but to his hardship our 'fellow, whose in vain was send on the front line there. With the aim have a handle on his story that he put in the picture for they: if he or anyone else seems to resist or dare of declining toward going to service in the forces, they would receive heavy punishments by that regime, where were treated as traitors. To the Italian man's tragedy, who was send to fight in Russia, where winter had emerged been nasty with extremely cold temperatures and windy, which resulted for those soldiers worn out, dressed in thin cloths, who had got frost-bites, or frozen to death. To reveal lacking of food and sleep took its toll—due the course of extension of thus combats. During the war time involving the 1942 battle, which was icy there so as to many of those soldiers, who had died from frost-bite, not only on the Germans' side, also among those Italian soldiers. He's stopped for a second, took a deep breath, and frenziedly is telling he's story what had occurred then when he was in Russia for about six months, and during all those times that he got through an ordeal. To tell more of Carlo's story that he lost so many of his comrades, with whom has formed a close friendships during that time, which had turned out being young lads, in fact. Indeed, many of them were killed in front of his eyes. He had witnessed every bit of terror pictures, how those become solders and civilians died, together with his friends, and all those horrors keeps coming back to hunt him ever since, until present days. During that ordeal Carlo was injured in his leg, and spent a long time in a hospital. Ever since often he still has got problems with his wound, and he'thanks God for Being a Life'. In the long run composing himself, and life seem of those who had being unable to survive thus terrible adversity and suffering. He had witnessed there corpses and flesh and parts of those dead soldiers, who had been lying in surround of 'the non man's zone'. There Carlo saw those, which dead corpses had lied in comb-military servicemen, women, and even children, who had also lied or being hanged up, awfully unkown. identifed of their country uniforms by means, which crowded of deceased: Germans, Italians, and the Russians, and other internationals in-between. This fellow doesn't stop, but powerfully puts for Borodins in the picture a story of he's life: after he's healing in hospital by the time upon his return back to Italy from the war, Carlo always has got a sore foot, even presently he is experienced ache from injury with a sudden attack of pain. In contrast, thus was less of his problem, which he came across to deal with. First of all, he couldn't find a good job for a long time to be able support he's old mother and himself. His family and he were never rich, nor owned a great sum of money at the banks, which life periodically could bombshell you with. Then surprisingly fate could make an offer, or less to get promise to be able enjoying luxury, with such golden opportunities to boot. While many years vanished without him noticed, when he grew older and tried to apply for a pension, the leaders between the Local Italian Government declined him an opportunity to receive benefits, but they had refused eligibilities for their retirement fund, absolutely not neglected those with Carlo among. Meantime, this old Italian became silent temporarily, he then continual and has also got acquainted the two with anecdote that he only being able surviving through hard working, as well Carlo happens to be a talented fisherman, else he was a first-class carpenter being making wooden worker. He then calmly, assumed that he is offered to help our family, who above all is willing, and capable working.

Its called for me to point at, this 'old Italian fulfilled his promise, when before pledged his words. Leonid soon was offered a job on the wharf. He would carry out with tusk for other fishermen with undertaking often either by helping with fixing their boats and vessels, or he just has made fresh paintings upon external the surface of these crafts. So early in the morning, around at 8 a.m. Leonid would take me to school, and then quickly he went straight to work that was located near by the sea on the wharf. Despite that Leonid was almost sixty-two, but had got through so much of ordeals in his life. Then again, he wasn't a lazy man, thus Leonid tried to keep up with indispensable job, which being offered him to perform there. It seems be the strength, which he had got, and wiliness to earn money for family sake, all that motivated and being kept him going.

Often when Alena would pick Egor up from school, they are walk along the beach of the Adriatic Sea, by a chance come across near the warf, where many times they are watched Leonid working there, where he would either painted some of the vessels, or was helping to fix them. Meantime, Alena soon has too undertaken a job, but it has not been the ideal provided work for her in order of supporting all of them. Shortly after Alena started working at the open Café near the train station, just where the entrance towards the park being located. Later she has also found additional job in a shoe-shop at the location of Lido de Centro station with her and Leonid earnings the family being able to afford a regular payments for their housing. 'Since we're living in Italy for few months, its become more stable, the family, and agreed buying sometimes for me that pictured in my mind—ice-cream.

One day Leonid wants to travel, so far as Ladispoly also settling town for most of those Russian migrants, who have chosen to be settled there. When grandpa has asked me, whether I can travel with him: I got excited . . .

Alena wouldn't mind, I she's being glad equally, but not without giving me a warning:—Egor you must be very careful, but you never leave grandpa's side, that is a command!-

At first Leonid and I being travelling on a train for a while, and when they are have arrived on the Central Station in Rome; then they have interchanged in a new direction towards town of Ladispoly. Even if, this train was accelerating, but it still took them over one hour on travel from Central station in Rome to . . .

Shortly after our arrival there they are saw this town Ladispoly, where mostly those migrants from Russian community have settled in. Many of the migrants have found jobs, still it ought to be casual ones, and basically for a short period. As for the living standard their situation have been much worse than they are having. The families ought to stay in one room and share within about four or five people within the members of these same families, as also they shared the community kitchen amongst the two or three families, like it used to be real in the Soviet Union, when during that time the community kitchens had existed or probably even worst. Some among them would find jobs nearby in Cafes and 'Pizza making' and other at the restaurants within different districts only people which being able to speak either a little Italian or in English. About the education many of those children of migrants ancestors there were unable to attend the Italian schools. Even so, incredibly positive was appearing there: they have got a functioned community centre, organized especially for those Russians, where they've been able to learn English. Since many of those migrants intend are travelling en route for English-speaking countries, as a result many of those Russians having attended set of English classes: from young up and about for those seniors or age groups. Meanwhile they're having searched for some of our acquaintances, whom they are met and saw few times on the market in Rome, while picking up the fruits and vegies the left overs from the rubbishes and organised heaps there. They've invited some of them few times before, but only on this time they are have been able to visit their family, given those have also arrived from the same USSR's region town that my family had, and so being our fellow-countrymen and women. After they have approached the building where our acquaintance resided, but are unable find them at first, instead have met other Russian migrants, who occupied one room per family, which could not be called a great living, conversely none of them seems be complained whatever thing with difficulties enfold on them. At last, the aimed family, whom they are being sicking for a while have found them by inviting to their place. The family sheltered at least half-dozen people, who arrived in Italy before they have waited for other members of their family, who are going to arrive from Austria to Italy in next to no time has been said by them. Their entire family have been placed in single but outsized room, where all of those members intended for got to exist: readily available, there it has emerge a tiny room, which looked like more of a former pantry, whilst their old Esther along with their youngest child being situated in there. The room itself be able to have room for only single bed, but they have struggled too fit in two stretcher-bed for their youngest kids to sleep in, and by some means they done it. Despite they are noticed in thus uncomfortable situation they have to be found in, but would not dare say whatever thing involving Borodin's, cause they couldn't spoil a friendly mood of this meeting between them. Instead it has made them discomfit in front of others, and unable to argue of their hard recent uncomfortable circumstances, which they experience they are too figure out from the start. And yet, Leonid was glad seen them once again, barring me then again have been ask to get outside and play with their kids. Within a spitting distance downstairs I have met other kids in backyard all those are in general also Russian-speaking, and they are enjoyed the time together playing soccer and other children's games, which I wasn't able to do that for quite a long time, all but forgotten how to play it. This day passed quickly, when Leonid and I are getting ready go home, which the hardest thing to part with comrades. Then one amid repatriates has asked Leonid, where do they're live. But Leonid acts in response, seen as those began laughing, and the other man is assumed:—How, in the world did you get across to settle in Ostia? They're all aware that at present our Russian community be intense in and around Ladispoly, cause they are not allowed to be able settle in Ostia. And, beside, they are all live here in Ladispoly or Santa-Marinella. It is strange, indeed. And have you actually seen any other Russian migrants there? Have they too being settled in Ostia or live there?—At this time my Leonid has begun to grin, when he responded:—Look, not everyone be able to afford a living and to settle in Ladispoly. Though, the worst case scenario for our family, is that: my wife is very ill, my daughter divorced in the USSR from her husband, and her being travelling with her son. There you see him, this little boy standing over there, whose only five-and-half years old. And now, answer me, what's in your opinion, they are supposed to do? Sleeping in the streets, that to leave out of the country and lacking of foreign language? And in the middle of winter?—This other persona, whom they are came to visit has spoken back to him:—Of course not, and I believe that you, Leonid, have done what was the right thing to do in a difficult situation, and decision be made, what was in the best interest for your family in yourself, particular in your circumstances.

Regardless what other people think or saying you have done a marvellous job for your family and yourself. Beside tell me, how's your other things are going? When they are have the time they would like to visit your place. Would your family and you mind if they'll visit you in Ostia? Will that be O.K. with them? Egor, do you think, will either your mother or grandma be angry—if they are come to visit you there?—Then I came back boldly with a reply as be poised:—Yes, I am sure my mother and grandma won't be angry. In fact, they'll be glad to see if you come to our place for a visit. They are live very close to the train station in the apartment number 22. When you gonna to arrive there, even as are happen to ask anyone where they are live, all the neighborhood will show you the way to our home, without you getting lost. Also please, bring your grandson, cause I'd like to play with him!—Those Russians, who are in attendance in the room including the one among them has come to visit looked toward me as being astonished by my words. But Leonid enlightens them:—Don't look at him to what he just said that you might find strange. Cause when you come to visit us, you'll be more amazed.—It's sound, as if those people have-not been really confided to hear that our family occupying two rooms Hostel-apartment, as became even more amazed to learn that they are stay in the same building with Polish emigrants too. Besides those Russians' have been strangely surprised to hear, that—time travel from Ostia station doesn't takes them nor more then thirty-minutes on the way to Rome. But Leonid would not give away our real living, by which our home compare to their was a luxury apartment not too make them even more jealous. before long they are said goodbyes to everyone there and left for the train station.

CHAPTER 33

It has been already arrived breathtaking colorful Spring outside with all over the places in Europe predominantly, seeking that "Passover" and "Easter" have usually being celebrated at this time of the Year, which they are lucky enough to view 'Easter' celebrating among Polish neighbors, who are catholic. Two sundays in a row our hostel has visited by the Catholic Prist. Seen in company with him have also arrived an escort from other confessions. All those Polish residents, who are lived in our complex buildings near by coming down from their flats in the backyard near the house, where those encircled and form it a big crowd of people, and have worn very fine fashion like outfits. One among the Polish neighbors knocked in our the door and invited they to come along towards backyard, as too by the Greeting of this Bishop and getting blessing from Him personally, as they have been waiting. Despite the fact that Prist not has been from the Vatican–City, or the world famous 'John Paul II' himself, its save to convince anyone for him being a main Catholic Bishop represented between those Polish migrants in Italy. Without doubt he was leading the 'Easter' Ceremonial procession in Polish lingo, follothey ared by him reading the Blessings from 'God 'in Latin', as one among those Polish fellows informed they too. The man also is standing along–held in his hands a large palm's tree branch accompanied by essential attributes for the proceeding of such great Ceremony as the Easter Celebration, which usually ought to be presented. Each person have blessed by 'God' and thanked 'Thee' for the bread giving to they.' After the ceremony everyone took sita around huge tables with stools, where they've been placed in the midst of a backyard especially for the Easter Lunch. Next these dishes being served for those Poles and alike in Catholic religions that symbolised the resurrection being of Christ, as prepared (on the previous day), particularly different types of dishes on the plates full with rations that being brought to the table for their traditional feast for everyone. As for the wine, which was part of the Ceremonial feast, as it is part of the Easter Sunday celebration. But prior to began the feast of the Easter lunch this Catholics Priest has made the blessings to God, and each person answered 'Alleluia', and so have they also.

After the Catholic Easter celebration the family be invited celebrate passover, where they could not find much of food, given to consideration that in Jew religion, the passover symbolizes to be some thought of the ritual fasting ceremonial. A prey in the Synagogue should be the most significant part of the Celebration, that be supposed to exist among every religious ceremonial traditions to bless our God for 'the Bread' giving to they and for all the good, which life gives them by all mighty'. Except that instead of bread, in accordance with Jewish sacramental traditions the nation ought to be eating motzas, in contrast: bread, or other sthey areets made from flour have been extremely forbidden, during the Passover. According to Jewish tradition, during the eight days of Passover Celebration those believer within, whose belief in it are not aloud to eat bread or analogous, along with having to drink either grape juices or water, but the soft drinks may contained acid gas that is forbidden too. What's important here, during the first few days of celebration of the Passover those campaigners, who happen to be either believers, or ought to drink only 'Kosher Wine' with the aim of celebrating the Passover, or among those its called Celebration of 'Passah'. And there in between for the Christian Orthodox cultura their celebration called—Pascha. The Russian or other nationalities, followers with those believes have the Christian Orthodox and ought to be among: those

Serbians and Macedonians, along with the Greeks, and the Ukrainians integrated, likewise, all those, who are celebrating Pascha. During the first days of their religious festivity they ought to bake special cakes, which those folks called amongst their tradition—Pascha. After Church Ceremony with the aim of would be ended on the next morning those folks served are to be served diverse dishes to devour for the feast, with the aim of celebration resurrection of the Christ, in the company of 'Him', whose returned back to earth to have the feast with his people. In the Christian Orthodox that public besides cook eggs and tint outer of that surface with diverse colors, as it's appears looked like more of a master piece art, then by holding one of each hand an egg they would smack with their eggs the other person sitting next or someone they would choose over. This other person, while holding eggs in their hands pass: he or she ought to pronounce:-"Христос Воскрес!"-, as the self before—that chosen one, so as to, a reply:-"Воистину Воскрес!"—In combination of means the 'Easter' and 'Passover' with festivities cover at last be drawn closer to its culmination. Given we have got an opportunity celebrating the festive season within many religions, and to taste lots of varieties of traditional cuisines, which ought to symbolize long-established rituals by every cultural fiesta!

One day mom and I are returning from Rome from Easter celebration, where the two of us spend more than half a day. At the same time as it's on the surface have appeared not very late, but sometime late in the afternoon. They both enjoyed the time, what they have spend to rejoice, as they are walking around differ places, which they are visited for the first time, since our arrival in Roma. While walking around Rome they are have admired the beauty of the ancient historical construction and also monuments, which come into view ought to be the world's oldest Historical construction. The History with their ballads and Goddesses secrets, which all thus building keeping in secrets forever come into sight to be fascinating such an captivating mystery for anyone to learn, at the same time.

given that Alena and Egor have taken a walk to the Vatican City, where 'John Paul II' residence be located, where they would as the main Catholic Archbishop and Monsignori lived there and ruled from, who were represent those loyal masses of the whole world, while their believes and denomination have bound along with the Catholic religion and with 'John Paul II' of Roma, particular on thus day when the Easter celebrations being on the pick, as for that reason all and sundry have the aspiration to be blessed by God only. They are become amazed by witnessing at the Saint Peter Square—surrounded by a huge crowd of people, who encircled the main building of the Pope—John Paul II residence, then again, it has been difficult for they getting through form encircled by with folks, thus after a long wait in the midst of square between groups within the queue, but they are have been able to get ahead of those. Surrounded and close by they are saw those guards dressed in extraordinary, but colorful unvarying, which might have be a symbol of old times measure up to with contemporary, when the Roman Catholic Church played a major role between all of those in European society and general public. As least amount, every time when they are would meet the local Italian public, who always put in the picture to they: with pride and joy of their story of the heroics endeavours. Of those tremendous challenges and thus glory of the ancients history of Rome amid those bold Romans who would have said their ancestors been. From the voices of those people they are heard the highest respect; by mixture of pride towards the heroic persons, their endeavours, for the period of those times when they used to live and made history for the new next upcoming generations. On top they have got a pleasure to walk around the ancient monuments and builds, as if thus could possible speak they would be able recapping many fascinating stories and Ballads about these previous days: for example: about the old Glory days of Julius Caesar, Augustus, perhaps even, which they have witnessed: the 'Fall of the Roman's Empire', with famous fire back then that destroyed a grander Roman Empire and other ballads, including the famous statue of 'wolf-mother', the animal had fed a Man's infants reminiscent of her breasts-milk, thus it's bronze commemorative plaque, which they were sighted at the hearts of Rome, symbolises inspired alongside by various of others fascinating Ballads with their heros. This duo has got a pleasure witnessing tremendous and breathtaking effort of the arts among some those finest Italian artists: Michelangelo, Leonardo Da Vinci, Rafael, and many others, nor less famous too. Discussion about the ancient history of Rome and the Romans' will take forever. In due course, being a little boy at the time I could not comprehend the pride of that Italian nation, how passionate they were talked about it's. I may possibly could not appreciate just than, how remarkable those old monuments, which come into view were, by way of being tremendously grand with assembled these ancient constructions the Churches. as the priceless paintings and tall statues actually have been placed and kept in the museums for Centuries, except marvellously panyless, and still to be found there. Back in the late 1980's, existing in Italy, and being a part of inhabitancies and their great ancient historical culture that represented, always made me excited with fascination. Italy is incredible and extraordinary nation, which made me being amazed, as I would dare say, who at least once have got the privilege visiting it. So, I have become very fond of these Italian traditions liking it very much.

CHAPTER 34

In the meantime, the day which I would like to illustrate what have happened just a few days before my mom's Birthday. Egor and Alena being travelling to Rome, as usual: at first they are joint a group with other curious tourists for the excursion and have been walking around these world's famous places in the city centre of Rome among the group. Alongside in the company of those being able visualising desirable study, and over look around these fascinating places too along with work-creations of the Italian traditional contemporary and ancient Arts: the city centre in the hearts of Rome. Back then on that day: the Sun has been shining, as for these white clouds they appeared to be fluffy with different sizes and shapes from knitted onto vapours up to berg, and it gave the impression of being like marshmallow shapes, which appeared to be seeing on top of that blue sky all together outside be wonderful climate. The sun-light as on top of the sky, and have sparkled with it's brightness while thus sparkle of radiance also reflecting straight onto the Shop-windows and inside other places too and even beyond. In that case a mother and son would go shopping to purchase some stuff on the Market, and they have also enjoyed every moment of an amazing Spring outer surface in view of the fact that its be the middle of April within sunshine outside prospect with a very warm day too. I have enjoyed every moment of surprisingly wonderful Sunshine outside gleamed from far above beyond with brightness the shop-windows being sparkling from that reflection, the Sky being blue and the result of a warm day that made the city and mood amid the population full with joyful radiance to boot. On the other hand excited but those two have felt a bit tired, but returning in high spirits back home to Ostia after a long excursion around Rome. They were in a happy mood and with full of joy the two went on the Train Station, as usual to catch the direct train towards Ostia. As they always have been done it before. As the two have caught the familiar route train, which been scheduled headed for Ostia station, in view of the fact that the Borodins already have stayed in Italy for over three-and-half-months, where they got to a certain extent being accustomed to values in a foreign land. On this particular day when this duo has entered in the interior of a railway carriages, where have seen full of those travelled in these same way as they are. Many of those passangers emerged being ordinary people they were returning from work, and as a result mostly all of thus seatings being occupied by them. Although, the train always stopped in advance on scheduled stations. Exact on the central stations such as the 'Fiat' factory, as they are as any other immense ones. The Company of 'Fiat' manufactured and exported their local Italian's motor vehicles have been made on the Factory 'Fiat', which were exist famous with at the end of the 1980's, indeed had produced into one of the largest car manufacturing Company's within Europe, at least where I have heard about. So in the train all those sits have been taken by those 'Fiat' employees and other working class men and women, who would eventually returning back home after a hard working day. At the end of 1980's the local trains have also had one bench, which being suitable to accommodate for up to three persons within there. As a result Alena and I are desperately sicking for any available sits in some of a train's carriages. But all the sits in carriage being occupied with passengers, then those two are decided moving to another compartment with hands full of bags and other stuff. As a consequence, they are kept walking ahead at the forefront, while the train being accelerating simultaneously. Being positive I observed quickly around compartment, whilst from a distance it draw my attention to an available seat, and thus I immediately learned about that luck for us. By approaching closer to that bench, they are didn't suspect whatever thing atypical at first there, with a laughter in a cheerful mood they are took a sit, since it's being enough space to be able contain room for both of they in. They're shown our faces looked glad, as being able to find a bench on that time of this day on the train, as they are even verbal communicated in Russian with each-other, but quietly. On the opposite site from them is sitting a group of three, whom among has sat a lady that emerged being with light blond hair virtually white, apparently she dyed it seldom. She has a medium haircut, where within her head tall of bushy in her hair. Also she is dressed in a black leather coat, while part of her shoulders and collarbones enfold as she covered by worn a silky green with shade of blue seen her scarf, which be placed around her neck, that same color as her coat she worn shoes. Egor doesn't pay attention towards other travellers, who are seated close by her, as there appearing men, as he due hasn't cared much. Next to the two is seated a young man in his early or perhaps mid twenties, with decanting in his black hair. Even if, color within he's eyes is dark brown, but being glowing. As for his complexion, I've not noticed then, if he was skinny or overweight. This unknown is atypical with his features, but he looks like an ordinary Italian guy. As he appears is a good looking young chap, with an olive skin; except for his being tan; likely he's having the skin texture affected from the strong sunray off remote. At first Alena and Egor don't pay attention towards him, as wouldn't bother to examine him meticulously. It appears that the two due have not noticed whatever thing been odd or suspicious about this lad. See he is wearing a dark jacket, when they having taken seats near him, except he pulled out under my seat a part of he's corner of his jacket. The guy is made wide smile towards them, he then has addressed me in Italian:—Come sta? Par'lare Italiano? Come si chiama?—Being naïve I have answered a little, as a result of my nature I was shy, also I have felt awkward talking to strangers. It appears that he has also become interested what language they interacting in, and Egor answers back that both are speaking Russian. The Italian guy then smirks again, and has enquired, whether they ought being headed for home. And I retort frankly:—Ci, Signor, vadose a Casa mia!—Next the Italian guy turns to face Alena—looking straight into her eyes, at the same time is examining her methodically. Next he enquired, whether I am her son. And she answed back:—Indeed he is.—This Italian guy then tackles me again, and has become curious abouts my father, while I responded that he is not here, cause doesn't live with us anymore and not in the future he will be. Both our answers seem to be satisfied him, when once more he deeply grinned, by which his white teethes became visible. Still the two are travelling monotonies for some time, while the train is accelerating. Except all of a sudden this Italian guy has put one hand into his pocket and took out a disposable syringe. Aafter he abruptly rolled up he's sleeves on his left hand, and without delay began to seek for veins around. He doesn't look pleased, though, for the reason that be unable to find a convenient spot into his vein. By his next intention of he has changed the position, when misshapen to his other hand and begun rolling up his other sleeve, and at the same time holding a syringe in his right hand in the air. Yet this time he is thoroughly examined both of his hands simultaneously. A hint that appears to be, where both of his hands enclosed tiny holes over his skin coat and around with these minor wounds, which have gone deep inside a pelt that possibly occurred from using syringes with needles very often. I couldn't figure out, but I felt confused, a reflection what the heck he is doing. When I looked at my mom—realized something is wrong. Alena has appeared—looking scared, seen her face dramatically changed to pale, after watching intensively for this guy's actions. This Italian guy, on the other hand after observing his arms still doesn't look happy, as he kept seeking, still being unable to find a vein 'to make a shot'. In that case he has curved round, and bends down shamelessly rolled his pans over, next he begun seeking again for the veins in that area, but now onto his legs, within muscles, where the cuffs and shin to be located. Around his legs particular, and up on where the muscles to be located visible dark red marks and few with blue shades spots. Else to be seen traces from previous wounds, and thus being distributed all around with on he's coat of skin spots. Me on the other hand, to being naive and a innocent as a kid, and by witnessing these red spots wounds, which appeared I thought to myself, how it's all happened, cause he might possibly got bitten by mosquitos. What a grotesque!—Interim, given that the guy has got himself occupied, except for me become intrigued by his impulsive activities. The two unaware, what's next could be expected from him? For now, they have watched cautiously for he's every moves. The Italian guy then looks toward them, has smiled, and said something to their surprise in a laughing voice, him being in a cheerful note. After he's intention when he subsequently moved up on his head, and began to seek veins on his forehead: at first on the left side little higher than fore cheeks, and then he realised, that they are have been watching him, eventual he turned with his back toward they. Despite of his weird behaviour, he turned his head towards us while the realisation might made him feeling guilty, maybe because of me; but I haven't got a clue, as he than draw back from them, but they are still watching him carefully, particular for every move that he made. Then I've caught the right moment telling Alena, while she is inclined a bit towards me, and began whispering in my ears:—They're needed to get up and quickly move toward another compartment.—On the same moment, as Alena tried to get up together with me, but this blond locks woman who was sitting on the opposite side from they grabbed my by the arm. Even though, she looked sternly toward the young Italian guy with grim, but once she has met mom's eyes, she began show a dodgy expressions, like the performance: imitating with her eyes: eye gestures, and turning her head from one side to another, and even winking. This Italian woman too made an expression, than has uphold her head straight, and then with scrag-end/back her materialized of the head rolled down, while her hair touched the collar along the back of her coat. Her face still shothey ared an expression with grimaces become visible upon it, and while holding tight her hand her index finger laid upon her lips such as:—Shish! Shush-, as she tried to warning they to be aware rather of undisclosed, at that same time for they to keep quiet, while not to make a fuss. She also sought they to sat still, precisely where the pair be seated, and not by any circumstance to move away further from this bench that they are occupied on that instant. Once the Italian lady assumed in the end that they are not intend to back off, as at first our intention have earlier been precisely that; she then put her hand into her leather coat pocket and taken out from an object, as there appears in her hand a silver badge, as the Police usually caring out with. By looking her in the eyes and nodded her head, I was still confused and could not figure out:—What the hell is going on here?—Alena becomes silent, like a thunderstruck at first, move, but as she could not even I tried to bring her immediate attention towards me, while she has been in a state of a shock, seeing she looked distressed, as I'm being suppose to . . .

Just before they have taken back the same sits, only swapping places with me, while sat herself near to the young Italian guy, but at the same time she taking place, as had shifted me closer towards the passage fare way. Likewise, they are sustained on the same seats and I tried very hard kept teasing her sleeves, and by bringing her attention towards me. When this young Italian turned back to facing they after all saw the same image as before, as he kept apprehensively seeking for the veins on his forehead. This guy stirred finger tips on top of the real skin texture, he then even moved on temporals of his head and still excessively always there. After observing 'the picture' at that point in time, I started thinking to myself, what's this weird man is doing odd? Still I become even more confused and have not said of his behaviour:—What the heck, that stupido is doing to himself?—For that reason, I asked mom to put in plain words to me the picture, that I saw:—Mommy, is the man not feeling good? Why is he injecting himself with a needle? Maybe he needs a doctor for a check up? Yes, mommy he does?—Alena at last turns her head toward me and smiled, but its act rather like with a nervous grin; she then has taken a deep breathe and started to talk again:—Yes, the man isn't well, indeed, besides, he is unpredictable. I'm begging you, son, not by any circumstances making him angry.—She also sustained of talking still insisted for me not to stand up and pushed me closer toward that passage, where the folks are in passing. She then moved even closer to me, and covered with part of her left side large body complexion. Meantime, once I touched mom's hand, only than I felt a tremble, that blood has nervously being running through her fingers. Despite everything, by watching her features none-one could suspect that, cause she hasn't shown any sign of it, on the contrary her behaviour looked suspiciously restraint. This Italian guy with a syringe in contrast, was neither restless, nor subconsciously calm. They are all sitting without doing whatever thing, but watching each-other closely, while the train—accelerating, as it have moved farther towards Ostia. It did not even occur to me at the time, that they are became unintentionally involved within prudent and unconscious in captivity at that train. I'm afraid even to repeat, what he might have done in order: the scenario could be similar to that, not only he has emerged being unpredictable and potentially risky, this guy most likely would stick the syringe into my mom's part of her body, or even onto my, in spite of mom tried to cover me up with a fraction of her complexion. But going back to that even, meanwhile in circumstances they were continued travelling, although, the train drive up and finally came towards the stop on one of the main train stations, which's 'Lido de Centro'. The instant that train stopped at the station, then this young Italian guy out of the blue has jumped up off his sit, and has began hurriedly moving at direction of exit. Those folks, who are sitting opposite from they too suddenly got up of their seats along with this blond lady, and start following this guy in the direction of an exit.

What happened afterwards those two were not aware off, cause they are have neither seen'the whole Picture', nor being at peace of a mind, even when the train begun moving away in full swing accelerating once again. After couple of stops they have finally arrived home. Only after that when they are both entered the threshold of our apartment my mom became nervous and was breathing frequently and heavily too. At home mom still could not get over the nervous breakdown, but it has not been far from over, as I couldn't imagine, cause it did not occur to me what is going on with her. Only in the evening, when they were watching TV, without prior notice the programme being interrupted by the urgent 'Italian News'. Readily available upon the screen they are started to hear, as also saw a footage about an incident on the local train and Lido de Centre station have appeared on the TV screen. From this announcement they are learned: that the Federal Police had captured 'the chain-series gang' of 'the drug possetions' and 'selling it' around the country, and even beyond. Amid those captured, which have come into view while being showing the footages on telly, for duration of that programme suddenly has appeared the young Italian guy, amid other strangers whom they were met on the train few hours ago. Alena and Egor din't mistaken, in fact, they both recognised him immediately:—He was visible on TV screen, except he has got surrounded by a large Police escort, in addition this Italian guy, in conjunction with it upon his wrists was wearing handcuffs. As the newsreader completed his speech and thus nasty pictures has vanished from the screen, only than I asked Leonid, what all these means that just saw. Apparently they are met that young Italian guy a short time ago, but Leonid looked with severity upon his face and then said:—Egor, you know something, son, your mother and you son—are very lucky, that have been able escape from this man. Please, promise me never get involved in any dirty business. Never, ever do rather shocking effects, and even try to take drugs, or other illegal stuff. I'm aware of, that at this moment you are only a little boy, still always remember don't act badly for your own sake and your mom's!

Will you promise me to be a good boy always? Yes, will you?-, I smiled with a bow, as am responded:- Yes grandpa! I'll be a good boy for all times, I shall listen to my mom and to you too. Yes, I promise!—Even though, the reporter from that television talked about this young Italian and informed all the views: so he was a criminal, and called him as a monster, they described him, or somewhat similar to it. There it also stated awful things about other members of the ring-groups. On the other hand, for mom and me, at least he wouldn't look like a monster. Apparently, they have not had a chance to see the dark side of his character. In the face of incident that had happened many years ago, but every time when Egor's reminiscence comes out; as he would look back, particular about that event. But it still does not click, as he could not interpret this young guy's behaviour, while holding that bloody syringe in he's hands?— With the aim of thus question, which always intrigued me all those years!

Despite this previous unpleasant incident that happened, at least the time had passed coherently, where they have resided in harmony with their neighbors and families of diverse origin and descents.

For the time being, Egor has continued attended School at the Monastery and even started to understand and speaking little in Italian. Some of these days one of those pupils have verbally abused Egor, and to he's misfortune got in a clash with one of them, given some of those individuals pupils are constantly bullying him then and there. It seems the fact, that after being tolerant from the verbally abuse I have become impatient, and seldom when those pupils would start, but wouldn't stop bullying him. Egor could not restrain himself by way of uncharacteristic behaviour. Triviality once he has got in troubles, but even started a fight with one of the pupil's in School, caused he couldn't help as to control he's anger. Then, he has got a warning from the school's Master of his undiscipline behaviour, just like that's being part of my punishment.

After that unpleasent accident with my fight with another pupil, as a result for my punishment I got dismissed for a short while from attending there. Egor eventually, had started attending School not as often as he used to be. After that horrible incident with this young Italian guy on the train, mom being not so eager travel very often with me, as before, as effect still was uneasy for her. Alena is sustained working at that time; but hasn't got time for Egor. Thus she's trusted that Leonid can take care of him. And so Leonid and I would catch a morning train by travelling regularly, and arriving at the Central Station from there they would change the route in turn by getting straight towards the heart of the city centre in Roma.

After a while I constantly being attending the Monastery school, while Leonid would pick me up from, or one in company of those Polish neighbor's were.

One of this day, my grandma, Esther arrived with our neighbor Marek to pick me up along with Janush from the Monastery School. When they would return home Egor has learned, that mom has not reappear from her second job. I felt a bit unexciting and changed from the school uniform, which depressed me—into my usual cloths. 'I have asked Esther Esther and she gave me her okay consent to play in the backyard with Janush, and since each of they have owned bicycles they are enjoyed riding around the building or elsewhere even within a distance far more away.

Once of the time came for both of them to go home eating dinner, my Esther has called up on me from the balcony and told me:—Egor, where are you? Dinner is ready. Come up back home. And too tell your friend that his dad was expecting Janush to get home!—When Janush heard his name called he asked me, whether he correctly understood what Esther told me, he was not mistaken, by having passed the massage to him, at least I began claiming the stairs and soon he followed me too. The flat, where Janush and his family lived and has placed on a level below from they, consequently it's being easier for him to lift and carry on his bicycle upstairs, quite the reverse it was for me. While I have eaten dinner over yonder in the neighboring apartment just behind the wall they heard the baby being crying. Close by behind wall has lived a family of four, and amid those are two little girls, one of them has being two-and-half years old and the other eldest girl, approximately my age, or maybe one year younger still my junior. The mother of those little children was the same age as mom, despite all odds she would leave for her two jobs in the morning and returning home only at night-time.

For that reason, those children being left in the care of their father. Esther has been an expert cooking traditional Русский или Украинский 'Борщ' и Блины, and she loved too making it. Few times on Sundays or other days those mentioned brood's mother, who name is Mavruzhata would smell their cooking; and would knock at the door and asking to give her a plate of this to consume. Since the Borodins were used to cook a full saucepan of that yummy 'Борщ' they would generously pour for her family a half of prepared cooking into Mavruzhata's saucepan, undoubtedly she couldn't cook these dishes herself, I suppose. Her husband and the father of her kids, Marek instead has obtained Doctoral Degree in Science at the Warsaw University in Poland, where he finished - was granted Post-Graduate in Classic Literature there. On the other hand, at that neighboring apartment over there yonder behind walls occupied by the Polish family something strange ought to be happening, since they are heard, that someone or else—had felt, while a little girl constantly being sobbing. At that same time the second girl began to cry, since both of their children have been making noise, over there something seems to be happening, for the reason that they are also heard a loud noise and fuss made coming from over there yonder via the wall inside our apartment. Abruptly over there yonder the front door closed with a loud clatter. A little while after, someone knocked in our front door. When Esther has opened the front door as both of us saw at the doorstep eldest of the girls from that neighboring unit. She looked very upset, her shoulders nervously shuddering, as her whole body anxiously is trembling, she than begun the cry. The second, as this Polish girl is appearing in front of doorway; as began speaking in Polish to Esther, still they have understood what she said:—

Бабцю, ходимо до нашего мешканя! Бо татку нема в дома. Моя сестра барзо плуаче. Бабцю, ходимо худшей! Юшто, допоможить моей сестре!—Esther saw desperation that she had in her eyes and asked her:—Где твоя матка? Завше не зателефонуешь до ней?—This girl visibly being frighten, but began sobbing again; and her stutters:—Мамцю нема також. Телефона нумэр невэм. Також невэм, колы мамцю пшийде. Барзо прошу, пани, швыдко идем до моего мэшкня!— Before Esther left to behind walls apartment, she's told me to stay home, and finish dinner, while she took the girl from neighboring apartment by her hand, and being stroking her hair, until this last calm down. The minute I completed my dinner I went to the neighboring apartment, and by entering in, I saw the previous girl and her sister, who has been younger than this last one, and seated on the sofa. While the older sister helped Esther to lift up a hefty luggage. On the spur of the moment Egor run towards them, next he has got involved with the needed help. Shortly after Esther tried lifting luggage up, as he recognised at once be their former luggage, which once had belonged to them: mixture of grey and light brown colors, that they have brought with the other stuff from Austria, thus, him being surprised to see it again herein. All the same, they are tried to pick up, but couldn't manage to shift luggage on the dinning table. In that case Esther has suggested a new alternative: to put it on the sofa over near, where this youngest girl has seated. Esther also is commanded me and the eldest girl to hold on with all the strengths to the suit-case, as soon as they are they are obtaining to lifted it up. Where beyond belief happened next follows that luggage has opened by itself, when they are looked over inside: where its contained well laid full with cash up to the top with those excisions of $US Dollars it. All banknote being tied up with covers and packed with bands around it. Being a naive child I have, neither ever saw these quite large amount of excisions, nor I ever came across accordingly dealing within such a great quantity of cash of $US origin in my life too, nor is I paying attention to danger, which has occurred here, either. And so in this situation, the main point for me was—helping the neighbors as well for this baby girl to stop crying, which apparently she's done, even before I arriving in their place. Esther looked unpleasantly surprised, hothey arever, she rushed and bend down, and closed it without delay upper part of a luggage, or front lead. By hook or by crook with the three of they remained, counting this youngster that has helped—together they are able too manage to lay down gear; then all pressed it down, as hard as they can, at last are sealed it. The minute they are finished with baggage Esther gave the eldest girl the keys from luggage that to keep it. She also warned the girls:—The minute your mother comes home, hand the keys over to her from valise, do you understand?—those two girls ducked heads in conformity.

Soon, after Egor Esther have left neighbors flat, while they're suddenly hearing sound, underway outside someone has been whistling. Anon has followed by an individual, who made fuss, then began climbing over our balcony. They are instantly recognized our neighbor Marek, whose being father of those girls from over there neighboring apartment. Despite the fact that, he emerged being drunk he looked bright and breezy to they, when he stepped upon the railing onto our territory balcony, but then boldly has walked on top of its surface. Since our living being located on third floor they are have been afraid, while assumed, that since he was under the influence of alcohol he has emerged uncontrolled to be unsteady, as a result he could slip over the rail and fall from such a height distance toward the ground. Bar to they are have mistaken about him, in contrast, he's being surprisingly adroit and quick within his moves, reminiscent of a gymnast, when swiftly he jumped down off that banister on our balcony he was fast there by landing near they and standing still. He then smiled and said:—Good Evening-. Marek was, asked for their consent first, next being passing through the room. Before he left, he shut the door behind with a thud. They have remained stunt, on or after his behavior, but didn't know what to make of all that.

Later that night, when Alena has retuned home from work Egor is excitingly given the lowdown of these previous incidents. Abruptly she became pale, and demand me with a serious tone of her voice:—Don't discuss anything, what happened today, and what you saw at neighboring apartment, not with anyone, above all to Janush!—Egor is stunned. even if I being inquisitive, when asked her why, but she reacted with in irritating voice, and her being fretful:—It's not of your business what's going on in someone's family mostly their affairs, or it's not of our concern either. Do you grasp? Do as I told you!—

The next day, Mavruzhata mother of those Polish girls from that neighboring place arrived with a visit to they, and has thanked for the help they are did. She has also expressed her delight, that they are did not discussed the incident with other folks, particular with those Poles. During talk with her, they both haven't mentioned about currency in luggage, that they are saw on previous night incident. Esther only said pleasant words about her eldest daughter, how brave and smart she really is. She grinned and looked content to hear that, and then unexpectedly had asked, whether Alena would like to come and work with her. It seems be a job that she predictable Alena agreeing, with the main duties to be a cleaner for an old Italian lady, who happen being rich and famous in Ostia suburb. This Italian lady has her home not far away from them my mom decided to accept that job. Though it hasn't been the greatest job in the world, mom basically be supposed to help this Italian lady cleaning up her flat twice a week. What's more, she payed mom hard cash in hand, every time when she would conclude with the task in the lady's flat. Alena also continued working in the 'Shoe shop' and has been able to afford buying me sometimes thus delicious Ice-cream to eat, that I was waiting so earnestly for a long time. They are not desperate any longer collecting thus unwanted supplies from the rubbishes plus from organised heaps of stuff, where they are would usually collect free fruits or vegetables, and other things from the market, but at this time not as often as before, perhaps on some occasions. Over time Borodins have become more secure financially, while are able buying meat every second day, as they would travel to Rome, not only for their scheduled interviews to the centre for migrants, but mostly have fun there as well. Since the Borodin's return to Ostia apartment house, and they would travel to special places where market be located right at the hearts of the centre in Rome. Being conveniently near they are detect a wonderful creations of diverse cloths, such as: leather made jackets and coats, different foof, which Italy is always was famous with their brand, plus many other objects and stuff. Leonid and I would travel to the Market, then one day before he has earned cash, Leonid decided to buy three different sizes men's suits. He explained to me that those three wonderfully created suits they are shall be given as a present to his nephew and one to his nephew's son, when they are going to travel in Australia. He has told me that we will be coming back next time, and buy incredible nice and modern cloths for me, plus for my mom to boot. Then Leonid opens to me a secret that in few days he is to be travelling, as far as to the City of Venice, with his Boss that has owend a boat and has invited him. Thus, he also asked me, whether I would like to travel along with him, because he shall be glad to take me over there. Egor began asking him question about Venice, in a location of the city, as well as if the city of Venice is a part of Italy or it's afar overseas, and many others. Leonid patted my head smiled, by which his look like golden, in fact these had been made from brass—teethes became visible, when he said:—Of course, Venice is a part of Italy, and when they're willing to get there you shall see for yourself, how wonderful and unusual this city really is, according to my knowledge of. Because the whole city of Venice is located on the water. Even so, the main convey there are vessels and gondolas. When they are arriving over there you'll be very surprised to see an old city located and build fully on water, in accordance with the conditions, thus standing, and mainly surrounded by water. Do you want travel with me towards Venice, Egor?—when Egor heard those news he became thrilled and probing him:—Oh, grandpa I would love to travel with you, but what about mom, do you think she will be giving me permission to travel with you? I want to go and see that city of Venice. But Leonid will you take me to ride on gondolas? What that means gondolas? And how they are travelling—in the city of Venice? By plane or on the train? Yes? Tell me all about how?—Leonid is patted again boy's head and within seriousness voice, than said to:— Egor, we're going to travel on a vessel the only problem is, that your mother may not be happy to let you go with me on the trip? She probably would be worried sick about you, I'm afraid that her answer will be negative. In any case, don't get upset, if your mom isn't aimed at giving you go-ahead to travel with me.—But they have made a deal, as on coming home both is going to convince Alena giving permission for Egor. Leonid has taken breathes, him then sustained have a chinwag:—Gondolas, resemble to a boat as it has advanced, and from what I heard the men were paddling with a large oar. I haven't got a chance seen it for myself, that's why I can't wait until travel there and you and I will see for ourself, whether it is true ot not?—The moment they came back home, the first thing what I did and I saw to mom tried to convince her let me travel with Leonid. While, he knew that I deceit mom about to travel on a boat has been bad, Alena and Esther absolutely not, but this duo lied to them, who are cautiously agreeing. After a long and 'hard battle', Alena eventually is given up, and has allowed Egor travelling with Leonid to Venice . . .

CHAPTER 35

A few days have past swift, while Egor uneasily be waited when Leonid would ask him to pack my stuff up and leave. Conversely, Leonid advised me to take only few needed things, but has also reminded me to bring along: toothbrush and a toothpaste, blanket, a hat, a jumper and a jacket, add to rubber boots. After Egor and Leonid finally board the vessel, there they've found a range of sleeping bags, plus pro every person from that crew has got stuff to be able maintain it, in case of the emergency—for the rescue purposes these basic things such as life jacket. Personally I has given a life buoy, in that case me being a child it was crucial to get that lifebelt with other requisite equipments for like this cruise at the open sea. It was very exciting add to it has been a new experience for me too. So I'm looking forward to that endeavour, while that voyage going to take me away in Venice. When their craft has cast off from the Bay our endeavour just began. In spite of all my imaginings of that endeavour via the sea its come out in contrast to me. Conversely, after a while I started to feel sick. I couldn't stay still cause, my whole body tempested from one side to another. Being a little boy, but seen with a slim build constitution, but I couldn't walk still, without being unbalanced, while walking upon the deck of this vessel. And yet, I have become scared and desperately wish for to see my 'mother'. Although, there has not been a storm at the Adriatic Sea, but needless to utter that also it's being my first experience on a real Vessel, not like used to read me those favourite fairytales, which I would imagine to be in a different way. In that way, I've been on the real voyage within 'the open sea', as I become anxious and scared, thus I've demanded Leonid to take me back to my mommy. In contrast, Leonid hasn't been pleased, and in serious tone of his voice he responded:—They're already hading toward the open Sea and enter it, and nobody would be able to do that for you, no-one is turning back to the shore!",—he plainly has explained to me. When Leonid has let me know I was nearly on a bridge of crying and collapse:—I want to vomit and I feel sick, my head is spinning round!—While Leonid gave the impression that he hasn't been paying attention towards boy's complaints, but he has said the same:—I worship the sea, and so equally do that crew amid sailors from this vessel. Those folks from the crew being called 'sea wolfs', as they ought to be able experts heading for the Endeavour for many years, and also have got acquainted with habitual sea caprices. But Egor has not been in humour to ask him questions what it's all these big and new words that he said actually meant. But I cared about my own they welfare. Although, he asked me, whether I feel that very bad, and will not hold on, until they are being supposed to arrive in Venice. Thus I ansthey arered him, anxiously:—Yes, I feel so very sick, please, grandpa help me!—He became really becomes worried about me, then they arent out and up on deck. Within a short while after a young Italian chap in his middle thirties appeared in front of them, had and offered me a tablet. I was confused, though, and didn't understand what is going on. But I already spoken Italian slightly better, than it's being expected for these time, since they are lived in Italy for a little while, I have got a bit more relaxed than and being able to estimate the situation. Italian skipper explained to me, that this particular tablets is for individuals, who have being in the sea for the first time, or for someone, who have got genuinely difficulties experiencing sea-sickness. This young sailer then shorly to Leonid the tablets, which offered him, but since Leonid did not speak Italian, consequently it was up to me translating for Leonid, about the tablets. On the other hand this sailor chap had re-assured they, that it could help me with the sea-sickness, as well as nausea, together with one-time issues. Leonid came back with a respond is nodding, which I identified meant of: that he gave me his consent to take tablet from a stranger with cold water. Shortly be seen that Egor really started to feel well again. By leaving behind a long crossing, in a short while they are at length arrived in the city of Venice while that vessel has been paddling towards it's bay. Its appeared being true what Leonid told me all before about Venice. Venice is located on water. Then Leonid shows me what gondolas look like. Occasion some of local Italians, who have operated and run these gondolas being coping with single huge oars on the boat with its extend nose plank, whilst they being paddling with a single oar. That oar has been big in size and a long one in length than usual ones. Besides those men, who usually managed the boats, while paddling with it's large oars along the water within the 'Gondolas' to be flouting one after another in a row, it's like standing in a queue on the ground. Whilst on the opposite side, if some amongst those gondolas might being homecoming back with passengers on board, they would paddle towards each-other where at the meeting place in the middle of the Canal from both sides of the opposite those sailors managed those gondolas, without any problem. On top those skippers would take off their hats, which emerged having long and distance across mainly dark color, with a slow bow, like part of their 'greeting ceremonial, for some kind of mutual respect intended for those, who are at Sea. While flowing towards each other and then apart apiece from, those men on gondolas would carry on paddling away along the Canal slowly, without stops. Possibly its because they have worked on boats for many years become true professionals in that field, which is Mediterranean sea. Once I approached that special station, where there usually sold the tickets, as tried ask over for cost for the single excursion on one of the gondolas. Next I clued-up Leonid about the value, he did not look in high spirits, instead enlightened me, that he didn't realised it's would be so expensive, cause he evidently hasn't got enough money for that kind of enjoyment. To our prospect those Italian who arrived with they have glad taken my Leonid and me in company with them at first on the crew, and yet on the gondola. Although there emerged a fifth members of that crew amongst they, apart from him that managed by hook or by crook to find room for everyone too fit in, are counting those. They have being flowing on the gondola along the Canal, whereas came to passing under the bridge, which remind it of a Arcade. They've kept floating along that water Canal, that being crossing with the main streets, on the both sides of the Canal they saw either old constructed buildings, or some of the main streets would appear there, as they arell as the city Square. The city Square in my indulgent called Saint Marks, where the whole area within the city being covered of dark color stones with an addition tint of marshy nuances among it. Perhaps all that must be my imagination, but I glimpsed those stones have emerged wet at the time, when the picture appeared in my eyes. There they are also saw many pigeons and doves mostly walking funny along the Square centre, with Seagulls flying above then landing on the surface ground or benches, or on foot wondering by the side of a pierce and seeking for food around the area. One amongst Italian men, who has seated in the same gondola with those. Out of the blue become excited as soon as a very tall building appeared in front to our right. I couldn't comprehend what is going on why those people made such a fuss becoming excited, but one amon those sailors explained to me, that 'Grande' and graceful wide construction, which appeared in front of they, have emerged the most famous Opera house not only in Italy, but in the World. That grande edifice, which they saw appears being a theatre, called 'La Venice Opera', where the most prestige's Singers from over the country and beyond, and also all over the Continent arriving here, particular to perform on its stage in this Opera House. Naturally, I being unaware on that Opera be supposed to at the time, but once that sailor mentioned singing I have a handle on, as a result asked Leonid to take me there. Apparently being a naïve kid, it didn't occur to him that, it has nothing to do with singing in a pre-school, in compare to with those professional Opera singers, who would perform on such as this prestige stage, as 'La Venice Opera' ought to be in the World of contemporary music. Having enjoyed the time of my life over there, but the only thing, by which Egor has felt unhappy, was that I only missed he's mom for not being there with. During our stay in Venice Leonid also helped those sailors with some ordinary assistance with an tasks that he's being given to perform, as a part of the jobs. But I on the other hand, under the supervision of those Italian skippers, whose brought they here, and also other gentlemen have either taking me with other kids to play with who either they're own brood, or close relatives for them, while they would disclose to me story, how magnificent and special this city of Venice for all the Italian's really is and what it means, or start re-telling me various of ballads about how this ancient city actually had been built . . .

In due course, by means of gaining a respect amid those local kids flattering me by becoming friends with those, who develop into many of the Italian skippers nephews or so, who have related with them sailors from the crew of the vessel, who have arrived along with those. Egor has enjoying every minute, that I spend time in the city of Venice. There it has not been boring for me, on the contrary, because continually I ought to be engaged in some kind of activities with my new local friends. Those local boys from Venice would take me with them to the city's Square of 'Saint Marks', or toward water Canal, from where all of them managed to get as far, as the main bridge, where being enjoying the view from straight down, and then deep into the water. After the gondolas ought to passing beyond they are would waive towards strangers passing by. My new friends and I would also run in the region of old city or centre with other places too, where I have witnessed largely major parts of the metropolis, by way of it's magnificent view and beyond, like its situated, while seal on my dispense. Some of the new places ought to appear every time, while they are resembling thus sites in the city, or experiencing by the view from beyond the roof: to the ancient architectural builds, antique statues and tombstones. Those have also done many other things together, as children invent new games where they get are play that, and so on. They are had have also the pleasure eating every day traditional Italian food: lasagne, spaghetti, pizzas, which the local Italians usually baked in an old style kiln, like food preparation process has being done in Italy for over centuries, in combination with other fabulous food for lunch, dinner and even supper. One of those Italian skippers even gave they to try the taste of their time-honoured traditional Italian wine, I was not quite sure, whether it's a good idea for me to follow their examples. And yet, when I saw other kids practically my age, who made toast next have drunk it, as becomes visible to be in a happy festive mood. Cause for them it's being just like normal and usual part of their routine rituals, then I have become more confused. When a few of those kids explained to me that wine is a part of their life and traditions, they have also advises me that it's nothing wrong to sip a tiny bit of thus great liqueur. Apparently it's being made from the high-yield grapes, which the Italian's ought to growing and cultivating that fruit. As soon as the right time arrives: those locals harvested thus grapes for all and sundry being able enjoying that taste of such deliciously-fabulous fruit, not only to eat, but also producing great Wine with their Italian trade-mark upon it. As I looked inside my glass, which contained less than half of quantity filled with their wine, which they are telling so much about it, eventual I have decided to sip a few drops from it after all, as a mutual respect towards their hard job. I just love it these traditional Italian dishes: spaghetti with principally prepared tomato sauce, purposely their happy Italian festive mood, which ought being contagious, though, but within a nice way, naturally. Still they are supposed to stay in Venice at least three nights, which they were informed prior to arriving there. Despite the fact that, they are spend only two nights there, but already one among the crew command from the vessel by informing they that they are have to get ready returning on the vessel to cast off, because they are heading back for Roma, to being more precise towards Ostia. So, to my misfortune, came the end of the third day of our voyage in Venice. They are having been clued-up to get on time upon the vessel and getting ready for our trip back to the Adriatic Sea, given a green light that meant they are supposed to be sailing off very late at the same evening. A short while later, Leonid has made the bunk bed for me in vessel's cabin, while signifying, that I should rather go to sleep, otherwise I might feel sea-sickness again. But I was in high spirit, as a result alone listen to him. A boy has felt asleep promptly soon after, the whole thing: with all the excitements and endeavours in Venice leaving behind . . . Although I've woke up in my bed where home being, I do not have off pat how I got back there in the first place. In the morning, it appeared, that I ought to be transfer back in time, it's being obscure—I imagined things, since by hook or crook, I already sleeping in my bed, at the Ostia's apartment. It's like I have never left our place, not got to navigate at different place. I was vastly happy to see my mom again and could not stop telling her the stories about Venice with their Italian traditional food, and many more stories about my adventures in an intriguing City of Venice.

CHAPTER 36

Once upon time, when they are come there at the org for refugees and migrants for the usual appointments. There they are had been informed by the chief in charge, that very soon many of the new Russian migrants, who arrived from Austria a short time ago, ought to be settled within suburb in Ostia.

In the last part of thus discussion it came as a real surprise for the family. Conversely, they are have not been so sure what to expect from all of the information, that they are received. After carefully absorbing the situation, they're given a good thought, whether it was intend for their the best interest?—In a short while eventually, towards the park, where my mom worked at the open Café just, just at a main entrance, they are first noticed, but next even hearing to facilitate it is taking place the beginning of a big construction side within the complex of the park. There, soon have begun arriving Engineers and other builders. Even as they brought with them special massive and heavy machines: tractors and elevated cranes, obviously convey these all the way through that park to for the constructions. They're also noticed trucks, who would travel backs and fort and ought to be caring plenty of built wooden small huts, which looked like boarding houses, as the whole site remind it more of a village in a tropical country. That coating of surface amid these undersized wooden huts have emerged dark brown with a nuance of redness on the surface, which be made from mahogany trees. Follows half-dozen days passed since construction begun, where is already build small houses have invented deep in the depth of this park that be reminiscent more of a forest by its grove.

In so sustained doing, shortly one morning they are started to hear noises, which have come from the train station; as they are become nosy; and decided taking a walk towards the place see to, what the noise and made fuss is about, what is going on over there, but being unaware set with their construction. Our town was a quiet and a slow living place. As a result, the noise and loud voices that be heard would come from these people, who they were arriving via the train station or else. Apparently the public, who made fuss upon their arrivals, which ought too become a disturbances amid those locals within Ostia, and encircle area. They're kept standing still, and watching careful; those Russians having settled in these wooden small huts. Among them being heard unhappy remarks and many are crying:—For hard journey, which they're having to accomplish. Not to mention, while they are all got through so much of ordeal already, and being travelling for a while to be able to come as far as Italy. Upon arrival they are must stay here, and now living like those people from the past, who had being forced to stay in "concentration camps".

At last Alena and Egor decided to go for a visit to the new Russian migrants where onto the park's grove being positioned miniature wooden huts. As for Egor who always being happy to get a chance talking in he's mother-tongue, as seeking other individuals which they couldn't imagined to see again, and turn out be our acquaintances. Because the only people that I'm being able having a word in Russian with those families, and amid for others, counting our neighbors: from Poland, Serbia and Bulgaria, who have not spoken clearly enough most of the time, I was guessing what they said, have and what precise it's all meant. Whilst, they are walking for at least ten minutes, next at last they have found 'that complex of a Russian Camp'. Upon their arrivals on the road to the entrance its appeared the area guarded surround it all through the complex, within a protected shield of metal fences round, which seemingly it was made as of aluminium material. Though, the whole thing around looked peculiar, but at same time, they began conversing straight with those Russians, by which rumour has it that were strangers, and they've spoke in our mother-tongue which the Borodins are also found wonderful. Those Russians, whom we only just met for the first time become very taken aback to hear that they are live in Ostia for quite some time, and to be estimated, less than six months. The Borodin's have shared the same common values that are hearing, they've got the news and in turn, programmed from their ex—homeland, while they also learned about immigration law, interacting between each other public or sources. Upon our next arrival in 'Russian camp' they are talking nineteen to the dozen about with some of the migrants who were our friends, and would start remembering those days of the past, back in the USSR.

For time being they would being often guests at 'the Russian camp'. I would go in the park nearly every second day just to speak with these migrants either with mom, or Leonid, even with Esther. They always were happy to see, when their family have to come greeting with contended manners there. Many of people being strangers to they, despite they spoken Russian lingo as they are have, and for that reason for they it's being as a test to get acquainted with them for the first time, but some of those families, who are already knew, because met them in Vienna. While those would greet they with warmth and openness, and in attendance these two families, who arrived from Kiev as if it felt like the Borodins went back in time home, one way or another those migrants were our fellow-country men and women, as a result they've got close with them in the camp, than towards others, who tried to help them, as much as they are could, because saw in what situation they stayed there in that camp. After hearing unpleasant stories Esther and Leonid just being able to declare only:—They've got through so much before, and are honestly earned the rights for being able to settle in this apartment. You have to know, that they are Russians, while being staying in Italy without proper documents, which might prove only, that you and all of them is, more than ever would be vulnerable to become subject for being exposed to the public. As to bring up, that you or those, who have arrived in a similar setting but got problems, and would be put in a black list as trouble makers too. Also, don't forget they're all waiting for permission travel to the country of their destination, but with such behaviour it'll look of a negative impact on any among them. I too want point out that can cost you your application, under which you're seeking positive results?—She continual and has said, that those international residents didn't become an obstacle for our family to be settling amid them. Its be explained to them what they have to get through, in order to gain a place. People by their nature usually are jealous and sometimes can't see truth beyond themselves, cause of egoism, like a blind folder has covered their eyes. Rumour has it that they chose not to believe they, what they are have been re-telling them, and they even thought, that they are almost certainly had payed a great ransom of money, to get possession of that living of ours. Even if, they are smiled, except for Esther that has felt hurt by their claims, to which she is responded civilly; but not without a hint and straight forward onto their faces:-You most likely measure people from your personal point of view, cause not everyone is the same. Ever since they are tried to survive, even though they are came from a provincial town, and have never saw those luxuries, and probably never will. On the other hand, people should always remain human, and behaving like human-being. And if God helped us in the time of need, they are should always remember too help others, if they should also help themselves !—This philosophical debate have intend of making those folks too become conscious, equally—its has not make sense for them, or unlikely some among them being predisposed to value, or to accept realism and kindness of the human heart. Alternatively, it has not our purpose to teach anyone, but they are simply tried act in response as human-being and possess dignity among them, who have not agree with they it's to be their personal business. As for they: one and all tried to survive as best, as they could of their abilities, or perhaps become conscious how to achieve it. 'This's our philosophy of life'—interpretation.

A short while after on the our conversations at the association some among the Russian migrants began to settle within the Hostel near where they are lived.

One family even occupied our ex—attic-room. When next the Borodins have a chat with this Russian family, who moved in attics not long ago.

Once they're having commenced with complain of apartment in comparison with their attic's, but they are made them to realize, that it has not being felt cold inside, like it was, when they are first arrival there, during the euphoria of cold winter time . . . Outside the climate by now has emerged being changing in front of our eyes, since that beautiful time of summer just arrived in Italy to everyone's delight, counting our family, as well. Besides there made present themselves previous Russian migrants, who also being waiting migrate to Canada, and likewise they not have search out in the least for earnings as bonus, and accordingly they have looked for jobs. Even if, Leonid offered to help some of them to find a job, but the Russian males have emerged gloomy with he's suggestion by rejecting his offer. They're met some of thus unlike characters, who ought to gave the impression of being of amusement towards their odd behaviour, and having tried to prove of all their intrinsic worth. One of the Russian women au fait with they hers be on familiar terms, which ensue with their family migrating to the USA. Given that in reality about a month time she had left Hostel, earlier than her family have travelled abroad.

They're clearly comprehend it, that in the future that may never come across to meet those people afterwards again, and Borodins tried to be friendly with them for the time being, as long as it's possible at these situation. Those residents from the Polish origin and other people likewise from these same communities, on the other hand have not been happy with so many Russians moving in these same buildings, or should I say to be more particular within Jewish ancestors, ought to be settling close nearby with them. Already used for their language now they called them—'жиды', while every day mood among the Poles grown more intensified with some thought of hatred towards those Russian-speaking migrants. Those Russian migrants of Jewish descent have not quite been excited. But tried to get alone with those Polish migrants either, and if there are supposed to arise of any conflicts involving those two diverse party, our family was always in the centre of thus conflict, and became like some thought of mediators between those community groups. The family, who occupied the attic-room turn out to are Russian speaking. In next to no time they become good neighbors with them after all. There also appeared other type of Russian wander with whom they are getting acquainted. And soon became friends. As with some who are tried finding the middle ground, given to consideration, as those still have behaved disagreeably with anyone. One Russian girl who was about eighteen years old has told they, that was she waiting to migrate to the USA, while want to become an hairdresser. She continued to speak up and has enlightened them, that she already started a training course in order to become a professional hairdresser, even prior to her leaving the USSR. Next she concentrates on me, if I want to become her client for a new haircut style. When I gave her my consent, a girl without delay is started cutting my hair. In a while, after I glimpse in the mirror, but I've become disappointed with my new hairstyle. While it appears that the girl has spoiled natural form of my mane that is resting on my head. With providence for my mother came to the rescue. In an unlikable instance, Alena is made adjustments so as to do fresh hair cut on top of the existed one, by which somehow she has corrected my new hair style, as much as she could, by that the girl has disfigured and herewith been visible it wasn't that bad, after all. As for Leonid in contrast, he didn't need a haircut, as his mane roots have surfaced virtually bold, like this he has nothing to loose, compare to me. In any cases this girl need practicing on some.

Beach Lido Di Castel Fusano

CHAPTER 37

Time has past. Borodin's have found out that an old lady from the Russian cam died, as she has endured dehydration, as an effect of having a heart attack. She was waiting to immigrate to USA with her daughter, Son-in-law and grand-daughter, but she passed away, cause the Emergency had not arrived on time to do the recitation and to save her. In the midst of the Russian-speaking, whose stayed at the same camp, alongside others, who have arrived from other suburbs to the park in the wooden huts camp felt for this family, and women, who have happened are not so very old in her early sixty years of age. All the same they are gave our respect to the remain members of the family of that deceade woman, by wishing them a safe trip to USA. Shortly after the funeral I become worried about my own Esther, thus Egor would hurry up, is running firstly upstairs to check up on her. As the boy was only five-and-half going on his sixth birthday, given that began identifying, who they were in similar circumstances that we all must take care for each other, as Leonid and Alena likewise are kept busy—working. Rumour has it that, to a certain extent almost similar happened in my family. One afternoon coming back from school me didn't go straight home, instead I have decided to stay at the backyard and playing with other kids. At last a touch of a logic sense has prevented me to carry on playing outside, source deep within my guts, or I should say sixth sense myself felt that up there in my apartment rather hasn't been right. For that reason, I enlightened Janush, whose being playing with me at backyard, directly went upstairs. Upon my return back to our apartment, I began knocking at our door, but none-one seems to be in a hurry to open it. Then I became worried and relentlessly have knocked amid my whole strength that I possible have on this door add too being screaming at the top of my lungs. Be aware that she should be home, but she hasn't open the door, which I found odd; me being again and again knocking, while sobbing at the same time. After a while I run down stairs and knocked to the apartment, where Janush resided with his family. Vladek has opened the door, by seen me sobbing and looking distressed, he then asked me:—Egor, what's wrong with you? Have you been crying? Tell me, did anyone hurt you, what's with you, boy?—I put in the picture for him the whole thing, that has arisen he without loosing a minute run together with me upstairs, only at length behind has followed by two of us Janush. Vladek then knocked at the door towards our backdoor neighbors then has disappeared in their apartment. Still I was unaware, what exactly he had done over there yonder unit, but later listening to this story that he was re-telling to my mother:—. . . the whole truth, what has really arisen in our apartment, I overheard them? Whilst our next door neighbors gave Vladek to go-ahead with, then him being climbing over the balcony, which has separated they from them, and visibly led towards our territory. He then quickly walks inside the lounge room in the interior of our apartment. But he couldn't find at first Esther there, he then stll looking for her, as dare enter my grandparent bedroom only over there yonder he has spotted Esther sleeping on a bed. Without losing a minute Vladek began talking to her, but she wouldn't respond to him. He next become scared fearing the worst, when has decided to shake her. After few attempts he's being able waking Esther up, but was so very deep into that eccentric sleep, according to her story: she seem has found herself being in the midst of two worlds and ready pass away. Besides she has been surprised that Vladek woke her up, and asked him to let her continued exist, cause she could not bear anymore thus horrific pains, which she experienced for the most part of the time: every day, every hour, or else. Apparently she then re-collected herself, and with the help of Vladek Esther got up off the bed, and has thanked him, she then immediately has opened the door and to let me in. After thus adverse accident with the deceased Russian lady, and challenging, that being prevented by our neighbor Vladek, they return got back to usual live, and few times have got visitors, Practically every day, they would either to play some of the old games, or would invent new ones in backyard or just playing jokes. They are also have have found long exchange of ideas about unlike issues, which is contrived to organizing dances in the evening like that times discos, which being popular in the late 1980's in the area of our hostel, or would walk in the park towards the 'Russian Camp'.

Meanwhile, here has got appointed a new manager of the hostel, who happens being a Vietnam migrant. It seems that they are have got quickly acquainted with him picky, hearing as he understood modest in Russian and Polish that it's being a relief for them.

Once again, they became in the luck, in view of the fact that soon they are able to gain a real car. It's turn out being a bolt from the blue for the family. One among our Polish neighbors, whose also being waiting with his family at their org for their procedure to process of the visa, in order to be able migrate to Canada. The man suggested to Leonid travelling along with him also offered his car that he also gain it. His name turn out being Piotr, which wasn't unusual for people from Eastern Europe to get names, while their first names, also should be likewise within it's similarity too all Slavic. Piotr offered them driving in the direction of 'the Fiat' Factory. After those three of they, counting Egor have arrived there unproductive locale an empty ground area, except for that site of an landscape, which owned by car manufacturing 'Fiat' firm that occupied a huge zone of space within the field. They are also found a few cars standing there unaided. That place has emerged being mostly for Italians those local or other folks, who willing to get rid of them very old brand, or just unwanted cars. They would leave their old vehicles alongside useless cars there within car-keys to be inserted into its ignition. And anyone, who ought to be interested to gaining those old sort of cars, who being able to come freely towards this place and choose among it. Leonid and Egor actually befall are stunt to find out, that something like that is possible for people, without getting in troubles with the Italian Law. Since living in USSR they were never even imagined that something like that could ever be achievable anywhere, especially in Italy, and they couldn't be wishing for anything better, and having a free gift to be able possessing a car. After thoroughly observing more or less Leonid pointed towards one of the cars and asked the Polish fellow, had brought them here, whose name and come to pass being Piotr. Apparently, Piotr became curios, for that reason being asking Leonid:—This car? The one which you see in front of that hillock, the violet color car to your left?—He then come within reach of the car, which Leonid has pointed towards, but after thoroughly probing it in the interior; then he has turned back towards them saying:—This car's engine looks not that bad, and I could possible fix it for you, if you want it. In a couple of days you shall be able to drive on. Leonid, you can drive, can't you not?—Leonid grins and replies him:-Yes, I can. But, I used to drive a trucks and also these cars which it has had the electric motors. I worked for many years on the factory in the USSR on the electric carriage. And I have been driven within the manual instructions. But I am sure I will be able to drive this car too.—Piotr looks with an interest and next asked again:—But do you hold a current driver's licence? Have you brought with you document from the USSR here, which can prove that you eligible to be a driver, and your photo ID onto it?—Leonid's face all of a sudden became serious and in an strong voice he said:—Unfortunately, I don't have here with me current licence, on the other hand, I still have some of my documents written in Russian, which can help me to prove, that I used to drive and there is also a current photo of me inside of it. I'm not quite sure, whether this document is going to be illegitimate to prove my rights to drive here in Italy, thus I need to inquire about this issue. But if you can possible fix this small car temporarily for us, and if you need any spare parts in order to changing, or help with repairs, or no matter which, let me know. And I would try to find these through this old Italian Soldier. Please, do this job for us, sorry to say, but they won't be able to pay you too much for the repairs. Once again, please, fix the car if can do it for our needs. And thank you in advance.—Piotr is bounced, and came back with a respond:- Yes, old man, they can make a deal. Then your car will be ready very soon. First: I am personally going to check this car, and then will testing it for a drive. Aso, old man you need to come along, and helping me to fix the car for you, cause I would be needed an assistant for this matter. Tomorrow morning 7.30 a.m. sharp wait for me downstairs, and we are both will drive here back. The earlier they are going to start fixing, the sooner we'll start to finish the job, the better it's going to be. If not, someone else will take the car away, and fix it instead. okay?—Leonid grins, has shown his teethes, and he nodded, as if some thought of consent between those two. Then Piotr is pitiless:—It's all settled then old man. Let's go home than, gus, and we'll talk about it tomorrow of some details.—Except for Leonid, whose providence of inevitable Egor going as he has taken out the car-keys from the ignition of this chosen an amethyst color car and put in his pocket. Only then they went in Piotr's car, and the last one had drove back to the hostel-apartments. So it's really happened for them, the Polish bloke has fix that undersized car after all, which ought to be of the old brand car's 'Fiat', and it's even has its trade-mark upon the surface shell from that company. Though, that car was not in the perfect proviso, but they're having come to achieve at least one dream to own a car, and by the way as the Italian would usually say "poco-poco", which means slowly-slowly come about to enjoy. So, now in Italy at least the family have a car in their possession, but they could not believe it, that it's happened in their favour for real. After all thus troubles along with hard working in the order of, fixing the car if its being not for Piotr they would have enjoyed that drive in all places, and above all around suburb of Ostia even farther than.

Given that Leonid has brought me a bicycle, I would also enjoy riding it on, while me being circling around. Many of those Russian kids tried to get hold of my bike. since being careful of my goods, since my childhood, and I wasn't that ego to lend anyone my bicycle. Thereby, one day Russian boys' got in a fighting with one of the Polish guys over Janush's bicycle, who is going to ride first on it. But something got wrong and the Russian boy broke his bicycle. Apparently Egor was just coming downstairs and saw a fight amongst them them, and suddenly one among the Russian boys has cry it out:—Это Егор поломал велосипед!—Janush looked towards me and said rather rude, then without warning jumped over yonder onto my side, and want to start a fight with me. Being confused and upset all the same of the interrogations, without prove my respond being:—Это не я. Януш, Я не ломал твоего велосипеда. У меня есть свой. Я всегда прошу позволения. Но мне нет необходимости. Я катаюсь на своём велосипед!-Egor bunged for a second, taken a deep breath, as my next respond in Polish:—А ты, Януш, ты ешьть не добрый! Ты, ешьть гупи!—Using these words Egor has left the ground, as been seen tears in his eyes.

CHAPTER 38

The time was passing quick, and they are still being visiting those Russians that were placed in a complex of the camp, located at the park. By-and-by, in Italy have already arrived the mid-summer time, and for the most wonderful month of June, within a great and a warm weather outside. Besides it's being a very important time particular for me, cause soon draw close to my birthday.

Vis-à-vis my sixth birthday decided to organize a birthday party, while she has invite, as many guests, as she possible could. Among those guests, have arrived individuals as from Russian camp and our neighbors from hostel, who too were invited since they being acquaintances of ours: that diverse community among others. Earlier on this day Esther and other people helped to cook traditional Russian food, which be placed in the midst of yard on a big settled tables, amid other dishes, which being served for guests, which have enclosed: by Italian lasagne, in the course of other yummy stuff to boot.

Apart from that food and soft drinks my mom had asked to help her baking a huge 'napoleon cake', which most of the residents only heard off and possibly to eat, but never actually themselves made it more.

Once Alena brought up this large size cake, and placed on the table encrust to being on a special plate, everyone grow to be so enthusiastic getting a slice of those delicious and wonderful pieces of cake. She also brought to the table French profiteroles, which being prepared with excellent technics and have thus great shapes within custard cream inside for all the guests enjoining eating it too. Even the Italian woman who worked there as a cleaner, Francesca, that has been a drug addict, couldn't resist to try that deliciously created dessert. Francesca being surprised, to find out that mainly of the cooking have being done by Alena, she was also baked it these delicious desserts and made a request to try the top of these layers. Exclude me be vastly happy, seeing as I haven't got so much fun for a very long time. With the party long-standing and Egor received great present from all of those guests, including: the Russian's, the family from Uzbekistan, who gave me for present a special 'Russian bingo' covered in a velvet bag, and from the different nationality, who have offered and in the royal etiquette handed me nice presents. They have so much fun there, and later that evening is organized dancing, not without the permission from a new hostel manager of Vietnamese origin. There're all enjoyed every minute of it; and have also invited him to celebrate with them. But the Vietnamese manager couldn't stay very long, on the other hand, he wouldn't mind to try a delicious piece of napoleon cake. every guests want to get a piece of that delicious napoleon cake. Among other guest he spotted an Italian fellow, who's in fact arrived uninvited at the party, but has brought me a great present for Birthday, with Italian Champagne.

Later that night those guests, who are present at my party, and the strangers, who have arrived uninvited too decided to organising a 'disco', when dusk started to appear, as the sky just only became purple instead of the Sun, that disappeared from above the moon was slowly flowing in along the clear sky. In the late 1980's all those are dancing under accompaniments of 'Disco' music, which was really popular during the late 1980s as even these uninvited guests they have enjoyed dancing under the tunes. And also since it was my Birthday to my delight I had been given consent staying a bit longer, then usual. Egor's birthday was coming to an end. Alena has left Egor, since I commanded her to make my bed, while I was on my way to place be in the care of my grandpa Leonid and grandma Esther, as they have continued staying in frontyard.

View a full moon-light is flashing straight through window, then is enclosed by what seem a cobweb to be glance beyond the clouds. Meantime being in apartment, Alena unexpectedly hears a knock on the door. When Alena opens the door to her surprise at doorway emerged the hostel-apartments manager of Vietnamese origin. Although he begins to speak by addressing her with a poor Russian pronunciation, but sarcasm tic tone while looking her in the eyes:—Ви мне давно не плятили за рэнд, если у вас нет дэнег, то ми можем что-то придумать. Вы не забыли, что должны были мне оплатить 3 дня тому назад? И что ви будете делять сейчас?—As she answers to the Vietnamese man that is walking into the room uninvited, as Alena began to speaks to the man, she looked worried, but worriedly her being listening:—Нет, я незабыла. Но если, вы мне дадите время до Завтрашнего дня, я постараюсь что-нибудь придумать. И оплатить вам недостающую сумму денег, что мы вам задолжали. Добро? Вы довольны моим ответом?—Next this Vietnamese man started slowly be in motion moves closer towards, at the same time grinned, as he's discussing with sarcasm, also leaning forward, but down, even though he wasn't very tall, within his height. He then stares onto her eyes and said:—Нэт, я нэ доволиен, или ви плятите мне severodnя, или я потребую вас висилить отсюуда, сегодня же. А типьерь тебе, понятно?— With his last words Alena on the go looking worried, as her face has developed into pale, while she being listening more anxiously and then has responded:-Я не понимаю, чего вы добиваетесь, я же вам по-обещала, что завтра я постараюсь достать деньги и оплачу недостающую сумму. Вам что не понятно, откуда у меня сейчас появляться деньги, тем более что уже скоро ночь на дворе? Пожалуйста, дайте мне время до завтра, и я вам верну?—But the Vietnamese man, instead has approached her, where she being standing, he bend a bit down, while he continued speaking by means of sarcasm, still is looking her in the eyes, as he said:—Ниет, мнэ нужны дэньги сегодня, но если ты нэ можэш отдать деньги севодня, я прэдлагаю тэбе стат маей жэнщиной, потому что, ты мне ошень нрависа. И нэ бойся—я мужчина женатый, и у менэ 3 ребёнки. И я себе сделал операцию—называется, вэсектоми, то есть, я могу иметь секс, и партнёрша не забэрэмэнэет. Теперь понятно, Алена, тебе, или нэт?—With one hand he grabbed her wrist, he then turns again reaching and has been pointing towards the sofa with he's the free hand. Alena still looks be worried, and more anxiously is listening, she than sarcastically began grinning too, as she spoken up in reply:—Да уж, всё понятно! Но я не могу быть вашей любовницей. Вы же сами говорите, что у вас есть жена и даже дети, или нет? Кроме того, какое мнение может сложиться у людей, живущих здесь, не говоря уже о моей семье и сыне! Я немогу вас оставить здесь на ночь.—In that case he reversed to the left, when has stepped forward, and is reaching his hands, he then caught her hand, he quickly began squeezing Alena's palms within hard to a grasp, while he's head being inclined, as him pointing toward a sofa-bed. This Vietnamese tried to kiss, but she tried to turn out and wrestle from him, when he began to speak in sarcastic tone; still his head leaning to the sofa, and so they're eyes too, as he said:-У нас ещё есть врэмья, пока усе унизу заньяяты ми может заньяться этим дьелом, и нэ терять время. Если ты не согласишса, всел семье нужно будьет уехать. Ничего тебе думать, давай раздэвайся. Тебе понятно это, Алёна?—Still Alena gave the impression of being bemused, still has by intrusion of a cynical tone in her voice:—Зачем же так спешить, можно это отложить и на другой день. Когда никого не будет дома, и нам не помешают. Ну что скажите, ам?-At that same moment someone began to knock on the door, and it happened to be Egor. Egor has been addressing towards Alena both speaking in calling her from the other side of the door:—Мама, мамочка, ты дома? Ответь мне!—I have made one more attempt to pull out the closed door-knob, but unsuccessfully, since it's being lock from inside, and anxiously spoken, when has addressed her over and over again that some thing:—Мама, мамочка, ты дома? Ответь мне! Почему ты не отвечаешь?—When she tried to make a respond, the Vietnamese man grabbed her hand, and began whispering in Russian; while with he's second hand and head being gesticulating to Alena and squeezing her hands via pointing to the door, forcing her to be silent:—Нэ открывай двэри, и молчи. Пускай идьёт отсюда! Иначэ ви все уедите. Поньяла?—Meantime, being outer the walls I have anxiously screaming, at the same time, and heard my voice making echos, as the volume has been exaggerated over yonder, in the corridor from my sobbing and scream, while pulling the door's-knob:—Мамочка, ты там, где ты? Дедушка, дедушка, иди сюда, мамы нету дома, пойдём её искать. Я хочу видеть мою маму? Мама открой, пожалуйста!—In that case Leonid began to stroke boy's hair, to subside he's distress, even as has spoken by a calm voice, at the same time as put he's left hand into the pocket:—Не плачь, Егор, не надо, я сейчас открою двери, у меня же есть запасной ключ. Да, ты успокоишься или нет? Мы сейчас разберёмся, добро?—Just before Leonid slowly taken out he's pair of keys, meantime on the other side off the door off the unit this Vietnamese man has grabbed the keys out of Alena's hand and has hurriedly run towards this door, seen as inserted her pair of key inside the keyhole. Apparently Leonid being unable to insert he's key onto the keyhole, which they both have found strange, and with cautious suspicion as they kept starring at that locked door. While Leonid, once again tries to insert his keys into the keyhole from it's door, eventually he's realizing, that his keys doesn't fit inside, cause already another pair is being stuck in there. Leonid made another attempt to insert the keys onto keyhole, but it's being helpless for him to open that door. He then turns toward Egor and began conversing with him, by speaking anxiously with tense, but Leonid has patted his hair and thus said:—Егор, я не могу открыть двери, но ты не плачь. Скорее беги вниз к Владеку, и попроси его прийти и помочь нам. Ты, понял?—When Egor has ducked he's head in agreement, while he spoken softly, but anxiously and more calm Leonid said:—Ну, всё, давай, Егор, беги, быстрее!-, After those words I left at once. While I have been running off the stairs with an echoes of my footsteps being heard around corridor, also it's vibration has exaggerated, like to be over-heard there yonder, as the sound passing through at apartment. Period in-between, behind that closed door, -over there yonder at the apartment this Vietnamese male being holding and squeezing Alena's hand tightly. I can't stir up memories what Vladek particular said, even so on my in the company of he's return back, on the doorway of entrance hall toward side of that place, which belonged to our family. In that case Vladek began discussion in a serious tone with Leonid; whereas in thus circumstances both parties have been standing, but spaced out. It sounds as if Alena being footing at the side of this manager in the interior of that apartment—while outside the wall Leonid and I together with Vladek outer the wall. As they are both just only revisit Vladek's place by coming back—three of they behind wall close to the door. Apparently, our loud voices from the corridor have heard over yonder in the interior, like volume from the echo being exaggerated from those three have made. Vladek suggested to knock on to our next door neighboring apartment, apparently by first asking of those permission to be able climbing through their balcony over straight into ours. Grandpa Leonid ducked in the agreement, and that's exactly what they are having done, as the next step of action. At some stage, there yonder in the apartment, Alena looks a bit scared, in contrast, she is not willing to distress me, her son, he is struggled keeping up with the Vietnamese man's unprovoked upholding her here. so she has decided doesn't want blaring, given that Egor might get scared. Shortly while Alena fail to deal with this Vietnamese man, and there be perceive sound that someone climbing over the rails at the location of balcony. Two of them within unit turned to the right side, where noise be heard, which led to the open door, where a balcony have been situated, they saw a man, whose appeared, where climbing over that banister of the upper tier separated they from that neighboring place. While the estranger made dins as their heads still being turned towards that balcony, they have anxiously watched, likely someone walked over the rail, and then quickly has jumped down off banister onto the surface. Still the Moon would stuck in the course of the sky, covering all over this cobweb like white cloud over it, as a large beam of a moon-light has shone through thier balcony in it's adjacent window, and falling straight onto, seeing as its reflection fell via the use of like unwieldy corner of balcony with ray fly-by-night hooked on the window directly inside.

At first both of them: the Vietnamese man and mom couldn't see them well, silluet of this estranger with a capacity of creating echoes may be. Ultimately there has emerged a person, who happen to be Vladek, given that visibility being clear enough to be able instantly recognize him. As soon as Vladek at length landed down over there yonder onto our territory of the balcony flooring, just towards the entrance hall room; he then walked fast inside the lounge room, stopping at the open door of its balcony. When Vladek observed, and its has sink in on the spot that Alena found herself in state of affairs he reacted promptly, and began to natter anxiously with a broken Russian accent, just as he's fist being stretched upfront and straight, as he exclaimed thus phrases:—Что здесь происходит? Слушай, ты, вьетнамец, Чего тебе нужно от них?—The Vietnamese manager became pale, as come back with retort, and he gave the impression of being a bit scared too, but confident, reacting:—Здьес ничего не происходит. Ето нэ твоё дьело. Это раз, а два—мнэ нужно нэ от них, а от неё. Они мене не интересуют. Идите лючше домой, и не мешай!—on that moment Vladek's expression has altered, it gave the impression of him being angry, while his act in response aloud, but by an annoying voice:—Я никуда не пойду, а вот ты сейчас же немедленно уберьёшся ис ихней квартиры, пока я не позвал сюда всех соседей, и ты не получил по мозгам. Ты, меня понял, или нет? Вьетнамец, отпусти её руку, и уходи отсюда, пока ты ещё цел!—Vladek then twisted to face Alena and has asked her in more quiet in a flexible voice, but still tense by gestures with his head leans to him:—Алена, с вами всьё в порядку, он вас не обидил? Если да, то скажите мне, и мы с ним—разберьёмся!—After all Alena began to speak in a soft voice, but with desperation:—Со мной всё впорядке. Не надо ничего делать, пожалуйста. Пусть манажер уйдёт, потому что нам не нужно никаких проблем. Откройте, пожалуйста дверь, и впустите моего сына. Спасибо, большое, Владек, вам—за всё!—Then Vladek is turned keys in anti-clockwise, when that door get wide open, as spirit of those three: Egor's, Leonid and Esther, who have joined, after Vladek and the Vietnamese man left their apartment. In that way, all of them than joint together on and enter into the apartment.

CHAPTER 39

The very next day when Alena supposed to work at the Open Café, in location of the entrance towards the Park was, and there again has appeared the same as the Italian man, whom they are saw yesterday at my Birthday party. It has been unexpected surprise for them find out that he has arrived long before they are, but not without help. Near him was standing another gentlemen whom they are never seen before. He was in the age of his late sixtieths, tall and upon his hair has been visible grey mane that made the color of his head, when looking on the sun with nuance of bluish, seen someone strew a whiteness on it that traces of living a not easy life. The new arrival approachs Alena, and introduced himself. Whilst, she shook hands with him. Alternatively she made gestures with her head and eyes turns facing the owner of the Café, as has asked to excuse her, and then she begins walking towards the side of her Boss. Even if, Alena's boss, being an Italian man, at the of late fiftieth or early—sixtieth-years of age. About his feature, he looked like a normal human-being, but in contrast, upon his left cheek has being located and visibly a big black mole. As for his eyes that emerged grey with a shadow be underlined of within skin sack; and shade of the facial appearance is light. Seen a middle age man is chubby, as by reviewing his complexion that would make anyone think he worked hard during all his life. It become visible that, he would begin to smile every time, when customers in close proximity, who happen to walk into he's miniature Café and occupying tables. He would demand from the employees, who have worked for him, to carrying out their duties, regardless what ethnic group those people belong to. Alena hasn't spoke Italian, but understood at least what her duty must be. The old Italian fellow, who came along with this man that being much younger than him, who previous have come within reach of this boss, while chatting rather mom has implied to him in Italian. This Café's boss nodded and has advised her to take a break for fifteen minutes. Once Alena stepped aside, bar so as to has asked to be made her a Cappuccino, as a bonus for herself. Those two Italian men my mom, and even I taken a seat around the table in the open café. After they're having felt at ease to converse with an old Italian man began to enquire, what language can Alena understands? Apparently he recognized that hers Italian isn't good enough to verbally communicating:— Can you understand French, Spanish, German, English?— Alena reacts without delays, but not without asking a contrary query:—I do understand German. What about Russian? Can you speak Russian, it would be better?—This old Italian smiles, then comes back with a retort:—Ih sprahe Deutch. Ih sprahe nicht Ruschen sprahe. Ferschtein?-And so, overture between those had taken a little while, then the old Italian gentleman has enlightened rather unexpectedly that put Alena in a state of a shock:—As you see the Italian man who is present here, but very much fond of you and your son. He is travelling to Ostia nearly every day mainly just only to see you. He want's to know, if you a free woman, or you're in a liaison presently?— Alena's face develops into serious, while her cheeks flushed with a spot of pink nuance, she relentlessly talks delicately, and still looking in front straight at her spokesmans eyes, she then assumed:—Well, it was unexpected, to be honest, it's being nearly two years, since I divorced the father of my son.—In that case 'interpreter', as he wanted to be called himself translated to the other Italian younger man eyes, and waited for his act in response. Just then a message has been comprehend by both of these party, as well as their mutual understanding being reached, given to consideration that foreigner requested to be called Interpreter. And so with help of the old Italian man, the last one began to speak again:—I presume this's your name is Alena, isn't true, my dear? And what is your son's name?-, followed by her reaction:-Yes, he is. And my son's name is Egor.—The old Italian man, who's happened to be a stranger, seems to be satisfied with her answer, while feeling confident, he then boldly continued his speech:—Alena, if you don't mind me to call you like an old friend, but it's needed to discuss in free manners, vis-à-vis on the situation. Alena, if you have been noticing, for a while this man, who is seating nearby, coming down to the café very often, and he also travels often here from another suburb mainly to see you. His name is Mario, and he's a widow. He's wife had died five year ago, and his Stepson from a previous Marriage lives with him. And he is attached to the guy. For the reason that he promised his late wife, who had passed away, to take care of her son.-, This old stranger has stopped looked to face the younger Italian—Mario, but with self-reliance and by the gesture, which meant consent from the last one, has continued his communication:—Mario is in possession of a grand house, and financially—can guarantee it to securing, providing with a good live and a stable income for you and your son. Mario is very fond of you and hold you in high regards as a woman, and alike opinion, you as a mother. Ever since he's wife passed away a few years ago he couldn't find the women of his dreams that he will be able to respect and love, as he does you. besides, he has brought for your son presents, brand new cloths. even if, as you, believed in past, Alena but since Egor's father is nor longer in your son's life, he can take the liberty as to adopt your son, if you agree to marry Mario. And since your son has the appropriate name Egor that in Italy shall be well regarded. What will be your answer in concern to this gentleman's proposal?—, Alena instead is carefully being listening,and the stranger, while talking tried to do it slowly. By taken a deep breath, she then come back with:—I'm flattered for this man's proposal. Even so, the whole thing you've said on Mario's behalf happen to be proper, first of all I would like to explain my situation to you: It is true that am, myself I—a free woman. But still, I'm bound with two old and sick parents, as I'm careful in relations to my mother, who is very ill and at this moment I feel like to safe her life. That's my first reason why we have left the USSR. My second motive is that I raise a youngster, whether this man will be a good father to my son I'm unaware of it. Causeof my main concern is about my son's future. At last, but not least: the important thing here is that they unable to stay in Italy for long, even if we wish for, since we all were not granted permanent residence here. Then, soon the family will be leaving for Australia, and that's where our plan is at present!—This old Italian seem to be staring at our side and face; then began translating the whole thing towards Mario. The other Italian man, Mario, happen to realize her indication then gets up as of his seat, and has approached they both, then patted my head, though, but I understood what he said in Italian. Once again via the old stranger-man, who has delivered the massage by that translation:—I really respect and admire your decision, I really do; and that approach as you have taken just before the situation come to mind. About your parents, you're still a young woman and have to build your own life, thinking first of all of yourself. Alena, you still forgeting that your son needs a father, as every kid needs a father figure, and so I make a marriage proposal to you, so that you and your son will be able to stay in Italy. As for your parents: they can travel to Australia, and one day we're as a married couple together with Egor can travel to visit them over there. I possess a big and comfortable house, and would like to built a family with you. I hope that they're can have our own babies. Anyhow, at present in my house lives my step-son from my previous Marriage, and I truly believe, for them both it will be an interesting friendship. But my step-son is nearly an adults, and sooner or later, he will be leaving our home for studies or unique, what ever he prefers to do if he is a barrier for that matters to you?—Her face looked a bit flabbergasted, still she is holding herself convinced. This old Italian new arrival then takes bags from Mario's hands, who materialized from nowhere, and those plastic bags he passed to me. These bags are not heavy; and I began to look inside them and to my surprise I have found a brand new suit, which fit my size in the tags and bar codes upon it, and other supplies contained by these. Meantime, mom bend down closer to me and told in a soft voice:—Don't you get attached to those stuff. Cause, you may give it back to this gentlemen. Put it down. Don't hold it in your hands.—After that upon Alena's face has appeared a nervous smile, as she began speaking German, which I couldn't understand:—I value your concern for my personal life and my familia, but, the truth is that I neither can't marry you, Mario, nor anyone else, for these matter's. At least for this time being, and not at this moment. My mother is very ill, and she needs me. And so is my son, who only turned six yesterday, Mario, you must be aware of that, cause you've been present on his birthday.—Alena stops, took a deep breathe, then has turned her head from one side to side, and in a heavy voice said:—And so, I'm declining your marriage proposal. I'm an independent woman and need to stay for sometime, or until my mother would be healthy. You can't imagine, what would like for her, being in a poor health arriving in Australia? I hope you realize what it means, ttravel to a mother-in-law? I'm trying to tell you, please, don't get angry by my refusal. I thank you again, for the compliment, and that is my last decision. If you excuse, me gentlemen, but I have to get back to work. Good afternoon to you!—She released my hands from plastic bags, and pass them back to Mario. Then again the old Italian man translated her respond back to Mario. Suddenly, face of this ex-fiancé Mario altered, while it's altered to pale and so being his eyes: brightness disappeared from it, as it seems that his eyes had become dull with a troubled look. Mario, in contrast re-collected himself and said, that he still wants to marry mom, in spite of the whole thing, which being said by her, and then passed the in turn through me, only then it struck me, what the conversation is all about. The old Translator, on the other hand has been listening carefully and then repeated the message to mom in German:—Don't be so categorical. Take your time to think carefully about my proposal. I'm eager to wait and travel with all of you if that's crucial in Australia in time. As soon as your parent will settle down there. If you change your mind let your Boss in the Café know about your decision. In fact you Boss will get in touch with me, via in he's turn can pass towards me. I do really have strong feeling for you . . . !-

Vis-à-vis Alena's private life: all these times, since her divorce from dad she has got lots of marriage proposals. This Italian manwas not the first one to make such a proposal of matrimony, and precisely wouldn't be the last one. As she resolved to carry her family through calamity to steadiness, been dogged to postponed with a matrimony to anyone, like this Italian man, into the bargain.

CHAPTER 40

A long these lines, few days passed, since Alena declined marriage proposal as of an Italian man—Mario. The Polish neighbors have invited Borodin for tea. There lived a family of three, a young couple, with a little girl, whose then was less than three years of age. Borodins were surprised at first of the invitation, yet, decided to except it. Later that day they have recieved a call from the Australia's relatives and by the tone of Alena's voice I comprehend it, that their conversation did not go as it planned. Although, she has looked pale and being breathing heavily; but has tried too explain the situation to anyone, but on other side of the line the one really tried to upset her, and expressed their unwillingness to except all of them as a family, Esther particular, only Leonid. The only person they want to see is—your dad—Said the man on the other side of the line.—Being standing nearby I was listening what man talked to mom on the other side of the phone line and I clearly heard every word that he said. He suggested, though, for the three of they remain Immigrating to the USA, or to other countries. When their talk ended, I have spotted that Vladek along with another residents being standing close by that phone-booth, which ought be used for all of those residents on apartments in the hostel, and mostly neighbours of a Polish descent. They say that Alena and Leonid also saw them, but bend their heads down, cause Vladek has drawn close, and got employed in discussion with the Polish, who being stand nearby and overheard the phone conversation. Vladek's air gave the impression of being grim, and also colour on his face has changed by becoming pale. He is concentrated on Alena with mixture of the Ukrainian and Polish:—Послухай, Алена, вам з мамой и Егором, незачем ихаты до той Австралии! До дупы далась та Астралия. Бо вас чэкаэ великэ горе, не треба туды ихаты. Поихалы з намы кращэ до Канады. Тоби буде кращэ з намы, мы не дамо, щоб твою маму хтось зобразыв. Ты щэ побачишь, що ци родычи зроблять вам? Послухай, нас, поидемо з намы до Канады чи до Амерыци. Побачишь тоби и твоим ридным буде краще з намы . . .—Once Leonid is drawn closer up, and starts to accuse Vladek to interfering within our Family's affairs, which it's not of his business. Vladek left though, but seem being upset, because he has felt for all of them, especially for Alena and Egor to boot.

The next day, when the man has approached her again with another man, who happens be our neighbours from the next door apartment Marek, who they are sold the dark grey luggage, they both began to convince, that she is making a mistake. And the other neighbour Marek has also told, once they are arriving in Canada he's family and he are planing to buy a big house over there, where they are all ought to be living together, as a family together with them. They also given they a warning, that if they are aren't listen to him, and come along with them—they are might regret it. As soon as Vladek left, Marek has returned back and said something different to her in a Russian accent:—I am aware that your mother Alena, and Egor saw the other day a large sum of cash. You act in the most noble and honest way towards our family. My family and I respect yours, and you Alena, particular. So, they are have trust in your family, even more than I have to face in my mother-in-law. You don't need travelling to Australia, it would be better, if you shall come along with us to Canada. As soon, as they are will arrive over there I am going to purchase a huge house, where they are all will be able to live—as one happy family. Listen to me, you will never regret, about decision, while they would never allow anyone, neither offend you, nor you're family. And in relation to your mother they will take care of her, cause there she will get the best medical assistance and treatment. Eventually she is going to get well over there, trust me!-

After that conversation with Marek—Alena has changed her mind, soon she clued-up about her decision to Leonid. Alas, he has become angry, as she enlightened him, what her recent decision ought to be, that those three of them likely to travel to Canada. As a result, Leonid has got drunk and at top of his voice made scandalous scene in our flat. was very upset and said that he is:—You etching me, papa, but I don't know what to do where to look for an assistant?—Everyone was telling mom not to go to Australia, amid those Poles and even some public, as have shown their face the council from the org, who looked after refugees and migrants called Caritas, with processed via uor travel documents. Although, Leonid insisted for the family to travel together, but secretly has a private and serious conversation with my gradma Esther, when has told her the truth about our plans. Given that Esther and Leonid were married for over thirty years, she precisely being attached to him, and obviously hasn't been planning to part with him. Hence Esther began pressuring and insisting for Alena's obedient to Leonid's will. 'And there mom was unable to change her mind, but mom hasn't got a choice, as being forced to unchanged the processing of our documents, in a bid to be able travelling either to Canada, or foreign countries, as refugees. In actual fact they have got an opportunity to choose any countries, where they're willing migrate to. Finally to be decided for those four airborne to Australia to build a new life over there from scratch.

CHAPTER 41

This time they are also learned that a Russian girl who arrived in Italy with her father has got missing for about three days. Her parents divorced in the USSR, whereas her mother gave her permission to be able traveling with that estrange father on the way to USA. Everyone amongst the Russian-speaking have been informed that she had disappeared from Ladispoly, where she lived with her dad, few days ago and nobody heard from her since. As father of that missing girl has been sick worried about her disappearance. But among the migrants all have been also worried about her health with her they safety, but people working for the association for refugees nut those migrants have feared the worst. While the lady, who's in charge for processing our travel documents referred to mom to ask other migrants, especially among those Poles migrants within other nationalities, or local people to inquire, if anyone heard or aware of the girl's whereabouts. She's referred to her:—Alena, being mother yourself, can you're imagine as this girl is not even sixteen years of age yet. They're all here, along with her father in particular very worried about her well-being and welfare. Not to cite, whether she is a life or not? They are fear the worst? With the news about that girl is a life, concerning her they arell-being she was unaware of and not sure. Still she has not being far away from Ostia, at least in the directions towards here, within isolated area outskirts of Rome. The woman's being also re-telling, what she heard, and has up to date of this missing Russian girl had left Ladispoly in a company of the two strangers, whose men then inclined towards her getting in the car, and after drove off in it. She continued and has also clued-up, that approximately whereabouts to be finding this Russian girl. Despite the fact that, our delight befall shattered by fateful news. In a couple of days they are learned that upon arrival of the Police on the mentioned place, the Russian girl had already been found dead. Father of this girls was crying, instead he has been forced to organize a funeral in Italy for the erstwhile girl. They've never had the chance to find out, what really happened to this girl, and whereabouts she actually being located, when the police found her, and also with whom she left, or why thus horrible news has happened with her. Who they were, being so cruel, as to kill a fourteen years old innocent girl. And the most vital: even more dreadful was to end up of such a young life, of unlawful and unprecedented ending that eventual being taken away from her loved once, by such horrific death, has ended up her life in such a young age. Obviously her blood has been left on someone's hands, when they had executed their attempts with no compassion. In spite of heartbreak evil, the girl's mother hardly had been allowed flying to Italy for her daughter's funeral that being organized at the same day upon her arrival in Italy, she was forced to return back to the USSR with her daughter's remained body in a coffin. Rather an awful had happened to this girl, which has unstated that the girl she being sexually assaulted, and then killed in terrible accident. Given that Italian Police went to this place, to find her alive, instead they found the girl's corpse. Where they never had a chance to discover more facts about that dreadful case. To pursue more shortly after this Russian-speaking man had left Italy and travelled to the USA, as of our Org and beyond everyone's topic has been only about mysterious gentlemen. Apparently they are learned, that gentleman, who left earlier abroad, ahead of all the immigrants, it turned out to be the same grieving father of that deceased young girl. But with what cost he was able migrate abroad? What a grotesque? The life of a sixteen years old was sacrificed; that he got opportunity traveling ahead of everyone else abroad? finally he hasn't got a choice, but to leave in terrible pain, of losing a beloved child, as have cried their eyes out.

CHAPTER 42

O ne day they went to the set camp in the park, with the wooden huts, as over there lived mostly Russian migrants of Jewish origins, who left the USSR, and traveled under the Israel's visa-invitations. Likewise they have lived in Italy upon their arrival to the countries which they have chosen to immigrate to different places. Those Russian migrants needed to stay in Italy for a short period of time, while they have waited for the procedure, while that process on filling up their travel documents, which supposed to be processed, as they have waited to get 'a green light'. Most of those migrants have already received permission to enter the USA, or Canada and/or other their chosen countries, under refugee status, this has included Australia too. Meantime conversing with those Polish migrants, who asked the Russians at some stage in of conversation, about their status and they disclosed to the Poles the truth, that made them very jealous and angry. Among those Polish migrants, which have converted into gloomy disposition towards those Jews, and with kind of anger amid those Polish migrants being decided overnight organizing a coup with killings of people, and innocent kids, as be supposed to destroy those huts of an existing complex of that Russian camp. Hatred amid the Poles are having intended for those Russians of Jews descent explicitly. If instead they accomplished what they had planned; it would made that complex camp alike ruinous. Those Russians existed in poor conditions, and in such smelling old wooden huts, which looked like more of a 'concentration camps', rather then typical livelihood. Not counting be evidence for some of Polish people, who overnight decided to repeat or bring back the history, when millions of the Jews were killed, during the World War II, as they prepared a Fascist group for thus kind of crime.

For the meantime, when they would approach the place where groups get-together, which were amid the Polish migrants, where between them I saw this lady, who had relieved my pain the first night upon our arrival at the hostel in Ostia. She was this same person, who made easier for me and my family, she even offered 'Russian Vodka' as first aid in attic-room for healing my burned leg then. They are been unpleasantly astonished as have learned about the dark side of her character. And yet, they saw that she possible be the one of their main leaders, whose intention being of organizing such a criminal act against human, who are Jews of the upheaval and unlawful coup. The Poles and other ethnic group, who were present at this meeting talked about their 'targets', amid them being converted into killers without doubts of those Russian migrants, as they have arranged the terrorists act against innocent people: amid them were children, too elderly women and men. Despite the fact that they saw them, who were acquainted with many of them, as the Borodins have been unpleasantly astonished to learn about thus dark side of her character. Could it be possible, that she ought to be the one of the chief Leaders to be capable organizing of such a crime against people, the upheaval and unlawful coup? At this instant realization has sent shockwaves throughout my body. Those Poles with other ethnic groups, who have being present present at that meeting talked about their 'targets', among their agenda without doubts have been: a Massive killings of those Russian-speaking, without a single survivors. They also freely discussed their 'killing targets', akin to they are getting ready for a 'hunt', by organizing an unfair and unprovoked act against innocents people, among whom have been: children, seniors persons, with other age groups of men and women, who they have become not only unprotected—then at risk, but too vulnerable towards the Poles real threats. Though, Alena became worried about what she heard, as if truth be told about that disturbing news, before it doesn't become too late.

As rumous has it that in org also had given they an advice to they're returning back to our apartment, and stay there, but not by any circumstances walking towards Russian camp, at least for few days.

As a few days has past Egor with family began hearing news—the Italian Carabinieri arrived at Ostia, and have surrounded that complex within Russian camp and installed around the whole complex area the metal guard from barbed wirer, which made it look like the protection shield fences. These Carabinieri have become present there for at least four days and three nights. 'Meanwhile, Alena and Egor couldn't stay home and have decided taken a walk towards the Russian camp, after all. Mom and I have found a place to hide in amongst trees, and underneath a large branch. Yet, they are observing the area, while have anxiously awaited, if it is happen there, in contrast being started capable of occurring to next there. Visibility be clear: sun shone, the sky over is blue, where white clouds, with its shape that looked like spider cobweb, which slowly moved hooked on the aerial and without stopping. Soon mom and I observed from a distance, as those Poles have appeared, who set in motion by draw closer. Then abruptly among those insurgents, there they are unstintingly acknowledged Vladek in company with few others there being of our acquaintances, whose emerged among a big group of those Poles, who also arrived, while approaching closer towards the Russian camp, alike wild animals would gathered going on the hunt. So, he and others come out into a view they being among our acquaintances. By seen them there from a not afar at distant, whilst they even moved from on top of on the hill down they are supposed facing those. Thus consciousness has just sent shock waves, it's alike nearly blood come to boil within the veins, as they are became very upset and frustrated to see him there—among insurgents, which have learned what he and others are intend to do, well know and to be capable doing such a inhumane thing. Meantime in Russian camp have stayed people, among whom being innocent kids, but the unprovoked act haven't been a hooligan fight in its place a terrorist act by means of a horror effect, like the Russian Jews might get killed on the way. As a final point the Polish insurgents came within reach of the complex camp, ans by the side they're possessing of: axes, knifes, and some of them have brought hand made sawn off guns which they covered it up. Carabinieri or the Italian military police barring already are waiting for the insurgents near the camp, and having surrounded the entire area of Castel Fusano, and too being brought on a high alert one and all between them. The Police have been awaiting for the other party if they dare to start, and to protect those innocent civilians: children and old people, with women along men among them too. While most of these insurgents understood Italian language, because they were located in in Italy for a while and they were easily communicating between inhabitants. For that reason, the Italian Police gave the Polish insurgents a fair warning, so if they are indisposed to stop those unprecedented attack on those unprotected Russian civilians, they would be facing consequences. Hereby, the Carabinieri prevented the Poles and given the last warning, in case if those last shouldn't subordinate to the given orders by the Police, by their willpower to be forced open fire toward those Polish rebels. Egor with he's family never had a chance to find out, if there those army got any casualties among civilians, but, one and all within Russian camp have being so worried and just could not wait until they got to get the 'green light', in order to be able to leave for their aim country, where they decided to migrate.

Soon after of that cited tragedy Vladek and his family have received a phone call. That call has come from Poles Org that up to date, he's family and him are to be leaving for Canada soon. He appeared disappointed, though, but said goodbyes apparently to each person, including our family too. Still, Borodins have wished them a 'safe trip and all the best in their future'. Even if leave-taking, Vladek once again reminded Alena of their travel to Australia and suggested not to go so far, instead the best thing, according to his phrases, be supposed to migrate to Canada, by meet with him plus other acquaintances, whose being over there. After Vladek's family departure, the Borodins were living in harmony and mutual respect with all those migrants. They're still visiting those Russians in the wooden huts it camp, alongside other nationalities.

CHAPTER 43

But everything good always comes to and end. Thereby, one afternoon they've received a call from the Org and them being asked to travel to Rome for an important interview. They are also have been advised to bring all of the documents, that they are possess of our disposal and to grant it to the Australian Embassy, as they arere informed, they ar e should be present those for overview during our appointment there. Although, the Borodins prepared everything for this important meetings, but couldn't recognize that it is going to be so soon.

In view of the fact that the next morning the Borodin's have left for Rome. At first they have travelled on a local train and followed by changed for a specific bus travelled towards the stop their being seek. Given that at length the family arrived to the place where they are this important meeting ought to take place They are being greeted by a Secretary of the Australian Embassy, where once again they've met a woman, whose come into view being responsible for processing our travel documents and who for many months and was helping our family, even though she spoken in a brogue Russian, but the Borodin's are able to figure out of her hassle.

Later on, after the translation and mutual understandings they are have been presented with the special agreements, which they have signed in. Probability payments, which they are supposed to make within seven days at the Italian National Working Bank—'Banco Nazionale de Lavoro', as to wrap up with their required travel documents, and requirement in accordance with the procedure intended for fill in the forms. The documents have been signed it by Leonid as the 'bread-winner' and Alena for herself and on my behave, given that Egor was under age, and so she has become his guardianship, besides to a 'trusteeship' for my future who happened being and always is by my mother. It was necessary Reparation papers towards the required payments in Italy, and for later on, when they are distanced to arrive in Australia and for our future settlement's therein. As they are've being asked questions, regarding the family in Australia, Leonid suddenly became agitated and spoken with a tone in his voice, that showed anxiety upon him and wiliness to fly over there right now. Critical to point that Leonid's actions has been unbearable, exacting during the last stage of the interview, and intolerant, cause he has mistaken, when estimated that with this kind of conduct he would be able speed up the procedure to fill in indispensable travel documents. He has made all of them more confused and embarrassed than to be, as the whole process was already complicated. Anyhow, the process of the documents finally has been completed and they are have being given 'the Green light' or permission to make the Restitution payments toward the Italian Working Bank, for an amount of money, which our family has been able to afford.

All the same, in couple of days my mom and I travelled back to Rome to find the 'National Working Bank of Italy'. They asked people for directions to the Bank, and after a short while walking they are finally found it. It's being happily located at the hearts of Rome's district. Those two spotted this old and great building with huge columns, which has sited in the original style, which has been painted in mustered color, and they have shined from the color, which being covered at top with linseed oil paint upon it, which made it's with more lacquer sparkling from the Sun-light. There they are also huge windows with a these same huge pretext up above the entrance. They are liked the build very much from the minute, as it has appeared in front of them, so felicitously situated fundamental to Rome, and they are with great enthusiasm walked in. After they are made the required payments to the Bank, though, it hasn't being easy for her to exchange a few words with the locals, because lack of language barrier. Alena could not understand what's being required of her to do at first. Eventually they are managed somehow making that necessary payments, and other things. They are both then left that beautifully crafted old Italian build. When they are walked out of that Bank and looked around which directions to go, so they are become disorientated and haven't even walked dozens of yards. Suddenly those two are hearing a noise, that reminded of a motorcycle, which has been riding on the move nearby. But, it's being actually a scooter, which has not been unusual to see on the streets of Rome or other cities in Italy, for this matter. Soon this rider on a scooter approached they from behind, and drove very close towards her. Then unexpectedly he or she tried to rip off the handbag from Alena's shoulders, where the handbag was aimed. Though, they are could not see the feature of the rider, if this person was a men or a women. Alena tried to hold on to her bag, but the raider was grabbing and tearing out pothey arerfully, as much as he or she could. Though this rider being speedy on the scooter, while by non-stop has drawn within the reach of driven slowly to. This scooter Rider being wearing motorcyclist's helmet, which also emerged dressed in the same suit as all the rides do, but neither of them could not see with the aim of identify's appearance, who looked like a human? And what sex that person he or she belong to? Anyhow, mom was wrestling with that raider and the later let her go, as a consequence, mom felt down on asphalt, before that she let go of my hand. In this situation she was laying down on asphalt, because she hurt her leg along with hand, but I being footing near and began to cry from the scare. This robber on the scooter has being planning the raid, when he or she assumed, that since they are came out the Bank that they are must have money. Though, the raider was mistaken us for an important person else, cause prior they are those two were rushing so as getting on time to the National

Bank—but not to make withdraw, instead to pay obligatory bills therein. At that time in the city of Roma has being always lunch-break for the workers at the most body of institution with business like or commerce corporations. At mid-day back there would usually be lunch-breaks for their workforce, as a result, mom and I hurried to the Bank to make payments, and to avoid the unnecessary long waiting queues in.

Upon their returning back to hostel she began to tell the unpleasant story to our neighbors about our ordeal, the Russian migrant have been in a shock, but the Polish and other migrants who lived in Italy for a long time they are not shocked, cause one of them told they a similar story, which ensued among other migrant:—The strange riders either on a scooter or motorcycle would unexpectedly appear or come from nowhere; then ripped off from your hands or shoulders handbags and purses then quickly driving away on their scooters.—None of the witnesses either saw the faces of the raid robbers, or even knew, whether those people being men or women, see his or her full body be covered with special riding suit, and this one's head was protected in a helmet. Polish neighbor prolonged and said:—. . . maybe it was well planned gangsters or a thief, as are working with the same approach and schemes. That Gang robbers or burglar wouldn't care about your feeling, or what condition people are, their goal to Raid, where they have to just grab or rip off bags from people's hands, but then rushing to drive away on the motorcycle or scooters!-

After thus unpleasant incident with this scooter rider robber, the Borodins have calmed down, and everyone is tried avoiding to talk with them about it.

The Borodins instead have got more important to deal with as to meditate on. They're having got pre-occupied, that them getting ready for a long flight to Australian shore.

Given the Borosdins have asked to get medical check ups, and when the results came back of those three: Alena, Egor and to our surprise Esther's—all being in good health. The test shown that they are healthy, as Esther's medical results has explained her being in a good health. The Doctor also added that Esther will be needed get to be done surgery procedure in the near future, once in his opinion: in her case—it hasn't being a life threatening situation, even, though, the entire family thought within a different light previous to. But its being good news at least. About Leonid's health: the results wasn't that good at all. The Italian doctor, who has got the results for his medical tests explained to what they have found out: that Leonid being ill with Tuberculosis in the earlier period, as a result he's X-ray has shown traces of the scars within the locations of his lungs, which being left after his illness in the past '. That doctor also continued and warned Leonid:-You have to be very careful in the future, cause Australia is really a Tropical country. Thus particular countries like Australia, which is to be located in Tropics near the Equator. Thus kind of weather conditions, with heat waves genuinely, can make an enormous negative affect with unpredictable effects towards your life. In general high temperature there, would be a danger to you're well-being, from my point of view. So, it's advisable for you're Leonid personally to live in a country with cool weather only.— He stopped for a second, and then added on top, by referring to Leonid:—. . . the climate change there for people, like you, who arrive from Europe maybe dangerous for your lungs, and also your for healthiness, and well-being.—This Doctor additionally has enlightened Leonid:—Still, you Leonid being obliged to facing former causes living in a Tropical Country, such as Australia is a very beautiful and a safe country to live in this world in the world, and people, which be in the world over there feel like a heaven. it absolutely doesn't mean that for you're family, above all for yourself it's a good idea. Cause you all just only escaped Chernobyl where the radiation level have and still is very high. As for Australia: you have to face new dilemma with X-rays radiation there comes from the sun, there is common experience heatwaves with erratic tropical climate contributes to the ozone layer, those factors could be, as harmful, alike Chernobyl for all of you. As the affect, which you can face again be there, I raise the problem for you to re-consider travelling to Australia . . .-

In spite of thus gloomy talk, with more advise from a doctor, then again that could not change their plans, whilst regular keeping up busy with all these preparations towards the Borodins future endeavour trip abroad. Soon after they have received airfare tickets for those four of them travelling in Australia, given to a reflection that I was only a child, by the time when the processing of travel documents began progress of filling up, while continued being in these forms I was five-years of age previous to. Readily available, my airfare ticket was only half the price, which had pleased not only they, but also the association, cause that wouldn't leave they with a large amount of debt for the prospect ahead. They were preparing for this moment for some days. Alena gave away her fur-coat, which she has worn for few years to one of the Polish woman, cause they are have been informed that Australia is a Tropic country after all, as a result the climate over there mostly for the whole calendar year must be the sizzling weather and heatwaves there. Hence, she assumed that the fur coat won't be basic for Alena to dress in over there, in Australia. As for the Polish woman, on the other hand, since she is going to travel to Canada, where the climate is really cold and snowy, she will be needing this coat, for sure. Given they are going learning to speak in English that basically those having assumed that in Australia there isn't going to be very easy to live. Also the news, regarding such a long trips on the plane didn't make me very happy either, and so was not my mom. on the other hand, the whole thing has decided and be supposed to fly in a bid to begin build a new life in that new faraway Country of Australia from a scratch. They are have not got time to dig up for more news whereabouts this country that they make an effort migrating to. While, they are haven't got the prospect to learn English either. 'As for me: I ought to be starting to learn at the primary school, where the Academic Year has began, as the duration of the Academic Year of studies over there already being beyond six months, because outside gave the impression of be gorgeous month of August. Everything they learned about Australia,from social and Economic states of living, with rules and principles, Law and loyalty 'down under' got them confused, it's looked weird and unfamiliar to the Borodin, which they haven't got a clue, what's to expect?

Sunset over Sea

PART–IV

To Start New Life From Scratch

CHAPTER 44

Finally came the day when the family is leaving for Australia. Given that a van is arrived to pick the Borodin's up, and convey them to airport in Rome. But the Borodin's weren't expected the neighbors would leave their flats, and being wishing to come downstairs saying goodbyes to them, there also arrived other migrants from the Russian Camp, and the even the Italian Leader, who has been in charge for all those long months since our presence in Italy. In reality it was really a deep emotional feeling to say goodbyes to all of those public, who became so close with they. The entire the residents from the hostel being standing within the backyard: those Polish migrants, the Serbian, as even the Bulgarian Family, apparently none of them has not gone to work on this day. Even that Italian cleaner Francesca, who lived and worked there, who happens being this drug addict woman, she has cleaned herself up nicely even dyed her hair, as the color within her hair became blond. Although she kissed me at my cheeks twice and wished they a safe trip, but at that same time persona Francesca emerged has being looking unhappy, when she said in Italian, that she shall miss our family very much. I have spotted this old rich Italian lady amongst countless of others, whom mom used to visit, or cleaning up her place; she was standing aside, being crying. They are also saw our new hostel manager who's being of Vietnamese origin, he did not look pleased and approached they together with another neighbor, whom they are acquainted with him - this man is called Piotr.

A Vietnamese man's wished they good luck. Next Piotr began to speak to:-You should not rely on someone's help—except yourself! Don't wait until any gives you a penny. But if you have to work hard to be able to afford everything that you want to achieve in life.—He stopped for a second, took a deep breath, then he non-stop and addressing her:—Alena you're making a big mistake travelling so far away country, which you're not even aware where it's located and what you ought to expect and do over there by yourself? Thus deal should be better off: for those three of you're, except Leonid travel with us to Canada.-, Piotr then stopped again, took a deep breath, where they've sighted tears in his eyes, said:—Look at my wife, Alena she is crying, I want you to promise us, in case, if something will go wrong abroad there. Come back straight to Italy, with Egor until they are here, and they are all will help you. And then they are all together will travel to Canada or USA. Remember that Okay, Alena?—

When the van arrived they are began to carry away our baggage towards the car, next one from the Serbian family and from the another from the Poles our neighbors unexpectedly jumped inside the Van and began to take out the luggage's out as well as they blocked our way and start to scream and tried to hold they up by wast the time, and also distracting they from getting inside the Van, while they kept saying:—Don't go, Alena! Babushka Esther stay here. They are all love your family. They are shall be worried about all of your well-being, about your welfare and future too, particular about you Esther. This country of Australia is not good for you?—He then goes round to face Leonid, is begun addressing him with irritation:—And you crazy, stupid Russian, you're family, Leonid over there will make you're family a living hell, you need to remember our words. They are begging you to stay with us, Alena. Let that old stupid man take that trip to Australia. He shall return back soon. You will find out that they are are right, old stupid Russian. Where the hell are you taking this great family of your's? If you want to see you Mother fly there by yourself!— Many of those migrants, particular the Polish there are crying, and kissing us, goodbyes mostly me. Even those Russian-migrants who came from Russian camp said goodbyes, and they are have been informed that one Russian guy is aimed at travel with them to Australia. In any case the Borodin's arrived at the Rome airport that drama and farewells in the Ostia's hostel, as the driver from the van, whom they are new for all those months in Italy, and who moved our family many times to varied places, also is said goodbyes to them but doesn't look happy. He is also shown they where they are have to go for the boarding. There also be that group at least of twenty people, who have spoke Russian. Apart from them there is standing, and by now having formed a crowd amid other Italian folks, yet among them being recognized an interpreter. View beside him a leader who has helped Borodin's during those long months of their stay in Italy. When they are joined the group the Italian lady asked mom to step aside together with me for a private talks with her. Farewell between Egor's family and those are touching, given that the lady hugged them and tears seen in her eyes. She also has repeated, what this man earlier puts in the picture for them, that in case if they are shall not be satisfied with Australia's style of life, or somewhat else should go wrong, not to hesitate calling, otherwise to get in touch with folks at the Org, since they will help Borodin's family return back to Italy.

Borodin's being instructed that their air travel to Australia won't be a direct one, since it's a very long flight, roughly 26 hours. With plane first stop is to be scheduled at Bombay, in India. For the airplane with next stopping is scheduled to be—in Singapore. Ahead of arriving in Australia the plane be supposed to make another stop over there in Melbourne, since they are travelling at the same flight together with other Russians, who will be disembarked in Melbourne. At the airport they are finally saw the young Russian lad who said goodbyes to his mother and step-father. The couple has been travelling to USA, but the lad has been travelling with they to Australia. He was at the age of his yearly twentieth years, or younger, but was upset to part with his mother. She's being crying and being telling him to come and visit her in the USA, as soon as he can, and get to go settled there. This Russian lad also travelled with they to Sydney where his late father's family and particular his grandmother lived. Given there've seen a few more couples along with their kids, which some of them, either are traveling jointly with Borodin's, or flew elsewhere, but the people who ought to be travelling to Australia, and tried too keep closer with each other.

CHAPTER 45

Eventually the Borodins have gone boarding the plane, our family being placed in the sits together with other Russian migrants, as close as possible, so that they are able to seen each others movements and intentions. Just before take off the plane they are asked the flight attendant to let me take the seat near window, it was an economy class compartment, though, but the plane itself has been 'L'Italia' of the Italian company airplane. The entire crew present being of Italian background, and so has being the traditional Italian food served, which flight attendants provide to they there. I have seated near skylight on plane, and enjoyed the view around and beyond. There I have watched the small like dwarfs houses, and did not realise, with many things which looked so huge on the ground would become pigmy's effects and tiny objects, when someone ought to look at those from above. The aeroplane be higher than varied cities flew through and beyond different: fields, regions and the country sides; tall mountains rivers and lakes, which looked like more of lacesfrom from above, rather wide, deep with extreme depth forests, while the views are breathtaking visibility from the windowpane with miraculous by me constant be admired to stare on over and over. All those new which would appear every time made excited, then the view has suddenly changed—became identical picture, and sustained at distance sideways, apparently pass, and still are flying above the sea, even the mountains appear scarcer, and later fade from the view at all. After a while that same picture became boring for me, when I asked why should we catch only view of the sea is visible, which is so big and long, Why won't they are see anything else, below the ground houses or fields, for example, even the mountains will do the trick. The flight attendant in that case has explained to me, that what I saw is called Indian Ocean; equally, I didn't care less.

From the time when we flew, I couldn't view anything else more attention-grabbing; then at the end—I have fallen asleep.

At the time when I woke up and looked into the window I still saw the same picture: up on the blue sky and white clouds, which looked like white marshmallows being moving parallel and straight ahead with our plane, but with those different shapes and sizes, as the flight attendant told me, that the Ocean also moved farther, in my opinion it's rather kept on the same place. And so it's became a peculiar for me, whether these huge Ocean ever to being complete it's flow to a different place?—I kept looking but could not sight thus prospect intended for a native land or big cities, which a stewardess has promised I'll be seen. But none of images appeared for the time being.

When out of blue the sky has changed from blue into becoming grey with those huge clouds, which at this moment looked like a grey curtain. Apparently the sun has disappeared inside a grey vast curtain from the other side of window. Unexpectedly is I witnessed lightning that struck, as it's blitzing has reflected onto my cubic-window being so powerful, and then the rain has started to fall. But this rain looked like a huge water fall with a thunder storm been in it's euphoria, which I never had a chance to observe close to the glass. Shortly after they have breakfast and stewardess let passengers know that all have to lock up their seats belt, because the plane is going to land in India.

Finally after so many hours of the flight not counting thus problem with my hearing, where at the same time my Leonid also started experiencing loss his ability of hearing during the flight besides. Our plane has eventually landed in Bombay, which is located in India, as I have been informed previously. The Borodins along with those travellers have been asked by a flight attendant to leave the plane, cause it's needed to vacuum cleaning compartments after a long flight. The travellers are have been also advised to go outside the airport's complex. By returning back boarding the plane—approximately more or less than two hours time.

Obviously the Borodin's aren't experienced flying at such long distance, too they being lacking of knowledge in English. So all those have made them confused and vulnerable. While one of the airport officials handed boarding passes for those travelers from that flight except Egor. The Borodin's are whither, where their lives being put on the line. As a result, at the Bombay airport one of their staff officials, who happen to be an Indian national, while waiting within the queue to receive boarding passes, which those airport staffs were handling to travelers from our flight. Neither Alena, nor any in my family was given a boarding pass by these officials for me. Yet not any of those none-interventional Indian Customs officials either has cared about missing to provide my family or me with a boarding pass. Given they are come from provincial, consequently neither of they, either innocently payed any attention towards their rules, nor to this important issues, or had been unfamiliar with their principles and regulations in Bombay airport complex. Now is turning point here with that value of the matter, by which I could play a vital role for those tourists, who are traveling abroad. So this would be for the Borodin's new ordeal. Each of those travellers, who already have left the plane, quite the opposite, every one amid those Russian-speaking including the Borodin's are kept closer to each other, and being following step by step one another. See next they've joined a queue, and stood behind crowd of their trip. Even as they've approached closer to view some of the items, which were presented on diverse displays for the customers, particular for the travellers, who arrived in India or with the aim of interchange there for another route to fly, all those included those Russians, plus my family. Leonid and Esther being on foot ahead of others, where they're all walking around Bombay's International airport and looked from side to side towards diverse materials and objects, which they are never saw in Europe, and apparently it's made they stopping near and to admire thus, but at these same time hold they back from buying. At the outset: the important issue here I must admit, that they are have lack of sufficient amount to afford all that beauty, which come across and attracted stuff and fascinated by—secondly: they wouldn't be able to pay money for these, anywhere. They have needed the chance to see so much of those beautiful cloths, there also be hand made different types of craft, these yellow gold or silver and white gold decorations, which sparkle with those colorful brightness of these lights, which have the power to be attracting consumers toward it. Still I never saw like this superb range of exotic things, which these materialized like an accurate decorative with hand made crafted time-honoured Indian garments and fashion outfits, which astonished all of they with that shiny golden and colorful knitting decorations upon it, which have the chance being presented itself that made it look like their attire suited for the Rajah, together with dresses for their women ubiquitously for the Palaces on displays. Although, they would observe diverse items, which they didn't even realise that so much beauty could exist anywhere else. 'Then our sight different modern televisions with remote control set, which they are never had a chance to make use of, though, they come across to enjoy in Italy, also diverse players, modern communication systems, into the bargain lots of diverse types bits and pieces. The next, which impede them at fist follows, and made them at a standstill, when they became amazed, when have ped near the Jewellery shop, who are offered folks fashioned costume jewelry, with chic invasive for brilliantly crafted watches and charms, which all along were made by hand arts and crafts. These items have being represented by whose traditionally folklore Indian Jewellers, which sparkle by altered colorful radiance, while it would attracted so many clientele those who are enthusiastic to purchase, counting them, as well. Who would reach thus destination of Asian corners from and all the over of the world perhaps never saw so much exquisiteness made by those with tremendous accuracy of those by brilliantly executed work crafts, signified by those gorgeous bits and pieces and objects, which have readily available being also presented on display for everybody to view. I also learned that those women dresses called saris and they worn them all the time, even during those heated summers, where the temperature jumps up to +40 Degrees C, even higher, where in tropical climate that becomes unbearable. The Indian women also y worn pants, which have to match the color, for those who would get dressed in saris. These excellently of creations with various diverse color along with fabric of saris are presented in the shop-windows by red, dark blue, swan lake green and other fine distinctions, which folks have worn it. Saw as well highlighted with golden or altered color costume jewellery, by which glass ribbons shined upon these dresses colorful knitting, with hand made crafts suits made by talented craftsmen, and its visibility gave the impression of being attractive. When next the Borodins saw the woman dressed in a white sari, with her head bent down, and tells that she read somewhere, about those women who saris is white are—widows, and the outcast for those normal people and without any rights upon 'Traditionally Indian society'. In harmony to the accounts, which has been re-telling of Indian tradition and ritual customs: the women and those men sometime also, who are wearing diverse and colors on their clothing are represented by the Indian Cast and made other to recognise to which of their Cast they belong to. Origination in Indian High Rank Cast persons—quite the opposite for the Low Cast have to conduct themselves, to drop below their heads, and don't the rights to walk ahead of a High Cast, which automatically think as their masters or owners as meet or if they pass by. As for those women whose husbands died or being killed, which made them widows; they have to cut their hair completely by becoming boldness, and too wear only white saris to the end of their life. Those women never even see other people or go to enjoy themselves, not to mention have the rights getting married again. Those outcast women if they being lucky staying alive, once they have aged, the Indian Government instead dishonours them from receiving any types of benefits or pension for that affair. Thus, the Religious Law, obligations and legal ruling, even present-day it have been forbidden for those poor women. The Law makes them outcast Widows, by which their Legal Rights were taken away from, Even their husband's relations would put glass bracelets upon their hands, which the ladies being dressed in, like the widows transpired on stage became immobile, and finally lifeless. Many of those Indians remind they of the Gypsies or Romales, which they are usually saw from time to time, either in the Soviet Union or even in Europe, while they are stayed there. And when they saw the women passing by in those traditional Indian saris they are tried to guess whose of them who belong to which Cast, belong to the High Rank Cast or whose to the Lower Cast. They are besides have sneaked pick upon those women passing by, who has upon their heads in the middle of their foreheads glimpsed red marks in the shape of a circle, which symbolised in Indian ritual traditions—they were married women.

By walking in changed places around the airport they have decided to go outside to glimpse at least a little more what's the life like in India. Still, they are have being unpleasantly surprised, despite the beauty of those cloths and Jethey arels and other stuff, the real life outside airport in Bombay to gave the impression of being quite the opposite, in fact the taxis, of which they are came across to see looked dirty, and when they are asked to get inside and began the trip they are felt a horrible smell and not only there. The air at the forefront on the streets, it seems there also 'spread' with thus awfully appalling smell has encircled the whole atmospheres, which made all of they adequate disposed into vomiting. By staring at scrupulously absorbing around the location count those are huge crowds, which come into view from now enclosed be not far from airport. They saw that kind of Indian conventional taxi', which they are have not came across to meet such a dare I for the first time in my life, because they haven't being used to see that kind of cars, in compare to the Europeans. These cars looked like more of the three wheels motorcycle or even three wheels scooter, but bigger in sizes, and with the roof upon them, still, all the dual carriageway automobiles are painted in either dark brown, or black colors with a shade of yellow or orange shades. Far above the ground on the air the smell has been unbearable, so they are able to glimpse mud with filth, as they are couldn't wait until would escape thus ghastly smell and overheated place. There, in contrast they are also distinguish a spectacle, where to be seen on the streets these odd type of cows, or ox. The Borodin's never bump into a breed that are lying in the middle of a main road, or right in the heart, where it's full of traffic, which could get jammed. I was just getting ready vomiting, by an effect then I put plain for mom to get me back inside the airport. Given I couldn't escape that weird place with it's awful stinky smell. Cause of that I kept wandering, if the weather all around India still would be the same?

CHAPTER 46

When the Borodins have found departure section, and they sighted outside the Russian lad, whose being nervously smoking, and looking around the airport area. Once he spots them—became bright and breezy while started resembling closer within them, as the lad began talking:—Where have you being? I became worried about you. All of us just come together to get ready boarding the plane. Come along with me, cause our plane shall be taking off in about thirty minutes time!—As the family strides, and next finally joined the group crowded with those Russians, who travel together from Italy, who are staying and waited in a queue, when per head is going to join another, talking.

When they are approached the boarding gates everyone among the passengers handed their boarding passes and would moving straight ahead. The next in turn came for they to do likewise, my mom along with myself have approached by one of the airport Customs officials, whose turn out being a woman, clad in khaki color uniform skirt along with top, most likely with a bit darker shade, while holding in her hand a black broom stick, which the airport security, or officials using mostly within that airport complex, or at the police forces carrying out. Alena with Egor by her side handed her a single boarding pass and when she tried to pass ahead the Indian woman stepped in the middle and tried to stop they to move. While mom being holding my hand and tried to move forward ahead, without realising that something is wrong. But here comes the turning point— one of those airport official, who's being a woman with the boom stick then without warning began to address them in English, whci they couldn't understand it. After a while she called another airport official, probably security and they both started pushing they back and out. She kept talking to they and they are in our turn also spoken but in Russian, and they are still couldn't understand each-other what the heck is going on here. This Indian woman unexpectedly heat with her shoulder and has ripped off from my mom's hand and grabbed it in hers. I became scared and could not figure out what is happening around. Alena tried to explain, but the only words, which she new in English:—No English, Russian!—They both continued arguing and everyone in their lingo, though, the Indian official spoken English, but mother tongue, Russian. A short time after in the airport official woman start to walk and has being dragging me away with her in another direction, while holding tight my hand. Suddenly it's struck me, that she wants to take me away from everyone, and than I began to resist. I began resisting, and in unison to scream cry, as also calling:— Mommy, help me! Mommy, don't let them taking me away from you!—Despite of mom's attempt to follow her those two airport security officers on the other hand—stepped up in front of her and guarded the way for her the and would not let mom follow they, and similar to me she was unable to resist the two big airport personnel. 'This Indian woman in khaki uniform—nonstop dragging me further away from my family; and they have already disappeared from my view, as I could not see them anymore. Despite just being a little boy, I kept screaming and resisting her frustration. She saw that I be resisting, in that case she has grabbed me aggressively apart from hand my cloth for me jacket, as too rough that befall beyond my power. In spite I was weaker in weigh against her, I kept blaring at the top of my voice.

But this Indian official has also grabbed me very tight, and began dragging me straight ahead. She is kept along along corridor; the woman official then turned to a door rear. At once they have approached an aim place, which seeing it I figured out that, het being determined taken me where on earth?

The moment this official has knocked someone might opened—followed by the Indian woman has grabbed my free hand, while her intention of time was to drag me quickly interior. Since I was a slim kid, and thus I didn't weigh a great deal. In that case the woman has picked me up in a flash, being under her own steam, and rushed with me seized—inside a murky room. By entering inside a dark room she placed me hard and quick into a chair, where it's been standing nearby the table. In spite of my hands is hurting, in that moment this woman has begun to leave and abandon the room. Then I start to run without delay after her to be able escaping, but when she saw my determination on rapid, it follows that she has pushed me away, and I fallen over on the base. Then the door closed with a thud behind her, and I've been left alone therein. Apart from being dark there room itself was without light without windows, while that place looked like it had got in it for interviewed room for detainees, like myself. It sounds as all around is hearing clearly that I couldn't stop crying, and kept calling:—Mommy!—If I'm being forced into the room. Despite the fact I was afraid, whilst the Indian official underestimated myself, but she was mistaken, once placed me there to facilitate within thus confinement, by also assuming, that I should fall under their rules and obey her or their treatment?—

Meanwhile, since my childhood I was always afraid of darkness, but to my hardship I've being left alone in thus circumstances, where I'm to stay and struggle in solitude in this dark room, like a criminal or even worst. I have kept here in an odd room, where there are only few chairs and a table; all by myself and deep in thoughts:—What's going on, and why dilemma happened to my family? And what shall be waiting upon my fate to ensue? What they are going to do with me?—Still, Egor was unaware what incidence have effect outside, where Alena kept arguing with the bloody airport officials. Until the Borodins saw the situation that, those Indians have disembarked the family's suitcases without their permission or word of warning. See their luggage were brought upfront and that have subsided them. By gestures, which the bureaucrat from Customs made towards Borodins, and ducking nod with their head, the family understood that airport officials will check out their suitcases. Indeed, she has thoroughly overlooked the whole thing inside our baggage. Where the Indian woman, who's being dressed in khaki, minus she then took away me in the solitary room nodded upon a tiny handbag, which being holding in her hands. Mom handed her handbag towards another person from the Customs officials.

Next a woman amid that staff has disappeared with her handbag somewhere:—You need to take up you're baggage, and walk after those airport officials—to the Customs compartment for X-ray check up?-

Once checking up process being completed those Hindus officials still couldn't let them leave and me to go free from this dark room. Still me being hidden there, but I start counting, cause it past at least two hours.

Period in-between, being within this dark room, where I have sit down and been observing squat near a wall—for how long I wasn't aware, but suddenly the door widely opens, and a beam of light start to flash in the darkness around the room. While it's brightness fall upon me and blind me for a second, while I still have not transformed the position, by at a standstill sitting down on that surface floor. I glimpsed at the familiar face of the Indian woman, who stepped inside. And yet, this woman put on the table a glass of water and some scone, which seem to be unusual within its shape, its like being rounded like a circle that I have not being used to eat that kind. I kept sobbing, as her presents made increase my distress and hysteria even more. Despite of her gestures with her head upon that food too, though in disparity I knocked my head for six against it, as bowed head in subordinate, still sustained with shed tears, but then said abruptly:—I want my Mommy!—She recurs like clockwork my shoulders, so that with my head and body simultaneously I've begun shivering and shuddering. Despite of my distress, I've held my head lower, but my sub-conscience, as I felt her presence, ahead affix on her every move. I could even hear irony, as she talks, as I undersood neither Hindu dialects, nor English for that matter. Here being heard some cynical tone in this Indian lady's voice, when she spoke for that matter and rather peculiar blitz, which become visible in her eyes. Still, I was only an innocent child, who left being defenceless as to become an victim of an unlawful and Illegal act of the 'willy-nilly' fates. I found myself in such situation, by which my fate, and even life have ensued in the hands of those, who already have made unlawful act against faith all Mighty, as me facing God known, what those foreigners have in mind to do with defenceless child, soon? In due course a new woman, who's one from those airport Customs officials—came back with a tall person that happen being a man. After a long wait, him being one of travellers, who happen to speak Russian; he appear at the age in his late fortieth, of he's hight like a giant, but with a thick and strong constitution where parts main of his body being concern; as for hair the color emerged dark with a medium short hair cut, and he has had blue eyes. He was asked by the airport Customs officials to translate for our family. While this Russian man is introduced himself as Alex. Besides he enlightened that he ought to be translating for them and for my family. He's being listening warily, apparently has delivered that translation for both parties. At this point being at the airport where mom standing near Leonid's, while a Russian fellow is sustained talking in English, involving with the opposite party. Whilst the opposite party have ducked at my family; then this man approached them, and began talking in Russian:—Вы говорите по-Русски?—He asked them and when they are responded positively, he then continued, and at that same time addressed towards the Customs officials. They also enlightend him in English, he ducked his head in some idea of familiarity; next he is addressing Alena and Leonid:—Уважаемые, Господа! Этот досмотр, касательно ваших вещей и—саквояжа, является рутиной проверкой, которая происходит ежедневно на всех Аэропортах, не только Бомбея, но и всего Мира. Вы не должны поднимать шум из-за этого. Кроме того, ваши чемоданы после досмотра будут отправлены из таможни назад в самолёт. Я сам—являюсь пассажиром этого рейса. По-этому, в связи с проблемой, возникшей у вас: никто ещё не был допущен на посадку в самолёт. У вас есть какие-либо условия, или вы хотите что-то спросить, или попросить у этих господ? Я могу перевести для вас по-Английски?—While he spoken it has been heard an irony in his voice, and sarcasm. He also be standing half turning towards the Airport officials talking and mainly referring towards them. They looked, as seems to being satisfied within he's translation and said amazing, which he did not translate, either too my or Leonid. But mom reacts in respond to him harshly, loud heard in Russian:—Я требую—немедленно, и без каких-либо промедлений вернуть сюда моего сына, которого незаконным образом утащили из моих рук, и держут неизвестно где? Какое право эти люди—имеют похитить его у меня! Пусть вернут моего сына!—By telling him that, Alena attends also towards those airport officials. This giant Russian, on the other hand looked amazed, but once again ask over, if it's true. Then this fellow began translating for the airport Customs officials:—Это правда, что вашего сына забрали? и вы не знаете, где он находиться? Когда и как это произошло? И сколько лет вашему сыну?—Although, the man kept asking, but still couldn't believe it. Apparently he understood, that everything she said was true, he then has changed the tone of his voice, and began listening carefully. After came a turn for Leonid to say:—Переведите, пожалуйста, этим людям: Они держут моего внука, как заложника, которому всего лишь недавно исполнилось шесть лет. И если они не хотят нам его вернуть, то пусть возмут меня, вместо него. А мальчика, пускай отпустят и вернут назад к его матери, потому, что она очень страдает. Я уверен, что мальчик очень напуган и тоже переживает и плачет! Переводите! Я готов пойти с ними, вместо него—а они пусть отпустят моего внука!—At the same time as Leonid completed last words his eyes looked with sadness. He then has taken a deep breath, stepped forward, as he was ready for rather unforseen. Alena, on the contrary, after a thorough consideration stopped him, as has also taken a deep gulp of air, as next allegedly implied:—Переведите, пожалуйста: что я требую привести сюда представителей Советского Посольства, и при чём, немедленно! Я уверенна, что Представительство от СССР—здесь есть! И мы хотим видеть кого-то из них. Кроме того, мы требуем позвать людей из Руковоства Аэропортом, чтобы поведать им какое безобразие, и те беззаконные действия, которые ученили с нашей семьёй. Однако, мы понимаем, что здесь Аэропорт, и эти люди исполняют свою работу, но это— не означает, что кто-либо имеет право, забирать моего сына у меня! Переводите, чего-же вы ждёте, Алекс? И не смотрите на меня так?—When she talked she also looked upon the Russian man and they've patiently waited, until he is obtained inclusive translation.

This time this Russian fellow seems to look a bit worried and peeped her in the eyes, as asked:—Простите, как вас зовут?-, when he asked her what's first name, and she responded him, that her name is Alena, he then began deal with translation to those airport officials. At what time that was unaware next he turns to face Alena again, meant:—Алёна, таможенники просят вас передать вашу сумочку для досмотра. И это будет последняя проверка. Пожалуйста, положите её вон туда на эту движующуюся дорожку!-, He pointed her with his stretched hand towards the conveyer belt, that look like a tread-mile, and yet he alone stepped aside. Alex then has unremittingly being listening to those Customs officials have significantly discussed with him.

When the Borodins routine checking at the X-ray Customs mechanism of a conveyer belt terminated, that staff is begun to check inside our suit-cases excessively.

As checking route at the Customs be near over, those officials began talking again to this Russian man. Soon after Alena has received back her handbag.

The time was passing and I kept sitting and being in a state of distress, as my pulse has been racing frequently, and I also often cried by calling "Mommy". In a while the door opened again and the Indian official, who had dragged me in here prior, she stepped inside and walked towards my seat. She is gestured me to get up with her hand in the air, barring I have been confused and could not understand what she wants me to do. Then this Indian official grabbed me up off the chair, as I is standing and facing her. She ducked her head and with her left hand points to the door, I didn't have a choice as to obey her command. She also took my hand and said one word, and I understood was 'Mama', and they are started walking at the direction from where they are came before, for that reason I have recognized the same route rear. It seem for now I stop crying took a handkerchief from my pocket and briefly wiped up tears from my eyes, by using fingers I have smoothed my hair.

Though she looks at me, and began smiling—then realization hit me from seen her expression: she is pleased that I'm being quick-witted.

When they have turned towards the rear corner I saw from a distance Alena and his grandparents—standing near conveyer belt mechanism, which looked like a trade-mile in a Sport Gym it's being peculiar, while it kept working in rhythm, when people would placed upon there their belongings among other stuff of their possessions—eventually it would disappear just in front from their view, it was interesting to watch this magic. Still, it didn't interest me at that moment, seeing as with all my strengths I pulled out my hand from this Indian woman wearing Khaki color uniform, and started running towards my mom. As soon as I jumped upon her hands and began to hug her tight, I would not let her go and leave her side. While mom kissed me, and I even heard her laughter, in a quiet pitch, and there're both of my grandparents, being louder. Actually I sneaked a peek at stranger tall fellow, but when I heard him talking in perfect Russian that comfort it me and calmed me down, even this translater was optimistically light-hearted. One and all seem being satisfied in spite of the confusion that have effect during a tough time for them. In a while sees the Borodin happily being strolling to a gate, where the four along with those from their flight have got through an airport check. Then all boarding up this plane.

'Shortly after my family and I boarded the plane and occupied back our seats. Even if, time was passing, but the plane wouldn't leave since they saw those two Hindus airport securities, who still being standing opposite from our seats rear there and both officials be apart from each-other as well. Those mature on this airliner have spotted decent, as usually on khaki color uniforms, except for their pale color turbans, which be fond worn on top of their heads. Even as, the two Indian securities are station apart from each other, as opposite of our sits, who have looked directly towards Borodins, as partially suspiciously contained by an eccentric, it's being rather a peculiar look, which been spotted in their eyes. Collectively seen there nor any sign for that plane to take off up the in air. Those travellers from their flight become apprehensive with impatient, when started blaming they for thus delay of the plane's that schedule to take off. They couldn't comprehend what is going on and once again I become annoyed with the ordeal, that I had to get through before, while my family and I have been anxiously awaiting until the plane should take off. Meanwhile those Hindus securities are staring towards Alena's handbag . . . A while after the Russian lad strides towards our seats, like has taken care of Alena, entailed:—Alena, listen up, these men looking strangely at your handbag. Why don't you open it and check inside. If not they will stay here forever? Besides,other travellers are've being waiting long enough for the plane to take off, and leave this bloody country.—Even as Alena listened to him and has looked with an interest towards his face and ducked with head. The moment Alena opens her handbag, her face become abruptly colorless, lying on her eyes expressed peculiar mix of bewilderment and impulsive shock, which paralysed her body. ahead, hers befalls speechless, but I still couldn't figure out why? 'Since I be near, but unaware what's going on around, also being curious by my nature I have decided to look inside her bag myself after all: but there I spot a lengthy piece of paper that symbolized this absent boarding pass; even I begun realizing the situation. Alena's eyes gave the impression of be unmoved, as kept staring on that boarding pass. Next she twists to face those Hindus officials with a peculiar bewilderment. In spite of the situation to be in our favour, mom could not move or speak for these matter, Alena merely looked in her eyes open-widely. Except this Russian lad, who's anxiously waiting for her respond, has then looked inside the bag also. This lad then advised her with out loud voice, cause seen that she has been in a state of a shock:-Alena, come on hold on yourself, keep calm, and give back this bloody boarding pass to airport officials and try to control yourself. Do you hear me? Or give it to me and I resolve to pass this boarding pass them.—It seems that she could not react as it should be, despite she emerged being sane, in that case Russian lad then has grabbed that boarding pass from her hands, and starts stroll towards those Indian securities. Once reaching them he instantly handed to those Indians officials this side pass. One among them first check up this; then have nodded. At that time they both in full swing are begun shifting towards exit. Anon 'I have heard Alena talking to Leonid and amid other Russians is a young lad, who's being telling them that she:—I'm still in shock, I can't get over it!What bloody hell, these Indian have done to our family. Why, they've tricked us, those manipulative witches, as they were capable into throw up in my handbag a bloody boarding pass?—When next she stops; then takes a deep breath, and progressing again, by too added:—It's their fault, cause it have being their responsibility to handing to me this shitty boarding pass which supposed to be issued, as a single boarding pass for Egor.

And 'they want to get clean hands out', after distressing us so much, particular Egor?—

A short while after the departure of these Hindus Bombay's airport security, they are up to date as to lock their with seat-safety belts via the loudspeaker. Soon after sense they're hearing an announcement by plane's Capitan, while, but it's became obvious, the in a row persons along for the ride are delivery—in favour of this plane to take off, with nonstop . . .

Only then the Borodin's start to breath in easier, when this airplane finally takes off from the Bombay airdrome—ciao, India! Seen the flight attendants became busy, by making fuss around all the passengers, counting Borodins. Once the plane 'L'Italia' has been already take off to the air high in the sky, that nobody will be unable to reach they above there, only then all amid the family felt a bit relaxed. In view of the fact that the next stop that plane be supposed to make a stop only in Singapore. The rest of that flight, Egor and he's family are observing through a plane-window by an aerial view: as the sky up there emerged be of a purple nuance, but clear, like velvet, the rain has gone, and been flowing up in the atmosphere. The moon-light is flashing short-lived through the glass, and it's exaggeration from those sparling stars, which shone not so far away above inside my window and beyond too. Seeing as this plane be up in the air, while thus aerial view subsided, since their flying course being in the direction of Singapore, where our next stop supposed to be, sooner than eventually they are ought to reach Australia's shores.'

Italy

PART–V

Master Of His Destiny—To Reunion

CHAPTER 47

It had past over two decades, since my long journey to Australia began. I'm myself still live in Sydney, and already have completed the High School 'down under'. I also had obtained University, and by now have accomplished with two Degrees over there else. I look with hopefulness towards my future, as I'm a 'Master of my own destiny'.

—So I'm finally landing in Berlin, Germany a week later than I planned, cause my dad couldn't get there earlier, due to he's meeting deadline at work. Better late then never, I guess? In a few hours after I disembark in Berlin airport, and I hope to see my father's side of the family for the first time in over twenty two years. I am feeling quite tired and anxious, and me not exactly sure, how this is all will turn up? I have fifty scenarious playing out in my head, I just hope they will like me, and accept as a part of their family. A few friends back in Sydney, who had found themselves in a similar situation told me not too do this re-union. Because, when they tried to re-unite with their long-lost families—they were rejected and left—heartbroken. All those years had passed, since my family and myself for the first time arrived in Sydney, still I have never had the opportunity to fly again abroad. Apparently today, I am beginning my journey to Europe once again, then I'm flying alone to Europe. Its visibly that now I'm an adult, not a kid anymore, where me all grown up. I'm flying away once again to meet with my father for the purpose of reconcile with him. With an advantage I want to see my other family, those folks are my from father's side, whom I haven't seen for over two decades: grandma Dora, aunt Tania and her family—the people I never saw up to that time, except for my cousin, who was a baby back then, when I was a kid myself. It seems that I don't remember her, but I look forward to meet with her again. Besides I want to get acquainted with her, likewise with her brother too, because they both my cousins. I certainly hope, that my other family will recognise me, eventually, particular my grandmother Dora and aunt Tanja with her family? Thanks God, that my grandma Dora who is still alive and well, as I pray that she would be in high spirit likewise for many years to come, for I hope that she can be proud of the achievements, which I made in my life. Its deep-seated in my heart about to my grandma Esther's health, who has undergone many surgeries procedures during all those years. She is still well, despite all horrors she had got through. since all those events have allowed her hang around, while she keeps physically healthy. Although, she has never regained weight again, but I am happy being together with her, and see hers still well-being alive in our day. In comparison with Esther my gradpa Leonid, had died less that five years after our arrival in Australia. Leonid'd suffered for few months from lung cancer, subsequent to was diagnosed by the doctors with thus horrible disease, and died in hospital, that was 'His last wish' before he passes away, that he didn't want they to suffer with him. Leonid's last words have some thought of meaning that I'm been supposed to carry out after he departed over - into another world. Before it's come to pass Leonid gave me a exhortation to be 'the Man of the House', he loved our family very much, me especially. When he has instead of being in a terrible state of pain, thus, he died in peace in a hospital bed, at the eventual stage before had passed away, Leonid was in agony. Despite of the tragedy, off which grandpa Leonid had departed forever, as a real man does—his last thought was only of the three of us—even at the last minutes in his breath of life he's contemplation being only of his family, only!

Resulting for this Russian man named—Alex Sher, who did help the Borodin's through a terrible ordeal. After all those years Alex Sher was chosen as the Coach to wrestling team. Then he worked as the Head Coach for the Australian Wrestling team, and there he had trained the athletes, who represented Australia during the "Sydney 2000 Olympic Games", as well as on the 'Athens 2004 Olympics'—in Greece. To a calamity Alex too had passed away few years ago after a long suffering battle with 'brain cancer'. Pertaining to this Russian lad, who travelled with the Borodin on plane from Italy to Australia—stopped along in India: after a few years lived in Sydney, he had decided move to USA with a view to live beside his mother. It appears that he has lived in New York along with his mother and Stepfather. A rumor has it that the lad was caught in the mid of 9/11 aftermaths amid crowds—I'm not aware of his fate. After the Borodins arrival in October of 1989, they had got closed the Russian camp in Italy, and I am thank God that neither of statements become horror-struck ordeal with terrible reality in my case, that in effect I've came across to witness there many victims. I thank God the Russian man—Alex, who had helped me in callous event—to re-united with my family, and mom . . .

CHAPTER 48

Since my family and I arrival in Australia throughout those few months, which was being there, I began study at the Primary school.

Rumour has it that a male teacher has held against me by saying incredible in English, which I couldn't comprehend, why he was cruel towards me—years ago. This Assie teacher then kicked me, and has sustained to do the same occasionally for the period of few months with his hand over my head, it's seems that he had verbally abused me regularly. As I can talk about nowadays thus on top of my bad luck the teacher would grab me by my hair and hit my head over the wall frequently. I was crying many times, except I couldn't dare tell a sad story to my mom, by effect that she has got plenty of struggles to her own on her shoulders to deal with . . .

It come into view that during the first month of my studies in Australian school this teacher always pointed out me to seat down apart from the other students—solitary over a single table, in the corner of classroom—away from others. In due course, being there it felt like I was some kind of carrier by means of an infectious disease, if not than what? Into the bargain, being present within that classroom I felt like being an outsider.

In sync I become emotionally upset, and a terribly lonely sole, on top being disallowed as a foreigner there. In the course of my extra studies there by destiny just in my class where I got to meet a Russian boy that turn out to speak in English very well, whose arrived in Australia few years, earlier than me, as he had begun attending school. This Russian boy evidently has interpreted for me the whole thing, what the same bloody English teacher assumed. Next this kid like me too gave the lowdown, and he has made clear toAlena, of facts for a whole story, about this Assie bloke, who was my Teacher back then; and in words has abused me with rough racial harassment language with an advantage of unfairness, what else can I sheer about it. My family have made an appeal to the school's principal, who's turned out being a woman. As a Russian boy's mother was a witness of, when she has translated for us and reported to the school principle the whole story enlightening her of the male teacher, who was unkind—but truth was specifics have effect, that him being teaching. It was triviality of predicament in school that the teacher being discharged from his job. Good readiness! What this bustard Assie bloke—educator in point of the fact—but really was there!

After that unpleasant incident had left behind quickly: eventually I completed primary school with 'Dux of the School'. Being a Russian-speaking boy I, amid other pupils was the only one, whose being able not only learning to speak English, but I attained high achievements in the course of studies. Also in my life, during my developements into scholarly—in High school, me being clever, by which I had successively completed my studies with three medals. As a results of my hard work in studies durable over those years, I began Higher Education next, and eventually completing it, which I had achieved been in University with degrees. Now I am delighted with all my accomplishments! Except for now I look with optimism, for the reason that I am "Master of my own destiny'. As I truly believe that Egor—transit passenger being central to this story, and except enunciating as it was not completed yet. It's just only in progress, forward and I believe all my future dreams look bright, which lie ahead and I desire for them too come true! After a long wait I am flying back en route for Europe, where it's all began: my voyage, as a transit passenger—was on the time without legal documents compare to nowadays, as I'm an Australian citizen gaining a passport by that. A foremost reason for this trip essentially is apart from travelling back to Europe, after many years that have past I wish to speak with my dad and reconcile, it's like to resolve our lack of correspondence and lack of contacts. I feel like to ask Alik, what had really ensued many years ago between him and Alena. Just like that I'm intend to make a fresh start without judging my father, and get to know him better. I need add that my ambition is to give my dad an a change for explanation, even supposing, mom hurt him leaving a scar in his soul, by means of vanishing with me, then she wouldn't let Alik together with his family to say goodbyes to me. In spite of a mess, which taken place in the past—he can be proud of me and all of my achievements. At long last my dad me and the family there can bond, as for my part time and again that I've prayed all those years, since parting with him and all of them, and I believe that will be event for us again at present.

As for Alena: all those years ago, she admitted has what went on before with unlike approach the past—then her main concern was before our exodus from the USSR: thus she was afraid that during our departure my dad would be capable in time to discover our intent for leaving, thus Alik's likely changed his mind to catch them in Moscow airport, it follows that his intention of taking Egor away from her for good. In spite of struggle, which bearably Alena has put great efford; she still is a stunning looking woman. 'I fled with my son without letting Egor say goodbyes to his grnadma Dora, his Aunty Tanja, and of course—Alik himself. I hope no-one will judge me for that: A mother is always right! I practically kidnapped my son. Alik had no idea of the exact day, when we were leaving.' If he found out this day—Alik would find a way to stop them from fleeing, and try to take Egor from Alena:—I had no choice only to mislead Alik. Maybe it was a mistake, but I believe that I did the right thing for my son's sake.' She was determined to leave with her family and Egor. Cause of Leonid and Esther's poor health: those two overall had got through many surgery procedures, five operations of which Esther alone undergone in Australia. In a tough situation, where be set all Alena's strengths in time were beyond her expectations wit in awareness be intelligent or ability that, she has raised Egor successively him to become a fine human. Apart from her struggle Alena has also being able to learn English—at her age. Here in a weird and wonderful country 'down under', meant to start from a scretch was an obstacle for her and Egor. Despite of obstacles, which she had to overcome, Alena succeeded through hard times, experiencing ridicule along the way and; except telling that she triumphs over dignity, even if her career was put on the line, and to tolerate upon rested for that's being for her moral fibre a 'hell of a ride'.

In life some families stay together some families fall apart, that's how it is. What I learned so far from my trip, and migration to a new country that you're not master of your destiny—it's destiny that rules us, and we have to accept it, and be grateful for what you have.

THE END.